endless —

A Novel of Holocaust Survivors

Editor: Sean Fordyce
Assistant Editor Researcher: Charles Foster
Cover and book design: Sean Fordyce
Distribution: Voyageur North America

Voyageur Publishing / Voyageur North America
4801 Charleville Road, RR#4 Prescott, Ontario K0E 1T0
Phone: (613) 925-2111
Fax: (613) 925-0029

Toll Free Order Lines (USA and Canada)
phone (800) 268-2946
fax (800) 444-5899
e-mail: voyageur@mulberry.com
Internet website: http://www.mulberry.com/~voyageur/

First Edition: August, 1997.

Canadian Cataloguing in Publication Data:

Karsh, Roma,
        Endless : a novel of Holocaust survivors
ISBN 0-921842-51-1
        I. Title
PS8571.A848E63 1997 C813'.54 C97-900554-X
PR9199.3.K37E63 1997

Cover film supplied by Gilmore Printing Services, Ottawa.
Printed in Canada by Imprimerie Gagné, Louiseville, Quebec.

endless

A Novel of Holocaust Survivors

roma karsh

Voyageur Publishing

Acknowledgments

I wish to thank my publisher, Sean Fordyce, for his insights, sensitivity in dealing with this subject and for enhancing the final version of this book;

Charles Foster for the care he took in reviewing the manuscript.

Fern, for her extraordinary perceptions in helping me create and develop the character, Sarah, and for typing my manuscript. I know it was a gift of love;

Yigal for his perseverance and understanding;

Leonard Feldman, who suggested that I write this book. Without his encouragement, this novel would never have materialized;

Mark Cohen, for his confidence in my abilities;

Angel Mealia who is a trustworthy and loyal friend who gave moral support — I thank her wholeheartedly;

Peter M. who has been like a guardian angel to me and whose friendship I cherish;

Ebenezer Sikakane, whose thoughtfulness has deeply touched me;

and Hugh Rendle for his graciousness in introducing me to the true Fountain of Life.

I wish to express my heartfelt thanks to the authors of *Of Pure Blood*, Marc Hillel and Clarissa Henry. If not for their book, the public may never have known the depth of another inhuman process taking place during the Third Reich — the secret organization of the Lebensborns, dedicated to the creation of a master race through eugenics. They were a source of inspiration to me. Regrettably their book is now out of print.

I also wish to thank the authors of *Master Race*, Catrine Clay and Michael Leapman for further exposing the Lebensborn program.

For Fern with love.

Part One
Sarah

The sound of screeching tires coming to a halt below their window was barely muffled by the snow that was now falling quickly on the city. Curfew meant that only the SS would be out so late. Yitzhak parted the heavy velvet curtains of the high window of the apartment's living room to look down onto the street. Below, he could see two ebony Mercedes, their engines steaming in the cold night. The cars remained silent and threatening for what seemed like an eternity, their roofs gathering snow. Everywhere else there was peace. Perhaps they would only stop for a few minutes and then go on to terrorize some other neighbourhood.

Without turning to look at her, Yitzhak mechanically motioned to his wife, Mindy. Resorting to whispers and handsignals, Yitzhak confirmed the number, identity and location of the cars. They didn't speak normally as if for fear that the police had superhuman hearing. A panicked gesture from Yitzhak confirmed movement. Three black figures stepped out of the first car and two from the second. Yitzhak stared in disbelief as one paused to urinate in the street. The heavy doors clunked closed as the figures reunited behind the cars. Mindy rushed to their daughter's room.

Sarah was sitting up in bed. The sudden silence from the living room meant that something was seriously wrong. She had become used to sleeping with the sound of her parents' voices, white noise, in the background. She was addicted to their agitated murmurings and would have had difficulty sleeping in the unusual silence. The look on her mother's face as she came into the room terrified her. Sarah remembered her parents' instructions for when the SS came. She was to climb out her bedroom window, up the narrow steel stair that was more of a ladder, and onto the roof and wait. After a safe time she was to run to her Christian friends and stay with them.

Swinging into action, Mindy carefully removed the window and helped her through the gap. In a few moments, Sarah found herself bundled in a housecoat and blanket up on the roof in the cold night air. She had been half asleep but the damp chill went through her, waking her, absorbed quickly by her small child's body. It was lucky that she hadn't slipped on the steel steps, greasy with snow and ice. The leaden starless night sky and the snow wisping down made the world surreal. Sarah sat leaning against the stone ledge at the side of the roof, melting herself a chair in the snow. What would she do if this were the night that she would find herself alone?

Every stair groaned a protest under the jackboots as the intruders tramped to the second floor. Yitzhak and Mindy didn't have to wait long once they reached the landing. With a thick guttural chorus of "Aufmachen" their door was crashed open, the wood splintering with the nerves of everyone in the building. Yitzhak had only a moment to wonder if his looking out the window had caused them to choose this apartment. Perhaps, he had allowed a thin sliver of light that had attracted them like insects to a flame.

The mirror in the front entrance was smashed, spraying shards of glass from the hall into the Horowitzes' modest living room as two men entered the room. One, a thin man whose smirk displayed ugly discoloured teeth, gestured to Mindy's curio cabinet, a small rosewood corner piece she had inherited from her grandmother that now displayed the lovely china figurines her family had passed on from generation to generation. Within a moment he had grabbed the cabinet, swept the ornaments to the floor in a hail of powdered porcelain and begun moving it to the door. Mindy leaned, reaching for the cabinet before Yitzhak could stop her.

The blow came so hard that she thought part of her face had been cut away. The owner of the fist that had struck her was now laughing, blowing alcoholic rage into her face as he leaned down to get a good look at the damage he had caused, Mindy having dropped to her knees. She screamed in pain as a coat brushed by her and a jack boot came down, hard, crushing the bottom of her exposed foot leaving a bloody impression on her sole. The same boot came up again this time striking her husband in the abdomen dropping him with one blow. With a revolver pressed to Yitzhak's cheek, the aggressor grabbed him by his greying hair and yanked him up like a puppet, gagging for air. "Jude!" he shouted, "show me your papers!"

In the shadow of the doorway the thin officer's face seemed transparent to the bone, a bleak whiteness with receding blue eyes, as if in his business, death had become infectious and blood vessels no longer circulated to the head. His lips were bluish, thin and pinched. He was about thirty, slim with narrow shoulders augmented by epaulets. Across from him, now fully-illuminated, was a round pasty face, all flesh, boneless with lips thick and glutinous. He was now twisting Yitzhak's hair, stirring him like a ladle in a thick soup — the poor man kicking his feet out, circling, vainly trying to relieve the pressure. Mindy retrieved the documents while Yitzhak dropped like a dying mouse from the mouth of a dog. Her eyes had gone dark, her frosted silver hair was losing what remained of its pigmentation.

No valiant effort on Yitzhak's part could protect his family. He stayed where he had fallen, not wanting to attract attention as the marauders looted the apartment. He stared at his swiftly aging wife. She stood still, holding up the wall with her back as if she alone could stop the house from falling down on her family. They watched helplessly as chairs were flung across the room, their glass menagerie smashed on the Victorian sideboard and their antique silver fruit bowls and a Russian samovar were stuffed into bags she had been saving in the cupboard.

With a last look around to see if they had forgotten anything of value and one last blow at Yitzhak, catching him in the shins with their boots, the bullies departed.

Sarah, who heard the cars leave, crept back in. Her mother struggled into her room and tucked her in, under the protective warmth of the covers, refusing to turn on the light.

Shortly thereafter, neighbours, having heard the noisy departure of the SS, dropped by to see if anyone had survived and to help sweep up the damage.

That night, Sarah, her mother and her father all cried silently, each in separate rooms, not wanting to see or be seen.

* * * * * *

Sarah yawned and stretched lazily in her bed. She glanced at her little clock on the bedside table; it was only ten and she was thirsty. Swinging her legs over the side of the bed, she slipped her feet into her houseshoes and crept to the door. As she was about to open it, she overheard her parents and Lena, their maid, talking. She stopped to listen.

"We should have seen this coming. It's been a nightmare since they took Cracow." It was her father, Yitzhak, sounding more despondent than she had ever heard him. "Now, they are going to lock us in a separate district. What's next? G-d help us!"

It scared her that this powerful man who had dried her own tears when other children called her names, was so close to tears himself. She stood behind the door unable to open it; unable to retreat to the safety and warmth of her familiar bed clothes.

Polish Jews who had lived for years in Germany, were snatched from the streets, children, the old, the sick, were thrown across the border like garbage. The excuse was a Herschel Grynszpan, a mishigine, who got a letter in Paris from his father telling of the family's suffering. "So this mishigine boy shoots an Ernst vom Rath, a minor official in the German embassy in Paris."

Germans never forgave Jewish businesses for being so successful after the war when loyal Germans returned home poor, maimed and humiliated. Jews now had mortgages on many properties in Germany. Even though many Jews had fought for Germany, the resentment and fury boiled over, carrying the burning oil of hatred everywhere.

"Twenty thousand already in camps; shops looted and destroyed; all the synagogues in Austria, burned — every last one.

Doctors I know, unable to see their patients, their offices destroyed."

Sarah could hear his teeth grind, a sickening sound more painful than his words. Like he was scraping bottom. Inhuman. Why do these people hate us? Why do they make my father like this? She longed for better times — when her father took her to the pictures or when they would watch the parades together.

"Maybe you shouldn't listen to the refugees. It would be better not to know. There is nothing we can do." Even her mother could offer no encouragement.

"Oh Mindy, we're being destroyed. How can we not pay attention? The German people know. It's no secret. Jewish ashes are being sent to relatives and they have to pay three marks to get them. There is no outrage! Prominent people are dying — the names are in the non-German press."

Sarah was still frozen at the door, her hand glued to the knob as if struggling to hold onto something she knew, something that wouldn't hurt her. She was so cold that she imagined her breath would form a solid if only she could release it. The last few days had been damp and chilly; even though it was March, it still felt like winter. Perhaps even spring would abandon them this year.

"The world doesn't care. Hitler has predicted the annihilation of the Jewish race in Europe." For the first time in her life, Sarah heard her father cry. It was like losing a faith. Her father had been all knowing, all powerful, god-like. Now he was no bigger than herself. She opened the door and looked into the room. The room was lit by a small lamp that cast striped lines of fragile illumination cutting the darkness into prison-like bars. Her parents' faces, partly in light and partly in shadow, were lit from below. Her father would have looked monstrous if he were not now crying pathetically.

Mindy reached over to wipe her husband's damp forehead with her apron. With her fingers, she made soothing strokes at the back of his neck all the while wanting to say the encouraging words that could not come out, for she knew that all he had said was true. "We'll have to bring in more coal. The fire will go out." Distracting him was all she could do.

"And," he ignored her and continued obsessed like a madman, "The British betrayed us. They are limiting immigration to Palestine for the next five years. They know what is happening here. We need to leave Europe — to go to our homeland. The British say the Jewish population must be no more than one-third of the Arabs and they are stopping us from buying land. There will be no Jewish immigration unless the Arabs agree. We must ask them permission to go home?"

Mindy gave up. There was nothing she could say to comfort her husband. She just sat nodding. Mindy knew he had to get it out. Otherwise, he would infect the entire family.

"And they say we started this war! Look at the war we Jews have caused. We caused Germany to invade Denmark and Norway with the enclosed ghetto at Lodz our reward? We can't even go out after dark. In Warsaw half a million Jews are crowded behind eight foot concrete walls."

Sarah's senses were overloading her, mixing her father's voice with the hateful ravings they heard daily on the radio. Those hysterical denunciations, so threatening, regularly consumed the family with helplessness and the dread of no escape.

Sarah was overwhelmed by oceans of love for her parents. Her breath came mechanically as her body demanded it. Otherwise she held it as if her silence would allow this all to pass over her and visit some other people at some other time. She thought of Josh, her brother. She wished he were there with her. He always reassured her.

Suddenly her mother, Mindy, interrupted her husband. "I know the facts. Jews have become limited in all avenues of life. Poles will have nothing to do with us. Since the occupation there's been nothing but torture, robbery and beatings."

Yitzhak interjected, raising his voice, "The Germans take us for any temporary manual jobs they need. I'm too old for this"

Lena, who had been quiet throughout the outpouring of suffering tried to calm them. "I — my family and I will help you any way we can." Her tone carried the respect and loyalty she genuinely felt for her former employers. It offered no hope.

The once charming, safe apartment looked hideous. They were dying and the world didn't care. The few gentiles who did, couldn't help. Sarah's people had become isolated from the rest of humanity, invisible to everyone but the Nazis. The apartment was cold and barren — forsaken. A picture of a cemetery infiltrated her senses. Nothing was certain, nothing could be trusted. She sank to the floor releasing the doorknob, letting the half-open door swing as if it had a life of its own. The little girl curled into a ball in the doorway. It no longer mattered what was happening around her. The Nazis might just as well have been monsters come to life from the stories she read. The floor was cold and after a few minutes she retreated to her bed, exhausted.

She never before considered a threat to her family and their comfortable way of life. She had taken for granted it would always remain intact — as invincible as her love for it. Fearful eyes darted about the sanctity of her room, her refuge. Here, she would leave the innocent purity of childish hopes and dreams, now muddied. Even here, she was no longer safe. From her bed she viewed her simple, birch dresser adorned with knick-knacks — her brushes and combs and coloured glass perfume bottles, her bookcase filled with schoolbooks. Her bed was shawled with egg-shell white, bobbled crocheted lace to resemble the cobbled streets amidst a littering of small wheels to represent the cycle of life, from birth to death, "to be reunited in heaven," her mother had explained when she was little.

"But when I'm in heaven, how will you know my name?"

"Souls recognize one another, no longer hidden beneath the costumes of our bodies." She had thought her mother was the wisest person in the world, they would always be together. Now she felt anonymous and the story no more than a bedtime fable.

She thought of school and the other children who were permitted to attend. Her family was trying to survive and carry on a family business and social life as best they could from their third floor apartment, only walking distance from Wawel Castle in an old but elegant part of town.

Since December 1939, each evening the family sat together after supper at the glass dining room table. Sarah did her lessons, coached by her father. The Jewish schools were closed and all Jewish teachers had been fired, including those working in general public schools. The teaching of Jewish children did not cease; elementary and high school students gathered in small groups in private homes to listen to lectures.

Weary of being frightened, fine-boned, raven-haired Sarah was livid. She wanted to blast in and rebuke her parents for having bided their time until it was too late. Nails dug into the white down pillow and as soft quills were released, she ripped it wide open and feathers blew about, alighting everywhere, until the blanched room was a field of snowy, broken dreams.

Her irregular, sharp, Semitic features had a certain razor's edge about them now. Her somber, navy-blue eyes became ink-black and rigid as stone. No golden-specked mischievous twinkle softened them now.

She was drawn to her dresser, and with sodden eyes, she pulled out an Austrian necklace strung with variegated crystal beads Josh had bought her. Was he safe? They sparkled blues and golds, with specks of white, wet and penetrating, before her. She felt proud as a princess whenever she wore them. She stared as into a crystal ball. Perhaps if she stared hard enough she would see her brother, where he was, what he was doing. When she held the beads she had always heard the melodious notes of Mozart that gilded her eyes and ears in aquatic hues; the beautiful notes coming from within her head. She would always associate this music with the best of her childhood. It sang as a happy fountain, sun and water merged into one radiance. Now, the beads felt hard to the touch, peregrine.

Sarah clutched the beads, as she thought of her twenty-four year old brother, whom she strongly resembled. She missed him terribly. He had left the University of Vienna when the Nazis invaded Austria and had completed his medical degree in Switzerland. His last letter said he was coming home but he never arrived. He wouldn't be so pathetic, so weak.

Poetic visions of Vienna floated before her — the city of impeccable, ebullient gaiety. Vienna was an old lady, eternally beautiful, who could sing and dance, proud and arrogant. She was all good things — wizened, ostentatious, and ardently seductive in the moonlight. She was an instrument to be played, the sun was there for her to dominate, rain applauded her — the world was her stage. And the world was at her feet. That's how Sarah remembered her. Unvanquished.

She surrendered herself into imagery, soft and shining billows of trailing music, intensified to ear pounding and swirling colours — the cafes, the taste of lindetorte from sweet to bitter cheroot. It was neither the gifts of food, nor the concertos, nor the glamour. It was sublime. A wellspring of happiness had been born within her. There had been intrigue that had bristled the hair on her arms. Adventure. The city had fastened itself to her as she had imagined a lover would, in galactic spills of rapture.

Her head now boomed with the music of a requiem rather than the gay music of a Mozart concerto. As she fought to retain her childhood, the current of the tide of her emotions, swept it away. Recent memories now seemed so undeniably long ago. Vienna was now a stranger having banished her like her brother.

Twice, once at age six and another at eight, she and her mother, Mindy, had taken the train to Vienna in the summer, to visit Josh. "My big brother, the doctor!" Sarah had called him proudly. He had suddenly changed from a rather shy, self-conscious, studious boy into a self-confident, mature, slightly arrogant man of position. He showed them around the baroque buildings — the Belvedere Palace, the Schonbrunn Castle, the Ringstrasse with the Parliament House. There were many statues, but her favourite was the statue of Johann Strauss Jr., the "Waltz King," in a park. They frequented the numerous pastry shops and outdoor cafés. Mindy had regressed to the state of schoolgirlhood and it was a delight for them all. She showed a side they rarely saw, romping through the coffee shops, openly celebrating the gift of life. There were the festive lunches with Josh's fellow students at Mindy's invitation. Rollicking, smothered in good food and gypsy music, it was a great hurrah. The last hurrah.

Proper Vienna had not resisted in her rape. In her fornication with the enemy, she lay ravished, the godly in her gone; an imitation of herself. Was she haunted by her former self? Did she know of her betrayal by her kinsmen who had whored her to the marauders?

The urgent babble of suppressed voices disturbed Sarah's sleep. The little clock by her bed said midnight. Her attention was drawn to her father, Yitzhak, an old man at fifty-five, was three years older than her mother. She had known him as an optimist. His words she could hear clearly.

"When I married you at twenty-five, I thought I was the luckiest man in the world. I knew I fell short in the ways of culture and etiquette, but I promised myself to change. And I did, didn't I?"

Quietly Sarah crept to her door again, opened it a bit, and peered out. She saw her mother huddled in the light, pale and drawn. Her father's pain-racked vocal chords registered that he had given way to defeat. Yitzhak was afraid. This came as a stupendous slap at the pride she had had for him all her life. There was no chivalry, no honour. It reverberated as a sickening disappointment on the fabric of her crumbling world. Her brother Josh would have fought!

Who knew what was to become of them? Mindy had always been an infuriating siren, heralding endless complaints — the town crier — she knew ahead of time that the housekeeper would chip her good dishes, the butcher would give her bad cuts of meat, the next door neighbours would never reciprocate favours — she gave everyone a hard time with her real or imagined miseries. Why hadn't she predicted this?

The sound of heavy footsteps running up the stairs startled everyone. Mindy's hand snatched Yitzhak's arm. Her eyes were staring in wide-eyed fright, arid lips worked the damnable word, "Gestapo." Lena poured her a glass of brandy. An attempt at normalcy was made. Mindy looked smaller and thinner.

Yitzhak, distraught over his wife's panic spoke to her gently. "You see, it was nothing." She just stared mindlessly into open space. Her hair was sweaty and matted to her head like a skull cap. He whispered, "I will always stay by your side." He was disappointed; he had expected her to be strong for the children. He pitied her. He knelt by her chair.

Mindy had of late, taken to retreats to the past. She'd browse through family photographs and go on about this or that occasion. In these minutes of amnesia about the present, she had closed the door to the future, a future she believed she would not live to see. Memories were the only comfort left her; they remained stalwart — she drew solace in what could never deteriorate, never change, never die.

Other times, she'd be on the verge of madness, crying out to the Almighty about the gypsy fortuneteller at a bazaar years earlier, who she now believed was sent to warn them of great misfortune. "There will be much wandering — I see danger and loss, then a desert; I am looking down on verdant hills, your children will ride out the danger..." The old woman became

16

reluctant to say any more as her forehead furrowed — she was bowed over her crystal ball.

Her hair, once regularly coloured at the hairdresser's, now was dirty snow. Sarah saw her father embrace Mindy, enveloping her with arms like wings. How could she stay angry at him?

He looked at Lena, glancing also at Nina and Peter, seeing them there for the first time that evening. They had been good neighbours for so many years. Yitzhak continued, while the neighbours clasped hot drinks that had gone cold hours before. "I am an honest man who has made an honest living. I began peddling my handmade shoes from house to house in rags; an empty stomach, for what? To take anything from anyone? I've worked for Christian owners, who own machines. Now that I have two businesses, one in Podgorze and one in the Jewish district, I have to make excuses for my existence and be penalized for it. It's a joke. Hah!" He angrily kicked back his chair and stood up. No one knew what to say.

Sarah stood listening. If only her family could somehow be held together, like the sun's pomegranate burst of fire in the horizon as it splashed westward and disappeared, yet lingered behind sepia-fretted eyelashes, to depart naturally, like a faithful friend knowing she would return.

Lena handed Mindy a sock to which she held fast and was now absentmindedly darning, a dull look on her face, as though awakened from a nightmare they had all experienced and didn't know if it might come back.

Mindy's plain countenance was the colour of porridge, her prominent, hawk-like nose standing out more demonstrably framed by her short hair which glinted like drifting silver as it was caught in the lamp's artificial light. Her short, buxom figure sagged heavily. Sarah could not imagine them not being together. Their love for each other and for their children was holy and preordained. She could barely recognize her father's stone-grey face with its new feature: numerous, spidery, wrinkles webbing its deathly surface. Only his receding hairline could offer her the comfort of recognition, tempered by the realization that he was getting old.

Mindy came from a family of eleven children, she being the third youngest. Her parents were religious and Sarah remembered her grandmother looking severe in long dresses with a large cameo brooch at the neck, and her frame wrapped in large shawls with which she covered her head while lighting candles on the Sabbath. Her stern looks masked a playfulness young Sarah brought out in her. They had lived upstairs and until Sarah was nine, she loved to scamper up the stairs to visit and eat homemade cookies and listen to stories of Grandma Miriam's youth in Russia. To Sarah, Grandma Miriam was magic.

For some obscure reason, Grandma had taken an instant dislike to Yitzhak and he was never invited. Then they died, her Grandpa when she was eight, and Grandma when she was nine. She still missed them, and their unconditional love, sorely.

The brooch went to Mindy, but she never wore it, saying it would be bequeathed to Sarah when she died. The jewelry resided in a bright blue velvet box that her mother occasionally took out to reflect on, always with tears in her eyes.

Those precious Sabbaths! Sarah remembered her Grandmother's plaintive voice, as though descended through the ages, murmuring the prayers over the flickering candles, after the waning of the sun, a small piece of heaven dropped into the old, musty apartment. And when Grandpa Israel returned from shul, Sarah felt her heart was a cup filled to overflowing with their mellow affection, sweet as milk and honey. At her tender age, she had taken for granted that they had been born old; she couldn't imagine them otherwise, and that they would always be like this, together until the earth would cease to spin on its axis.

How quickly these affirmations had rushed away. Sarah would go up and sit by their door in the aftermath of her grandmother's death, as though intense longing would cause her to materialize. She would tenderly place her palm flat on that door, as if it were the gateway to heaven, and she'd wait. And she was still waiting.

Sometimes they came to her in dreams, just as Grandma had promised. She'd be in her shawls and would place a gnarled hand on her forehead as if she were sick and it was so real that Sarah would awaken, calling her name. Life had been an Eden. Now they were outcasts.

Mindy's entire identity was in her family, it was her reason for living. And she had ruled with a firm hand, literally. They had reeled from her slaps, and then her guilty kisses. The kids knew she was only as strong as those who loved and obeyed her. They witnessed her generosity to the needy, who were never turned away hungry and who often sat with the family at the table.

Sarah was feeling very sleepy now but compelled to get her housecoat and go up the stairs to sit by that beloved door. When she did so, her mind began to wander and she closed her eyes.

Then she was on the other side of the door and her senses were assailed with the wonderful odours of grandmother's cooking. She could smell the stewed chicken and the freshly baked chalah bread and see the white damask tablecloth laid out. Her grandmother was lighting the candles and her grandfather was holding a glass of red wine, just as he had every Friday night. The two elderly people were watching her in a half-light that glowed warmly and she felt saturated in their love.

Their eyes were wise and gentle and she wanted to go to them. She could not take her eyes off the candles. Their radiance was drawing her in as was the sweet smell of the food. The transparence of the love she was receiving, the breathlessness of her dream come true, took on a holiness that made everything shine. Their home looked enchanting and timeless. There was the fire of youth in their eyes and translucent rosiness on their faces. So this was heaven. She stared into the firelight. Closer and closer she found herself delving into the inner work of the flame. The dreaming child tossed as though her entire body were learning something both wondrous and terrible.

Then she was inside the flame. There was a desert with palm trees of great, green leaves embracing the wind under a vivid aquamarine sky. Beside the desert and in contrast to it lay a moving sea even though the air was still. Her footprints were in the gold dusted sands that stretched for miles, and as she wondered how they got there, a second set of prints, much smaller, appeared and she knew they belonged to her own child. She did not know how she understood, but she did — everything.

The sun above her, was the centre of the flame and more brilliant than any waking sun could be. There was a symphony in the movement, a rhythm to the incoming and outgoing of the tide. Images of children spilled from the water. Some were as yet unconceived, others achingly familiar. All were real and waiting to pass the delineated line from heaven to earth, unearthly in their joy to tumble and toddle in the dappled Monet sands. One child she was drawn to, and when she looked into the vision of this little girl, radiant, with dark eyes framed by mahogany curls, she saw her Grandmother Miriam.

* * * * * *

Over the tufted, blue divan were paintings by local artists of Cracow. Heavy velvet drapes blocked the windows and the view of Wawel Castle. Silver-framed photos of milestones in their lives dotted the furniture.

Yitzhak was still delivering his monologue with a bellicose smashing of his fist on the table. "We are alone," he yelled.

In 1940, the Germans ordered Jews to be at work and open their stores and offices during the high holidays of Rosh Hashana and Yom Kippur. The registration of all Jews age sixteen and over started in November 1939. The order to have the Magen David on the right arm came on December 1. On December 5 and 6, there was a special search in the eighth quarter of Cracow. "We were prepared for that search but the thieves came back."

Peter, a neighbour for many years, said, "You can trust us and we'll help any way we can. We'll safeguard Mindy's jewelry until this is over." He was a gentle-minded man of sixty who owned a grocery store. "You'll not go hungry, that I can assure you."

"We're not taking charity." Yitzhak was uncomfortable.

"Bah, wouldn't you do the same if the situation were reversed? I have good connections with the farmers who bring produce. It doesn't cost me anything." He squeezed Mindy's wrist. She looked weary, with a wan and vacant expression. "Don't you be concerned with issues of etiquette. These are not good times. The Germans are hauling off anything of value. They are looking everywhere for Jews, including basements and attics."

"Do you know," Mindy sadly added, "that during this two-day curfew the synagogues were robbed?"

Yitzhak was screaming again "We are being thrown out of our homes for Germans coming in like never before."

Mindy began to cry. He had gone on too long. Lena implored him to stop, "Please, you're upsetting Mindy. I can assure you, we will all try to help."

"For the sake of..." Mindy urged, "for the sake of our Sarah, our child, we must do something..." She couldn't bear to mention her son's name.

Sarah had come back down the stairs and had been listening again to her father's ravings. Half-formed visions of harm coming to her parents, spun about in her head. A film of perspiration covered her forehead and under her arm pits. She crept back to bed. Never had she been so alone. Bedtime stories told during her happier childhood collided with the nightmarish bedtime conversations of late. Hugging her pillow tightly, she prayed fiercely for her family, her brother, her dry lips moving until they could move no more, for sleep, blessed sleep, overtook her.

* * * * * *

On March 21, 1941, the Horowitzes moved to the ghetto of Podgorze, minus their Sarah, and from then on no Jew was allowed to live outside the ghetto. For Mindy and Yitzhak, there were few illusions. After careful planning, they had delivered their most treasured possession, their remaining child, into the hands of their former charwoman, Lena.

"Mama, mama, no, no! I won't go! Please don't make me go!" Sarah had known Lena all her life. She had been nursed by her, bathed by her, diapers changed and doted on by her. Sarah only knew that her parents were exiling her, that they would no longer be there for her. It was inconceivable that they had decided this.

Her parents knew that they had to be expedient in this brutally painful time, or they would weaken and not be able to let her go. In a world that hated them, that held only evil and shame, they had to act heroically. They had already mourned their son for they did not believe they would ever see him again. His last letter from Switzerland had given such hope but the silence that followed meant he had likely been killed on the way home.

"When this is all over. It can't be long, and then we'll all be together again." Mindy was crying quietly and smiled through the tears. They held each other, sensing it was for the last time. Mindy was wearing her Sabbath finery of black silk and then, they finally turned away. Her parents were not going back to their house. Her home was gone.

Lena stepped forward. "Come Sarah." With those words she took the girl's hand in a firm grip to lead her away from the place of good-byes. In the darkness, everyone seemed like goblins. Even the street was silent. The disappearing figures of Yitzhak and Mindy were quickly consumed by shadows. Only the faint scent of roses emitted from Mindy's perfume lingered.

With a well-packed suitcase in hand, wearing her good boots, her wool coat into which Mindy had sewn part of her black mink for extra warmth, she walked away from what had been her home. As they walked to the poor apartment which Lena occupied with her husband and two children, Sarah could find no solace. She raised her eyes upward and through her mist, the sky resembled stained glass, which made her think piously of a synagogue and if He pondered their pain.

"Sarah, you will stay with us for one week at the most," Lena told her. "Cracow is unsafe for hiding a Jewish child. Neighbours and friends will know and could report me to the Gestapo. Christians harbouring a Jew suffer the same fate as a Jew. I'd be shot on the spot or sent to a death camp."

"Please let me stay with you! I don't want to go to strangers!" Sarah was on the verge of hysteria.

"It's out of the question. Maria, my sister, lives in Tarnow, a small town not far from here. She's agreed to take you. They live in a small apartment and they farm potatoes and vegetables during the spring and summer. During the winter, Lech, her husband, makes shoes. He was a good tradesman and he used to arrive in Cracow by horse and buggy before the war, to do business with your father, and sometimes spent the night with your family before going home the next day. When he was in financial trouble a few years back, Yitzhak helped him and never wanted the loan repaid. This all happened before you were born. Lech wants to show his appreciation."

*T*hree days later, Lena answered the knock at the door and Lech walked into her shabby living room. For the first time since her arrival, Sarah crept out of her hiding place behind a large cupboard. Lech stepped forward, picked her up and gave her a big bear hug. He didn't waste words. "Is everything ready?" Lena handed him the suitcase and a bag which contained cheese sandwiches for the trip to Tarnow.

There was little time to waste on formalities. An embrace from Lena's family, a warning to Sarah to keep quiet and Lech and Sarah were gone. He had sneaked the suitcase into the wagon and when he was sure nobody was looking, Sarah was covered with a big, burlap bag and deposited into the wagon, a mattress placed over her. Then, the long, slow ride began. Sarah heard Lech call out a friendly greeting to the SS guards as they left the city. "Next week your shoes are ready," he shouted.

"They're not cheap either. They should be lined with gold for that price," the German answered. "Just have them ready. I have a Fraulein that likes to go dancing." Lech gave a self-deprecating wave of the hand.

Once, Lech stopped to eat a sandwich and to urinate in the forest. As agreed, Sarah did not budge from her hiding place. They couldn't take the risk. It grew very dark and cold in the forest

Chapter Two

Tarnow
March, 1941

but Sarah was well-protected by her fur-lined coat and the mattress above her. She could hear the cry of a distant wolf proclaiming another animal's loneliness. In time, the rocking of the wagon caused her to doze off and dream fitfully. Sometimes she'd awaken, believing herself sheathed in the comfort of her own bed with her parents watching her lovingly, and that seemed the reality. She'd awaken to a nightmare of the swishing of pine trees and the whinnying of a horse.

Embarked on the crossroads of her life, she thought about Josh. Maybe he was dead. He would not be so selfish as to worry her parents. No, he had to be alive and safe somewhere, maybe still in Switzerland and his letters lost. But what about her Jewish school friends? What about Rachel? She was the same age and her very best friend. Who knew anything anymore. Two of her Jewish teachers had been shot along with many Christian professors — the intellectuals. What could the Nazis have against cultured people? The Germans were a cultured nation. It made no sense. She dozed off again, and so the night went.

Who allowed all this to happen? Her parents had thought that the sleeping Sarah had not overheard their usually hushed conversations in the night. But she had.

"What can we do, Yitzhak?" One night, her mother had sounded frantic.

That night her father tried to sound hopeful. "We shall find a way... If not for us, then at least for our children."

Her mother's nagging voice went on as if she had not heard him. "And lately the stories coming back by Poles who have been there and know. Maybe this is what will happen to us. Oh Yitzhak, I'm afraid I'm losing my mind. Have we lost Josh? Where is our son?"

"No, it is the world that is insane. Yitzhak's voice had become hoarse. He leaned back in his chair dejected. Oh, how Sarah remembered that night! Her father, for the first time in their marriage, slapped his wife, the woman he would have readily given his life for, desperately trying to stop her hysteria.

Sarah remembered another night when David Cantor, a close personal friend of her parents, dropped by and told them that the Germans want to leave in Cracow only those Jews important for economic reasons, about 15,000 out of 68,000.

What were his words?

"Remember, the Jews have been warned that after August 15, families forced to leave will be limited as to the belongings they can take out. I'm so sorry to tell you this!"

Sarah had spied on them from her bedroom door slightly ajar and had seen this very dignified man hang his head. More and more Jews were forced to leave Cracow and by the end of 1940 the community was small, beaten and tortured.

Another night, Sarah heard her father at the kitchen table say, "There's an order from Governor Vachter to create a special ghetto for the Jews. It is to be like Warsaw and Lodz where the Jews are already locked behind walls in special Jewish districts."

Her poor mother was whining. "Maybe we should have left Cracow. Being locked in a ghetto means the end of our freedom. Oh Yitzhak, we are now totally dependent on the enemy!" Her emotion had magnified Sarah's terror.

Sometime in the middle of the night, a travel-weary Lech slowly trudged up the two flights of stairs to his modest apartment, with Sarah sleeping in his arms. Maria opened the door. Sarah was partially roused and in her disorientation, the walls of the ominous, dark night clung to her like living, liquid tar. The remoteness of this alien place came achingly into focus. Her staring silence accentuated the white linen of her face. Beneath the girlish curls of sable lashes hanging heavily over puffy lids was a new expression — animal wariness. "I don't belong here!" she bawled, clutching at the blanket about her.

As she shivered and cowered into a corner of the upholstered daybed that served as their sofa, she broke into heaving sobs. Lech stood motionless, not knowing what to do.

"I want to go back. I want to be with my parents. It will be all right, if I'll just be with them." Desperate longing rivered tears down her face.

Maria disappeared, only to reappear swiftly from the small kitchen of the bland apartment bearing hot tea and bread with jam. Placing the food and drink on the tiny coffee table, she wrapped a large, muscular, peasant's arm around Sarah, wiped away her tears with the back of her hand and said: "Sarah, I'm going to tell you the truth. You can best help your folks by their knowing you are safe with us." Sarah nodded her head in negation. "Sarah, if you would be in their place, what would you do? Think about it a moment." She obeyed.

Shortly, she answered in a feeble voice, "I would send my child away."

Soon Sarah, at first forcing herself, not wanting to seem ungrateful, nibbled the bread and sipped the tea which together lumped in her throat as she fought back tears. The warmth of the tea eventually loosened her throat and finally she gave in to her hunger. Holding the hot mug in her cold hands, she drank trying to think only of the steam that surrounded her face.

"You must be very tired," Maria said gently to her. "Finish eating and we'll get you to bed. You'll have plenty of time to get to know my children better." There was a pause and then she added, "You're home, Sarah. Our home is your home."

Sarah was as tired as she was unhappy, as she was defeated. All she wanted to do was to sleep, to escape the baffling present. The simple divan she was sitting on looked very inviting as the exhaustion hit full-force and her head fell on the pillow. She was barely aware of being covered with blankets, as she drifted away.

Even as she fought it, sleep overtook her. She was comfortably warm on the daybed until daybreak came and she awoke to the sounds of a rooster and trickles of light filtering through the window. Her new life had begun.

Soon there were the hushed voices of children inquiring about her, footsteps in the corridor of the apartment, and the familiar smells and sounds of breakfast being prepared. Curiosity got the best of the children and they quietly wandered into the living room and Sarah found herself staring at them, appraising them as they appraised her. Ten year old Danuta glanced at her with a mixture of curiosity and amusement in her large green eyes. She looked just like her mother. It was incredible. She had the same broad, open face, the same honest and friendly green eyes, and small pug nose with wide flaring nostrils. Pale gold hair framed her face. Speaking directly to Sarah, she said, "Please come to the kitchen for breakfast. Mama told us to come and get you. Oh, don't bother about getting washed first. How old are you?" Danuta said all this at once and in one breath.

"I'm eleven years old." Sarah was feeling peculiarly shy and still trying to get her bearings.

"Goodie! We're almost the same age. I'll be eleven in only three months, so we can be friends!" Sarah felt relieved. She hadn't known what to expect. These were good people.

Anje just watched and listened. He also resembled his mother, except that his skin was darker and his hair black. He would be tall like his father. Sarah knew she was here because her parents were taking care of her still. She felt a little better.

At the table Anje opened up with a million questions and Maria had to hush him.

"For heaven's sake, let the poor girl eat. She's had a hard journey and I'm sure she is still tired. You both can talk to her when you come back from school. Now, the two of you, move. I won't have you getting to classes late."

Eventually, Lech came to eat. "Today I make the boots for the Germans," he growled. "Soon will be spring, and the farming begins." He munched on a piece of Polish sausage and drank black coffee. Sarah noted that he lacked much in the way of table manners. He talked with food in his mouth, slurped the coffee and wiped his mouth with the back of his sleeve. She thought of how her mother would have set him straight but these things no longer mattered. The goodness of his heart did, inasmuch she was comparing this peasant to her more sophisticated father.

Later, while Lech was diligently working on the boots in a tiny back room, Maria said, "Sarah, come and see your room. The noise you heard was Lech fixing up the little back room for you. It is the safest thing to do. If Danuta's friends come to visit, they would realize someone else was there and might tell their parents. We can't risk you going outside and being seen by anyone. Neighbours, friends, people passing by in the street could report you to the Gestapo. You'll have to remain hidden, away from prying eyes, indefinitely."

Maria quietly explained all this to her, as Sarah gazed at the tiny niche that would be her own from now on. Two narrow mattresses, including the one she had been covered with on the wagon, sat on the floor, making her bed. A warm comforter lay on top. The room was a narrow rectangle with no window. A small desk and chair occupied one corner and a wooden cupboard that had housed Lech's tools stood empty. Ugly, faded, yellow wallpaper covered the walls. Sarah glanced about like an animal about to be caged. She understood. She would not ever go for a walk, to the library, or to a movie. School was out of the question.

Why shouldn't Jewish children merit the right to study or participate with other children in normal, social activities? If at least it would all be explained to her, then she could examine it and possibly understand. She wondered, was she seen by others in a way she could not recognize? Was there a distortion to her mind or body not evident to herself?

For what reason did well-intentioned Maria have to tell her, "If invited or uninvited guests come to visit, you will stay very quietly, making not a sound — no coughing, no sneezing — hidden under the mattress, until you get the all-clear. The stay hidden signal will be the kitchen tap suddenly turned on and off along with two coughs. You must remain quietly in your room until someone comes in to tell you it's safe."

Maria brought the suitcase into the little room. It became obvious to her that Sarah did not know what to do with it. She sat at a distance from it, as though it contained her family's essence, which on opening, would escape, like the genie in the lamp. There was nothing left of the life she had had before now, except what was in that case. In the physical space of that magic lamp of old leather, was her universe —everything that was and ever would be of import to her. Not daring to disturb its preciousness, she did nothing at all, but sit beside it, dry-eyed. Maria came and crouched beside her. "You're just a child; you're in the spring of your life." She wound her fingers through Sarah's limp ones. "Just because that door is shut to you now, doesn't mean it's forever." And with a flick of a finger, Maria opened it.

Right on top, was an envelope with her father's neat handwriting, saying simply, "Sarah." It was light, containing only a page or two. With a lump in her throat, she tore it open, then read:

"My darling, dearest Sarah." Maria offered, "Would you like to read it together?" Sarah merely nodded. It went:

> We beg of you, do not live in unhappiness. Be at peace with yourself and grateful that such fine people as the Jasinskis have taken you into their home as their own. They are good and decent people.

Perhaps, G-d granting, we shall all be together again and we shall speak of these terrible times as something of the past. On the Sabbath Mama will, as always, cover her head, and bless the candles, and thank G-d for bringing us together, just as it should be. But, if it should not be so, my Darling, then you must be strong, and carry on what we taught you. You must love yourself firstly, for if you don't, then you cannot love others. You must love life, be thankful for it. You must study and someday you'll marry someone who cares about you. And you must cherish this man with your whole heart. And you will have children and your husband and children will be everything to you, just as you and Josh are, always will be, everything to us.

We pray that one day you will live in Palestine as a free and proud Jew. Don't aid in the enemy's victory, by becoming weak. This is just what they want. The young Jews must continue this race, must create a permanent homeland. The Nazis will be damned and I want you and Josh to see that day, even if your mother and father won't.

Our advice for now is, live for each day. Appreciate it and what it has to offer. Help Maria. Learn to cook and sew. She knows all these things and can teach you. There is something that can be garnered from every person you encounter, even if not immediately evident. Become friends with the children, especially Danuta. Most of all, love these good and brave people. They have earned it.

Your mother and I want to write a few words to the Jasinskis, but we are at a loss for these words. Nothing can be said that can give just credit. Thank you seems so small in comparison to what they are doing for us.

I can write no more. Love this life. Enjoy it. Be a part of it. Your mother and I will love you for eternity. Forever and a day,

Your mother and father.

The dark commiseration from a dying parent under iron self-control, brought the threat of the morrow into wrenching prophecy. They knew they were going to die! Both were overcome with emotion, and they cried, Sarah on Maria's shoulder. Finally Maria spoke, with her actions. She knelt on the floor, crossed herself and began unpacking the small suitcase methodically, her large crucifix of gold dangling over her full breasts. Sarah crept to the same position beside her, helping.

With their removal, the belongings became holy sacraments. There was humility as each item was held, the sweaters, the shoes, the nightgowns the well-worn edition of Grimms' Fairytales. The food her parents parted with, without thinking of themselves — including a tin of all the cocoa her mother possessed and a bag of biscuits — added to the handful of symbolic sacrifices. And then, reverently she was pressing her father's talit to her face, filling herself with the scent of him. How often she'd seen him wear it! The prayer shawl had belonged to his father and his father before him. And the sterling silver bejewelled kiddish cup they drank from on the Sabbath. It brought a hot tide of yearnings and a bitter flood of tears. Her parents were giving her the gift of life.

At the bottom, in two envelopes, were several family pictures. Sarah looked at them. So many memories — a mother — a father — a proud brother, little and then in a white coat — baby pictures.

The profound yearning, the longing to be reunited made the need even greater until it felt that it would envelop her and ultimately destroy her. Sarah realized that she would never see her parents again. What hurt so terribly was that they had also believed that and were determined to save her.

From that day on, Sarah fell in with the routine of the Jasinskis. Maria left home at six each morning for her job at the warehouse, Lech worked at a friend's home or in his bedroom and the children went to school.

Still, Sarah's heart carried a heavy burden of loneliness and fear. The Jasinskis were kind and well-meaning, but they weren't Jewish and no one would come to take away or kill any member of their family because of who they were.

She realized that this brave family was taking terrible risks and lived with the knowledge. Sarah, afraid of being an even greater burden, chose to keep her fear and worries to herself. She didn't want to worry them and she didn't want them to change their minds about keeping her.

S pring came. The sun shone brightly. Colourful leaves grew on the trees. Flowers blossomed jauntily everywhere, amidst fruity scents. Lech went to work in the fields and Sarah insisted on earning her keep. The Jasinskis had been adamant — "Sarah, you are our houseguest and houseguests don't work, especially such young ones." But she needed something to do with her time. So they accepted her floor-cleaning, ironing and baking. She surprised them with mandel broit, made just like her mother had taught her, the finger like dough laden with orange juice, orange peels and nuts.

The merry, Slavic girl with candlelight in her pale eyes had adopted the fugitive girl and viewed their unique friendship as an augury. "When a black cat crosses your path, something bad will happen. I always cross myself. Your coming to us must mean we were chosen to do something especially good, for I haven't seen a black cat in a long while." Nothing could mar their relationship. Like all girls their age, they kept secrets and Danuta would update her about school, the students and town gossip. Maria and Lech grew accustomed to the youngsters conspiring. Danuta even sneaked Sarah out of the apartment a few times as spring began.

Amid the joy a welcome spring after a hard winter always brings, there were dark thoughts.

Chapter Three

Tarnow
April, 1942

31

Sarah was sometimes envious that Danuta's family was safe and had no reason to despair. She would have been jealous, if it were not for the visit of some acquaintances of Lech who talked about the Jewish ghetto of Tarnow and how a Catholic family who had hidden a Jewish couple were shot by the Gestapo. The danger they were putting themselves in was brought home to Sarah and she felt ashamed for begrudging them a peace of mind they could no longer have, thanks to herself.

"Oh, Danuta, don't come with me. It's too dangerous for you." Sarah had a frown on her forehead, for Danuta was insisting on accompanying her outside.

"Don't be a goose. I want to come." Danuta's fresh, mischievous, ever-present smile was a Godsend to Sarah. She was a born gossip and her mother's friendship with the town doctor's wife, also the town blabbermouth, gave her material that she embellished, Sarah suspected, with her lavish imagination. Who did what with whom was cheap entertainment and it didn't seem to matter if it were malicious or not. By the time Sarah heard it, she believed it had been exaggerated enough that it could be called fiction.

One Saturday towards the end of summer, 1942, when nobody was home, the girls went on a secret mission. They smirked knowingly as usual as they left the apartment, checking left and right that they weren't seen, and then darted off down the hall and out into a pleasantly cool late afternoon. This would be the third time that they weaved in and out of side streets, peeked around corners, then skipped all the way to Bolek and Sandra Bolewski's farm about two miles out of town. It was there that a young Jewish man was being hidden.

Sandra Bolewski, a squat, large woman, in simple peasant clothes and a stiff, white apron, opened the door and the girls ran upstairs, two at a time, to a small attic with a boarded-up window. Engrossed in one of Yan's medical books, Henry Reichman looked up and smiled. He nodded at his cot with grandiose gestures. They laughed at the princely invitation, which automatically put them at ease.

The diminutive space had a dank, chilling odour and a woebegone atmosphere. Wrinkled books and untidy papers were strewn on the floor of the prison, cell-like room. By the time

Sandra delivered plates of potatoes and red beets and a pot of tea, the small room had become a boisterous party, with the girls venturing forth an assortment of questions, giggles over town gossip and then silence as they sat hanging on to his every word.

In the dim light, they could have been on a camping expedition, with straw for a floor, as they scrambled onto the cot. He still looked gaunt and haggard from his ordeal but he had a sense of humour, even in tragedy, that captivated the girls. While they ate, with cheeks full of unchewed food, Sarah begged him to talk about his life.

In a subdued voice, he cleared his throat and began. With a winsome smile to them, he then turned involuntarily inward, his expression becoming absorbed and melancholy. "At twenty-four, I had the distinction of being in that rare minority of Jews who were accepted and then graduated from the medical school in Cracow. I braved the beatings each year in the fall when classes resumed. Once, in my second year I saw a fellow Jewish student flung from the second floor stairs by gentiles." Here he paused, exhaling heavily.

"He died instantly. My parents pleaded with me not to return to school each year. We had terrible fights over it. You see, my father wanted me to go into the furrier business with him. But my dream in life was to be a doctor. I would not be satisfied with anything less."

His eyes had fixated on a small, rural painting on the wall, and as he spoke, his gaze remained riveted there with a longing for the freedom of nature it offered.

Sarah found his presence most pleasant and she looked upon him with the fondness of a pupil to an adored teacher. He reminded her of her brother. Physically, Henry was short, no more than five and a half feet tall and delicately slender and small boned, boyishly appealing with an unmanageable fluff of black hair over the centre of his forehead. His hands were in perpetual motion as tools of expression, conducting the air. His fingers were long with the beautiful tapering of an artist.

With self-deprecation, he held them up and said, "My Jewish colleagues would advise me to control this ungentile affectation, but this is a part of me and who I am." He chuckled, "Where was I? Ah yes, you see those books? They have become my literary prayers. I was always a bookworm. Now, I relish the free passage to places I can't go physically. I'm an armchair adventurer, but not by choice, no not by choice." He sighed mystified by the girls' silent interest. "The printed page is a great invention."

He found his thread again. "I showed them, my professors, that this Jew was indeed worthy of becoming a practising physician, that these hands could perform surgery."

"You were in a camp?" Sarah asked almost frightened to hear the details. And yet she implored him to continue. His voice echoed in her ears as she listened intently.

"No. I escaped that. My parents went into the Podgorze Ghetto. That same day, the SS came to the hospital where I worked and took me along with many other young Jewish men they had rounded up and put us in cattle trains on a transport to the east. I knew my parents and I would not live. However, during the night, the boys who had been cooped up in the cattlecars were let loose in the woods. Then the SS began to shoot and beat us at random until there were about a hundred dead on the ground. I ran for my life, along with two teenaged boys. Terrified, cold and hungry, we ran blindly for hours until we came to a small farmhouse. Out of breath and wet and dirty from a heavy downpour of rain, we knocked on the door. As luck would have it, the farmer felt sorry for us. He gave us warm food, drink and a place to spend the night. All the boys could talk of was running away to Russia and joining the army there. I decided to take a chance and walk to Tarnow. I hoped that Yan, a Pole and a gentile who I'd studied and graduated with, and who had always been decent to me, might help me. I had nowhere else to turn. Moving only in darkness, two nights later, with the screams of my comrades from the train still echoing in my ears, I arrived on the point of collapse, at the farmhouse of Yan's parents, Sandra and Bolek Bolewski. It was late evening when I knocked on their door.

"I was half dead with exhaustion, defiled, filthy. The door ran in a blur. I had reached for it as for the golden gate of heaven. I was prepared to die, just for a momentary confirmation that there still were human beings who would look upon me with compassion and not revulsion. It was a pivotal event. I wearily accepted there was no exit from the maelstrom of annihilation. I would not emerge alive; I had no energy, no courage, no way to go on. A transport to the east, was unavoidable.

"My first sight of Bolek, was of a divine being, unreal and bathed in white light. Later, I learned a lantern had been responsible for this strange illumination. I lay crumpled on the doorstep before his feet in my wet rags, shivering. He leapt into action, carrying me like a small child into the house, calling Sandra to come and help. I was placed on a warm bed on a comfortable mattress and covered in wool blankets. I thought I had died and gone to heaven! There was the sound of feet padding about and the sensation of being bathed in warm water. My dirty, soaked tatters were stripped from me. A pillow — soft and wonderful — was placed beneath my head, as a warm mug of milk was put to my lips. The sweet, soothing liquid spreading slowly through my vitals, replenished me. I was alive, I thought. Exhaustion intoxicated me. I just wanted to sleep. I became disoriented. Coming straight from a death train, squeezed together with decaying corpses and human excrement that turned us into one homogenous, unspeakable mass, where even G-d wouldn't go — there I was beneath a portrait of the Virgin Mary and her baby, Jesus.

"In her arms, I imagined myself, as crazy as it sounds. My mind was climbing over itself. It occurred to me, that the Almighty had sent me to hell — that that train was hell and the decomposing mire, that insane abattoir, was for me to be purged of my sins, and this lovely bath was my mikveh, to cleanse and purify me. There could be no other explanation. And then I thought of the others and I knew I would remember them always, for the rest of my life — their cries, their terror, and the unbearable indignities imposed upon them in the manner of their deaths."

Sarah listened to the raw emotion in his words while staring into his grave olive-black eyes. She thought that she could feel the soundless pounding of his heart. The loss of her own young innocence had made her more acutely sensitive to his story. A flush was creeping up her neck and the girls sat nestled against each other, legs crossed. Time flew for the two exiles and their young compatriot. Sarah urged him to go on. Her high, sweet voice, full of purity, lit a spark in a sightless place he thought was dead. It stirred him and made him uncomfortable. Henry was enjoying the sound of his own voice and the attentive audience which made him feel more valued than he had felt in a long time. He choose his words carefully as if this were a speech to a crowd.

"The next morning brought a glorious sunshine. It shone directly on me, illuminating the room, making it appear cheerful and inviting. It had been so long since I'd paid any attention to the countryside, which I love so much; to the changing seasons. That day was different. All my senses were unnaturally keen. I wanted to live. With all the abnormal circumstances, my heart had become a desert. Now it wanted to be fruitful again. I didn't want my life to have been in vain." Sarah pondered over the similarity of their parents' destiny. Both of them had lost parents.

A familiar, manly scent of spicy shaving cream, caught in her nostrils. It was the same as her brother's. It was so powerful that she actually believed she was at home with her family, with Josh. It was so comforting that she let herself be swept away by the warmth of its waves. She inhaled strongly, head thrown back. She could taste its sweetness, like melted molasses. Around and around, her head spun. So sinfully lucky she was to be sharing with one of her people, to have this sense of caring. She bathed in it. And like the sleepy child she was, she yawned and rubbed her eyes and felt her body go slack, to his mesmerizing voice, rhapsodious to her ears.

"Here, let me cover you, sleeping beauty." He was smiling down at her, pulling the fleecy comforter over her, and she thought again of how much he reminded her of her brother. She didn't want him to stop talking, she was clinging to him, to the moment, before it too, slipped from her fingers.

"When Sandra and Bolek heard my story and that I was Yan's friend, they volunteered to hide me. From that day on, I have lived in this attic, spending most of the day reading or writing scientific papers and waiting, for what, I didn't know."

"What about your parents," Sarah wanted to know. Henry hesitated, as though afraid to tell her. But Sarah saw his fears. "Please. You must tell me. The Bolewskis gave me news of what was happening in Cracow."

Sandra appeared at the attic door. She was carrying a bowl of fruit and handed it to the girls. "I see you youngsters are having a good time," she said grinning and hurried downstairs, not having paid attention to the tightness in Sarah's face.

They ignored the food. Henry shifted his position and continued. "The ghetto is an enclosure for the Jewish population — they put twelve thousand in there. Conditions are bad. Unrelated families have to share a single tiny apartment. There is never enough air, especially in the summer and no grass. At first you could come and go, even daily, to work in Polish or German factories. A few friends, via 'passeurs,' had false papers made and some escaped to Russia. The movements in and out meant that some food could get in. But slowly and surely the contacts with the outer city became limited and the guards became strict so that food and supplies became scarce. Prices skyrocketed.

"I knew my parents had moved into the ghetto, just like all the others. They were allowed to take everything but furniture, which had to be left for the Germans who moved into their homes. Shortly after, the Gestapo arrested me, passage in and out of the ghetto was limited to those with special permission. Cracow Jews had to either leave the city or move to live in the ghetto. You should have seen the endless procession of thousands in trucks, wagons, carts and on foot that crossed the Podgorze bridge into the ghetto. Before moving, most sold everything they could that was not necessary for living there. Paintings, carpets, suits, fancy dresses, luxuries you cannot imagine were purchased very cheaply by the good Christian citizens of Crackow. The pitiful families tried to move into the ghetto with as much food as possible. Books that had been handed down for generations from father to son, did not have any use now and were left in empty apartments. Jewelry and gold coins were sewn into clothes and smuggled in for use later."

Sarah stared unblinking, the bottom of her throat burned. She clutched her neck. Henry offered her a drink of water and she took a few sips. Faith was all that was left, faith that somebody somewhere would put a stop to the horror.

Henry swallowed, as if thirsty, and continued. "Word spread through the underground and Sandra and Bolek continued to bring me news. In the ghetto the Jewish police sold out our people. Jews hate them as much as they hate Germans. They arrested fellow Jews sent them to their deaths.

"Eventually Jews could not send packages through the mail service. These packages had been a lifeline to the ghetto, a stream of food that the Germans cut off. When the war in Russia got going they demanded our furs and fur coats for the German army. Also warm shoes and ski equipment. Life in the ghetto was horrific beyond belief. By the end of last year, deportations and deaths happened constantly — a daily event. Those who survived were no more than a living cemetery — skeletons with skin, hollow, dehumanized eyes and their voices. Corpses, many dead, others still moving. The stench of decomposing bodies, adults, babies, children... When someone died the family had to remove all clothing and throw the body in the street, since, if not, they had to pay the Germans a high burial tax which no one could afford."

Henry wiped his face as if ridding himself of dirt that wouldn't come off. Henry drove in his pain with merciless, self-speculation. "Why didn't we see it coming? As a group, a particular race, throughout history hated, we should have sensed we were endangered. Animals do."

Sarah had paled to the whiteness of a ghost and a draft whizzed through her as if she truly were one. Her inner voice asking more questions, Were her parents alive? Or were they better off dead? Where was Josh?

Henry continued. "Earlier this year, for a time I could no longer stay in the attic. The Bolewskis knew it was unsafe. They tried to keep the increasingly bad news of the Jewish situation from me. During the day, I usually stayed in the barn, with the farm animals, lying motionless at the bottom of a hayloft. On very cold nights, Sandra would bring me into the house, and sneak me back to the loft before sunrise.

"The SS searched the ghetto in order to check the identity cards of everyone. Some identity cards were stamped and those with stamped cards could stay. They refused to stamp cards of anyone over fifty-five. This last June, as Sandra came to take me to the house to share supper with the family, I instinctively knew something was wrong. When she told me of my parents being sent on the June first transport to Treblinka, I broke down. Sandra held me. She smoothed the hair from my forehead as she must have done so many times for her son, Yan. It was the first time a person had touched me that way in years. I knew she understood that a part of me died that day. I couldn't eat and then, Bolek coaxed me to drink hot black coffee. Later, I was strangely calm. Do you know what I mean?" Sarah did.

For a moment Sarah grew frightened of him. She looked at his stiffened veins rising to the surface, altering the composition of his features. They became hard, livid red. The hulking words, the evil they conveyed, the thickening of his voice as though through mortar, projected him, in her perception, as brutish and unpredictable. She realized that his long speech had reminded her of her father's obsessed monologues. Both of them, in their pain had gone on for hours, had seemed unable to keep track of time, to realize that they were speaking to people who knew what they were going through, people who were on the same side. Is that what the Germans do to us — turn us into raving lunatics? She felt guilty for having been so angry with her father those nights when his rantings had kept her from sleep. These observations made her both timid and fascinated. She surprised herself by the need to reach out her hand and lay it on his.

He was driven to distraction. Henry, shocked by his own vulgarity, realized that he was suddenly attracted to Sarah. What was he doing, having such thoughts of a homeless child? He was swept away with guilt.

Mozart's Eine Kleine Nacht Musik came up from below like a kind ambassador. Sandra must be listening to the gramophone. The three of them sat motionless listening to the music valuing the moments of wordlessness. Briefly, it seemed as if they were suspended in time. Nothing could happen to them.

Below, Sandra was calmed by the music which reminded her that, however awful the circumstances, she was still a person. She knew something important was happening upstairs and she did not belong there. At first she was astonished by her own tears and then grateful that she could feel something.

* * * * * *

Sarah often made her way to see Henry, sometimes with Danuta, sometimes alone, when the household was away. Because there was no news of her own family, she listened to Henry's stories as a substitute for her own.

Each time she came, Henry told Sarah more of his story. He told her of when Yan came home. "Two weeks after I discovered my folks had been sent to a camp, Sandra came to the barn to tell me Yan was home. In the house, Yan gave me a big bear hug. I didn't know what to say. I wanted desperately to unleash all my bitterness, but I didn't want to upset Yan. His parents had done more than enough, endangering their lives. Yan was understanding."

Henry was sitting with Yan and his family at the table, silent as though at an open crypt. All of them knew that Yan would begin when he was ready. Yan spoke slowly letting each word mature before he went on to the next. "It's getting worse. I saw it first hand. I was forced to work in a German military hospital. I hate their mechanical villainy; the frequent, high-pitched outbursts. The whole place was inhuman. I didn't recognize them as people. Do you know what I mean? The SS uses any minor infraction as an excuse to demonstrate their cruelty."

Henry understood what it meant to not recognize them as people. They didn't see him as of the same species either.

Yan poured them both thick, black coffee and gulped his down. The ensuing news, now delivered in clipped agitation, fell as grenades on the family.

"Convoys of Jews, thousands and thousands of them, are seen everywhere and aren't heard from again. They just disappear." Yan bent closer, his voice conspiratorial, "I've heard hush-hush reports from a chemist, that they are using the bodies to manufacture chemical products. And there's the suicides, Jewish families have taken to throwing themselves out of high windows, before deportation."

Yan was recounting some of the latest Nazi crimes, when he just happened to describe an SS attack on a small town near the Polish border where a young woman, Elana, whom Henry had been in love with for years, had escaped to with her relatives.

Henry paused when he was telling Sarah the story of that night and that far-away look Sarah had come to recognize was there again, a look that emphasized the distance between them. Then he spoke deliberately, forcing himself through the facts as if he had some need to unburden himself in front of this child-woman.

Henry told Sarah Yan's account of the night when the SS rounded up the old and the children and took them to the market place and forced them to lie naked on the stones. There they were run over again and again by the SS trucks. Whoever survived was shot. The remaining townspeople were marched outside of town and forced to dig their own graves, stand at the rim, and then embrace each other as the bullets brought them death. As he would talk Henry looked away towards a corner of the room so Sarah could not meet his gaze. Every so often he would look back to see if the story were too much for her. She remained passive, her hands folded on her knees, the only indication of her pain, the clenching of her knuckles as the graphic details were being described. This is no child thought Henry. She has already been robbed of her innocence. I doubt if I could shock her if I tried.

"Elana... we had planned to marry after the war. She was twenty-one, an artist. She had studied in Paris... why?" Henry did not have to describe his emotions on hearing the dreadful news. Sarah witnessed them as if he were hearing it for the first time.

"In July, Yan came to visit again, with a letter for me from a convent. I sat, disbelieving, reading it over and over. I hugged Yan and cried with joy. Elana was alive!"

"Dearest Henry," the letter began. "At long last I can write to you. I write with tears of happiness that you are indeed alive, not like the others."

A convent in the area had come to her aid. They took her in, cut her dark, bobbed hair very short and dyed it blond, along with her eyebrows — and she became Sister Gabrielle.

The convent has been very good to me. They took me in when I had no hope. I am Sister Gabrielle and if you'd see me, you probably wouldn't recognize me. My parents and sister are all dead and I live each day with the knowledge that if it were not for mama's coaxing I would be dead with them. My own mama, a week before that terrible massacre, went to the convent and begged them to take my sister and me. Finally, mama refused to take no for an answer, the sisters agreed. I begged Angelica to come with me, but she refused. I could do nothing but go alone. The good-byes were terrible. When I heard of what happened, I wished the SS had killed me too. The sisters comforted me, and wisely, got me working right away. They got me scrubbing the floors I have never seen so many floors so intimately. I began to understand the monks and the nuns who seek salvation by living in poverty and hard work for others. I begged them to give me more work. Anyhow, one day while I was nursing a patient in the hospital, I saw Yan. He looked like he had seen a ghost. I spoke with him and he agreed to take this letter. He is a fine young man, Henry, a very fine guy.

Please forgive me, but I am so very tired. We work day and night. There are so many dead and dying and sometimes I can sit for half a night just comforting someone.

I tell myself each day that I wake, Henry, my Henry is alive and that is all that matters. I pray for the day that we will be reunited once more, and then I'll never, never, never, ever, let you go, my love.

I kiss your eyes, your hair, your lips,

Your Elana

P.S. I will try to write soon again.

Henry kept the letter and reread it and when he was lying in the hayloft, he kept it close to his body. Her love kept him going. Yan, every month or so, came home for a visit and usually brought with him another letter from Elana. Henry devoured every word and shared many of the letters with Sarah. It was a vicarious existence. She helped him to endure the days that blended into weeks and months.

One day at the end of 1942, the Gestapo arrived at the farm. Sandra, although disintegrating internally from fear, managed to freeze an outward smile on her face. They searched her house and basement and the wood shed, but not the barn. Frantically, she ran to the barn when they left. "They're gone," she sputtered.

Henry could not bear the sight of this kind woman's terror. "I will go," he said simply, removing hay from his clothes.

"No! It would be the death of you. The Tarnow ghetto has been evacuated and sent away to Auschwitz on a cattle train. It was horrible to see." Just the mention of it made her cross herself violently. "We are devout Christians and under our roof, no harm will come to you. I truly believe G-d sent you here to be with us."

Henry shrugged, "If I am to die, then I shall die as a man and not as a coward in hiding." And as an afterthought, he said, "I shall try to join the Resistance."

"Are you mad? Just days ago some people in the Resistance were hunted down and killed. It is probably the reason for the search. There is nothing you can do now. If there were, we would have told you. If the Gestapo catch you, what will become of us! They would torture you into telling them about us!" Henry knew she only said this to keep him there, and that she was worried about him not herself, but her logic made sense even if he felt sure that he could never be made to give them up to the Germans. He was overcome with frustration. Knowing she was right, he furiously kicked the farm tools that lay about. He had to wait it out. But, Oh G-d, for how much longer?

Henry still came every evening for dinner with the family. Then Christmas approached and the Bolewskis invited relatives and a few friends for Christmas dinner. They had a pine tree in the living room which Yan decorated when he came home for a week. And that same night, with the guests gone, boisterous and a little drunk, Yan brought Henry to the house.

"You don't look at all well. You're so pale and that awful cough! Let me take your temperature. 104 degrees Fahrenheit." Yan got him to gargle salt and water, gave him aspirin, and Sandra insisted he go immediately to bed in Yan's room. Henry stayed one week in the house, with the drapes drawn. Visitors who dropped by were dismissed and told that Yan was ill with a bad flu. Henry's temperature fluctuated between 102 and 104 degrees for three days, as the new year began, and then he got better. Sandra fed him chicken broth with noodles, hot camomile tea with sugar, or honey and lemon. He ate potato dumplings and boiled chicken as his health returned. But the cough remained stubborn, especially at night.

About a month later, as the entire family sat down to supper, they broke into an animated discussion of the progress of the war. Yan and Bolek excitedly were talking about Stalingrad, the best news they had heard in a long time. On the Russian front the

Germans had suffered their biggest and bloodiest defeat: Stalingrad was liberated and almost a quarter million German soldiers were dead, wounded, or taken prisoner. News filtering in from the Pacific was good as well. These days they talked more often about the progress of the war now that the news was frequently good.

Each word was music to Henry's ears. Each word spelled what he had been praying for. Each word confirmed the inevitable: German defeat.

The year 1943 came and went in the Jasinski household and soon it was the summer of 1944. Henry's latest news was that the Russians had moved westward into Poland, forcing the Germans into retreat. With the battlelines coming closer, thousands of Poles joined the ranks of wandering refugees, with only the belongings they could carry or put on a wagon.

Sarah, now fifteen, had blossomed into a young woman. Her hips and breasts had rounded out and her face had matured. As she stared at her reflection in the bathroom mirror and a young woman stared back, she shyly smiled to herself. Mama and Papa wouldn't recognize their own child if they would meet her after the war — whenever that was.

Seldom did she allow herself the luxury of believing that her parents and brother were still alive. She had come to accept the worst possible fate for them. The Jasinskis and the contents of her suitcase were all she had left. It was like the effects of a powerful drug, the high of optimistic thinking was never worth the desperate low that would follow. A suppressed sob choked her as wild imaginings took hold. She tottered to the edge of the bathtub and sat down.

There was so little to be grateful for. So little that felt good; the visits with Henry, the

Chapter Four

Tarnow
Summer, 1944

warm feelings she had for her hosts. Her young pride in her burgeoning adulthood.

Maria had a flair for any handiwork and she patiently taught Sarah whatever she knew. She also had a talent for thievery and as 1944 drew to a close and warm clothing grew scarce, she stole whenever she had the opportunity. And she was proficient at it. The result was an ever-increasing store of goodies: cocoa, sugar (stuffed in a sagging bra as she left work), bed sheets, a pillow, wool for knitting, thread, light bulbs, sausage, tea, canned fruit. Everyone was amazed at her. "Mama," Danuta said, "One day they'll catch you."

But Maria safeguarded herself against this too. Sarah sat in her little room, her knitting needles clicking away on a small sweater reincarnated from the combined wool of two old children's cardigans. Maria would slip it to one of the guards whose young niece would be the lucky recipient. With these trades the household got cooking pans, stockings, flour and embroidery thread. Every little bit counted, and Sarah felt relieved that she was able to contribute. She felt like an adult.

Danuta and Sarah became inseparable. Anje, now seventeen, worked with his father in the fields, but avoided school. He was afraid. The Germans were taking strong, young men like him and sending them for forced labour for the Reich. Some of his friends had answered a knock on the door, only to be taken away by the Gestapo. Many of them died from the grueling toil and abominable living conditions. The Poles now hated the Germans like poison.

The new year, 1945, was celebrated quietly in the Jasinski household. Maria surprised everyone with a plump turkey, baked potatoes and canned vegetables she had been saving. Gifts were exchanged at Christmas. Sarah and Danuta had crocheted a black scarf for Maria and she wore it immediately, waltzing about the salon, a gay, unworried expression on her face. For Lech, seeing his wife's carefree expression reminded him of what life had been like before the Germans came. He had made a pair of shoes for Danuta. Anje gave Sarah a book of poetry, and both girls got pretty, floral cotton fabric from which to make spring outfits.

During one of Sarah's visits, Henry broke down crying. He had just received a letter from Elana, one month old. Unable to

talk about it, he simply handed her the already well-worn paper.
The letter was written in a fine neat hand.

Dear Henry,

I've fallen in love with someone wonderful. You don't
know how difficult it is for me to write this letter. All at
once, I feel desperately guilty and ecstatic beyond
anything I ever imagined. Aaron was one of my patients
in the hospital and for a while I didn't know that he was
Jewish. Slowly we revealed the truth about ourselves. He's
a fugitive, like me. His family was sent to an
extermination camp. We can only hope that they
somehow are surviving.

For the first time my life is complete. I hope I haven't
distressed you terribly, but is what we're doing so wrong?
You're too honest and I just couldn't lie to you. Oh, please
don't hate me, Henry. I've been so alone. I only hope that
someday, you will find your happiness too. I wish you the
best.

Always your friend,
Elana

Sarah kept looking at him over the page as she read the grim
letter. His eyes were dwelling on some point in space, his profile a
granite chiaroscuro of planes and angles. Just as she read the
elegant signature, the candle was extinguished and he
disappeared. The coincidental obliteration of his and the tallow's
light seemed to her a terrible omen. Matches were found and as a
wavering light was restored, she found herself gazing into the two
empty chimneys that were his eyes.

Sarah was deeply wounded, but didn't know why. And she was
very tired. She felt that she could not bear to be there any longer.
She got to her feet and numbly mumbled, "Maybe this isn't a
good time." Slipping into her warm coat, she put on her boots
downstairs and left the house quietly. She did not want to go back
— ever.

Night was quickly approaching, but she gave it no heed, just
as she failed to notice a black car far in the distance. It was only a
meaningless speck of dust and no more, just as she saw herself at

that moment. The cold air was biting and she dug her gloved hands deep into her pockets.

Her tiny world was crumbling about her, as the weighty, frosty lace fell silently, and her boots plodded on, head bent in despair against a bitter wind that pushed her back and ripped at her face. Henry was mourning Elana and the Jasinskis had each other, and the aching loneliness nipped at eyes which couldn't cry.

Preoccupied by inner visions of horror, she gradually recognized a more immediate danger. Looming way up the road was an unmistakable Mercedes. The SS! It was too dark and cold for anyone to be out! Who were they looking for? Fear and hate assailed her. The SS must be searching for her. The great Nazis on a mission to hunt down a dangerous, homeless, freezing and hungry little girl! In a gesture she knew they were too far away to see, she shook a fist and watched as the car stopped at a farmhouse. Henry! The Bolewskis! She had to warn them!

Trembling, she began to run, falling again and again in the foot deep snow. She had to get back to their house, but she also had to stay off the road, close to the protection of the trees. They were her only allies now. Did they know how afraid she was?

Now she was sinking and now she was pushing ahead on acutely freezing limbs. Ice was forming on her back, hands and feet from snow that had gotten into her clothes. It penetrated her skin, cut like knives in welts. Then she saw the Bolewskis' home, a plaster, ghostly structure, the sallow eyes of its windows alit, its inner warmth a desire beyond description. She was pounding on the door, a scurry of steps, and Sandra opened it, her eyes startled at the sight of Sarah.

"My G-d, Sarah!" Icicles had formed on her eyebrows and had extended her nose like a glassy Pinocchio. A band of ice haloed the hood of her parka. As she attempted to speak, a beard of snow broke loose from her chin. She was a bushy-eyed snowman and she was quickly melting. Sarah, through chattering teeth, managed, "Gestapo!"

Sandra was at once up the stairs and momentarily Henry was at the door in coat and boots. "Quickly, into the woods!" and the door closed behind and they were in the hellish void.

Together they stumbled off, helping each other. They lay down in the snow together and waited. Soon they heard a car stop at the house. It seemed to take forever, then the vehicle left. The visit was probably no more than twenty minutes. Then Sarah felt herself being dragged to the barn where they both fell asleep on a bed of hay.

Before dawn, Sandra ventured into the barn. Laden with boiled eggs, bread, and steaming coffee, she said, "Tonight, you come back inside the house. You both stay here for now. The SS were searching for someone — not you, so don't worry."

Under the hay they remained until dusk. The snowstorm had covered the world outside in heavy dunes three feet high and there was no visibility. Half dragging her, and falling under his own weight, Henry wrestled the two of them to the house.

In a few minutes Sarah lay by the fireplace, having the circulation rubbed back into her limbs. A hot water bottle was placed on her chest and then hot coffee was made. Together they sat drinking silently with only the sounds of the whistling wind and burning embers. The deathly beauty outside still managed to rouse fear and wonder. Then the two snowbirds slept deeply with the night, by the toastiness of the fire, in a nest of blankets and elusive dreams.

The snowy gridlock remained uninterrupted throughout the next the morning. Sarah woke first and tiptoed to the silvery stencilled window. Her fingers reached out to trace the design. The monochromatic scenery was otherworldly and fantastic. Unblinking, she gazed longingly at the entombed houses of ice, shingled in thick tiles of snow that exaggerated the shapes beneath, and up at the cavernous lofty grey eye of the sky. The trees and ground were upholstered with down-like fluff, piles and piles, smooth and unflawed. How guileless nature was, with her veil of mist and flakes. It appeared to condescend to her insignificance, reducing her. She placed her face against the glass and her skin burned. How dare there be such calm amid chaos! The day was hiding its shame magnificently, the great grey eye who refused to testify to the unspeakable cruelty it witnessed, played accomplice by covering the bloody tracks well. How obsessed with guilt it had to be. How haughty, how sterile.

But then she couldn't forget altogether the joys she had known, playing in its softness, rolling in it. Once upon a time, winter had been her mammoth playmate. She had revelled in it, ridden its surf and laughed. Now it was forbidden. Others would be sledding, building ice castles, sharing in its bounty, carefree. But for her it was an nonnegotiable, impassive, white moss.

She suddenly realized that Henry had come to sit beside her. "You look a million miles away." She gave him a rare smile. He looked at her damp eyes, glanced timidly away, and then placed an arm about her shoulder. He just understood. Home wasn't a place, it was who you were with. After a time he drew softly away returning with two cups of hot coffee. She wondered if from the little good in her life she would awaken into a cold hell. They had escaped physically — so far — but the running and the hatred that caused it were too much for her.

She turned to Henry, she opened her mouth to speak, but couldn't, and then to her surprise, her head dropped onto his breast and leaked out all the hurts.

Sarah returned to the unshakable goodness of the Jasinskis, to the reassuring muskiness of leather sheaves, to the comfort of their home. She continued to help with the cooking, studied Danuta's school lessons, enduring the stunting of her own education with resignation and resentment. The homework she did with exuberance and self-imposed discipline.

Occasionally, she huddled frightened in her back room, fearing for all their lives when unexpected knocks arrived at the door. And always afterward, she felt moved by the magnanimity of their unflinching courage and she'd bow her head in humility. The shabbiness of their apartment reinforced the grandness of these simple people and she tried all the harder to earn her keep and their respect.

Henry also felt the need to make whatever gestures he could to his hosts who risked so much for him. He made himself useful as a handyman, fixing leaky pipes and anything he could see that needed attention. He built a closet and carried sacks of potatoes and coal and pickles in brine to the barrels in the basement.

* * * * * *

The latest news was filled with a tragic hope. The Russian army, under General Zhukov, stayed on the eastern bank of the Vistula, while the Germans destroyed the uprising of the Polish partisans, and then, Warsaw. Meanwhile, the Russians replenished and fortified their army. The Germans battled the Western Allies on the western front and sustained tremendous blows from the air to their industrial plants in the heart of the Reich. When the Russians finally crossed the Vistula early in January, they were ready to take Warsaw, then move on to Germany itself. By the seventeenth, Warsaw belonged again to the Poles, that is whatever was left of it. About 250,000 Poles in Warsaw were dead. Miserable and hungry, hundreds of thousands, were homeless. By the nineteenth, Crackow and Tarnow were in Russian hands, the German forces having fallen back over a five hundred mile-long frontier. A week later the Russians entered Auschwitz.

Sarah and Henry now had freedom of movement but could not feel liberated until the Third Reich surrendered and passed into history almost four months later.

By May the Russians arrived at the ruins of Hitler's chancellory. One day in May, amidst the Allied planes roaring overhead and the sounds of shelling, the radio declared the war finally over. People ran out of their homes into the streets, hugging, crying, singing, shouting.

Danuta and Sarah had heard the radio and together they ran out into the sunshine to the field where Lech and Anje were working. All Sarah could think of was that she was finally free. The brilliance of the sun-flooded field stunned her. She fell to the moist soil and breathed in the fresh fragrance of the buttercups and lilies of the valley. She held them against her cheek and then got up and ran around and around the field, skipping, jumping. She was free and alive! And alone.

The Jasinskis would go on with their lives and she would go home. What had happened to her home, to her parents? The questions rolled over her in cold, sweaty waves, despite the warm weather. She had found a safe harbour here for a while, but what now? Her parents were gone and now that there was no reason to have to stay with the Jasinskis, she was more alone than ever.

She swayed unsteadily on her feet while the scenery revolved around her as the ground grumbled to the swooping and dipping majestic steel vessels ploughing the sky. There would be no victory without her parents and her brother.

She floated dazedly to the road in this landscape under siege, perplexed, searching. She started to run, passing peasants hard at work in the fields, and she waited. A young boy pedaled by on his bicycle as she sat by the road. Some time passed and she stayed there because she didn't know what else to do, then a strange and beautiful phenomenon rolled down the dusty path. A Russian jeep with three officers in it, but to her it was no less than a golden chariot sent down by the Almighty Himself. She blinked through blurred eyes, immeasurably moved, then wiped them haltingly. She looked again as the sun brightened the vehicle and its occupants in proud streamers of light. She had seen Russian soldiers for over three months now but on this day they became real for her. Everything became real, her losses and her recovered freedoms. She had wandered through the previous four months as if asleep never certain of an end to the nightmare until now.

A young officer swung out of the jeep and into the crescent of yellow, and in so doing, drifted out of his world on a different plane, to cross over into hers. It was a heralding of the ages when she blurted out that she was a Jew from Cracow who had spent years in hiding and was so happy to see him. And then he answered her in Yiddish!

She was immediately in his embrace, crying childish tears. A Jew was one of the liberators! The words came chokingly from a deep hollow within her. "I want to go home. I want my mother and father," she muttered. There was something in those somber eyes, a tragic compassion and it scared her.

"I have to go now, but I want to help you. My name is Abraham Rabinowitz. I am from Livov. When the Germans attacked our city at the end of June 1941, I escaped with the retreating Russians. Here I am returning with them, a soldier in the Red Army. You can reach me at headquarters. I'll try to find out what I can about your folks. Give me a couple of weeks." They parted company warmly with a hug and as he drove off she sent her desperate hope with him.

She would find out that Abraham had pitied her for good reason. He was still in shock from the horrors of Auschwitz, which he had helped liberate. It was a hell light years beyond Dante's inferno, one he relived every time he closed his eyes to dream. None of his family had survived and he believed they had died there. Sarah reminded him of a lost sister just as he had made her think of Josh. Her pain was his, but he had seen the instruments of destruction first hand. He had seen the bodies. And the smell — Oh G-d the smell. that was the worst of it. No photograph could ever be complete. When they went among the camp's buildings there was no place they could put their feet down without walking on a layer of human excreta, rags, filth and decomposing bodies.

Human mountains of naked corpses, just grey skeletons, victims of butchery impossible to describe, lay around the factory of death. He retched when he realized that some of the bodies were still moving. Then he and the other soldiers feverishly pulled apart the bodies to sort the dead from the ones that were alive. He had found a girl, Sarah's age, naked, emaciated and almost dead underneath the body of what had been a large woman before she had been starved and eventually killed, her body left to rot on top of her still-living compatriot. His heart almost broke when the young girl he thought he had saved, died hours later. This girl visited him in his dreams; standing, saying nothing or asking him where her family had gone, or why he had taken so long to get there. She became a metaphor for millions of others, including his own family. All asking him the same questions. What if he had fought harder? What if they had arrived one day earlier? Who might have been saved? He had seen mass graves. How many had been buried alive with machine gun wounds not severe enough to grant them instant peace?

Indelible images — there were bodies still hanging from their nooses, tongues protruded. The survivors looked worse than those who had been relieved of their pain. Ravaged by typhus and dysentery, skin oozing with pus and gangrene, they stared at him with eyes so sunken and black that he could see no expression in them at all. But the pupils followed his movements. Some would lift an arm from a shoulder that jutted out of a fleshless body. They looked like death itself. Many of them died within the first few hours of the Liberation. Why did G-d help them survive to see the collapse of the Nazi state only to let them die within hours? Perhaps some could not live with what they had seen and the idea of returning to a life without their relatives and with their nightmares was too horrifying. There was ever present the stench of putrefying flesh. He learned for the first time, that it was possible to dream a smell.

How was he, only months later, to tell Sarah that her own parents had suffered the same ill-fate, years before at Treblinka.

And how was she, when the truths were finally known, to believe that her mind would ever dim enough to mollify the grief for her loved ones, for all the others who met their fate with the monstrous evil of the Third Reich.

To accept her parents' death as well as her brother's, was too much for her, so she left herself a measure of hope — or perhaps it was more of a dream — for now secret, and she busied herself in the fields, working like a mule, from dawn until dusk. One day, Lech came to her on behalf of the family, tentative, uncomfortably shifting from one foot to the other. "Sarah, we... the family, that is, have always tried to be good Christians and do what God-fearing Christians should do. We hope we have done right by you and we want you to know that you are welcome to stay here for as long as you like." His words painted his face red. He was embarrassed. She didn't know what to say, she was feeling his awkwardness sharply. "You're very lucky to have survived, Sarah. Very lucky, indeed."

At no moment did he look her in the eye. Her own eyes dropped to her shoes in mounting anger. He was speaking as though she were a criminal who had managed to escape punishment. It stung. She was confused. They saw her as a Jew. She was indignant and felt her face burn and the veins in her neck pound and throb, revolting against all this simple and ignorant man did not know! By keeping her, they could continue to nurture a love for themselves. In exchange for the so-called compassion and charity they bestowed on her, they were trying to buy their way into heaven. They cared about her and respected her no more than the Nazis had.

She was filled with the shame of having taken charity from them. This man would never know that the world was now poorer because great and learned men had been murdered. It came to her that there was nothing holding her to Poland. She would go to Palestine and fulfill her father's wish.

To go forward, she had to go back, this one last time; back to the Cracow she had loved so much. She needed to prove to herself that it was the way she remembered it. The nightmare had lasted so long, she needed to be reminded that her former life had been real. Most of all, she needed to say good-bye to her memories, her childhood and her beloved birthplace.

Abraham couldn't have been more gracious. He drove her there one rosy, late afternoon. She became giddy as though drunk, when she felt the knobby, cobbled stones beneath her feet. The war had not left the town unscathed; the Nazis had taken anything they felt was useful. Public statues her father had taken her to as a young girl were missing. The Liberation itself had come at a price, a few of the buildings were demolished and there were holes in her beloved streets although the city had fared better than most under the Nazis and escaped with minimal damage. Later she learned that the Nazis had mined and wired the city for destruction but at the last moment Polish partisans had cut the wires to the detonators.

The people themselves showed the strain they had endured under occupation. They went about their business restoring the city, accounting for the damage and removing whatever traces of the Nazi regime they could with the same grim-faced stoicism that had been with them throughout the war. They, like Sarah, knew that their ordeal wasn't over but their joy in the defeat of the Germans could be felt like electricity in the air. Abraham had been reluctant to bring her. He had warned that it might be too emotionally taxing. In her volatile state, it had been important she carry it through at once, before her shaky courage failed her.

They had arrived in an officer's car with Sarah chatting nervously, but when she could see the familiar streets, she was so enthralled, so famished for "home," that she begged him to stop the car so she could stand on the street, and feel its strength through her shoes. Then she ran like a small girl, the Sarah she had left behind in Cracow, her leather shoes clap-clapping on the stones just the way she remembered. All the while, Abraham followed in the car behind. The cobbles resounded in an arpeggio of feet and stone knuckles rapping out a percussion-like, almost musical beat along the familiar streets. Instinctively she ran into the market to face the tall, ancient houses in St. Mary's Square, wept at the walls to the right of Our Lady's Church, where Sundays her mother had taken her to buy vegetables and fruit.

Now it was empty, lifeless and smaller than she remembered.

More people passed by, poor and haggard and preoccupied. Buildings seemed to have aged, shops were missing the hustle and bustle of better days. She looked about. What presented itself before her, was bleak, faded, and unremittingly cold and indifferent. What had she expected, her thoughts suffused in a juice of bitter herbs that budded distastefully in her mouth, a welcoming committee? There was only beggarly repression on the outward face of her city. Unhappy, the city was, even though Judenrein.

Once she stopped running and dreaming, she couldn't get used to how fiercely ugly the town seemed. It was languishing. Sarah felt dizzy as she turned about and worried that she might not be able to find her home. How was that possible? Had it been a hundred years since she last saw it?

Abraham had left the car when she stopped running. Now, he put an arm about her and suggested they turn back, that she had had enough. "Never," she stubbornly answered. Cracow was dead, as were the grey, lifeless figures that shuffled along in the street. Ghosts, except for the clopping sound their feet made. Cracow stank from the stench of the dead that it had helped bury.

Her feet carried her, more reluctantly but determined, and they walked on, through the open graveyard that had been her birthplace of joy. Along Grodzka Street, they made their way toward the Wawel Castle, the staunch witness to all that had been, who attested to the former existence of the people she had lost, whose floors surely resounded with the imprint of Mindy and Yitzhak's footfalls onto the stony ears of the walls that had to crack from the sheer force of the tears it held. The edifice still stood, undestroyed. Listen, she whispered, you're now mated forever, in the roundness of each teardrop, in the circle of no end. On they stepped, imprinting the sandy banks of the Vistula River, Abraham offering her an antidote to her monumental disappointment, with, of all things, a boat ride on the river.

Not without the pilgrimage to her home first. The walk now was a death march. There had been no memorial service for her parents. This was it. Her palms became sweaty and she wiped them on her dress. Strangers passed by indifferent until a stout woman stopped dead in her tracks, open-mouthed in disbelief.

"Sarah, my G-d, is it really you?" They hugged and hugged, then wept.

"Abraham, this is Elizabeth... we used to buy fabric from her shop down the street..."

"Wait here," Elizabeth urged, "let me lock the shop and I'll go with you to your parents' apartment." A minute later they were on their way. Elizabeth explained, "You see, the Germans took all your folks' furniture, left it bare to the walls, a donneveter," she cursed with raised fist. "My daughter was taken as slave labour to Germany, and they made an old woman out of her. A poor man and woman live there now, and they're out all day working. I know them, but not very well."

She knocked on a neighbour's door for the key and Sarah braced herself. Surely there had been a grave mistake. As sure as her abiding love, was the certainty that if they were alive, they would be waiting. Surely! The moment she had imagined in every cell of her being, was here. The door fell open on a creaky hinge, on the holy of holies which represented their home.

Humanity had left this place as it had everywhere else. There was no mark, no sign, that the Horowitzes had ever been and Sarah fell to her knees on the bare floor and wept tears that tasted like blood, then lost consciousness. She was carried to Elizabeth's store, where cold water splashed on her face revived her and she drank strong tea as Elizabeth talked with her, told her how sorry she was about her family, about her own troubles. Weakly, she begged for news of Josh but there was none.

In her mind she made an escape to her beloved castle, her temple of joy and the keeper of her earliest memories, this benevolent watcher. She was the torchbearer of all lost, wandering children and within her a fire illuminating all their life forces in convergence together. Abraham could see her face aglow and kept quiet so as not to disturb the moment.

This was a candied elixir that she chewed in her mind, as they drifted off on a small boat on the Vistula. Somehow she recognized that she was embarking on an odyssey to understand the meaning of great suffering and death.

The sun descended as they rowed away, the steady motion of the oars rippled furrows of water in wider and wider circles. The medieval fortress was receding into the background and a quirky reflection of the river embraced the castle. Looking at this, she imagined that her imminent exile could make a castle disappear, make birds stop singing, and make grass and flowers stop growing by a sun that would cease to cast its shine in their direction.

The castle, the humming of the cars, the vigilant waterway with no harbour, the wind-chimes through the branches of the trees, the home of Polish kings, already cloaked in the grey, shadowy mist, was already in the past, intangible and transitory as her dreams, but was hers to keep for the rest of her life, in a timeless place, to remain always fresh, immortal.

* * * * * *

Sarah returned to the toil of the fields and worked from morning until night. The work was like an anesthetic.

Seeds buried in the ground sprouted into life, the earth seemingly a caretaker of existence in all stages, the ripe, cherry-hued tomato in her hands, its fleshy roundness succulent and eaten, thereby halting its inevitable progress to atrophy, to join the earth, only to resume again the cycle. These thoughts came quietly, wordlessly, as both girls bent over the potatoes, tomatoes, green peas, scooping them out from the moist, dirt bed and laying them gently as newborn babes into wicker baskets. Their faces were bronzed, their eyes like white painted glass with chocolate centres; gypsy girls with hair tied up in brightly-patterned kerchiefs and Danuta's gold earrings twin twinkling hoops bouncing in the orange rays of the sun.

The phalanx of neatly striding rows of vegetables, represented the fundamental honesty and simple goodness of nature that she would not debase by unkind judgements of the Jasinskis. She regretted her mental probing and examining of people who had risked their lives knowingly. From the daily newspapers she now knew that enough Christians, just like them, had been caught by the SS and added to the merciless slaughter. Hell had its angels.

The two teenagers talked about the crops, the weather, fashions, yet it was what they didn't say, that meant the most, just as in a letter where one reads between the lines, the seemingly idle banter was a reassertion that their bond remained unbroken.

She saw Henry almost daily. He worked on the Bolewski farm and at night, bone-tired, they'd eat a late supper or just keep company. They would spread a blanket on the sea of grass, a sprawling of satiny, emerald and the lone moon a topaz island in space. He had been journeying into Cracow frequently, had been telling her of his own dream to go to Palestine to begin anew. He spoke with conviction, "We must have a Jewish homeland, Sarah. We were foolish enough to believe it wasn't necessary and for thousands of years we wandered. I will not live in the Diaspora and be at the mercy of gentiles who will always make it clear I don't belong, that I'm not one of them. I want to be with my own kind." And then he'd look askance at her, and say he was sorry for his outburst.

After a time, Danuta asked Sarah how she felt about Henry, since she spent so much time alone with him. "I do think he's rather taken with you."

"Oh, you're silly."

"I am not," she said evenly. "I've watched him look at you when he thinks nobody's watching."

"I would know if that were true. He'd say something directly."

"No, he wouldn't, because men are shy — shy and stupid. That's why they need women to tell them what to do with what they're feeling. Mother told me — she told Dad what those urgings meant, if you know what I mean," she giggled, "and that's how women get married, and she's been telling him what to think ever since."

"Well, I certainly don't know what to say to that."

"Well, if you don't, Mother can tell you what to say. She has the experience."

"Oh, do let's get back to work," Sarah said, bending again over her vegetables. She was glad her face was hidden beneath her straw hat, for a cobwebbing of prickly blood vessels was reddening her, as though she had baked in the sun for hours.

Sarah and Henry met again, the next evening, over borscht and potatoes. Later, he sat leaning against a tree, his jaw firm and set in profile. "I heard from a cousin, well, actually, a cousin by marriage, who lives in Palestine. Their gates are closed and still under British mandate, but he's a powerful army man and has arranged for me to go.

"I won't be treated as needy, stateless and inferior. I've wondered if we had wanted a homeland as much as the Nazis wanted us dead, if then maybe millions of European Jews would still be alive today, in Palestine. We could have done more if we had made this promise." He was standing, his arm flung at the turquoise sky.

"Have you thought about what you're going to do? I mean, Poland betrayed us. There can be no love left, only pain." He faced her with eyes of tarnished, liquifying silver, searching hers. His hand touched her hair and shied away simultaneously, his stance a mixture of male restraint, humbling before her. "You're not grownup yet, I know, but you can become an adult with me. You make me feel young. It's something I have to relearn. Teach me to be young again, Sarah, teach me." He looked at her with such abandon and then he fell to his knees, buried his face in her dress, and she felt arms encircle her legs through her sheer, cowslip dress and she drew away abruptly.

Sarah knew he was entrapping her with the offer of a way out from loneliness and isolation. Facing the future unprotected scared him too. She cringed as though they both were confined in a sealed, deserted place, for he was tempting her with something that she was supposed to want that he could give. How was she to be so certain that she desired his coveted prize, when she had no concept of it? And she was expected to say yes, thank you, please — at once. It was a marriage proposal in a monumental package — start a new life in a new land and begin new emotional ties with a man who, in so many ways, was a stranger to her. She was enticed and threatened.

"I, I — don't know," she blurted as she turned away from him. She was backing away from finality. There was finality to such a decision. And finality made her think of death and of the deceased, who couldn't be here now to tell her what to do.

Henry realized he had asked too much, too quickly and said apologetically, "Oh, I am a brute pouncing on you like this. Take time to consider. Take all the time you need, but say yes, please say yes." He couldn't help himself. He could not lose her now. He walked her to the Jasinskis in a shy, shared silence.

It was well past midnight, yet Sarah sat hidden in shadows, a portrait of abstract contemplation, her elbows on the ledge of the open, mullioned windows. She was utterly alone. Maria and Lech were away with the children, visiting relatives. The door to the apartment was ajar, letting in trickles of lamp light. Without the usual warmth that only human company can generate, the space was sharply poor and coldly unfamiliar. The starkly indifferent home in the full moonlight was streaked in drab, lifeless patches.

She sat bridled by the intangible ropes of indecision. She could neither dismiss the implications of the evening nor free herself from the affliction of Henry's face, the kind, intelligent keeper of piercing eyes, which followed her like breaths of iced fever trailing in the air. His desire made her crazy.

Henry had as much as promised himself to her for her to take on unequal terms. He was older, smarter, crafty. How else could his mere touch cause her brain to soften like melting butter on the stove, as her entire body became more pliant, ready to bend as easily as a freshly baked, Sabbath chalah. Even here, at a distance from him, there was an emerging sense of excitement quivering in her veins. She had rebelled against the power he was able to enforce over her person. Sarah had become the prey that was afraid to be devoured and that was why she had run from him.

Her narrow outlook had not counted on her seeing him as anything other than a surrogate brother. Oh, her dear Josh. If at least he could have lived to be with her now, to shield her from carnivorous men. How frightfully devious it was for Henry to tantalize her, to plague her with resolute, cannibal eyes!

She didn't see the door open, nor hear the patter of uncertain miniature feet pad haltingly into the room. And when she did realize the waif was there, gazing with saucer-sized, innocent eyes, the laborious whistling accompanying his uneven breathing, her face softened and she was upon him, wrapping him in her arms. "Stephen, kitten, why are you out of bed?" He was the neighbour's five year old, who had asthma and was so tiny and thin, he looked only three. He had developed a habit of wandering to the Jasinskis at night, where Danuta, who was fond of him, would heat him milk in the kitchen. It was an adventure for him and for anyone who would see his eyes light up at the vision of the box of old toys in the closet. "You're lonesome too, Stephi, come on." She took him by the hand, touched by the skinny wisp of a child.

The wisdom of babes. In the total naked trust of a lamb she made her decision.

Upon returning Stephi to his home, Sarah lingered outside. Something primitive and elemental entered the surrounding, stagnant clime, a gathering of suppressed forces, mounting. Her other self that came to crude awakening, jumped within her and she knew, felt, Henry was there, behind her, by the shed. Rooted to the ground, his breaths were the lifeline to his wellspring from which she had to drink or she would die and her futile attempt at words to convey this, lay parched in her throat. Her ears boomed as blood rushed to her head. She studied his eyes focused on hers, and the glistening joy expanding his face, his admission of selfless love and willingness to make her custodian of his soul. And there, she made her commitment.

For Sarah had become a true believer who trusted she had a mission in life, and that it was to go with Henry to Palestine, for the children, to teach and guide the children, for they were not only its future, but the rebirthing of an abandoned people — from out of the ashes. Henry drew her tightly into his arms in an unhalting smothering of kisses that took their breaths away. She closed her eyes in reverence of her newfound knowledge and him.

They married in a civil ceremony. The Jasinkis and the Bolewskis were there and Bolek said just before the small reception in the living room; "This house is a blessed home now." There were tears, promises made, and Sarah and Henry stayed for two months more on the Bolewski's farm in a small farmhouse and worked the soil. They could not face living with their memories in Poland and in late 1945 they left for Palestine to begin the life of pioneers.

In 1947, the couple settled in Rishon le Zion. They bought a two-bedroom house in Shunat Abromovitz, an area surrounded by fields of orange groves. There were a few pleasant streets. The Cupat Holim of the Histradut, the health care system of the organization of the workers of Israel, gave Henry a loan of $2,000. With no imports, the furniture was Israeli-made and Spartan. Kitan, a linen factory, produced plain, white linens of poor quality. Living conditions were a far cry from the elegant standard of living, Sarah and Henry had known in their past.

For entertainment there were two rundown movie theatres, rat-infested and without subtitles. A separate film roll ran on a separate projector, with the Hebrew translation, and usually the operators didn't understand English well, so translation was not simultaneous with

Chapter Five

Tarnow,

Autumn, 1945

the conversations in the movie, resulting in outbursts from a frustrated audience. Rats as big as cats scurried between people's legs, frenzied by the smell of carelessly strewn remnants of food, even cheese sandwiches. Many of the people seemed coarse, no less frenzied than their furry friends. Sarah learned to sit with her legs tucked beneath her to avoid nasty scratches. She'd substitute their high-pitched complaints for memories of concerts in the parks of her childhood, and sigh to herself and Henry would take her hand and squeeze it reassuringly.

They had to endure the punitive, scorching sun, relentless during the days from May till October, with its piercing, burning amber rays, refusing to bleed even a drop of rain. When finally nightfall descended covering the small town with its black, star-studded canopy, relief came. Sarah confessed to sleepwalking through daylight hours, waiting for the night, the very same darkness mantling Europe and the secrets which she dreamed would one day be revealed to her. She thought constantly about her brother, for whom she continued to harbour hope.

With the War of Independence of 1948, several hundreds of thousands of European immigrants poured into the new state of Israel. They were a bedraggled, shabby lot, who had arrived at the end of their world to begin a new battle for survival. Living conditions were very poor. There was a lack of accommodations, food supplies and services such as hospitals and schools. People lived in tents, huts made of tin or wood in centres usually within city boundaries.

From the wet and windy Israeli winters these tents offered no protection. Sometimes tents blew away with the wind or collapsed and the families were left with nothing, except their obstinate determination to survive in a land of their own.

The newly established Israeli army took a major part in building camps for the immigrants and maintaining them in emergencies of which there were many floods and storms. They strengthened the communities' infrastructure, roofs, and sometimes they provided food and shelter. The financing came from the Israeli government.

When Sarah and Henry came to Israel, they settled into a hut made of wood. Henry was taken into the army for the compulsory army service. After six months of basic training, he spent another one and a half years working in an army hospital. In 1950, he began his permanent job, working in the central medical building of Rishon le Zion. He was paid a little more than factory workers. However, Sarah and Henry were happy with what they had, a home, indoor plumbing and enough to eat.

The hospital, Asaf Harofeh, was built and Ayelet, their daughter, was born there in 1949.

In 1951 they moved to a newly built residential area in a suburb of Rishon. Called a 'shikun,' it consisted of about one hundred similar, bleak, grey concrete houses. It had two bedrooms, a small kitchen, and a shuttered, spacious sunroom. The walls were grey plaster and the floors were concrete covered with paving stones, strong and insulating against the heat.

Many of the residents were middle and lower class immigrants from eastern Europe — Poland and Russia and they were, on the whole, blue-collar workers, working in the wineries, the glass factory and in construction — mainly brick laying. Many worked in the orchards, picking fruit. Sarah spent sweltering hot, backbreaking days for a few years, in the orchards, picking oranges and grapefruits.

During the early fifties, there was a shortage of food, so a period of rationing ensued. This did not provide enough food for a family. People living in apartments would go to farms for food and the prices were high, resulting in a black market. The farmers benefited the most. Luckily, Sarah and Henry had created a fruit and vegetable garden and so were less dependent on others.

Clothing was scarce as well and what was available was of poor quality. Some people got packages from relatives in the United States and western Europe. Sarah was grateful for the sewing lessons she got from Maria. She bought a sewing machine and made most of her clothes and bed linens. Evenings were spent knitting sweaters and baby things for Ayelet, often in the company of her neighbours. The atmosphere was warm and friendly, and people usually were kind to one another.

Sarah's other wish had also been fulfilled. In a one-storey, grey schoolhouse surrounded by cypress trees, she was teaching the children. A course completed the year Ayelet was born, enabled her to instruct the new legions of Israel. Her new family in the just-built bungalow, was to her the idyllic image of pictures she had seen of cottages in Provence, with its copses of savory lemon trees, a haze of daytime stars aglow, fuzzy peaches and ignescent oranges tangling with wild roses in the hedged quarter acre. The fronds of flower and fruit beautified their lives and she humbly considered their luck a gift from G-d, their greening home a barricade against the dead years. Sarah could see herself merging into the exotic untamed landscape as one of its sabras, tough on the outside, soft on the inside, just like the green fruit she cultivated. It was here, she vowed with ardent romanticism and obstinate devotion, that she would remain forever, for it was where they belonged.

During a brilliant, windy, rain-filled night in February of 1951, with friends gathered in their living room around a portable, benzene heater, the subject of the Holocaust was brought up. Claps of thunder smacked the windows violently as she remembered her brother, her loss. Over time she had come to accept her parents' deaths but she had never known about him. This not knowing was more painful even than the certain loss of her mother and father. Hope would tease her and torture her until, feeling guilty, she would ask for deliverance in the form of any news, even if it meant knowing that he was dead.

Lightning played with her faculties so that his face actually appeared to be projected on the glass as a living photograph, and she cried out to the tormenting clarity of that vision and to the preciously small, ever-haunting hope that he could somehow be alive somewhere in the universe.

Sarah and Henry were walking along the beach and she was remarking on how pleasing the sea breeze was in the dawning hours of day. He held her close and their lips were kissing in soft trilling motions, while his hands were around her bare lissome waist. They had just made love lying in the shallow inundating water, mated with nature. They always responded to each other with ardent passion. Her deepest inhibitions were shed in the openness of the sea and in the cleanness of the salty air. Her body would unwind and stretch, like a cripple who has lived in the narrow confines of a wheelchair and has suddenly been cured. There was nothing here to remind her of Cracow or Tarnow, nothing here to frighten or sadden her. Her habitual, morning excursions were meant for her to go outside herself and feel total freedom. Here she was more than an extension of her parents and all that had happened to her family.

Her feelings of guilt for surviving and her anger for their leaving, as illogical as they were, remained embedded in her soul.

The trauma of the war was never far off. Sometimes, on the beach at night, she'd tell Henry how horrible it was to see her parents walk away from her and disappear for ever. He would listen to her story again and again, sometimes with more interest and patience than others. She needed to talk about it — even if she had already used every possible word in the world to describe it. Henry wanted her to move on, to concentrate on their new life. He felt sorry for her but he too had lost family and her preoccupation seemed like an obsession to him. It is a frustrating recreation to dabble in past events that cannot be changed, he would tell her.

Sometimes he could be so understanding, comforting. Or he could be so close to her pain that he was unable to help her and instead wanted to shut her up. Their common past both made and broke their relationship. And just when she thought that everything would fall apart, he would show her an empathy that would colour love for him that she would only remember subconsciously the next time he grew distant.

She would almost drive herself mad torturing herself with images. The sea, then, was the River Styx, the darkness, a cryptic co-conspirator, and her mother and father solitary figures walking in the valley of the shadow of death. She had had to be restrained from following them into that gully from which no one ever returned. And out from that amorphous blackness came wicked men in ebony uniforms, who smelled of decay and fought for death, not life. Sometimes she managed not to think about them only to punish herself with guilt later. All that was left of her parents were her memories. If she didn't keep them alive in her mind, she would be killing them more totally, more permanently, than had the SS.

Preparations for the Sabbath remained for her a message of survival and a triumph over oppression. Her ancient soul would ache with joy, as she cooked, baked, tidied the house, and then lit the candles in long, silver holders, her head covered, murmuring the words of prayer. As she moved about the house in the Sabbath ritual, she would think of her Grandmother without guilt for she had died a better death. She had not been obliterated. She had been spared.

When Henry came home, she'd bask in the timeless comfort of the ritual of the affirmation of the Almighty, in clinking glasses of red wine, the inviting table setting and savory dishes set out, and in the much needed reassurance of her healthy, relaxed family.

Sarah sought meaning in everything that happened in their lives. The first house they had lived in had become a Mediterranean Noah's Ark, complete with an auspicious sign, in the form of a pigeon (Yonah) not a dove as was stated in the Bible, that took it upon himself to nest in their tree when she was pregnant. After the birth, the messenger-bird had left, mission accomplished and Sarah proclaimed that soon they too would leave the boat for a permanent dwelling.

When Ayelet chose to come into their lives, Sarah believed a miracle had occurred. Like a brief glimpse into the far past, she looked into Ayelet's eyes and she saw the night sky of Cracow with stars, and in her gabby loquaciousness, the Vistula River.

The rooms of her life were homed in Ayelet's and Henry's body. They would look at each other as old and dear friends. Sarah knew in every cell of her being that they had been preordained in the great expanse of the cosmos, to touch once again. She was conscious of the pure joy that one held for the other. In this vast Age of Aquarius, soulmates had reconnected.

Henry, in honour of Ayelet's birth, had presented Sarah with a pair of diamond earrings, but Sarah told him Ayelet was her first stone, a rarer gemstone, the sign of a talisman from the angels — of rebirth, pure and pregnant with the promise of life.

Women all over the country were vessels producing many more jewels. From out of the ashes, like Joshua who covered the burnt city of Ai with stones, a memorial still there today. Their children were living rock-gem memorials being issued, testaments to covenant renewal — from the outposts of Dante's inferno, its graduates, like Job, were the pioneers of restoration.

Her beloved home, though, also doubled as a prison. She alone, had erected the bars and fashioned the key. Not until she had proven herself different from her family — stronger, smarter, and nobody's victim — would she ever feel truly free. Her core was fuelled by lapses of heartrending grief, combustible, self-destructive. For all the intenseness and great emotionality that filled their home with warmth, love and beauty, Sarah lived with the stigma of her parents' inherent weakness and childish naivete. She was by virtue of her past, a rich patina of heroism and crushing fear, soft yet toughening, an original of her own making. Sarah despised her parents' impotence, their passivity. At the end of their life, they were as helpless as newborn babes leaving the responsibility of defending the world to those who took risks to keep others safe. This was unforgivable as was their abandonment of their children. These feelings were not about logic. It was a struggle to blame someone, not a whole country, and to find a reason for what happened. She never saw the men who killed her parents. She didn't know their names. If it were her parents' fault, then she might be safe, able to avoid the same fate the next time the world went mad. If she blamed her parents' killers, there could be no hope for her.

Sarah could never look at children's clothing or toys and not shudder at the millions murdered. The documentary films awakened in her visions of demons wearing swastikas, whose faces frightened her with their sadistic glee. The Nazis, after all, were in Israel too, even if only on celluloid. Their images triggered in her, old patterns of survival, almost against her will and reason. Footsteps outside her home caused her, before she was aware of what she was doing, to stand guard, armed with a knife against Gestapo agents about to storm inside. The walls of her perception kept her from escaping the shrill dithyrambs that came from without and within. "Release me from myself," she begged, and she'd go coax Ayelet out from under the bed.

Trains were cattlecars. A packed knapsack for a children's sleepover reminded her that the event was a ruse to fool the parents — it was really a roundup. She didn't need Dr. Mengele, she would push those buttons listening to a friend's experiences in the camps and then would fling herself into the sanity-inducing rituals of mundane daily responsibility with cannonball speed and purpose.

Ayelet was an outgrowth in Sarah's unique Tree of Life. Sarah knew her astute daughter pitied her — the terrible pain and fear was measured in the child comforting the mother. "Come, Mommy, don't cry. I'll protect you." And Ayelet would sit by the guarded door, a small arm on her shoulder. At five, she'd bring her a cookie to make her happy. And Sarah would smile through the tears.

Her ordeal from a time before her daughter was born was forcing a new generation to grow up before its time. Her personal Hell, already had proscribed Ayelet from the normal childhood Sarah most wanted to give her. Ayelet felt it her duty to be cheerful at nearly all times in order to not disturb the balance and upset her mother. When Henry was away at night, Sarah insisted on sleeping with the lights on, and she jumped at any sound. Sometimes she paced back and forth nervously, imagining all sorts of dangers.

Ayelet was the miracle that Sarah's hopes and dreams were lived through, and this was a great responsibility. It made Ayelet intense, serious, frustrated and with a vague but real sense of inadequacy. Stories of Hitler's Europe put her in awe of the survivors; she could not imagine herself surmounting such odds. She knew Sarah saw in her everything she wished her own parents had been — fighters risking all and on their own terms.

Driving up the mountains to Jerusalem, Sarah passed orange groves and long, snaking jets of water irrigating green fields of crops. Then closer to the mountains, crumbled, skull-like boulders and rusting armoured cars lined the sides of Jerusalem Highway in memory of the Israeli War of Independence. It rang of battles and pilgrimages. There was a history that went long before the Holocaust to an era when Jews had fought as equals, army against army. The forests rising out of mountainsides were symbolic of family trees restored. Everything she did had a meaningful connection. Just as after the flood, a piece of earth was bestowed on them as a ground luminous with opportunity to plant seeds of a new life, to harvest and offer all the seasons unceasing.

Death was part of a beginningless and endless movement. Sarah saw the Israelis as magnificent mountain eagles, who soar above both life and death, and see them for what they are, in all their mysterious intricate interrelationships.

Liberation from the camps entailed more than physical release. On liberation day, the guards were gone, but their image was printed on the retina of the inmates. To this day, those that have not been released in death, still feel imprisoned and tortured, are still prisoners to that image.

Sarah now knew pioneers who came to Palestine in the '30s and concentration camp survivors. Tovah, now her closest female friend, told her on occasion of her sleeping and waking dreams — of the Lagerstrasse, the north and south road that dissected Auschwitz. No Jew, except for Kapos, were allowed to walk along it. Chain-link fences still remind her of the electrified fence surrounding the camp. The wet, cold winters brought nonending upper respiratory infections. The past was more aggressively clear than the present and became a tight weave, woven with shots, screams, barks, lashes of truncheons and whips and runny with human blood and excrement. It was a hell tapestry continued by eyewitnesses afraid that when they die the truth will die with them.

Already many people all over the world were refusing to believe the Holocaust ever happened. Where Hitler's police obliterated their bodies new Nazis wanted to obliterate their memory. Survivors, in order to become functional, would try unsuccessfully to lessen the vividness and immediacy of their memories. Others would cringe at the depth of human depravity and turn away. Even the Allies who fought for that Liberation Day would prefer to not have to examine their roles in the Holocaust. They knew they had refused entry to thousands of Jews trying to leave Europe before the death camps were built. They had full evidence of the extermination programmes early in the war yet made no specific effort to interfere with the Nazis' efficient killing machine. Everyone had a reason to want to forget.

The black smoke of crematoria had been washed into fleecy whiteness.

Sarah found no escape in time. Time does not heal all wounds. Now, years later, she discovered that she could no longer eat meat — it was cannibalistic — it would be like chewing on inmates' bones.

Part Two
Elfriede

ow hard it had been! Elfe found herself in front of her ornate, brightly-painted cuckoo clock of blues and reds. She had carved it herself to replace the one she had as a child and it was her focal point in the oasis of the room. It sat on the shelf her husband had made. She had made a home for the delicate, olive-brown, white breasted, wooden bird at a time when her own home was falling apart.

Staring at the clock, it drew her inside, unlocking the past. The years fell away and she was eleven once more in her family's ancient house of stone, on the outskirts of Munich. Like a sentry it proudly stood amidst chestnut and linden trees. Oh, and the flowers! They were everywhere in jewelled sheaths, proliferating, heavily scented in their beds, in window boxes. Ivy wound around trellises up the sides of the house, peeping through windows, edging along the porch in this garden of paradise.

The interior of the house was splendid, dramatically panelled with stained and polished oak. The furnishings were ostentatious in their baroque grace. Richly-detailed oil paintings and tapestries, depicting pastoral scenes of orchards and sweethearts embracing life sensually, hung on the walls. Delicate porcelain willoware gleamed from the Viennese, black oak, handcarved breakfront in the dining room. The

Chapter Six

January, 1997
Summer, 1941

beautiful possessions played tribute to happier days when her papa, an educated man and professor at the University of Munich, who had been born to wealth, understood how his wife's humble background had created her craving for material possessions. How dearly he had loved her!

Now she was five and her mother was putting her to sleep with "The Six Swans," her favourite Grimm's Fairy Tale, or with the myths of the Norse gods; Odin, the ruler of Asgard who quested for wisdom through suffering, he even went to the Well of Wisdom and paid for a drink with one of his eyes; and of the goddess Frigga, Odin's wife, the source of her own name, Elfriede, for it was said Friday was derived from Frigga. Her mother had delighted in retelling the story and Elfe had never grown tired of hearing it. She had felt especially proud of her namesake's great wisdom and silence, for Frigga told no one, not even Odin, what she knew. In an old, well-worn book, her mother had shown her pictures of Frigga at her spinning wheel, where she spun threads of gold and her secrets. Elfriede's mother would then brush her heavy, honey hair and Elfe would imagine herself a wise, beautiful goddess.

Bad timing and unforeseen events had stripped Elfe's mother, Katherina, of a family she cherished creating wounds she thought would never heal, but did. She had grown wise enough to appreciate that steps could not be retraced, relived. She had discovered that in order to enjoy who she was, it was necessary to remind herself of whom she had been, so she would know where she was going and not be afraid.

Katherina Boldt's beginnings were humble. She was an orphan, left on the doorstep of a church when she was only two days old. She led a life of misery in different orphanages. But she was talented and always dreamed of becoming a successful painter. In this way she was fortunate, for in the late 1800s Munich had become the true powerhouse in German art.

As a young, struggling artist barely out of girlhood, her life was full of camaraderie. She expressed through her work the ideas that obsessed her: social justice, the cause of peace, the fathomless mystery of death.

In 1933 Hitler was named German Chancellor and artists like her were forbidden to teach. Life increasingly became a

nightmare. Some found a degree of solace in the music of Bach
and Beethoven and revelled in their city's culture. Impressionism
was then strong in Germany. Beginning in February, 1933,
prominent radical artists, writers, and anti-war leaders had to flee
the country. The ones who remained were ousted from their
positions and denied the right to show or sell their works. Jewish
artists, including leading figures in the art world, were bitterly
persecuted, and even ordered to stop painting and drawing.
Katherina became repressed.

One day, in a coffeehouse, in 1929, she caught the admiring
eye of a young, fierce-looking man who found her intense naivete
endearing. They met every afternoon when he was free from
teaching, usually going to the coffeehouses to meet friends or to
the art galleries. They frequently made love on the creaky bed in
her modest room and a few months later they got married.
Katherina became pregnant and in her happy domesticity she
once again began to paint gentle, pastoral scenes, filled with
children in the familial settings she had always imagined but
never experienced. People even bought her paintings for modest
sums. With the birth of Elfriede, her home life was complete.

Elfe's upbringing had been elegant, cultured, filled with
ballets and concerts. When her legs were still too short to reach
the floor from her gilded chair, she was captivated by the music
and the lithesome swans in Tchaikovsky's Swan Lake. The world
was introduced to her as a magnificent, fairy tale place with
heroes and heroines who were always seeking justice — and, so
long as they were morally pure, they found it.

She craved knowledge, excelled in schoolwork, took piano and
ballet lessons and could not understand the word "bored," heard
so often from her girlfriends. And she had an obdurate need for
her aloof father's approval. She was a precocious child of whom
her teachers spoke highly. When they informed her parents that
she had liquid abilities, that she flowed from academic subjects
with ease to artistic endeavours skillfully, she felt ten feet tall.
When her watercolours were hung on the classroom walls for all
to admire, she thought she would burst with joy. She was deeply
hurt when her father failed to congratulate her himself and instead
addressed her mother in regard to her scholarly possibilities for
the future. She had overheard the conversation when they were

retiring for the night. "Do encourage Elfriede more on the sciences. The universities have higher requirements and now's the time to prepare for the future."

She hadn't caught her mother's muffled voice, but she so yearned to please him that she hung onto every word of praise, albeit not directly to her, like a drowning person holds onto a lifepreserver.

Lavish dinners were frequently held at their home; the silverware was polished to shine like mirrors, mullioned windows were cleaned, and the odor of delicious delicacies mingled with the fragrant arrangements of flowers in vases. Ladies and gentlemen breezed in beautifully dressed, silk skirts, fine dinner jackets rustling. There were glimmering occasions when Elfe joined the guests.

After shopping expeditions to Paris, they would return on the train, laden with boxes packed into steamer trunks containing the very latest fashions to fill all the wardrobes. It was as though Katherina was filling the emptiness in her daughter's heart with material possessions where a father's love should have been. There was a lonely air that hung like low fog over the laces, ruffles, and velvets with each crinkle and rustle like quiet, embarrassed voices.

At the beginning of November 1939, the Gestapo arrested the professors of Cracow University to send them to concentration camps inside the Reich. For the large number of individuals to be liquidated, the transfer to Germany was too complicated for this procedure to be followed. The "General Government" didn't want the intelligencia in German camps, nor need the tiresome correspondence with the families. Matters were simplified.

The action was carried out by the chief of police, the Gestapo and the SS as a simple internal operation of pacification necessarily carried out outside the frame of regular procedure.

Her father, Herman, was devastated to learn that the faculty of the University of Cracow — about 180 professors — had been assembled in the courtyard under the ruse that they were to be advised of the rules under occupation and instead herded into vans and sent to Sachsenhausen and shot to death on New Year's Day. He had befriended three of them years before, as a student on a school trip to Egypt. For the first time, the war came home to him.

It caused Katherina to tend to him with patience and overprotective kindness. While she sincerely felt sorry for him, in a way, she was grateful for his renewed ability to show emotion. His anguish had made him more like the man she had married than the one she had lived with for the last ten years. She understood that for all his aloofness and stiffness, he was a lost soul clinging to the values and morals he'd been brought up with, all of which were now being swept away. Despite the bravado he displayed amongst students and colleagues he was a confused and frightened man now having difficulty with his pride of country. His tenseness and depression escalated into sporadic bouts of rage misdirected at his wife. His guilt for this only made it worse.

He would become frustrated in his useless innocence, in his beliefs in the prodigious progeny of the Prussians and in mankind's inherent goodness without dark shadows and became distraught and confused at the apparent contradictions. To him, the world was a school, life went by the book, and there was no real evil — there were only flaws in education. He never understood that the evil mind was incorrigible, for it filtered the outside world and information differently, resulting in a grossly distorted picture. It could have education, but no knowledge, for that would involve sharing itself with others.

Herman was too spoiled and selfish to dirty his manicured hands and dig below the hygienic surface of academic life to reveal its soul, a raw and filthy, amorphous thing. He wanted his gentleman's safe life where he could easily accept himself and others — on his terms — non-judgementally. Katherina believed he was rushing to suicide, just as were the plotters, murderers and the foolish followers, in an apocalypse where honour, loyalty and patriotism were useless words.

She watched with dismay as he became a recluse, sitting for hours in his study until she pulled him, pleading, for dinner and theatre. Guests arrived more frequently, to prevent necrosis of his spirit and to encourage compassion rather than anger. She told him he was wasting his energy, his wrath, on soulless men. They had so thickened with prejudice and hate, that they were trapped as though in stone. It was too late.

He would stare benignly at his wife. She'd get up and kiss his cheek and he'd give her a lambent smile. Other times, a fire roared in him and his shocking diatribes would cause her to tremble briefly, regain composure and say quietly, "Please don't say such things, dear, it hurts me."

The mad rantings of the public at gatherings of the Führer, the delirium of his people, the marching of the storm troopers, all had terrible impact and he felt that he too was at fault for his part in things having gone so far. The nights weren't a time for rest any more, they were dark daytimes with the rumblings of soldiers, police, their vehicles and loud knocks on doors signaling searches for Jews and traitors to the regime.

Such a night wakened them and they found themselves in the kitchen sipping coffee. "What has become of us, Kathie?" he said, wiping red eyes beneath his horn-rimmed spectacles. He had become terrible to look at, facial lines were deep crevices, a saddening geography of a soul. He looked at his walls and held her hand so tightly, she winced while he seemed to be crawling up them mentally, taking her along.

Herman, embittered over the loss of his friends, felt betrayed by his countrymen. Goebbels and his massive propaganda machinations, in which his philosophy was taken as a new and brilliant religion, wasn't new at all. The power of suggestion had been subtly and not so subtly implemented since the beginning of society. Mankind was divided into two basic groups psychologically — leaders, and followers — most choosing to follow. Hitler and Goebbles were clever; they elevated the losers, criminals and psychopaths, giving them uniforms and power, and let them run loose through Europe. Murder and thievery on a grand scale gave glamour, position, fame and honour to those who before had been cowards, felons, delinquents, convicts and hoodlums. Their small, distorted, limited world, previously in the corners of civilized people's minds, expanded into grotesque, terrifying proportions. The poison was disseminating, unchecked, uncontained and cloaked in disingenuous semantics. The Dark Ages were back, with the Jews depicted as agents of the Devil wearing a secular disguise.

Herman was becoming a spiritually and emotionally old man plagued by shortness of breath and peripheral coldness and numbing of fingers and toes. Katherina watched over him, her hands, human feathers of gentleness that rubbed the deadness to life.

The bullets that ended the life of his friends and comrades, had gotten him in a vital spot, as well. She tried every way to calm him. She'd read him Goethe and cook dishes he liked. At night they'd lie in the four-poster bed and she would bring apple strudel with tea and they would talk about friends, in particular those who had escaped from Germany for a new start in France and England. He'd listen, eyelids growing heavy, her words a massage for raw nerves; then he'd fall asleep with letters and photographs from friends scattered on the blankets. Katherina was invaluable to him. He could not have coped without her. She had become his filter for ugliness and chaos. The strain of this role was wearing her down. She welcomed the chance to prove her love to him but it was aging her noticeably. Her hair, once a uniform honey colour, now had white streaks that would hang off her head like icicles. New lines were growing on her face and she had stopped smiling to herself as she used to. Now, all of her was spent as an emotional crutch to her husband.

Elfe, he regarded with impatience. She would brace herself at dinner when he'd quiz her on schoolwork. He was an undemonstrative man brought up in a home of little affection which he had craved as a child and been denied. He learned to reroute those energies into intellectual pursuits. Time healed those wounds but also dried up any attempt at interpersonal displays of affection. Katherina gave a great deal more than she received, and even then, her rewards were nuances — a winsome glance, a tone of voice — she kept them all, like tiny pearls constantly added to a long string. Herman and Katherina had their own secret language. Elfe was Herman's personal project because she was an outstanding pupil and she wanted badly to please him, arriving to supper often with butterflies dancing in her stomach. Katherina, sick and tired of the mealtime routine scolded Herman, "This is neither the time nor the place to discuss matters." She gave him a stern look that he hated and he proceed to eat in silence. Her eye, which she knew unnerved him, did not waver until he looked up from his soup said, "What are you staring at me like that for? I feel like I'm in a monkey cage at the zoo, picking lice out of my hair in front of hundreds of people."

She knew she had won and gave Elfe, who had been sitting there as usual, subdued and silent, a long, sleek smile of commiseration. Bolder, she continued, "I must say..."

"You wouldn't care to keep it your own little secret..."

"...that your manners at the table are deplorable. Not only is the dinner table a classroom, it is also a dentist's office. If you must pick your teeth with those toothpicks you insist on buying, then do so elsewhere."

He slammed his hand into the table once, to show he was in control, then, like an admonished student, he continued eating with his face fixed on his plate until dinner was over.

After supper, Elfe's parents would sit in the molded oak-panelled living room, in the dim tangerine light of the teardrop crystal lustres. The dark, polished wood floor resembled brown marble, and the old Tabriz rug of garnet, grey and sepia added to the overall aura of wealth and exquisitely burnished autumn colours. The room was framed by the great, shadowy talons of the linden trees which Katherina always said, were soaring wings of eagles, free in nature yet deeply rooted to the ground, protectors in the coppery light of the lamps where Herman abandonned himself to solitary reading and solitary thoughts. Katherina knitted or embroidered as if she too, were alone. In this way, she believed, they were closer to the Almighty, attempting to solve grievances and problems with themselves. It was human nature, that when one communicated verbally to another, responsibility for actions and decisions shifted to the other. This way, they had to answer only to themselves. She greatly revered the holiness of silence and the monasteries that advocated it. How many wars could have been averted this way, she often said.

Herman had never identified with the suppressed and oppressed. He had felt superior to the ignorant bourgeois, above the crowd. Now he was becoming enlightened and it made him frantic. A monumental lynching mob was growing and its members couldn't see beyond a hunger for blood. They needed a god to guide them — a fanatic, a megalomaniac who in his madness, believed he was the Almighty and that his existence depended on his followers and his followers depended on him.

Katherina firmly believed that everything was predestined but that humans had the unique ability, above dumb animals, to surpass it with actions to improve destiny. Her convictions were arms around her soul, and she was stretching them to include her husband. She had tried to understand Herman's lack of bonding with Elfriede. His own parents had been cold and distant and birthed him to continue the family name, and he who had resented this, had become the same.

Still, there were times when Elfe slept, that Katherina would catch him standing by the door to her room gazing at her with fondness and tenderness that magnified his eyes like radiant water, and she would think with a catch in her throat, "He loves her. If he didn't, I don't think I could bear it." Those times, she could see in him, the young, stern man who quoted poetry under the stars and had swept her heart away.

Katherina had long ago determined their home would be a place for a child to thrive. It was an affluent upbringing, filled with ballet, piano and painting lessons. They went to the theatre, opera, concerts and enjoyed vacations all over the Continent.

At a recent piano recital, Herman applauded Elfe for her rendition of Mendelssohn's Songs without Words and nodded in assent to a Robert Schumann concerto. But another girl, brilliant in music, stole the show with Chopin. They were all walking home in the dusk and Elfe was dispirited over her unworthiness in his eyes. Second best would never please him. She knew she could have played better, but her hands had trembled. Her true love was in colours and textures. That was how she saw her world. But she had so wanted her father's approval tonight.

His silence created a hollow inside her for the chill of rejection to flow through. Her disappointment stretched with the shadows and played on her like long, dark ivory keys of melancholia. He walked on the cobblestones lost in his own unemotionally textured place of which she played little part, and in her mind, an insignificant one.

Her father was a glacier. Even his organs were nothing more than water, a monolithic freeze. Perhaps that was why he wouldn't warm to her. If he did, he'd just evaporate into nothingness — there was no soul to leave behind. That must be it, the explanation. If he had any courage, he would take the risk in order to love her, even briefly, then he'd have a soul. Then he couldn't become extinct.

Then there was an art fair and Elfe won first prize. It was for an enchanting winter scenery of snowcapped mountains surrounding a glassy lake on which glided children skating. In the distance were houses alit with Christmas decorations. Her parents attended the fair and when her father looked more closely and recognized one cottage with pitched roof as the very one he'd been born in, in the Bavarian Black Forest, he coloured vividly. Katherina said in a serious tone, "She loves you. Elfe painted this from her heart for you." His eyes were wounded; he rubbed them and nodded his head. It looked like tearless crying.

"She's your child, your flesh and blood. You don't even know her. She's begging for your affection. You're a foolish condescending Prussian."

Herman became agitated, "Let me be." His voice had a rough edge, but he was moved. The teachers had gushed profusely at Elfe's talent and found her promising under the right tutelage.

Katherina sashayed over to him, hands on hips, "What did I tell you! Painting is her music! Elfe is not like any other child. She is Limoges porcelain amidst terra cotta."

He was florid. "It's war now, and you want to prepare her for one great party. Let her become a starving artist, at least she'll have fun!"

Katherina's eyes filled with angry tears. "Are you so afraid to think with your imagination or feel beauty and give it importance? Let the destroyers destroy and her create. There is enough ugliness. It would be a sin not to develop what the good Lord gave her. You won't stop her! Do you hear me?"

"I am insensitive, hard-working and pragmatic, and it has allowed you to live in fine style. I haven't heard you complaining, either!" They eyed each other, two bulls in the ring.

"When she draws, pieces of heaven descend. She's an instrument that must be finely honed." Katherina was begging now.

He flourished his hand, "Europe is full of disappointed and starving fine instruments, as you put it."

"The Continent was always populated with misfortune. That doesn't mean Elfe has to be. You comfort yourself with pessimism as if it were a friend. I'll use my connections and anything that'll help her and I won't hear any more nonsense from you. You're so cruel." She recovered.

Herman wasn't going to let her have the last word, he continued but more quietly, "I'm not the enemy here. I won't be the one to exploit her. You're forgetting it isn't I who made the world unkind. Sentimentality doesn't prepare you for life. Oh, why do I bother. It's all been turned upside down, if you haven't noticed. The intellectuals and cultured are a threat despised by the new regime and garbage rules the New Order. The Germany we had has slipped like sand through our fingers."

When your enemy can be your employee or neighbour, people you have known all your life, you aren't free to trust your own perceptions. He had said too much but his pride couldn't let him recover the words he spent so foolishly. Now, his anger was directed against first himself and then the new world he reluctantly lived in. Perhaps, creating a bit of beauty would serve a purpose. He looked at the painting again. Katherina's words, "She paints like a musician," echoed in him. He scrutinized it more closely. Each stroke of the brush was a note from a chord in his heart inspired by the genes of his ancestors, his Teutonic blood.

He was listening to his wife as she pointed to the broad strokes on the canvas. "There, you see rhythm, order, but not the diseased type we're now being inflicted with." Katherina was whispering. "When people sense their feelings are the same, they trust each other. What is art, if not to share emotions and to love and trust one another?"

"There is no honour, only hate and ignorance and parasites to feed off the Dummkopfs." Katherina could take no more. She ran home crying. What was happening to them? The man she had married was atrophying. Evil was devouring everything that had been good. Elfe would shine as a great polar star, immaculate, bright. She would see to it.

The gods of puberty had visited Elfe, thirteen, bringing the usual distortions of perception that came with the alterations of body contours. They were so distantly removed from her old self-image, that she suspected her former child's body had somehow died and been replaced by a mature one with new and confusing emotions.

When the sleepy winter awakened and throbbed to life, so did she, similarly roused by nature's laws. She was magic, a budding woman, on top of a rainbow, cried to by the tumescent winds, bowed to by the limbs of trees, lovely as the loveliest spring blossoms.

In the picture she painted of herself, Midas had bathed her in effervescent gold, her skin, a peach and pink sun. Her breasts were bobbing fruits. Her satiny skin narrow at the waist, broadened at the hips and thighs, her legs were muscular and well-shaped. Her body flowed like a graceful river. Her carriage was regal, her molded, heart-shaped face was aristocratic with a long, slender, patrician nose and rosy lips that when parted, revealed perfectly white, glistening teeth. She was proud to say she was uncommonly pretty and she could say it through her candid, wideset, aqua almond-shaped eyes to every mirror she passed.

Boys began to pay attention, girls were jealous. Elfe fluttered about vivaciously and exploited their insecurities. Boys carried her schoolbooks home, sharpened her pencils, and she rebelled by bringing the nasty-looking ones home to horrify her father. She attacked her art with inspiration and energy coming from the hormones rushing through her young body. She would go to the park at the break of dawn to draw the rising sun and galavant in the dewy grass.

Her station, she took for granted. The poor were born to be servants and she was born to be served. It never occurred to her that the cook had a life outside of the chores she did for the family. Her hair was washed at the beauty salon. How else could her heavy, crinkled, waist-length forest be coaxed into sophisticated bobs?

The respectability of old money was everything. She wrote on French stationery and slept on starched white, monogrammed bed linens with detailed hem stitching. Flowers abounded in silver vases, only vintage wines were stocked in the cellar, the antique furniture was pungent with age and lemon polish, a violinist played at their dinner parties. Her father was her only disappointment, tall, handsome, remote, aloof, and never satisfied with her.

She dreamed of running with the wildly rushing Isar River where her heart felt free. It rolled rapidly from a spring under the blue glacier ice, like her father — whom she visualized as having been born from that spring, toward the enchanting Danube River. One day, she dreamed that it would bring her into his heart. She had sketched the banks with its many gardens, waterfalls, brooks and miniature lakes during infrequent outings with friends.

There were times she felt wretched and sulky, spending many hours studying, painting and practicing the piano. She still tried to please her father, to get his approval, but to no avail. His sad disillusionment was a stone wall between them that she was attempting to plant flowers in.

Elfe filled her life any way she could. She became obsessed with appearance and diet, a devotion to clothes, and showed her craving for attention with overt friendliness to guests, patting and hugging them, giving them kisses, listening to their problems. She danced and teased and laughed at parties, collecting the nectar of admiration. She volunteered at charity functions, gathered used clothing for the poor and helped out rolling bandages at a hospital. When the needy kissed her and cried in open gratitude, she was embarrassed and felt a twinge of guilt.

Childhood left and the activities of a young aristocrat took its place, with stylish clothes, uplift bras that she practiced wearing in front of a mirror, jewelry, snobbish cliques and ballroom dancing. When the girls talked about snaring a proper suitor in time, they usually stopped short of what actually took place in the bedroom and it was a conundrum of bewilderment. She just could not reconcile a proper young lady doing something so unladylike, vulgar and messy. That her stern and glum father did that with her mother was incomprehensible. Like her girl friends who whispered amongst themselves concluded, their parents had only done what was necessary to conceive and then never again.

And then one day, her life became a harvest of pain and sorrow, sullen and troubled, the house a chilly, dreary tomb. The joyous sounds of the laughter of family and friends so often in their home was silenced. A tragic automobile accident carrying her mother and a friend to a party crashed into a railing, overturned and burst into flames, killing the driver. Katherina escaped the clutches of death but not unscathed. The flames had scorched her eyes, permanently blinding her.

For a year her mother's wings seemed clipped forever. They wept storms and then accepted that a benevolent God had spared her mother from death and it had to be for a reason not immediately evident. And so, they took account of how much they had left. Katherina began to work again, this time carving from wood the birds and animals she so dearly loved, entirely from memory and the sense of touch. And then, Elfe baptized them into life with her paint brushes and built them into cuckoo clocks for children.When mother and daughter were work-weary, Katherina would tenderly brush and braid Elfe's waist-length hair, while Elfe would read aloud.

Elfriede had become to her mother as the stars are to a navigator, helping him to find the position of his ship. And even though Katherina could no longer see, she continued to be the flint that kindled Herman's spirit, travelling across space to become candles.

Her beloved house remained a sanctuary of sorts, while a plague was spreading in Germany. Isolation from humanity had become their lot.

In 1944, life was to deal another blow, for one night their home was bombed by the Allies and forever Elfe would wonder if her mother had, during those last moments, blindly stumbled about alone and frightened or if she died in the arms of her husband, each supporting the other, having made their final peace before they greeted their Lord.

She often thought of her deceased father's hopes for a daughter he had not learned to love and she always thought of her mother whose daughter had been her dream come true, until the dreamer suddenly came to her end.

*E*lfe was at her Aunt Gerda and Uncle Frederick's farm when she learned about her parents' deaths. Her life seemed over. She went to stay with her friend Hedwig in Munich without even going home once.

Shortly, Elfe was invited to stay with her Aunt Gerda and Uncle Frederick. With their son in the military, they had no grand illusions about the fate of the war. When she got there, Auntie kissed and hugged her, as if she hadn't seen her in years. Elfe was taken in by the atmosphere, the collective enthusiasm, the warm cordiality. Quickly she fell under a wonderful spell that dismissed the terrible present time. Her aunt and uncle were simple people. They lived only for the land and for the family. They grew apples, peaches, and grapes, with apricot trees trained against the whitewashed walls of the modest farmhouse. Everywhere there were flowers; petunias, geraniums, marguerites in their neatly-tended garden surrounded by a metal fence covered with thick ivy. Sheer enchantment.

Despite the wartime, and perhaps to get them through it, her relatives held traditional rural get-togethers with everything a wartime economy could lay on. It was at one of those rural get-togethers, where the men got dressed in their lederhosen and the women wore gaily

Bavaria,
Early Summer,
1944

decorated skirts and tied their hair together in thick braids, that she met a childhood acquaintance who would change her life. There was folk dancing and music, and all the neighbours came. Long tables were put together and there was food and drinking and the singing of old songs, with arms wrapped around each other's shoulders, everyone swaying in rhythm, side to side.

Elfe was immediately a part of everything, helping with the food, picking herbs from the garden and filling the house with flowers. Outside stood a barrel of beer and there seemed to be an endless procession there for refills.

The neighbouring families came and soon there was feasting, folk dancing in the yard, the children had a ball. They played games and the parents laughed. The partying was expected to go on throughout the night when finally everyone weary yet revitalized, would drag themselves home, carrying their children in their arms. Aunt Gerda and Uncle Frederick would stand proudly at the doorway, an arm affectionately around each other. No one wanted these evenings to end and when they left, it was reluctantly.

In the quiet summer countryside, in the company of family, under the powdery-blue sky and poppy-red sun, with the early afternoon permeated with poignant scents of fruit trees, relaxation bathed her from head to toe. Children skipped rope, threw balls, and chased each other amidst squeals of laughter. There was a return to sanity as the kitchen became a hub of activity. Bushels of ripe apples were washed and grated, walnuts were cracked, pastry dough rolled out for the baking of apple streudel. A large cauldron boiled with vegetables for the soup, cooked ham was sliced, and Elfe took a break.

From the moment Gunther arrived, he did not take his eyes off her. He followed Elfe around, helping with the food, all the while flirting, flattering her. He even made her a nosegay and went after her as does a bee after a rose.

Her cheeks resembled ruddy apples and her eyes were grapes of lilac, prompting Gunther to monopolize her company on the porch while they nibbled on cheese sandwiches balanced on their knees. Over sauerkraut and ham plates, beneath the gaze of his unwavering eye, her mind wandered to the Gunther she knew as a child, at his folks' old farmhouse with the steeply pitched roof,

Bavarian style with timbered ceilings overlooking the Bavarian countryside of gently rolling hills. In the infrequent visits, she had romped with their two dogs and picked flowers and berries to bring her mother. The ladder to the loft had been the scene of a few upsets when he removed it, trapping her for hours in the dark crying. But he had also played checkers with her and they'd hiked in the fields.

She had often found him beastly, and being eight years her senior, she'd been no match for his pranks. At eleven, he went into the Hitler Youth and she hadn't seen him until this day, when she was conscious of his knee pressing hers and the peculiar new rush of ribbon-like sensations.

Gunther's family she had never gotten close to even though she knew them from early childhood. They were of the common sort her parents and their pretensions kept at arm's length. They lived outside Augsburg, northwest of Munich, near Dachau.

His father was a labourer in a chemical plant and his mother was a hausfrau. They were of an odd sort, even among their fellow peasants. His mother's sister was a thin rail of a woman with chronic stomach ailments from swallowing solid food whole. She had lost all her teeth years before and the familial penuriousness prohibited her from being fitted with dentures. Another of his mother's sisters also suffered from emaciation, due to abdominal cramps. In her case, she had chronic diarrhea. It was suspected she found it rude and embarrassing to tell the doctor. Gunther himself had had his escapades with bizarre ailments when he drank the free beer they got from the distillery that his mother mixed with soap to wash her hair in. She kept the mixture in the fridge. When he became very sick, she switched to shampoo.

He had been feared and hated at school for his temper and had been known to break chairs over student' heads. He had left his autograph in the form of stitches across bodies from class to class. But now Elfe's demureness attracted him. Her rabbit eyes verified she was a virgin and the thought of the inevitable pain and blood she'd experience for the first time, while he was orgasming, was an enormous aphrodisiac.

Each April 20, on Hitler's birthday, boys of ten were admitted into the Deutsches Jungvolk. A ceremony combined with Hitler's birthday celebrations had as sole object the captivation of their minds. They remained in this group till age fourteen, spending a year in one of the four sections meant to progressively lead them to the Hitler Jugend which would prepare them for the army or the Party formations. There, their minds were perverted in order for them to become professional murderers. Some minds needed more perverting than others.

In 1939, a law made membership of the Hitler Jugend compulsory for all children. Any child not a member could be taken from the parents. Elfe, however, had been given special dispensation to look after her blind mother. Others in rural communities were passed over. From the age of six, the child was subjected to a continual barrage of Nazi propaganda and ideology. From this tender age when the personality is easy to mold, the Fuehrerprinzip was implanted in young brains. A little later began the training which would reduce a human being to a state of total subordination. This "culture," was the grounding for the Hitlerian creed.

The friendly Babel's chorus of children's voices and drunken villagers' ballads resounded in the night with the chittering of the crickets and the excited drumming of Elfe's heart. The prevailing cool breeze made her tremble; she shook like a fragile leaf and Gunther drew her close. Her temples throbbed as she fought unseen chains of restraint. His hands cupped her flushed face as his inflamed eyes hypnotized hers. The motioning trees and his proximity were dizzying and she shut her eyes to not betray their longing. "You're so beguiling. I must kiss you," buzzed the bee.

Tiny, barely perceptible, delicious stings fell all over her bare neck and naked shoulders as he pulled the sleeves gently away as if they were petals. His open mouth clamped stickily over hers as his tongue searched. Confused, yet desperately wanting it, Elfe drew back.

"You're not a child anymore — don't act like one." He looked disappointed and unaccustomed to being denied. It was as if she was meeting him for the first time. He was so much older — twenty-four — and already a member of the police. He was now dangerous and that made the experience oddly more enticing.

New feelings replaced sadness, monopolizing her with their conflicts as he held her in his arms beneath a tree's branches that defined the heavens of her small world.

The cues unrecognized, they stood up and strolled through the grass. Now as her world was defined by greater physical space, she began to remember who she was, who he was and what divided them. Oblivious to her secret musings about her patrician superiority and his lack of acceptable social class and graces, he hurried her down his path as he walked, holding her hand firmly, only slightly faster than she.

He had his hand around her waist. she was wearing a simple, pink cotton skirt and a matching, shortsleeved, embroidered blouse that was clinging to her breasts. "You're absolutely blooming, my little flower," he said as his hands descended from her shoulders, his arms pushing her to walk a little faster. She was now firmly in his control. They strolled with his jacket gallantly wrapped around her shoulders against the cool, brisk breeze. Then, she became the aggressor, her fingers clinging to his thick, closely-cropped hair now pulling him along before her patrician mind would change.

He laughed and the night filled with his laughter, the sound echoing from the darkened trees veiling them. "Let us not be alone tonight my little angel. You've grown up so quickly. Nobody's at my cousins' farm. Come, let's walk there in the moonlight. There's a gramophone and cider there. Come on."

Once in the house, he fell upon her, lacing their lips wildly. In a rasping voice he declared, "I'm going to make love to you." A fireball exploded inside her which, until then, had been dormant. He took her hands and slid them over his bodily contours.

Elfe tensed uncomfortably at the bulge between his legs. Then he led her to the bedroom, taking a bottle of whisky from the kitchen with him. He drank from it and offered the bottle to her. The liquid fire spilled down her dry throat and splashed over her blouse. He yanked it down so Elfe was semi-nude, and his teeth suckled on her nipples. With his face crimson and puffy and his breathing laboured, his eyes shut tightly as though in pain. For a moment the spell was disturbed and a kaleidoscope of bits and pieces of words and feelings came through. Oh, how he had led her down the primrose path, so cocksure of himself.

His stocky build reminded her of a farm animal, his sweaty body profane and what she was about to do, so repellent. But with Gunther she'd gain experience. With him she was prepared to endure the shock and embarrassment and awkwardness of being subjected to this most unladylike, ungraceful act. It was so humiliating and undignified. Yet it was attracting her.

Sex and childbirth seemed so far away. A cut to the abdomen like Caesar's mother was for the upper classes. Pregnancy never entered her mind. That was for trollops and peasants. Her body remembered its heritage and would behave accordingly. Gunther's genes were inferior and most certainly his sperm too weak to worry about.

Gunther drew back for a moment as if sensing her hesitations. For a moment she actually wondered if he had been hearing her thoughts, what he might do to her. When he spoke, she was so relieved at the knowledge of the preserved sanctity of her private thoughts, that she did not dwell on the meaning of his suggestion.

"Let's go to the barn, have you ever lain in the hay?" Later she would wonder again if he had known her thoughts, that he was removing her from the house, a familiar world, to where he would be in his element, in control.

Then they were in the barn with the smell of hay, the shadows behaving as a maiden's shy veil and he was again pulling her blouse down her senses invaded by the musky odor of animals and dung. His mouth was on her breasts and she could hear her heart pound. There was hidden carnal promise and hunger; his nostrils distended like a primordial beast. His chest was hairy which both repelled and attracted her as she buried her Graecian nose in it and felt his canine teeth nibble her ear. "You are my angel," he whispered. The hay-bed became an altar on which her childhood died.

Afterwards they returned to the house, groped through the dark rooms to the bedroom and lay side by side, under a soft eiderdown comforter while he stroked her hair. The world was quiet except for the rustle of the starched bedsheets and the crickets outside, relishing each other, devouring each other. Later, Gunther walked Elfe home, reassuring her that she would be his forever.

When Gunther refused to see her, Elfe blamed herself. What had she done for him to break his promise? She became bitter and remote. Aunt Gerda and Uncle Frederick tried to cheer her up. When tenderness and humour failed they pleaded with her. Everything had changed. The fairy tale had become a nightmare. Many times she buried her face in her hands and cried.

"Now, now, liebling, don't despair," Auntie would say. "You are young. You have your whole life ahead of you." But Elfe already knew that was a lie adults give their children knowing that each life's journey is of unpredictable length and consequence.

Embarrassed with her wretchedness, Elfe again went to stay with Hedwig, staying there for two months until Aunt Gerda invited her back when she learned Elfe was pregnant.

Elfe did her best but could not escape the depression. After helping with the chores, she moped about. It was vexing to Gerda, so she'd cook special meals to get Elfe to eat. "Eat," she'd say, "think of the baby." But being reminded only made her more nauseous. "Nerves," her aunt would coax, and then sit and watch her like a hawk until she'd cleaned the plate.

Since Gunther was a distant relative of her Uncle, Aunt Gerda took it upon herself to talk to him. Elfe was too ashamed and too guilty.

Until the confrontation, she had been a chick inside the eggshell. There had been a small opening and Gunther had filled it when he had entered her. Now she was drowning in it. Birds had a shelter when they emerged; they had home, a nest. Every animal had its place; she had none.

"It was an accident," he said and he would have her sent away — to a Lebensborn — away, away. What was this Lebensborn? Vaguely there had been reference to a SS maternity home, Steinhoring, but not much was known about it.

At Gerda's house, he dominated the kitchen in a threatening stance, as though they were in trouble, not he. He was a bloodless, cold machine. Elfe was caught off guard. She didn't know what she had expected, but the total detachment struck her dumb.

She tried to control her nerves. Gunther's cold grey eyes gleamed like chrome. Her hands convulsed and she hid them in her apron pocket. She was in an absurd situation. Aunt Gerda remained steadfast yet seemed to be searching for words. Elfe wilted.

He stood like a piece of formed metal, feet clicked and then parted, his large hands clenched. Everything about him was cold except for a fuse that lit his eyes. The machine knew them as an instrument of danger and intimidation. He had killed, of that she was sure.

Here stood a monster, inhuman. Blood did not flow in his veins. He was shining metal with a coiled steel spring inside instead of a heart. Whatever had made him this way, was most definitely irreversible.

Elfe attempted an outwardly calm facade, which to Gunther made her look weaker, but ladies of breeding did not show embarrassment nor hysteria in disgraceful circumstances. They also did not sleep with the likes of Gunther.

Gerda had believed meeting him on her turf would throw him off. She was wrong. Before her was a trained, professional bully — every territory, his. But she was determined. "What did you do to Elfe?"

His nostrils flared and his lips retracted from his teeth like a dog about to attack. They recoiled before he moved. Then a foot lashed out violently kicking a chair sending it crashing against the wall. Veins throbbed in his temple; his Adam's apple protruded, he kept a brutal stare steadfastly on Elfe. He was trained to identify the weakest point of any defense. She cowered, shaking and ashamed. They would do whatever he said. A menacing, sidelong glance remained trained on her burning through their defenses like the sun under a magnifying glass. She thought she might have to throw up.

Now she understood how she got pregnant. It wasn't the Gunther she knew as a child; that Gunther was impotent, but long gone. He had been a mealy-mouthed but ordinary lad. Standing before them was a monster who posed as the old Gunther. This impersonator lived to destroy — not to create, and not to negotiate with. Pregnancy was the result of her sin for sleeping with him. Without emotion, he spoke of the Lebensborn as the extent of his moral responsibility.

The blow to her vanity left her reeling. This common brute had gotten the best of her. He had struck her down as thoroughly as if he'd picked up a plank of wood and smacked her over the head with it. She was sickened, remembering how he had laboured and sweated and groaned over her, drenching her with his perspiration. It had slithered like wet worms down her body.

The reptile-machine had won.

It occurred to her that he hated her. Hated her for being all that he was not. Why hadn't she thought of that before giving herself to him? What had those malicious but otherwise lifeless eyes witnessed? She wanted the ordeal over, for him to leave. She implored her aunt with her eyes to end this fiasco. The machine missed nothing. When he bid them farewell with icy finality, they let out heavy sighs of relief, but could not talk for several minutes.

A few weeks later a letter arrived at the farm.

"Elfe, Elfe, come at once! The letter has come from Munich, from Steinhoring, I think!" Aunt Gerda was rushing to the garden where Elfe was picking flowers. Anxiously the two women scanned the pages quickly. "This is it. I'm going to Steinhoring." There was a catch in Elfe's throat. How could she ever repay those two old, kind people. Aunt Gerda made it all look as if Elfe had done them a favour instead of the other way around.

On that last day Gerda took Elfe's two icy hands in her warm, work-worn ones and said, "Take care of yourself. That's all that matters. Have a healthy baby. That's all you have to worry about. You're so terribly young to have gone through so much. Just think of what your parents would want for you now. Think of that, and you'll be fine."

Elfe's memory of the journey to Steinhoring was as if she had seen a newsreel of it. The details there, but the feeling that it was happening to someone else. The car took them through rolling, green landscape, the quaint little houses strewn here and there in clusters round their churches and farms. A wagon drawn by a workhorse carrying fresh fruits and vegetables to market, passed before her eyes as she was driven away from the farm. She cherished this countryside and the excursions she had here as a child left indelible remembrances locked and sealed in her heart. The clucking chickens in the yards and the peasants seemed unchanged. She saw no swastikas or SS uniforms. At least here the scenery remained unchanged.

She shivered even though the air was warm. She huddled in the back seat of the black Mercedes, her wool coat around her shoulders and her two suitcases beside her, filled with all the clothes she owned. Some Auntie had given her (sensible, practical things) and the rest were stylish, big-city fare, bought in happier times. She envisioned the many idyllic hours spent in art galleries, admiring the fine, old oil paintings, as the innocent, dutiful daughter of an artist. Now she was damaged, ravaged by fear of the unknown, and guilt for her obvious impropriety; fifteen, expecting and utterly alone.

Removing a small compact from her purse, she studied her face. It seemed no different except for her eyes, which were still timid. She couldn't keep that. No need to have the Third Reich doubt one of their privileged specimens. The familiar landscape was speeding out of sight, bringing her closer to a new life for which she was unprepared.

Tears, lonely singular ones, escaped from her eyes. How safe she had been, in the modest farmhouse with the simple folk. Now it would be so different; the mystery of the Lebensborn made her more fearful. Too many stories told cautiously by word of mouth gave indications as to what kind of place it might be. She had never expected to find out first hand. It wasn't like her. She was just a girl, not grown-up at all.

While wavering between the present and her thoughts, Elfe had been ceremoniously driven into the park that surrounded Steinhoring. It was heavily guarded by the SS, imposing uniformed figures at the entrance with their German shepherds. She was grateful for the security they offered. That they were there to keep her prisoner, did not occur to her as where else would she have to go?

As the car approached the building, Elfe thought of some of the things the Lebensborn promised. She remembered that she was assured, in fact, guaranteed utter secrecy. The Lebensborn staff could never reveal the presence or identity of any of the women here. There was a special sworn oath. She had been told that unmarried women were given the right to change their names or that of their children, and were entitled to be addressed as "Frau" not "Fraulein." Other than in the Lebensborn, they could withhold the names of the father and the birth certificates of illegitimate babies born in Lebensborn were only available to the mother and father.

Elfe's stomach churned and churned the milk she had just taken, before the drive, into butter. She didn't belong at

Steinhoring, but now, she didn't belong anywhere. The booted footfalls, the arrogant tramplings of young SS men in their dapper uniforms, like prize horses' hooves, prancing and strutting as if on parade were foreign and threatening — someone else's army.

What also had struck her profoundly, was the tribute to the beauty and dignity of motherhood, presented at the entrance, in the form of a statue of a German mother breastfeeding an infant. It made her think of the Madonna and Child.

There was an ominous grandeur to the grounds, to the Bavarian, chalet-style home. Her senses became infused with the sounds, scents, and textures that seemed to murmur around her on a conspiratorial breeze of the burnishing fall. It was all so unreal, her feelings ran so deep, that the soft crackle of the turning leaves, the sweet cries of the birds overhead, were oblique innuendos for her alone to hear, by small, rustic creatures bearing news that caused them shy discomfort.

Elfe's internal depression blended with the unnaturally sterile, steel grey of the office creating a sickly combination. Her body was cold and clammy, and even the gem blue of her eyes was muted to a pseudo-anemic grey. Years later she would try to remember first walking into the building but she could never unlock that memory.

Even in her wretchedness, she was glad that the long-winded rambling monologue was not a personal exchange. While she was desperately lonely for human interaction the woman who stood before her seemed not to qualify. She was resolute to conceal and safeguard her true self as though it were in a strongbox of determination.

The barking was coming out of a pugnacious bulldog face, loose jelly flesh hung from jowls of a faded, sallow, middle-aged woman whose thin, coppery hair straggled hopelessly behind her ears and neck in a bun, just as those eyes were skimming over her own physique. The red-veined, jealous eyes networked a quick examination, and then the mongrel breed of a human being triumphed in the obvious surrender of a thoroughbred girl who was now an unmarried breeding mare at her mercy and to live under her rules.

Rules! The only rules Elfe had ever known were the product of home-grown, private schools reinforced with the aim to create a maiden for ostentatious and easy living, who hired people like this one, to clean her house. Elfe stood 170 cm tall, ramrod straight and proud. She was everything of beauty and breeding and grace. The woman before her was not, and they both immediately, instinctively, recognized it. Elfe clenched her fists. She felt dirtied, insulted in this derogatory presence. And yet she had made her choice. All that was gentlemanly, sheltering, mannered, was gone. A Lebensborn, with its tawdry implications, with its peculiar respectability and mystery, now jostled a young girl who'd been cloistered completely, who'd never had to wonder where the next meal was coming from. Anyhow an imitation of grandeur was easier to adjust to than poverty, managing like a peasant with a bastard child. Even the idea had filled her with abhorrence.

The breeding mare braced herself for the submissive, pretended eager to please, easily trained, role in the face of personal defeat. Here, she would still be privileged. For a spoiled, immature, homeless, orphaned teenager, this way would be easier, whatever it would be like.

No one had told her that someone so very young could know tragedy. Her mother's accident should have been her first warning. Then a war and her parents' deaths, so fast and she was confused, sad, angry. It wasn't fair. No one had warned her that life was often unfair — that the trappings of class could be removed.

She recalled the pretty past with the pretty clothes and her own ingrained ladyness and her tainted virtue. That something inherently noble flowed coldly, resolute, as blue as the Danube, through her veins, there was no doubt. If her illustrious ancestors had been standard bearers in this unfamiliar room now, she could not have felt them more acutely. A wry smile curled her lip upward. A cruel twist of fate had dethroned this princess.

Thoughts rolled over one another, like the cobbled stones of her beloved Munich. A cavernous wheeze brought her back.

"I'm the head nurse, Hilda," the face pontificated. She continued on in a practiced monotone, to list the various rules of the home and its unique importance. A swamp smell lingered in the room, radiating from Hilda, from her heavy-set, gluttonous body and the dribbling beads of perspiration dripping from her pudgy brow which had soaked into her clothes.

The grey office began to carousel around Elfe. Hilda, unbelievingly, was now insinuating a buddy relationship with the Führer himself. "Ah, yes, the Führer pops by to visit us and then the cook brings fresh kaffee and kucken and we talk..." She was pointing affectedly to his large portrait on the wall.

The grating voice tread on Elfe like railroad tracks as she longed for the old-fashioned, charmed life of which she had been lucky to be a part of and from which she was banished forever.

Swooning, in meek, stupified silence, she met the second, disagreeable-looking woman who stood like a scarecrow. "This is Anna, one of my secretaries," Hilda spluttered, spraying the thin, wiry, thirtyish woman's face with spittle. The submissive, birdlike woman barely blinked. "She'll show you to your room." She nodded to the scarecrow, "Introduce her to her roommate," and she was through with a dismissing wave of her hand and a Heil Hitler.

They proceeded down the hall, the scarecrow woman leading the way quite literally with her nose which she used to acknowledge the presence of those they passed, her weak thin hands not worth involving in unnecessary gestures. The SS could be seen everywhere, framed pictures of the Führer hung in the main office, in the bright corridor and on the walls of many of the girls' rooms. She was in the lion's den now, with the heathen, treading on rich, Persian carpeting. A staircase dressed in a red rug, led the way upstairs. In the right context it would have been regal but here it was like blood dripping down the stairs inviting her to its source. As Elfe was led to her room, the odious display of spidery swastikas galvanized the fact that this was very much an SS establishment and sinister. The flag itself looked harsh, unsophisticated, plebeian. The sudden chime of a grandfather clock in the hall and the pusillanimous beating of her heart decried the pendulum of her life, swinging from joy to sorrow. Clocks break. What if she were left here, waiting for the return swing, all her life? Homesickness tugged at her like metal wiring.

From an open window, church bells, like angels' harps, strummed the minty air with reverberating piney clangings, shattering against her ears like delicate crystal.

Choking back hot tears, Elfe reminded herself of her sentence. She pushed back an orgy of reminiscences and marched down the hall. Momentarily they stopped in front of room twenty-four. Her fingers sweatily fingered the handles of her bags worrying them until the threading that seamed them together began to come undone, just like her life she thought. But this was her new life. She willed her fingers to become still and they gripped the handles, hard like rigor mortis.

The door sprang open and Elfe was facing a tall, plump, ungainly blond with a rubicund circle of a peasant's face, typical of those she had many times seen milking cows, on her outings to neighbouring farms. Eyes mischievously danced around a complexion flecked with numerous red freckles. Sheaves of wheat surrounded her head, caught with a red ribbon and tied coquettishly over one ear. A silver, heart-shaped locket dangled on a chain about her neck. She cracked into a wide, toothy grin and snatched Elfe's hand with a roughness as if it were a farm tool. "I'm Gisela Schulz," a high treble voice rang out.

The clownish creature was an affront to Elfe's eyes which actually hurt trying to locate the person underneath the garish display of hot magenta that spread from the top of her head and dizzied her now reddening face as they scrutinized each other. Her roommate occupied an expanding figure of about six months pregnancy in a flaming tent-dress. Elfe became suddenly weak as if she had walked the many miles, rather than been driven here. Her hand grabbed a wall to stabilize herself, as her stricken eyes roamed around the tumbledown room.

"Well, what are you looking at?" It was a stentorian farm animal squawk, like that of a giant hen, as Gisela glared at the secretary. Elfe

Bavaria,
Summer, 1944

was relieved that the inquiry wasn't directed at herself as she had at first feared. A glance of mutual disgust was exchanged between the two. Bristling, Anna left the doorway, as the door slammed behind her. "That crow will have to learn to treat me with more respect," said Gisela continuing to size up Elfe, her forehead encrusted with Indian red eyebrows arching defiantly with her large hands resting on her stomach.

"Was there a fight here?" Elfe whispered as she stood in the middle of a scattered hovel. Strewn all over were mangled clothes, unsorted laundry, and mismatched shoes. On one of the two double beds, lay dresses, silk stockings and an iron.

"Nah, relax, it always looks like this," Gisela said, busily scooping up articles of clothing and dumping them on a chair.

Aside from the mess, the room was large and comfortable with a roomy pine armoire and a gay, floral oriental rug on the hardwood floor. As expected were the obligatory framed photographs of Hitler hung on the white-painted walls. The beds were covered with simply embroidered, white cotton bedspreads. There was a heavy mahogany, dresser with a big square mirror against one wall, of the same wood as the headboards. Beside each bed was a mahogany bedside table and on top of each sat a Chinese export lamp. Orphaned cut flowers lay on the dresser. Best of all, were French doors with waving curtains of coloured bands, that opened onto an amber sun beating down on rolling, velvet meadows and a glassy lake.

Gisela began to chatter volubly as Elfe unpacked her suitcase, feeling desolate and almost ready to cry. She was wearing a light lavender skirt and short-sleeved, cotton knit sweater with a tiny collar — city-girl style as were some of the dresses that came out of the valises, along with sensible country fare.

Gisela's eyes grew round. "Wow, you're a classy broad, nothing like the fanatics we get from the BDM, thank G-d."

"What do you mean?"

Gisela was practically drooling onto a silk camisole on the bed. "That's fancy-shmancy stuff from Paris! Oh, most of the girls here are only too happy to bear children for the Third Reich. Sleeping with the SS in order to get pregnant, for them, is the loftiest job in the world!" Her eyes narrowed shrewdly. "You're not the type."

Elfe nodded her head from side to side. "You look my age. I'm fifteen."

"I'm one over you. Hey! I wouldn't mind borrowing that..."

Elfe was hanging a linen peach skirt, beautifully cut.

"Who am I kidding? If I'm lucky, I could fit half of my butt into that." Gisela was posing in front of the mirror. "I'm a big, fat cow, but of pure blood. Listen, you look so glum," said Gisela cheerfully, her straw coloured hair with auburn streaks made a golden frame about her face. "I'll make us some tea. We can drink it on the balcony, okay?" She winked and her lip curled crudely.

An odd idiosyncrasy, thought Elfe. She gasped when she stepped outside. "What a marvellous view!"

"Yeah, sit down." Gisela patted a wicker chair beside her. "Let's get to know each other." A kettle whistled and she went inside leaving Elfe for a moment.

Gisela returned with a pot of tea, lemon slices, biscuits and a box of cream-filled chocolates. Once they were comfortable, Gisela pulled out a packet of snapshots: "This is my family. That's my mother and my father. And that's my pig, Porkchops." Elfe, unaccustomed to the company of one so forward, was content to let Gisella monopolize the conversation.

Strains of Mozart's Magic Flute floated from an open window over the lake, while footed mermaids waded in the cool waters, creating green, shimmering ripples. What was the music of aristocrats doing here? What could the Giselas of the world know of culture? Elfe stood up. She couldn't believe she was here.

What was smashed could not be rebuilt. And, as though in assent, the delicate opera stopped, and it too, was gone, just like her home into the past. Gone like a white sail into milky clouds above the earth while she, earnest and melancholic, was fated to be anchored with those on land. She shivered, notwithstanding the warm September air, and out of some purgatory, came the voice of Gisela and the slap of a glass into her hand.

"You can use some of this." Out came another glass and a bottle of schnapps. Crystals clanged together and Elfe, unused to potato liquor, coughed and Gisela laughed and then Elfe realized that she was hearing her own laughter. What at first burned like poison, now felt tingly and welcoming. Her sad thoughts dimmed as the alcohol misted her faculties.

The grand music restarted and seemed to mount the stairs with melodious foot falls, singing of solidarity and continuity. She shut her eyes — she could almost see them, her elitist Swiss ancestors. Her chest swelled with pride just as it had years before when she had gazed at the Lion of Lucerne. The inscripted words in the rock, Fidelity and Courage, she had something to prove to them, to herself now. Music had never had such feeling. It was as though they had risen from the grave to walk beside her now. Tears fell into her lap but there was some comfort in them.

Gisela came from a farm in Bavaria and so had escaped the notice of the BDM. She showed photos of fruit trees, chickens and geese. Her father and brother were on the eastern front. She sighed heavily, "My mother and sister have managed as best they can. A bomb dropped near our farm, but not much was destroyed. Now my grandparents from Berlin, who were near starvation, moved to the farm so they could all be together until the end of the war."

Elfe was relaxing; some of the loneliness had left her. The girls saw something of themselves in each other and it united them. Her manacled heart felt freer. The air was balmy and she took a deep breath and let herself be bewitched by the magical countryside that she loved so much. The meadows were belted by pines and enhanced by evergreens bordering the soft grass. Here and there honey-coloured cows grazed peacefully — a pastoral scene, dreamy, Arcadian, blissful, timeless.

She wasn't alone in this captive cell. Life mattered again. With half-closed eyes, thoughts were dissolving as a faint, pastel sky mellowed her mood — helped by the effects of the alcohol. Meadow blossoms, creamy buttercups, lacy-like white and yellow parsley; dainty, delicate, multi-coloured butterflies flitted about, landing on each flower and then fluttering on to the next. One flew through the window and alit on a daisy in a glass vase. Gladsome birds glided through the trees. What a celebration of rural beauty. A silvery stream girdled the meadow, etching the slopes as it swam over shiny rocks.

A little later, the two girls sat on Gisela's bed and Gisela, her hands on her swollen belly, talked of how she came to be pregnant. "An SS officer seduced me. I was lonely, went to an acquaintance's get-together one evening, was bored, left and went to a movie. There I met him. I was taken by his charming manner and thoughtful gifts and attentions. I thought he really liked me." Briefly Gisela's composure left. "The cad got me pregnant. I wanted to get married. He was a cute guy, but he said he already had a wife. I wanted to barf in his face. I really did. I trusted him, so now I'm here." She patted her stomach.

"I'm so sorry."

"Nah, let's leave it." Silence ensued. A quizzical look crossed her face. "How did you get here?" As Elfe was about to speak, Gisela held up her hand and sniffed the air. "Do you smell food?"

"No."

"Go on."

Suddenly Elfe felt an overwhelming need to tell her everything that had led to her arrival at Steinhoring. In one sweeping motion she spun around to stand at the French doors, a distant look in her eyes. "You can't imagine what the weeks after my parents' death were like." Her face took on an expression of carved marble, delicate and hard at the same time. "Rage and despair were all I felt." Her blanched face gave an impression of a fountain figurine repressing tears of anguish. "The sunshine had gone from my life. At times I blamed myself for not dying with them, at other times I was guilty for being glad that I didn't die, that sheer chance saved my life." Elfe's voice became anxious, words, memories and feelings spilling out freely, desperately.

"Go on, please. It will help you."

Elfe told her about Gunther and his cruelty, how she came to Steinhoring. Suddenly there was a loud cracking noise and Elfe turned about. Gisela was already removing the pulp from a bag of walnuts and wielding a giant nutcracker in her hand.

"Every woman should carry one of these in her purse. They'd stay zipped and scared — mostly scared — and then they'd, well they'd take us seriously! Yes they would."

"I don't know about that."

"You don't know too much. That's how my mama has kept my papa in line all these years. She's threatened to cut it off, and with her temper, he's never too sure. Many times I heard him crying behind the barn, trying to piss after she let him have it with a cooking pot. Anyway, don't let me disturb you. Go on." Elfe was shocked by the crudeness but found it fresh and liberating. That there was another being growing inside her was bewildering — it sat within her in purblind darkness. That she had been invaded by a troll, a mongrel, a lout, was incomprehensible. But how could she explain this to a woman of the same class?

Gisela interrupted to ask, "But how did Gunther hit the target? You know what I mean." Gisela pulled out every detail.

Dusk fell silently for the girls. A breeze gently rustled through the trees and the newly-acquired friends spoke now in hushed tones. Preening against the window pane, there appeared a plain, brown nightingale. Like a travelling minstrel, it was singing its heart out, full throated, sweet, its melody echoing through the woods. Its purity made the girls feel unworthy. With a reverence they laid bread down for the bird; it ate graciously, then flew away. The maidens sighed simultaneously.

"Gracious me!" Gisela exclaimed. "It's past suppertime and I'm starved! Hold the fort! I'm going to make us some sandwiches!" With that, she sprang like a giant-sized, fluorescent bouncing ball to the small table and a stash of food and began cutting thick pieces of dark bread, stuffing salami in between, all the while popping chunks of food into her mouth.

"You like your sandwich with cucumbers?" She was choking and food was falling out of her mouth as she turned to Elfe.

What a pig! She had to control herself from laughing at her. "Yes, please," she managed with a smirk on her face.

"Great! You're finally smiling! Here's a sandwich. If you want another, just holler."

Presently, the two, a bacchanalian portrait, were munching, sipping hot, strong tea, and dipping into Gisela's cache of cookies hidden in her bureau under her underwear. "I need these keks. Those buffalos in the kitchen can go to hell. I'm sure they steal food and sell it on the black market."

It grew darker outside and the girls decided not to curse the darkness with electricity. Instead, a candle was lit and they were swept into a dreamy mood. "Let's talk. Let's talk all night. I feel great! Continue the story." Gisela looked eager, kind, and most of all, absurd lying on her bed now, her hands folded on her tummy schoolgirl fashion, her middle looking like a globe. Elfe poured out until she felt like an empty vessel.

"Elfe, hon," Gisela said, eventually, standing up and stretching, hands massaging her back, "I've just got to go and take a nice, warm, long bath. My legs are killing me and junior here thinks my tummy is a playground. Forgive me." Gisela left the room. For the first time at the home, Elfriede was alone.

It was suppertime on a deceptively quiet evening shortly after her arrival and Elfe and Gisela were headed into the busy dining room. The aroma was inviting. "Mm, mm," Elfe sniffed the air, "chicken and roast potatoes and apple strudel. I'm starved."

"Yeah, me too," Gisela said, eyeing the table near the window. Presently the room was packed with the SS and pregnant women. Amidst the clatter of dishes and animated voices, a tall, pregnant blond woman entered the room. Glancing about, she headed straight for Elfe and Gisela's table. "Damn," Gisela hissed into Elfe's ear, "Here comes buttface."

Monika eased herself into a chair and the girls passed the plates around. They looked away as she tore into the chicken, gouging out a leg. Then she dumped some potatoes and vegetables onto her plate and proceeded to eat with both elbows on the table. Juice dripped down her chin. She was a stout, coarsely featured woman of about seventeen, with an enormous head and protruding forehead that shadowed two asinine, cunning eyes. Her bulky frame shook like a massive aspic that was removed from the refrigerator too soon. The way she wheezed and snorted, gave the impression that a little evil person was behind all the blubber and had difficulty getting out.

Around her fat wrist, the girls noticed, was a fine, tripe-strand pearl bracelet with an unusual clasp of highly polished rubies. Gisela couldn't help remark, "That's a striking bracelet you've got on." Monika dropped the wing she was devouring, and wiped her hand on the tablecloth.

Thrusting her wrist proudly at the girls, she boasted, "It's my favourite. And you know why? Because it used to belong to a worthless, stinking, dirty Jew!" Gleefully she looked around as though she had won it in a raffle, having defeated unworthy opponents. "My uncle is a guard in Dachau. He has to go there and endure the terrible stench of those dirty Jews. My aunt complains he has to strip himself naked and wash himself head to toe, his clothes too, every day when he comes home from work.

You know what that smell is of course." Here she paused for a moment, and then enunciating very slowly, said, "It's their rotten flesh burning in the ovens." Her upper lip was snarling.

Elfe felt dizzy and forgot about her food.

"Anyhow, this Jew family with a bunch of lice-ridden children arrived by cattlecar at the camp. The husband and wife begged my uncle to have compassion for his bastards. Huh, imagine those Jew pigs trying to get sympathy! 'Please, save our babies,'" Monika squeaked, gesticulating. "They offered this jewelry and my uncle said, 'None of you need anything anymore.' Straightaway they were sent to be gassed. The sooner those Jews are erased the better!"

Seeing Elfe's panic, Gisela too, became alarmed. Excusing themselves from the table, Gisela and Elfe walked back to their room. Elfe tottered to her bed, her face grey. Underneath the bed was homemade moonshine from the farm. She grabbed the bottle, gulped and fell against the pillows. In hating Monika she had to look at herself.

These were her people doing this. She was no longer above them having fornicated with the lowest in the country. She hated herself, but most of all she hated the thing growing in her belly, growing for this purpose. Her voice strangled in her throat. She couldn't explain this to Gisela who appeared more shocked by her reaction than by what they had just seen. Perhaps she too would get used to it.

There was a hubbub of booted footsteps in the park, boisterous laughter, male and female voices and car engines starting. The noises came to her as the buzzing of wasps, black, the builders of a new, monstrous fabric for the universe, with its own particular pattern for future generations. And these women were living in its nests as the queen mothers of the new colonies. The colony's prey would be devoured to make room for those chosen to propagate the species, the superior generations. Her hands flew to her heated cheeks that seemed to have turned to fire. After a few minutes Elfe managed to describe her feelings.

Gisela was subdued. "There isn't anything we can do."

Elfe looked around the room and considered how small her world was, safe and full of light. It seemed like the most protected place on earth, whose purpose was to create and celebrate new life. But it was made by the creators of death machines, who dedicated themselves to taking life and light away. She thought of the irony and of the German soldiers lost on the Russian front, and of nature's bitter cold revenge.

Returning from the bathroom, she applied a wet facecloth to her cheeks. "Since the age of twelve, I've seen the Jews wearing the yellow Star of David with 'Jude,' on the sleeves. I saw people beaten by the Gestapo and I chose to look away, because it was unpleasant for me to see. Maybe that is our punishment — to see and to know, and keep that knowledge forever."

Elfe glanced at the open window. There perched a nightingale, cooing a sweet madrigal of perennial purity. But she could feel no kinship with such innocence. In the song she heard reproach. Her parents seemed to come alive watching her from the photo hanging on the wall. They had given her life, but no useful tools to cope with it.

Gisela made preparations for bed. Starched sheets rustled and pillows were plumped. Then, while folding away her bedspread, she said, "Listen, you can't be too surprised by Monika. After all, we are in a Lebensborn home. These homes are run by the SS Fuhrungsamt. The medical superintendent, the head nurse, yeah, Hilda too, the administrator, and the secretary are all members of the SS or of the Party. Himmler himself — I've seen him here a few times — acts as registrar of births and deaths, and is responsible for keeping order here. He's in charge of the files too, which he keeps locked up. He's head of the SS. Need I say more?"

Inside, the room was quiet except for the rumble of water in the kettle getting ready to boil. Laughing voices vibrated in the hall and a navy, almost onyx colour filled the sky like paint. Topaz stars dared to twinkle in suspension. To Elfe, the dark opaque sky represented one reality and the voices outside their room another; she was caught between the two. Her mind sped on like the wild Isar River that she loved and now began to resemble. Her thick eyebrows were dark blond hedges with a troubled, vertical valley between and her insightful eyes had cooled to a glacial aquamarine blue. The lone candle, they had come used to lighting, shifted a ghostly, trembling light on the taffy-coloured polished floor and reflected on the white walls. Arthritic creaks in the floorboards answered the drones of the cars in the gravel driveway, the shiny, metal monsters revving up. Someone lumbered heavily up the stairs. The kettle started to scream and fume its gaseous vapors into the air as Gisela bustled to make tea. Elfe took a sip of the strong, sweet, soothing liquid. Monika's contemptible words stuck like icicles to her body. She thought of the stylized black flag fluttering at the entrance, an oppressive insignia she was hiding beneath — a rock hiding underneath a bug.

She felt very, very tired, and could not fight off memories from her childhood — Jews being forbidden to enter parks, museums, concert halls and certain streets. Store windows broken, Jews herded onto trucks and cattlecars to unknown destinations. The fear in their eyes was looking into hers now. In Munich they were not permitted to buy food. All this was public knowledge, just like the impossibility for them to get medical attention in her city because the Jewish physicians had been arrested.

A maelstrom of emotions wrestled with Elfe. In her loathing of herself and her people she included her parents. She said to Gisela or to nobody in particular, "If I think of my father without my daughterly blinders, I know that he was a stereotypical professor engrossed in his books. Education didn't help him put theories into practice. He sat on the sidelines of life and viewed people's behaviour as though their maliciousness and unscrupulous manifestations were merely signs of misguidance and could be corrected. He just let things happen. When he finally saw the bitter reality, he fell apart. He was a dead, defeated man before the bomb was ever dropped. I'm afraid I'm like my mother — a peaceful dove with ruffled feathers who used to live in an ivory tower with useless innocence — never having to be responsible for the matter from which my world is made."

Gisela looked at her blankly, Elfe could see that she was truly confused. She glanced at the patternless night and then at her friend and then just sat numbly staring into the darkness.

Gisela muttered lamely, "When I first showed up here, I got quite a shock. I believed most of the women were fleeing the wrath of relatives or were classy girls in trouble who had to hide out till they had their babies, or had nowhere to go to have their baby in good conditions, like me." Meeting Elfe's glance in the mirror, Gisela said softly, "Better face the music. We're in the minority here."

Elfe knew her better than that. Gisela loved her internment at Steinhoring. If not for Hitler, she never would have been elevated to a higher station. She bustled and twittered like a chipmunk, drunk with gorging itself on the fruits it burrowed and hid. She bossed the staff around with grandiose gestures and they suffered her. She rode her position for all it was worth.

Gisela conducted herself with chipper authority which made for meanness, coldness and hostility by the haughty married women whose husbands were SS officers. Women who never would have crossed her path, now were paying attention, albeit with nastiness and rejection and Gisela got a major rise out of it.

When she walked into the dining room, their heads turned and returned to their cliques, snubbing her. She'd sit at the next table and loudly squawk that the father of her child was a married SS officer, "Why, he could be any one of yours!" These insinuations would be tossed like clumps of dirt and she enjoyed the irascibility she aroused as they lost their composure and wriggled in their chairs as though they sat on heaps of manure and were forced to pretend otherwise. She knew they detested her and whether they acknowledged it or not, they had lost their exclusivity with their spouses. When she smiled maliciously, her large front teeth gleamed with predatorial delight.

The next morning, Elfe stretched, yawned, then rolled onto her side to drift into lazy slumber again. But something moved inside her stomach, then slid up into her throat. Frightened, and swallowing a sour tasting liquid in her mouth, she jumped from her cozy bed in a sprint to the bathroom, just in time to vomit, retching violently, a dark yellow fluid. Again and again, she gave in, kneeling over the toilet, both arms grasping its sides. When it was over, she was drained. Wrapping herself in her bluegreen bathrobe, she opened the French doors and stepped outside.

The sun had shied away and was hiding behind grey, striped stratus clouds that could not contain themselves and were bursting open. The earth was thirstily drinking in the silvery crystalline water. Shade was offered to emerald meadows and trees, their long, brown legs wrapped in a taupe mist. Branches nodded to one another assiduously.

She couldn't stand to eat now, but a hot, strong cup of coffee would settle her. Minutes later she was in the living room cradling the strong, aromatic, hot liquid. With her she had brought an artist's pad and pencils. Aimless women wandered about, sway-backed, hands on hips, gigantic bellies jutting out. She was ensconced in a velvet armchair amidst idle, gossipy women obviously engaged in pettifoggery, listening to their copious outpourings of jealousies and suspicions of one another.

There was another war inside the War going on, thought Elfe, disgusted.

Just then, a loud, agonizing shriek emanated from way down the hall where the labour rooms were. It was followed by moans and groans and scurrying feet. A few women left the living room to investigate. There was a flurry of activity as a doctor went in and out of the room.

Elfe found herself all alone until Monika sauntered in, nibbling on cheese and pumpernickel, like a rodent, Elfe thought wryly. Elfe tried to ignore her, pretending to be preoccupied with her drawing.

"You know, I like you," Monika said, chewing. "You seem nice, not like those married bitches who treat us like shit. What do they think? That what they've got down there is made from gold! You're different. Would you do a picture of me?"

"I don't do portraits, just sceneries." Elfe wanted nothing to do with her, but she had to be careful. "Do you know what the hullabuloo was all about?"

"Yea, that bitch what's-her-name, is married to an SS officer and thinks she's Queen Shit. She's a few hours in labour and begging for pain killers. There must be Jews in her blood. No respectable German woman would agree to any artificial aids to deaden the pain. Only degenerate Western countries. Hah, listen to her howl! She sounds like a braying wolf in the wild!" Monika laughed, then she continued laughing, slapping her sides, then she roared like a lioness in heat, and rocked back and forth till she was red in the face and gasping for breath. She leaned closer to Elfe and whispered cryptically, "I won't be asking for any injections when my time comes. Gazing at the portrait of our beloved Führer will be enough." Her eyes, sitting too dangerously close together to be aesthetic, softened.

Monika, popping a plate of cookies on her expansive lap made herself comfortable, "You know, I was in the BDM," she declared, "My family is very proud."

Elfe knew that many of these girls were her age, fifteen or sixteen, and considered racially "pure." Some girls were older and from varying backgrounds, but nearly all of them had one thing in common, a fanatical desire to present the Führer with a child. She also knew the BDM was the female equivalent to the Hitler Youth.

Monika continued, "You must be very proud to be allowed to stay here at Steinhoring, one of the best out of many highly secret SS organizations for the purpose of producing blond, blue-eyed children by mating men and women carefully selected from the best Nordic specimens in Germany. All the young men are members of the SS or the police." Monika sat up straight as if on a throne. Elfe mused over the term "stud-bulls" she heard whispered in the village. The women were sometimes hissed at and called "lazy whores" by the villagers.

Monika's voice continued with the rapidity of a hammer pounding a nail into wood, each clipped word enunciated exactly the same as all the words before, with no difference in inflection, a machine with no changing tides of emotions — a tool for the using and as useless as a doornail otherwise. And surely that was how she too must perceive the reality she now lived, Elfe thought dismally.

"Well, the BDM teachers were very proud of me. My school marks were good and they said I had real leadership qualities. One day my leader approached me and said, 'With your blond looks and wide pelvis, perfect for childbirth, have you thought about giving the Führer a child?' Then she explained about the home of the SS foundation, the Lebensborn. I was thrilled!

"The home I stayed in was in a lovely, old castle in the Black Forest. There were about thirty girls, all teenagers. We did not reveal our names nor where we came from. All you needed was a proof of Aryan ancestry back to your great-grandparents — of course I was accepted. Each one of us had her own luxurious room. I had one overlooking the grounds. There was a mahogany bed and a matching dresser. I had a gold brocade bedspread and drapes. You should have seen it. The maids made sure to keep the vases filled with flowers from the garden. We had game rooms and a cinema, even a lake for rowing, swimming and sailing. There were horses and some girls went riding. There was a gourmet chef and lots of servants.

"A senior SS doctor examined us when we arrived and we had to declare that there were no cases of hereditary diseases, dipsomania, or imbecility in our family. An SS officer explained that Heinrich Himmler had been charged by the Führer with the job of pairing pure, Nordic women with SS men of equally pure stock to produce a pure racial breed. We were introduced to the SS men who were very tall and handsome. We had fun with them, going to movies and having parties. After a week we had to choose the man we liked. We weren't told their names. Then, we had to wait till the tenth day after the beginning of our last period. We were examined and allowed to invite the SS men to sleep with us at night.

"I chose a terribly virile-looking guy who slept with me for four nights that week. The other three nights he slept with another girl. It's a pity, I would have loved to have him every night. He had a voracious appetite and we did it all night. He barely needed to rest between.

"I got pregnant right away, and had the choice of going home or moving straight here. I chose to come here so I can just relax and do nothing till the baby comes."

Elfe sat stiffly, her clear, sibyl eyes a celestial, translucent hue, her soliloquised umbrage treading the sea of disdain. She turned Monika's words over and over in her head like vomit that reeled itself from stomach to mouth and then stayed there. How advantageous it sometimes was, she silently observed, to be endowed with a vacant mind, incapable of seeing past one's own immediate needs. She had listened to dimwitted Monika, in all her glorified grandiloquence, a pathological parasite, quenchless in her many appetites, coasting along, making no friendships, indifferent to others except for the services they can render, and discarding them just as easily as a used rag. She felt more in solitude with such company than when alone.

I shall become like her if I stay here long enough. Her imagination overtook her and she fancied a Medusa with hideous teeth and claws, blond hair braided with hissing snakes. She even felt she was turning to stone as she listened to Monika.

The cold rain transformed the ordinary windows into mock stained glass of all hues of garnet, amethyst and gold. Candle flame and stiletto sparks, struck like distant pistol shots. Mute, melting wax was kissed hotly by the orange flame. Fire and glass cast a lingering spell of false comfort. Elfe despised the place. The half-eaten kuchen on the small mahogany tables, the strawberry torte left on a chair partially devoured in a corner, the silver Swiss chocolate wrappers crumpled on the floor were all luxuries unearned. Had there been warm human beings with compassion inhabiting the home, it could have been animated charmingly, instead it leered tawdry and gaudy, the de-personification of the hard, self-serving harlot, layering herself with showy possessions, yet unable to generate anything of true beauty.

A smattering of noise broke through the pattern of rain as the home's heavy, rusty gate fell back on its hinges and the impetuous, angry barking of the German shepherds grated the air abruptly. The driving rain pounded invisible fists on the windows and doors. Elfe kneeled at the fire and rubbed her hands while red patches blazed on her cheeks. Monika continued.

"We were told that a baby born here could be handed over for adoption to a good SS family or I could keep it and bring it up myself. Why do I need to be saddled with a baby? I've got more important things to do," Monika said, checking out the remains of a chocolate box.

Elfe laughed to herself sarcastically. Yes, it was more important to sleep with the SS.

Monika rattled on, "A few more weeks and this cargo I'm carrying will be gone. Then I'll be free. For giving the baby to the Führer, I'm going to get that allowance they give on leaving the home for post natal exercises and beauty treatment." Monika was posturing in front of a small mirror on the wall. Elfe shuttered her eyes in the capering heat of the dancing fire.

The hands of time moved forward in a loud, booming bellow from the grandfather clock in the hall, heralding the arrival of late four o'clock afternoon and the entrance of a wild-eyed, Bohemian Gisela clad in a provocatively wet, clinging maternity dress and jangling a collection of bells in the pockets of her coat. Accompanying her were several other women and they all immediately descended on the fireplace.

"We got caught in this miserable rain and then our ride got stuck," Gisela said, to the fire, her teeth chattering.

"Hah, your boyfriend probably stood you up," Monika jeered.

"Listen, dung heap," Gisela retorted, turning around to face her. "Why don't you take those elephant legs upstairs so that monster in your belly can rest and where we don't have to suffer looking at you."

Monika jumped out of the chair like a mad woman. "How dare you!" The other women intervened, as Gisela and Monika glared at each other.

"No need to behave in a way unfit for a German mother," one said.

"Come on, Gisela," Elfe yawned, "let's just go upstairs." The bells had become a passion for Gisela. The high, treble tympanic sound, reverberated prettily in its own unique musicality through the corridor, as the two girls mounted the stairs.

Munich was famous for its unusual and interesting industry of church bells which their foundries sent to different parts of the world. A small shop near the village made small ones for display, from porcelain, in bright colours and the children loved them. Their lively chime brought squeals of glee and now many of the children wanted them. Even Dr. Ebner kept a whole row of them on a shelf in his office.

"You must give Monika allowances, Gisela," Elfe remonstrated as they entered their room. Gisela was about to answer, her mouth half-opened, but she just waved away the subject with her hand. Elfe quickly skirted the room, lighting candles.

Through the window the wind pursued the leaves and the squirrels fretted audibly on the branches. The Lord's wardrobe was bare; even He was penurious now. She could not bar her thoughts like the windows. Their fleshless reminders could summon her any time. She didn't want to think now. Even the sun had abandoned its responsibilities today. The fountain of the sky gave its hysteria a rest. The orange, halcyon, flickering lights freshened her mood.

A snack was made of pumpernickel bread and butter. The kettle whistled and hot, strong tea was poured. A mischievous look smeared its way over Gisela's face. "What do you say, we've been forced to listen to that wild animal orgy every night. Look at these rings under my eyes," she demonstrated, her eyebrows flying up. "I look like a raccoon." Kneeling on her bed, she began pounding her fists into the wall. "Inge, are you there?" she screamed. "She's been here since forever." She was pointing accusingly at the wall, smiling, obviously envigorated by any hint of intrigue. "That Fraulein has a man in there every night. He's made her pregnant for the second time. I don't know why they don't get married. He can't seem to keep his hands off her."

Elfe giggled. More sandwiches were made with thick cheese. Gisela was stuffing food into her mouth, her words coming out muffled as with cotton wool. Elfe had to concentrate very closely.

"I can hear everything. You're lucky you sleep like the dead, but I don't. They fuck almost every night, and if they wake me up, I knock on the wall with my fist and they quiet down — unless they're right in the middle, and then they have to speed up. She's pretty quiet, but he groans like a bear, he does. He can go on like that for about twenty minutes. He's so impatient sometimes, that things get knocked off the furniture."

Elfe was trying to connect subdued, shy Inge with a ravishing sex life. Gisela pounded again. "Inge, are you decent, ha, ha! I'm coming in with my roommate."

A minute later, they were in Inge Fink's messy room. She was huge, even for someone full term. Her stomach looked stretched to the maximum. Elfe couldn't devise how she could make love at all, in this state. Inge looked about twenty-eight and seemed friendly and down-to-earth. She lay on the bed with difficulty and Elfe noticed how swollen with edema her feet were.

"I told Elfe about your live-in boyfriend." Gisela's tact was known to all the residents. Inge blushed tiredly, her face puffy.

"Inge, are you feeling all right?" Elfe asked, concerned.

"I'm two weeks overdue, I can't sleep any more, there's no comfortable position to find. It's dragging me down."

Gisela teased her. "You ought to get the big lout to marry you. Tell him he gets no more sleeping privileges and you'll be a married lady faster than you ever believed."

"Inge, where is your other child?" Elfe was curious.

"In the creche downstairs, but I don't like it. More and more children are arriving here from other homes and the overcrowding isn't healthy. My little Heinz always has a cold. He gets sick from the others. As soon as the baby is born, I'll move into a small flat with Arthur and the children. You know, Himmler himself is a friend of my family. He visits me when he can."

Why they hadn't lived together till now Elfriede was hesitant to ask, but Inge seemed to read the question on Elfe's face and answered, "We don't have much money. Arthur wants to open an office." She sighed painfully. Elfe noted her lips were chapped. "Times are so bad now, but we'll manage. My parents will help with whatever they can." The two younger girls exchanged consoling looks. Inge knew her immediate future. The girls possessed no such crystal ball.

In the days that followed, Elfe got more used to the place and the routine. In the morning, breakfast with the other women, about a hundred and fifty in all, then clean up time in her room where she and Gisela cleaned the floor and did laundry in their bathroom. Gisela often remarked that the room seemed bigger now that she was sharing and had to keep it tidier. After chores, they'd go out for a walk in the countryside and then back to the home for lunch.

Meals they usually had with Inge. "She's a good sport, that Inge. I'll hate to see her go." Gisela often spied on one of the other pregnant girls talking with her SS boyfriend. "You see her? When G-d gave her those big tits, he forgot to give her any brains. She's nuts about him. Well anyhow, so is every other girl here, and he knows it. Gorgeous, isn't he? He's the stud-bull in Bavaria and probably papa to many babies. She thinks he'll marry her, just because he gave her a tumble. Christ, what an idiot!"

One restless night, Inge, pale and haggard, eyes hollow and stricken, crept into Elfe and Gisela's room. Turning on the bedside lamp, it was immediately evident that Inge was having her baby. The bottom half of her nightgown was wet and Inge's voice was weak and incoherent. She whispered, "It's time." She was about to faint, when the girls grabbed her arms and then supported her between them.

Soon they were in the labour room in the care of the midwife.

"Too bad Arthur isn't here to see how easy all this is," said Gisela quietly to Elfe.

Inge was writhing in bed, overwhelmed by the savagery of the pain. Her bitten lips bled. Her hands were gripping the bedposts.

Spasms caught her in their clasp, then let go, only to start again. The midwife was firmly telling her to rest between. The girls were told it would be a while and they left.

Early morning delivered a son, small but healthy. The next day, Elfe visited Inge in her room. The baby was sleeping in his basket. Groggily, Inge welcomed the visit. Sitting up in bed, Inge suddenly said, "I had to have an injection for pain. I just had no more energy to give."

"I'm sure it didn't harm the baby, Inge," Elfe answered.

"That's not what upsets me." Inge sounded depressed. "Those damn, crazy women accused me of cowardice, of not being a true, strong, German. What business is it of theirs?" Inge was irate. "You know, most of the girls are from the BDM or the Reich Labour Service and they're very young, usually fifteen to sixteen. They want them that young because they're inexperienced. Guinea-pigs! They're so damn easy to brainwash!" Inge's exhaustion made prominent the planes of her face. "Those virile girls!" Her face was a white mask. She looked ill and miserable.

"Inge, don't do this to yourself."

"Oh, I shouldn't care at all. Soon I'll be out of here. But it just makes me so mad. I'm horrified at the way these young girls are being used as production animals for the State. I'm flabbergasted and amazed at the total lack of sentiment or affection for the men who are the fathers of their babies. For these girls, sex is a duty to the State and has nothing to do with pleasure."

Yawning, she went on. "SS men are supposed to be devoted entirely to Nazism and not be burdened with worries of pregnancies and marriages. They are free as birds. Arthur told me that married SS men are expected to have at least four children and at the same time be relieved of any responsibility. They also are supposed to have babies outside the marriage. So imagine what's going on here. The Germany we knew is gone forever."

Elfe fingered a piece of bric-a-brac absently, her face in her hands, veiling her emotions. There would be nothing to look forward to, at least not for decent people.

Inge could hardly conceal her contempt. "Nothing is sacred between a man and a woman! I'll break both his legs if he thinks of sleeping with another woman! Damn this place."

"I thought you liked it here," Elfe said.

"That was before I knew of the many conveniences our men get." She voiced it with the vehemence of a woman determined to protect her turf.

It was open knowledge that the furnishings, drapes, linens, crockery, clothes and so forth, were confiscated items from "the enemy" — the Jews and whoever refused allegiance to the Black Order. The buildings too were requisitioned — from the Rothchilds, the Hapsburgs, from religious orders and Jewish communities.

The storage room at Steinhoring received periodic shipments that came from Cracow and even German-occupied Russia. The staff stole whatever they took a fancy to and even carried home oriental rugs and furniture.

Gisela always kept an eye open for an opportunity to snatch luxuries that were sprouting as if from a bizarre garden. The garden was kept in abundance by the railway line from Dachau to Steinhoring.

When Elfe recalled the lovely clothes and antiques that were reduced to communal cremations along with her parents, she became entranced with the promise of vindication. It surfaced as an urgent, insatiable hunger that insisted on satisfaction. On imagined contentment, she didn't need much encouragement from Gisela. She joined in the pilfering wholeheartedly.

Elfriede's instability that resulted from the shock of loss of family and financial security, gave her a grave sense of unworthiness and humiliation. Steinhoring was no more than an SS poorhouse in her eyes, and the communal dining room and the cooked porridge for breakfast (something Himmler ordered for its nutritional value and because he suffered from stomach pains), the grub of beggars.

With everything gone that she had loved and that had identified her class, she was taking back what was rightfully hers, just as a robbery victim retrieves his stolen possessions at a police station. The irony, that she felt justice was served in obtaining seized belongings of deported Jews who had committed no crime, made her clutch the items to her breast no less strongly and with no less passion, for, to her, it was only fitting and proper that these reassurances of wealth and position should go to her and her unique problems, from other special people who ultimately would understand. That this rationalization was similar to that of her entire nation was lost on her.

The idea of being bereft of all monies, was so degrading, she feared it was visible, that everyone at the home knew. The Empress had no clothes! Shame would colour her hotly, until she remembered the policy of secrecy. She snatched at the dresses like someone stripped naked in public. The fashionable items were a barricade against rejection, ridicule, and loss of prestige. It was the act of a forsaken, frightened and unhappy girl who saw herself as a pitiful orphan.

For Gisela, an opportunist and co-conspirator, who would have found it sacrilegious not to take advantage of any advantage that came her way, they were of like mind. But of opposite sides. Gisela rejoiced in the ousting of the upper class by the working class with whom she had hated and envied the wealthy aristocracy. Elfe belonged to a species that she hoped would soon be extinct, for the liberty that previous class distinction had refused to allow, was now here. A new society was being invented that offered to be prosperous and entirely in her favour.

Later, Elfe was upstairs with Gisela. They were making an inventory of linens they had collected. "Will you look at these treasures? We could probably sell them and get good money."

Gisela turned to face her, twisting her straw-coloured hair on top of her head. "When I leave here with my baby, I'll take their allowances and I'll buy toys and anything else he'll need. Wait till they see me at the farm! They'll turn green with envy."

Elfe looked at Gisela without comment. What would happen to her when she left? Steinhoring had become a safe haven. She had tried to hold back all thoughts of leaving and now her eyes filled with tears.

Gisela asked, "Why don't you go to your aunt's farm? Listen, at least there you won't be imposing, there's always enough food to eat and you can help out." But all Elfe could think of was the pain of forever parting with a lifestyle they knew nothing of.

On one woolly, snow-laden, December day, when the barren earth had gone through its transmutation to far-flung monochromatic, maquette white, Gisela, as strong and wild as the mountains, almost effortlessly produced her son, Thomas.

She had ventured into Dr. Ebner's office before lunch, complaining of menstrual-like cramps and back pain and quickly it had mounted into labour. Afterwards, she had told Elfe that the birth was likened to mountain climbing, out-of-breath but making that difficult extra effort to the summit. Thomas, now, was the zenith of her life.

Snowflakes fell soundlessly from the sky. Nature's jewelers dangled tear drop icicles from the bony arms of the trees, and bleached, starched sheets coated the unconsecreated grounds of the home.

Increasingly, Elfe was dismayed at the lack of justice and morality in Germany. Sordid stories from the scorpion tongues of the SS guards at Steinhoring, cursed her mind. They spoke quite freely about the Jewish Dachau inmates that they brought sometimes to work on the grounds of Steinhoring. Only the strongest would be brought to work at Steinhoring. She saw them herself and they were no more than living skeletons, dressed in horrible, coarse rags and torn, ill-fitting shoes. She was sickened by the cruelty of the SS. The slaves were constantly guarded and not permitted to have anything to do with the villa and its inhabitants. SS officers with binoculars, watched them from the windows. She was revolted at the situation of these pitiful, fellow human beings, stripped of all dignity. Every value she had ever believed in was under assault. Anyone and anything resembling human dignity and decency had been annihilated.

Before November, 1944, the girls' freedom to come and go as they pleased without an SS escort, would have been impossible and dangerous since the SS ran these homes and everything was always accounted for. By the end of November, 1944, the children born in most of the other Lebensborn homes were being hastily evacuated to Steinhoring. In the East, the Red Army was getting closer. Doctors, nurses, pregnant women, women carrying babies, toddlers, were transported on SS trucks or special trains and sent to Steinhoring in Bavaria.

That winter, Steinhoring became the last refuge of the children of the super-race born at a time of military disaster. Because the house was in the heart of Bavaria, the SS believed it would become the famous alpine redoubt in which Nazi Germany would be able to hold out. They believed that this region would never surrender. Steinhoring had to survive. During this time, restrictions on the girls' movements were relaxed as the SS were preoccupied with more urgent matters.

Early each afternoon, the two girls would leave the villa, in spite of the December cold, for a walk, leaving behind the imposing, six foot, stone walls. They plodded arm in arm in the phosphorescent snow into piney sunlessness. Winter stared as though stunned at the glossy pile on pile of polar whiteness. It invoked calm and the girls felt like forest handmaidens. The minty freshness of the air waltzed with the moans of the winds beyond the frozen margins of the ground and the varied, wrinkled textures in the snow were like shaved apple morsels. Rugged trails became truant paths for vagaring feet. Icicles tinkled like tiny bells and the sun winked sporadically at the panting girls. Steam came from their mouths. They were outcasts, hated, disgraced. Their fellow Germans didn't want them anymore, were ashamed of the Lebensborn girls. Elfe and Gisela, were ashamed themselves.

"More and more, we're drawn into a bottomless, insane pit," Elfe began the familiar conversation involuntarily.

Gisela didn't know what to say. She knew where the conversation was headed and wanted nothing to do with it.

Elfe continued, speaking into the air, inconvertibly. "The staff are poison. The SS are ruining the country. Look at what they have done to the Jews. What will happen when the war ends? They will hate us. Everyone will hate us."

Gisela answered softly, "We can't help anyone. We're powerless."

The strychnine words of a Gestapo nurse replayed themselves. "I worked with a Gestapo squad in that town we liquidated. We were very efficient in the mass executions and the Jewish babies were killed by a shot at the back of the neck. Some babies were just slammed into walls, their brains splattered all over."

Elfe was seething with anger. "And the doctor didn't like the story, only because he considered it inappropriate for pregnant ladies to hear. You've heard the stories the electricians tell who go in and out of Dachau to work. Mass executions, every day." She was breathing hard.

Gisela added, "At least, we're relatively free to do as we wish, and we must remind ourselves of this every day. We're very lucky. Wouldn't you say so?" Gisela turned to Elfe.

Elfe couldn't help but nod her assent.

Time went on, torpid days drifting and blending into nights, weeks into months, a strange, surreal life. Elfe felt like an understudy in her own life, that the real star would come and relieve her. She prayed that one day she could plunge into the darkened audience.

Almost forgotten images of her family and lost life would overcome her when she least expected; the longing would cloud her eyes with hot, salty tears. They would stream down her face, choking her; trickle down her neck, falling to the damp, moist moss of a dewy soil.

She would think of the tiny child she was harbouring inside her, safe and warm, and wonder what kind of life she could offer. She desperately wanted the war to end before her child was born.

One particularly lovely, cool, late afternoon, at the beginning of March, 1945, as Elfe lazily strolled back to the villa, laden with a basket of wildflowers and her knitting, the alarms were sounded and the women and the SS headed, as usual, for the basement. Bombs fell, exploding in the garden, on the stone wall, and on one side of the villa. She couldn't make it to shelter in time, so she dropped face down on the ground near some underbrush and bombs exploded all around her.

She knew that when this occurred, the concentration camp inmates remained outside. Afterwards the dead would be taken away to the ovens in Dachau. This ghoulish thought made her dizzy and nauseated and she closed her eyes and took a deep breath, inhaling the smokey, dusty air of destruction.

When she opened her eyes, before her was a hellish scene of mutilated, newly dead bodies and among them, lying prostrate, skeletal limbs like dry branches with bony appendages, clad in coarse pajamas, crowned by a shaved skull, was an old man. He was slithering on his stomach, like a captive caterpillar, moving by an instinct of survival, toward a hole just created in the wall by a bomb.

Elfe's eyes were glued to the wraith and his death march. This was the enemy? For agonizingly long seconds she watched him struggle over the ground, coarse with shattered rock. A wave of self-hatred broke over her as she recognized the perverse attraction to watching another human being struggle. She thought of her mother, blind crawling through the fire. What if someone witnessed a struggle to get out of her burning home? And the words of hatred that she poured out for the war and regime of her countrymen until poor Gisela would want to shut her up but was too embarrassed to. Was she the greatest evil? A hypocrite wanting no part of the responsibility but unwilling to do something? She made a decision to make her country, not this man, the enemy.

Mechanically she closed the distance between them. She could help, or watch him die. She fell beside him and began tearing off his tattered striped pants. She should have spoken to him, to tell him that she was there to help not to torture, but she was unable to speak. She met the gaze of unimaginable, wild animal fear in the dark, hollow eyes of the gaunt creature. Never before, had she been face to face with one so alien — he was neither beast, nor man, nor dead, nor alive. What had been done to him, he was so fleshless, shriveled and withered and now trembling. He was so thin, that she could have picked him up in her arms like a baby. As if acting from outside herself, she tore off his miserable shoes. With both arms, she pulled him through the wall, and into another dimension of her life, slinking him to cover and the safety of nondiscovery, to an underbrush in the woods behind the house.

Time being crucial, though it seemed to have stood still for her, she thought of the safest place where she could hide him. Dragging him along like a rag doll as quickly as she could, she brought him to a thicket, completely covering a small cave she and Gisela had by chance come across one day. They had thought about hiding some of the loot they had stolen from the SS there. She knew she could keep him there, but she would have to bring him clothing and food. She recoiled at the sight of his emaciated body, marked by numerous beatings.

Looking down on him, she knew she was committed to him. She had never seemed so close to G-d as she did now. This is how the angels must feel, she thought, wiping her eyes.

A long, skeletal hand cautiously reached out, touching hers. Looking downward, he tightened his grasp, as though it were she reaching out for help. Elfe met his eyes for the first time.

As he slid through the bushes and into the tiny cave, shame and compassion swept over her. He shook his head in disbelief. Neither could believe the other was really there. Her expression was determined yet warm, her lips a pencil-thin line. For once, there was a usefulness to her life.

It was as if Nature had been watching this interlude, for the trees seemed to pulse back to life with colourful butterflies and insects, buds were opening on trees — the entire forest hummed now with an assortment of birds. For the first time that year, Elfe recognized spring. She whispered "The Gestapo will think you died in the bombing, when they find your rags and shoes." She read the question in his eyes. "All the others are dead."

A trembling, hollowy sound muttered, "G-d bless you, G-d bless you." The entire skeleton that housed this voice shook uncontrollably from head to foot, a lone leaf in a breeze.

Elfe swallowed uncomfortably, her mouth and throat dry, "I will come tomorrow with food and clothes." She got up to leave, brushing grass and leaves from her dress and as she did so, she felt his hand once again touch hers. She fled the cave.

Elfe made her way back to the villa, interrupted when she got close as once more, the sky exploded in an avalanche of stones. Windows rattled and drummed to a curious beat. Broken roof tiles rained down on her. The hell-storm had not ended before she moved again. Crawling, she pushed a door open and sat on the stairs until the fury broke and then crept upstairs to her room.

Shortly, the sounds of an animal stampede shook the floors and walls, as countless feet clambered through the hallways along with a crescendo of voices. The door fell open and a frowning Gisela stumbled in with one month old Thomas cradled in her arms. He was crying bitterly and she was comforting him as best she could. Her eyes were frightened, her face haggard. "You're delicious, my peach, my parfait, my little nix." It was a pretense of calm as she cooed and ahed over little Thomas cocooned in his blanket. Elfe watched him relishing in the motherly attention.

Deftly, Gisela then washed his face, changed his diaper and put him to her shoulder. As if on cue, Thomas burped. "I'm sooo proud of you," Gisela cooed. She marvelled at everything he did, from eliminating, to eating and burping. When he slept, she kept vigil by his side for hours. There was always the fear that he might not awaken, and it haunted her like a ghost. Finally, Gisela spotted her friend's anxious expression. "Okay, what happened to you?"

Elfe put a finger to her lips and saw an eyebrow rise in curiosity.

"Let me put Tommie in his bassinette and then we can talk." She covered Thomas, who was already sound asleep, straightened her dress in one swift motion, and nodded to Elfe to sit down on the bed and with the door locked, Elfe told her her secret.

"Don't worry about me. I won't tell anyone. But how long can he last out there in the damp and cold? What if he gets sick?"

"His only hope is that the war will end soon." Both girls became immediately preoccupied, lost in thought as how to save Elfe's charge.

Straight after supper, they retired to their room, now collaborators determined to help each other. They were whispering into the wee hours of the night.

"Elfe, this war can't last much longer. look at the heavy losses we had in Russia. Germany has too many enemies now with America, Britain, and Russia closing in on us." Gisela went over to the armoire and from beneath some blankets, she pulled out newspaper clippings. Handing them to her, she simply said, "Read these!"

"Hey, this newspaper isn't ours!" Elfe exclaimed. "It's Dutch! How did you get it?"

"Annie gave it to me and with her handwritten translation. I wish I had your brains, then I'd understand better what all this means."

Elfe read slowly, then hid the clippings back in the armoire. "We have lost the war, but how long the battle will go on, nobody can say." She lay down on the bed, her arms clasped behind her head.

"Let's hope all this ends soon. I feel like a caveman every time I crawl out of that cellar." Gisela sighed heavily.

By morning, the girls had definite plans of how they were going to help their charge.

"We will bring food and clothing during our afternoon strolls in the woods. It'll be easy." Gisela was confident and excited about the prospect, taking it as an adventure. That first day, Elfe helped Gisela get Thomas ready. He was a healthy, robust, goodnatured baby with large, grey eyes and fine, blond, curly hair. He slept a great deal except when he was hungry; then his angelic, peachy face would turn red as a tomato and he would howl until Gisela would put him to her breast.

At the moment he was very pleased with himself, gurgling and cooing, his tiny body all curled up in a ball. He had just had his meal and was falling asleep. He reminded Elfe of a kitten. Thomas was an easy child, sleeping most nights peacefully in his lacy basket, and days content with staring at the ceiling or snoozing in the pram on his daily outings.

When afternoon arrived, the girls demurely marched out the door of the villa with little Thomas in his perambulator.

"For beginner thieves, we're not doing badly at all," Elfe giggled.

"What have you got?"

"In that pillowcase there's a loaf of bread, a jar of jam, and two cooked potatoes. In my knitting basket are two pairs of wool socks, a large flannel shirt of mine, trousers I stole from the SS and a rolled-up blanket. I'm knitting him another pair of socks."

Shortly they made it to the cave. Elfe went in while Gisela watched the path. She knelt down and found the man shivering badly but his eyes brightened when he saw her. His teeth were chattering from the cool air and soon Elfe had made him comfortable, dressing him in the flannel shirt, and wrapping him in the blanket.

While he slowly ate the potatoes, she watched him. Only when he was finished did they speak. "Who are you?" Elfe asked.

"My name is Joshua Horowitz. I am from Cracow." He was studying her, remarkably with quiet dignity.

"I am Elfriede Clauss. I'm from Munich." She saw him glance at her middle. "My parents are dead. I am staying at Steinhoring to have my baby."

She gave him a jar of hot tea that had been wrapped in the blanket. She had to help him drink, he was shaking so badly. Observing him, she sensed that this was a person of enormous strength, for while he shivered, there glowed a fire in his dry eyes. He had beautiful hands, with long, slender fingers and square tips. These were honest hands, aristocratic. This was no ordinary man. What shocked her, was how she had misjudged his age in their first encounter. He was no more than thirty.

"You are very kind." He was cupping the warm jar with both hands as if it were the most precious liquid in the world. Those haunting eyes —so full of suffering, so full of tragedy.

"Is there anything else I can get you? she asked. She saw he was shy and reluctant to say.

"I would like... Well, you see, I have nothing left but my faith. I was wondering if you could bring me a Bible."

"I will find you a Bible. I have to go now. But I'll be back tomorrow. And every day." Their eyes drew into each other and with that inner picture, she left.

Each morning Gisela and Elfe in hushed voices planned and executed the pilfering of food for Josh. Gisela gave in to her free spirit, with her mischievous blue eyes mirroring her lust for life and uninhibited nature. They found ingenious ways to acquire food and clothing for Josh which Elfe brought him almost daily.

"A few months ago, this would have been impossible." Elfe straightened up, her hands supporting her lower back. She had just finished arranging her "knitting bag" to take to Josh.

"Steinhoring isn't the classy place it was. It's a zoo since the winter. It is all happening so quickly. The army is retreating, no doubt about it." Gisela spoke without sadness for her country's certain defeat.

"I'm with you, girl," said Elfe rubbing her lower back. "And it isn't a moment too soon." They were living in a trap that was getting smaller all the time with hundreds of babies, young children, women in labour, as well as dozens of nurses and a large number of SS officers and men along with members of the Lebensborn administration all sharing the villa and huts. Each day became more impossible; confrontations were more frequent with the women of 'pure German blood' resenting the Norwegian, French, Dutch and Belgian women who had arrived in the last few months. It was a filthy, overcrowded, blood-curdling noisy camp.

Gisela nodded in agreement, "what's really terrible is that I think I'm beginning to get used to this house of horrors. After all, the stench of the babies' pots" which were filled to overflowing, sometimes for days, "is easier to take than the savage women who fight over chairs by a window." Gisela inhaled with difficulty, her upper lip curled with distaste. "It's the lack of privacy that bothers me. On a farm I was used to wide-open spaces. Here it's wall-to-wall women and then some."

The aroma of fresh coffee and cinnamon drifted into the room, moving aside its own smell, and the girls, like sybarites, followed the sweet smell to the dining room and put deafened ears to the chorus of crying babies, shouting children, and the prolonged shrieking of women in endless labour.

A pall lay over the humorless house. There was no joy, no happiness, no sense of renewal in a home where every day Hitler's elite, obsolete, children were born. The SS strutted around like roosters and the women clucked in a frenzy over myriad complaints, engrossed in their needs. There was no organization. Some women stayed only a day, others stayed for months. And in the changeable weather, even the sun couldn't decide if it should stay. Sometimes it would hover, then disappear. There was no honour, no fraternal link between anyone. The war had mercilessly exposed all that was ugly and pestilent. What could have been propitious bonds of blossoming friendships, became instead the heavy, crippling prison chains of distrust and greed.

Like a child dragging her security blanket, Elfe wrapped her raw emotional cravings in a pad of paper and coloured pencils. She drew not only what she saw but what her mother would have seen, for these ties were immortal. She brought out the genius of creation with the innocence of the inner child. Newborn depictions tumbled out of sleeping faces, infants nursing or playing in the creche. Directly from her heart to mothers' hands and bedroom walls. Each picture was a revelation, an act of cleansing, a gesture of showing the holiness that was every child's legacy, before suffering and corruption spoiled their freshness, eroding all that was pure and beautiful and spontaneous and bright. Cherubic features were fleshed out and given life before their angelic expressions were irrevocably lost forever.

Elfe was transported to all of the yesterdays, with blind love, dissolving as with a mist, the flaws. She thought of the house and how it captured gold and heliotrope colours in the sunset as though kissed by the gods.

Elfe stared through the window at the wind-driven snow smacking against the pane slantwise. Spring had retreated leaving the field for one last counter-offensive of winter. In mad arousal, the glass was being battered and thumped as if repudiating the home's very existence. Debris sailed into the sky like kites, only to become impaled on the weary branches of stooping trees. Gisela came panting in, looking beset, eyes wide and frightened like a deer trapped by hunters. Her lips trembled, her face was pale.

Elfe was lighting candles in polished brass holders. "What happened? Are we having schnitzel again tonight?" There was soft mockery in her voice, eyebrows arched upwards in mirth. Just then, Annie, a Dutch girl they befriended, came through the doorway uncharacteristically whistling a lively tune.

Suddenly Gisela was sobbing in loud outpours. Gripping her sides, she doubled over, continuing to cry more softly, her figure twisting unnaturally. Suddenly she sprang to the bathroom to vomit. She returned, only to move about disoriented.

Watching her pace in dizzying circles, was like intruding on a caged animal who was suffocating from an internal obstruction that would not be released. The aimless movements of her hands and quivering mouth answered none of their questions.

Annie, their Dutch friend, herself full term, waddled over to sit beside Gisela and implored her to reveal the source of this terrible and unexpected interlude. Elfe brought her a glass of schnaaps. Gisela lost her facade and they became voyeurs, staring in on something very private. An aristocrat with pretensions, she was not. She was ordinary, unworldly, now struggling and utterly exposed. Surrounded in her darkness with pinched lips and exhausted eyes she was unaware of them.

The girls had pledged allegiance to the club of tasteless luxury, of devotion to self-love and conveniences, pampering and self-indulgence. And it was almost sacred, for there had to be something to the fact that there were agonies too numerous to mention inflicted upon a multitude of men, women and children. Yet these girls were lavished on by a ceaseless reservoir of nutritional delicacies, clothing, medical care, in an oddly glorious setting.

Galas, symphonies, ballets, long gowns — glamour — was Elfe's world of awareness, not the sad commentaries of the poor and luckless. It was simply not her universe. She despised this shared characteristic with Gisela.

The air was gauzy in the waxen light and Gisela's ashen face had the texture of painted paraffin. Beyond the French doors were moaning winds mimicking her lapsed state.

Gisela closed her eyes, seemingly entranced in an insistent and private pain compartmentalized in her. Her hands twisted in a mindless, disembodied way, the silver locket on the chain around her neck. The girls blinked as the catch flipped open. Gisela drew back so overcome that at first she could not speak. More schnaaps was poured. A tiny picture fell to the floor, and she went grovelling on hands and knees in a lunatic brushing of the rug with webbed fingers until she found it. She was unconsolable as she presented it for them to see.

Perspiring as though the room were overheated, she dripped with tears in hot silence at the rosy-cheeked, curly-haired, cherubic infant. "She's my sister who died in her crib when she was one year old. Just like that." She snapped her fingers. "I killed her, but I didn't mean to... G-d only knows I didn't mean to. I was only three and the day before she had accidentally broken my favourite doll. So I got mad and yelled at her. I said I wished she were dead. Little Agathe cried. Lord knows, I didn't mean it. I loved her!" She pounded her chest.

"The next morning my mother screamed when she went to the crib. Agathe just lay there not breathing. She shrieked and shrieked and everyone came running and I took her and kissed her and begged her to wake up. My love and remorse didn't bring her back. Everything was different after that. Guilt took the place of my sister, and mama was never the same again, becoming just a shadow of the woman she once was. Do you know, her hair turned stark white overnight! She was only twenty-five." Now she stood up and faced an invisible scene on the wall. "But it was I who expired in that crib with Agathe that awful day. My final memories of her alive are unforgivable. Three people died. Only one was buried."

She responded only to the glass of schnaaps. With caution, Annie tried to tell her that crib deaths were well known in Holland and G-d's will shouldn't be doubted.

Gisela rambled on, oblivious. "There is a sign, it's roaring in me, a curse on my family." Her voice was now hissing. "It's gone on for generations. My grandma died young, as did her mother, and other relatives — only the women. From the time I could eat solid food, funerals were a more reliable ritual than birthdays. The coffin maker wasn't nice to anyone, but he was to us, always sending us Christmas presents. He carried a measuring tape and asked us how much we grew. It's destiny; the more we run from it, the closer we get to it.

"I was meant to remember. The baby clothes downstairs were omens, reminders that I murdered her. I killed her, surely as the curse of early death is upon my family and there is no escape, no one to appeal to except the Angel of Death. Earlier downstairs, there were all these children's items on a table. They were being sorted and I suddenly felt a cold hand on my shoulder, so I spun around, but nobody was there."

Elfe said, "Superstition isn't reality, come on, Gisela, this isn't like you." But Gisela was inside a nightmare. The unpardonable crime she believed she had truly committed occupied all of her mind. Carefully placing the photo inside the talisman, she clutched the replica passionately as though it were the infant Agathe herself.

A nnie Nicolaas was a tall eighteen year old Dutch girl who had become fast friends with Elfe after starting out as her model. According to Elfe, she was a topographical study of Holland, with an attractive flat face, with large, blue brooks for eyes, ash eyebrows that moved expressively like the cloth sails on a windmill and curlicued, scarlet lips that were shaped like a tulip. Her teeth were an even row of opals, her flaxen hair was a blanched shade of corn, knotted into a thick braid. Full term, she was a garland of soft pink clouds that swayed (not ungracefully) beneath a starched, embroidered apron edged in ayelet lace on its rim and on the straps. Often she was the image of a garden statuary, her arms laden with blooms that she cultivated in their small nursery.

She was a funny girl and very homesick. Rather than her adapting to Bavaria, Bavaria adapted to her, at least partially. On moonlit nights, the dark sky was the North Sea that overlooked her beloved canals, flat green meadows and forests. The moon was an ice rink in the image of her lakes. She would trace imaginary, winding channels with a finger pointed at the landscape guarded by romantic Quixotian windmills of Cervantes' legendary giant men waving giant arms stretched to pick up every breeze in order to drain water from the

Chapter Ten

Bavaria,
February, 1945

land and grind corn. Annie's escape from loneliness was in reveries of her beloved Amsterdam, on the Zuider Zee, which was like Venice, she said.

Storytelling was her forte. Pastel-coloured nostalgia was woven into misty wooded hills onto the banks of the Rhine River of Arnhem, where her family moved to when she was eight, to be near her grandparents. Her father, Gerrit, was a high school teacher and Dory, her mother, a housewife. She had two younger siblings, an eleven-year-old sister Jeanne and a thirteen-year-old brother, Philip.

Annie missed ice skating and had brought to Steinhoring her skates, which hung on a nail on her wall. She also brought pictures of the tulips, hyacinths, daffodils and narcissuses that carpeted the countryside between Haarlem and Leiden during April and May. A little Holland was recreated in her room with live flowers in vases, a splendid traditional white lace cap with upturned sides and wooden clogs that were displayed on her dresser. The staff seemed obsessed with the fact that Eva Braun's favourite flower was the tulip.

In May, 1940, Holland was invaded by the Germans. The royal family escaped to England, and London became the seat of the Dutch government-in-exile.

In February, 1944, in a restaurant in Arnhem, Annie met a single SS officer, Fritz Kohl. She didn't want to have anything to do with him, for her parents would have been furious as well as their friends and neighbours. But he was pushy and came calling to her home. When she refused to come out of her room, and when her parents tired of his courting them with chocolates and flowers and steely persistence wrapped in charming manners, she gave in. It wasn't as if he didn't realize he wasn't too welcome. Her father had said so in those words but Fritz was not to be deterred and promised he would win them over. He was a carbuncle on their spirit of negation and with time he did grudgingly gain their acceptance, if mainly through attrition.

Starvation now assailed the Dutch and for the sake of the children and the Resistance, her father was now a part of, they accepted the ration coupons and food. Annie was receiving letters from Fritz and they became small flames that fed her passion. His occasional phone calls were breaths of intoxication and she basked in them as if they were pieces of stars that lit up her life. And that persistence of his resulted in her getting pregnant in April, 1944.

In July 1942, the occupation authorities had begun rounding up thousands of Jews and shipping them out of the country. The underground heard they were going to be murdered. To avoid deportation and death, they had to go into hiding with a gentile family.

Early in 1941, the persecution of the Jews in the Netherlands was mounting. They were excluded from hotels, restaurants, theatres, libraries, public parks and recreational facilities. Signs warning "Jews Forbidden" were springing up everywhere. Jewish students could not attend regular schools.

Annie's parents lived modestly in a row house of red brick. As Calvanists, they were taught to respect the Jews as the Old Covenant people. Annie's parents were members of the Reformed Church and they taught their children to love all of mankind. Religious affiliation affected all aspects of Dutch life; Catholics and Protestants had separate schools, labour unions, political organizations and social facilities.

Annie experienced religious prejudice while attending elementary school. Walking to school she was verbally harassed (and saw her schoolmates reciprocate) and she learned to identify with religiously alienated people and to have compassion for them.

In April, it was decreed that all Jews must wear a yellow six-pointed Star of David sewn on the left side of their clothes, over the heart, as big as an adult's hand with the word JOOD printed on it in black Hebrew type letters. The Dutch were offended and men began tipping their hats as a sign of respect to those wearing the star. And so the Germans issued another edict; threatening prison or death to anyone assisting Jews. More decrees limiting the lives of Jews followed, respecting the confiscation of Jewelry and bicycles, and outlawing their use of public transit and telephones. Curfews were imposed, travel was restricted and limited times for shopping in the few stores allowed to serve them were established.

During the summer of 1942, six thousand Jews were sent to the concentration camp at Westerbork, which was a transit centre for sending them further into the Reich to concentration camps. In August, nightly raids began and three to five hundred people were captured every night and herded into vans. The underground press carried horrifying reports of shootings and gassings.

Through a friend, a fellow teacher, who Gerrit suspected was in the Resistance, he learned of a large-scale effort to rescue Jewish children from Amsterdam. These children and their parents were slated for certain death. Gerrit earlier, had helped former Jewish pupils find hiding places. Now he contacted an organization of university students in Amsterdam who were taking children out of a day-care centre.

The police were taking Jewish families to a large theatre in Amsterdam. After a few days, most were then sent to Westerbork for deportation east. A Children's Shelter was set up across the street to care for infants and young children. There, Resistance workers cooperated with underground workers inside the Jewish Council to take children from the shelter to hiding places out of the city.

Each morning the children were taken for a walk by German girls. The students would step in among the groups of walking children, grab one child and run away with her or him. Annie's father succeeded in getting members of the Reformed Church and other people to take these children into their homes. He would receive a telegram from Amsterdam that a parcel would be arriving at a certain time. The students would bring the children in groups of four to eight. Homes were found for about fifty children. Most Reformed Church families took in at least one child.

In February, 1944, Annie went out with Fritz Kohl and he never realized how well those rations and gifts were used. They helped supplement food for Jews in hiding. In April, Annie got pregnant and in September 1944, she arrived at Steinhoring. Conditions in the Netherlands were desperate and while the decision meant that she would be taken away from her family and from the soon hoped for liberation of her country, it gave her child a chance at survival. At home, thousands of Dutch citizens were starving to death. Annie felt guilty about abandonning her homeland and was eternally homesick.

Shortly after Annie became friends with Gisela and Elfe, she was heading down the stone steps to the cellar for a bottle of beer which halted, when consumed in small amounts, her nausea, when she tripped and fell, landing in a heap at the bottom. Two SS officers heard her cries and rushing to the scene, rescued her and carried her to the infirmary.

There were cuts and bruises and the possibility of a head concussion but the only thing that had broken was the amniotic sac. Word got to Elfe and Gisela about the accident. Rushing to the labour room, they found her in lamentable shape. She looked like she'd been beaten, with her face convulsed in agony, her nose bleeding, her lips torn. She was gripping her belly and drawing up her legs in spasmodic movements. She seemed more possessed by an alien monster bent on vengeance, than participating in the arena of incipient motherhood. A nurse was beside her, trying to make her more comfortable, when there was a great heaving and she lurched forward as though the earth had quaked.

The doctor sped in, nurses were whispering in agitated tones to each other. Gisela trembled like the wind outside. Somehow Annie's situation further aggravated Gisela's raw feelings about Agathe. Elfe wasn't surprised when Gisela took flight as though deadly fumes had been discharged and were at her back, propelling her to the staircase.

Annie's tremendous love for all living things was all-encompassing, from the lowliest spider that she found indoors and gently returned to the garden, to stray cats she fed from the kitchen. She would not give birth so her offspring might die. Her womb had been, in her mind, cradling no less than a portion of divinity, uncorrupted, angelic, and although she embodied the cradle, it was the hand of G-d that rocked it and ruled the world. This had been her reason for leaving her country and her family, unless she returned with a baby, there was no point to going home.

That it was a life threatening situation, was evident in the doctor's worried expression, in the hurried comings and goings of the medical staff, in the evil odor consuming their nostrils.

Dr. Ebner was a man of logic and reason and he knew that not all babies had a recalcitrant desire to survive. He fought vicariously with them, for the unborn were the future, artless and innocent and had not yet learned of the wickedness that was in all men. He intervened on nature's behalf and was in awe of it. In spite of the centuries of famines, plagues and natural disasters, the human race could not be wiped out.

This baby was a sign of man's survival and the Reich's surmounting all, a fighter who wrestled, then defeated the Angel of Death. The first battle would be won. Of course it would; he was a veritable little soldier!

"There is nothing to worry about," a nurse was saying to another woman in labour across the room. "Having a baby for the Fatherland, ah, now what greater pride can there be." The nurse was smiling proudly at the picture of the Führer on the wall, the same picture the other patient was gazing at, with the same fanatical love. Annie was aware of none of it. Deliverance from the wrenching, knife-like butchery ripping her insides used up what little strength remained. Arrowheads of pain smote her murderously.

The good doctor was, with all his intimidating abruptness and stiff militarism acknowledging the superiority nature had over man and medical science's inability to conquer it. He also had great reverence to these feminine temples of life and he devotedly tended to them, for if the purveyor of the fountain would run dry, then the hope for the future, in the form of heroic German soldiers, would die.

The purpose of his life was the production of perfect human specimens; each child he delivered was a source of pride and joy and the source was very precious, to be protected at all costs. There was artistry and beauty of proportions, form and colouring and he felt as a sculptor does when he completes a handsome statue, with each delivery. That they were living monuments rather than still art, preserved on walls of museums or standing motionless in parks, undignified, their main function, toilets for birds, made him feel grand.

Hours passed and gripping Dr. Ebner's hand, Annie, weakened, face bloated, eyes glazed with suffering, made him give his word that if it came to who should survive, it would be the baby. It would be her gift to them, to bestow on them.

Just then her eyes bulged, her back arched and a scream was expelled through her purpling lips. It pierced the chamber, the halls like shaking hearts. The doctor lifted the sheet to expose her veined belly and massaged it to aid her muscles to help expel the fetus. Examination in the contracted muscles of the birth canal, showed a cervix insufficiently dilated. On further examination his growing pessimism changed. The child could be reached by forceps. Annie's pleading, insanely tortured face had a gas mask placed on it and she was delivered from further pain.

The infant boy appeared from between her legs, bluish and pasty, covered in blood and would not breathe. The good doctor released tired tears of frustration. No wonder she couldn't deliver. He was over eight pounds, a Nordic princely specimen beautifully proportioned with a tangle of blond curls on his head. No, he would not lose him! His fist banged the counter. He picked up the slippery cold body and inserted his finger into his mouth and extricated a gooey lump of blood and mucous then proceeded to give mouth to mouth artificial respiration, breathing in and out of its throat, his hand gently pressing the tiny chest. He was ordering the child to live. Live, he kept commanding silently, live!

Then, with the renewed sound of wind on the windows, Dr. Ebner's own heart leapt with joy. A frail cry was heard, then another, and then another. It was no less than a heavenly choir singing in a great cathedral, to his ears. And lifting the babe gently as though made of chaste gilt and belonging to a high priestess, he ceremoniously placed him in the mother's waiting arms.

"No, no, she'll be fine," was the answer to Elfe's query.

How could any of them ever be fine again. Elfe cringed as she glanced inadvertently at her own swollen belly. The Jews weren't considered human beings by the Third Reich, but neither were pure-blood Aryan girls. They were machines, baby machines. The Jews were given numbers to deny them any worth, to make them invisible. But what about the Lebensborn girls? The stupid, brainwashed girls were foolish enough to believe that they were superior beings, when in reality, it was a hoax. We're nothing more than expendable pieces of property!

The monotonous voice of the nurse went on. "There were lacerations during the birth and she lost a great deal of blood, but she'll recover." There wasn't the slightest indication of pity in the cold tone. A figure with a wooden heart crisply left the room.

But Annie did not recover. She died knowing her child had lived, but that she would never be there to take him away from the horrible regime he was born into.

Something was the matter with Elfe. A dryness clutched her throat. Through hazy eyes, the room whirled and all of a sudden, Dr. Ebner was there. She tried to go towards him but the floor became an undulating sea, threatening to swallow her. She gave in and slid downward in a faint.

That night, Elfe and Gisela could find no peace. Anger consumed them. They could only think of poor, so naive, so gentle, Annie. Their nerves were threadbare. In tremulous voices, feeling like tumbleweed after a severe windstorm, they talked of Annie. They twittered about their room, ghostlike, arranging bedding, rearranging bedding, making tea, all the while chattering nervously, compulsively.

Finally, they crept into bed, chilled by the recent event and talked well into the night. Gisela eventually fell asleep. Elfe lay in her bed and remembered Annie and the stories she had told her of her beloved Holland. Images of flowers, tulips — thousands of them crowded Elfe's mind as she drifted into slumber. She saw fishing boats and windmills and Annie's beloved graceful canals and bridges, green meadows, skating rinks and skaters. The Vincent van Gogh flower fields that she had seen in photos as a child, now came alive as something immensely personal. She was sharing Annie's nostalgia for a place she had never even visited, except now, in her dreams.

Annie had said "I loved to visit Arnhem when I was a small girl. My grandparents lived there in a small, red brick house with a thatched roof, huge windows with black shutters and a lovely garden. Grandpa worked in a tin refinery and Grandma gardened. She would take us on strolls about the many fine, old buildings, and the town hall. Many townspeople called it the "Devil House" because of its strange devil figures that support the entrance gate and bay windows. My sister and I used to pretend that devils really lived there and Grandma laughed at the idea. We had so much fun there."

"Devil House," Elfe suddenly thought of the strange name, yet a picture of Steinhoring, with its SS black flag fluttering at the entrance and its SS guards with their killer dogs, and the imposing, high walls to ensure secrecy flashed before her eyes. Then she saw an image of a small, cozy, red, brick house, a thatched, old-fashioned roof, and cheerful, large windows to let in sunshine — life, and welcome spelled all over the faces of those waiting at the door. A house that was a home. With a sigh, Elfe reached over and turned off the tiny lamp on the bedside table, looked at Gisela and snuggled into her warm blankets and lay there imagining what it would be like to have a real home again. Elfe, her tiny baby asleep within her belly, fell peacefully asleep.

The next day, Gisela watched her friend slowly, heavily, collect her "knitting bag" and saunter out of their room.

Two hours later Elfe was back at the villa.

"Back so soon?" Gisela was breastfeeding Thomas and he was making happy gurgling sounds.

Elfe heaved herself carefully onto the bed and sighed. "I'm getting so tired and I feel so sluggish. I just delivered the goods, talked with Josh for a while, and turned back." It seemed that she was going to rest, when she began, "I was curious as to what sort of person he is, this man of such observation, who studied my middle and said I must be due soon and I was taking good care of myself. So I asked what he did before the war. He shrugged and told me that he had led a privileged life in Vienna and then in Switzerland. For three years before he escaped to continue his studies at Bern University, he walked with fellow students along the wide boulevards surrounding the Austrian capital. On sunny days they'd stroll along the Ringstrasse, the city's most famous street. A circle of splendid parks edges this boulevard. After classes at the university, they would visit the Museum of Art. Occasionally he went to the Opera. This is no ordinary man.

"As we chatted, I had the impression of a somber man. His dark eyes became two shining and penetrating beams. I asked him what he studied. Do you know he was a medical doctor? Got his degree in 1941 from Vienna University.

"'You are a physician,' I said. His answer was so pitiful 'I *was* a physician. Now I am no one, who has returned from the world of the dead. I know death — how it looks and smells and feels. The city of Bern declared him a learned man. When I said this to him do you know what he said? 'You are my nightingale of the forest, and the cave is my sacred, sheltering nest.'"

"Poor Elfe. You are such an idealist," Gisela chided, "I think you have a crush on him!"

Elfe ignored her. "I wanted to be careful asking about his life. He has built a wall between himself and the world. I walked back as in a dream. Over the winding paths, I spoke my thoughts aloud, as I admired the richly plumaged birds in the trees and the buds growing on the branches. I am eager to save this strange man and have him tell me of his sadness and the turbulence within him." Turning to Gisela, she said with exhilaration and ardor, "It is our duty to help him and give him hope."

Gisela, lost in shadow, brooded briefly, "You do have a crush on him!"

Elfe felt drained. She sighed heavily. The days were becoming harder with frequent reminders by the athletics of the being inside her, anxious to make his entrance into this very complicated yet beautiful world.

Gisela put Thomas back in the bassinette, made some cocoa, and the two girls tried to relax, stretching out on the bed, Elfe became lost in thought.

"You look troubled again. Out with it."

Elfe shrugged wearily, staring at the ceiling. "Oh, it's just... All right. The other day I was in Inge Fink's room. We had a long talk and do you know what she told me? With the enemy advance, all these Lebensborn homes were evacuated quickly. It's taken them often weeks, travelling right across Germany by special train to reach Steinhoring. Women gave birth during the trip but they never lacked food. Inge's boyfriend told her in sheer disgust, of how hungry German refugees would try to storm these trains, begging for a little food, not even for themselves, but for their children and they would be cruelly, brutally beaten back by the SS." Elfe glanced over at Gisela, scowling. "Each morsel of food I eat is like biting off a piece of a hungry child." She was shaking her head.

"I know. Go on."

"Well, you remember when the first babies arrived, last autumn? Well, truckloads of all sorts of things — food, clothing, furniture — arrived here. Villagers, who by the way, are starving, saw these truckloads of coffee, sugar, cereal, cocoa, fresh fruit and vegetables, canned fruits and meats. They hate us. Of course they can't say anything. How can they not resent us, especially with the rest of Germany suffering? To make things worse, prisoners of war deliver these goods from the station to Steinhoring.

"And you know something else? It's the Allied raids on Munich that brought the entire staff of the Lebensborn headquarters here. Some live in a flat upstairs and the rest, as you know, are staying in huts built in the park by Dachau prisoners. All the files also were brought here. The SS still believe Hitler will win this war."

Gisela looking pained, said, "When I look in the mirror, I'm afraid of what will condemn me there. I'm frightened of seeing their hunger in my eyes."

Elfe was getting bigger and bigger and moved slowly, her edemic feet swollen, her energy sapped. "I don't look like a Teutonic thoroughbred," she said miserably. Both girls prayed for the war to finally end but they didn't know what they would find once it was over.

One day as Elfe and Gisela were about to return to their room with some food they had stolen for Josh, half a loaf of bread, a small jar of jam, a knife, spoon, and a bottle of red wine, they noticed the head nurse, Anna Beck, quarreling with one of the doctors over a fur coat. Unnoticed, they hovered behind the partially open door and could hardly believe what they saw. Laid out on a bed were things that both girls instantly knew had to have been taken from wealthy Jewish homes and estates.

"Can you believe all this?" Gisela stammered, round-eyed. Before her lay furs of mink, grey fox, wolf, and sable, the finest of linens, beautifully embroidered, and silverware — sparkling, shining entire tea services and cutlery. "They are squabbling over who gets the set of sterling silver cutlery with the Rothschild family crest. They're going to take away everything from here and leave us with nothing! Well, I'll be damned if they think we're all that stupid! We'd better get out of here before they see us!" Gisela was speaking to deaf ears, for Elfe's mouth was gaping with a surging thirst that tensed her entire body. Her nails were digging into Gisela's bare arms like tiger claws.

Deeper inside the room were stacks of oil paintings leaning against great marble commodes. Gracefully carved, upholstered chairs were stacked one atop the other in a gruesome mating position. There was more: sets of lovely porcelain dishes, Graecian urns, fine figurines, heavy, brocaded draperies and bedspreads.

These luxuries spoke low prayers to her, beseeching her to adopt them. Only she, with her blue blood, could truly appreciate them for their proper worth. She was near collapse just from her personal appraisal, as she gazed lovingly, her eyes caressing each fold of fabric, every texture, detail, colour.

Walking back to their room, Elfe reluctantly pleaded with Gisela. "We should stay out of this, please. We know how cruel these people are." Gisela was trembling with excitement. Elfe's own greed was spreading, overcoming her fear. Elfe could barely restrain her desire and knew it would be an unpardonable sin not to, at the first opportunity, to retrieve something — she had lost enough already.

Elfe was thinking about Josh, his people were the source of all this finery. He had told her a little about himself. She had had to ask him his age. He was much younger than she would have guessed. She had sensed refinement. It seemed that all of his family were dead. That was what he believed. He had been closest to Sarah, his sister. When Elfe spoke with him, it was to his soul, for his body was more dead than alive. And yet she remembered an instance when she had probed too deeply, albeit inadvertently.

Coming one afternoon to the cave, she found Josh in the depths of despair. With a gentleness, she busied herself unpacking something for him to eat and drink, attempting to perk his spirits by chatter. He looked like an elderly, wrinkled person, with sunken cheeks, limp torso and badly swollen feet, that were out of proportion on such a gaunt, emaciated body. Suddenly he said, "I have been reading the Bible."

"Does it give you comfort?"

"I have lived with death. My heart is black. And you ask a question of Life?"

"But you are alive! you must live!" Elfe was vehement. She would not let him give up.

"Do you know what I have seen?" His face grew rigid. He was about to permit a glimmer of light into his bludgeoned soul. "Murder was committed every day as part of the usual routine.

Mothers, fathers, grandparents, babies, rabbis in their long, velvet coats — all forming endless lines for death, day after day." He moistened his lips and continued his lament. "They were brought to the edge of an open grave, shot and buried and the next group laid down on top of them. The daily tortures, the public hangings of men, women and children. All this I saw and more!"

"Please stop!" Elfe pressed her hands to her ears, her eyes tightly shut as if she could block out the ghastly pictures. Tears seeped out from beneath her lashes. Tenderly, he reached out and took her hands in his.

"Don't cry for me. I am an epitaph of sorrow many fathoms deep. And you... You are the sun. Even hell has its seasons." His intelligent, sharp eyes, stood starkly against the sickly pallor of his skin. His forehead furrowed as in deep contemplation. She could easily envision him in the noble, esoteric calling of a doctor who loves his fellow man in unconscious brotherhood.

She spoke. "What kept you alive?"

"Hope. Hope that one day I would be reunited with my family." His eyes dimmed into an unseen distance. A wry smile crept around his mouth, in tiny lines. "You probably believe I had given up all hope. But it's not so." He pointed a finger to the outside. "My heart joins in the rebirth of spring, something I believed could never happen again. For me joy and sorrow are united. I look in wonderment at the aged trees who survived yet another winter, at the newborn birds, at the scampering field mice. They all attest to our ability to renew ourselves. While I hope, I expect the worst."

"Don't give up your hope, Josh. You will be reunited."

"That is sweet of you, but I have few illusions." He exhaled heavily. "What they don't understand, is that they killed the least important part of us. They can burn the flesh, but its treasure, the soul, is released and preserved. The name, each and every one, need not be written in stone, for even stone crumbles, yet the name is forever inscribed in the heavens, to be used again when the soul seeks another covering! It has always been so and so it will always be." He gestured with palms upward."

Shyly, she uttered in a whisper, "I pray for you."

She felt gratified, remembering how he had looked when she had first saved him and how he now appeared. He had become a little healthier and a bit stronger. He had even gained a little weight.

* * * * * *

"Hey, come back to the world!" Gisela said.

"I was just thinking about Josh. You know, his German is excellent — as good as mine..." He never failed to inquire about her health and her pregnancy. He cared. They had become friends. Elfe had to lie down on her side on the grass to talk to him. She told him, "Someday we'll remember the cave, when you're a famous doctor, and we'll laugh." The six long years of a seemingly never-ending war weighed heavily on her now as did her full-term pregnancy. Each day she hoped there would be news of the end and each day she was disappointed. "Yes."

"What? Yes about what, Elfe?" They were in their room and Gisela was tending to Thomas.

"We're going to think about ourselves too. We're going to have to take what we can from the supplies before there's nothing left for us."

Gisela was observing Elfe. "You've hardened. There's a new toughness in your face and manner. When I first met you, you seemed like a major snob, too good for the rest of us. But you can be sort of a regular person."

"I suppose that's a sort of compliment." Elfe sighed wearily.

For the next few days, the SS drove back and forth to unknown destinations, probably their homes, with the loot. This new activity did not go unnoticed by the women in the villa.

Elfe was lying on the bed, her swollen legs supported by pillows. She was in her ninth month and everything was becoming a burden to her. The nausea had returned. She felt heavy, sluggish and tired all the time. "Those pirates aren't going to take me for a fool." She was obsessed.

Gisela was fixing a hem on a dress, exclaiming "damn!" every time she pricked a finger. "That treasure is bothering you; Hell, it's driving you crazy."

"You're damn right. I'm getting in there first chance I can."

Gisela became irate. "Those villagers are right. We're whores, parasites, profiting from what isn't ours!"

"When I think about it, nothing is actually owned by anyone. Everything is on loan — even lives." Elfe wasn't making excuses for trying to survive the storm by dropping anchor here, but she had compromised herself. She began arranging things for Josh. He was her saving grace. The shame that had washed over her receded. What a peculiar world! She thought of her countrymen in the Wehrmacht, who fought and died on foreign soil in heroic defense of their country, while others, the spoilers, willed them to die in the name of greed. "I believe Josh was brought to me to keep me from self-pity," she said, thumping her chest dramatically.

As she spoke, a breath of air floated through the window bringing with it the pungency of new grass. Thomas murmured and Gisela bent over him, crooning and coddling him. His tiny body wriggled in contentment, he drooled and yawned, a tender bundle of sweetness. A gift in a troubled, doubtful world.

Later that day none of the guards stopped the two girls as they left the grounds, Gisela with Thomas asleep in his pram, and Elfe, a covered wicker basket in hand. Gisela, as usual, watched the path, waiting by the road, as Elfe quickly went to Josh in his hiding place and gave him the supplies. He was glad to see her and they automatically clasped hands. After she had chatted with him for a while and kept him company while he ate, she said, "Josh, the doctor says I'm due any day now. I want you to have enough things in case I can't come for some days."

Josh opened the towel she had brought him. Inside he found a warm shirt, a pair of woolen, handknitted socks, bread and wine, and some dry biscuits. Also there was fresh fruit — apples and grapes and carefully wrapped in paper, half a cooked chicken. He was so desperately hungry, he devoured part of the chicken immediately and drank a little wine. "This should keep me for a week. In the camp one miserable slice of bread and no water plus indescribable hard labour sustained me for three days," he told her. "You're putting yourself, and Gisela too, in danger at an enormous risk for a Jew. I will each day carefully ration the amount of food and drink. On a colder night I might have a drink of wine, wetting the bread into it."

Sometimes Elfe had brought an apple or peach for him. Three days earlier she had salvaged a nice piece of sausage. Josh had relished every delicious bite. "You girls are keeping me alive. I don't know how I'll ever be able to repay you."

Elfe, a little embarrassed, retorted, "Who knows, maybe someday you'll save my life." As soon as she said it, she blushed.

Josh, ignoring her tactless words, said, "I'm concerned now for you. You deserve a life better than this. I wish I could help. You're so young."

"In a way you already have. You have made my loss seem so much smaller, in comparison to yours... I loved my parents very, very much." She felt the back of his hand wipe away a tear that had escaped onto her cheek. Again she realized that her words were unfair.

"I only hope that someday I will be able to thank you properly. Don't cause unnecessary danger for yourself. Promise me you'll think of yourself and the baby first. You must take care and not worry about me. No one seems to know about this place. I see only crickets, butterflies, and birds who sing to me. I had forgotten how beautiful and wonderful life can be. Life and fear were one and the same for me for so long." His face was full of compassion. He moved to help her sit on the blanket.

In the dim light of the grotto, in the presence of nature and fewer restrictions, nothing stood between her and her conscience. The eccentricity of the situation loosened her ego. A rise of wind prompted her as though it were her own breath, to ask, "It's true, isn't it — what happens in those camps?" She held her breath. The moment was long. The planes of his face became a tragic land. New fragile leaves rustled on the trees. She wondered if a tree felt pain or loss. If burnished fall colours were actually rage at man.

On returning to the villa, the girls noticed, near the infirmary, a door ajar. Sneaking inside, they spotted packed crates. Prowling through them, they found bags of sugar, tins of cocoa and tins of coffee. Slipping some into the wicker baskets, they looked further. There they found a treasure of expensive collectibles.

They madly dropped linens, a pair of silver candlesticks, a beautiful antique silver tray, and a few flashy baubles into Thomas' carriage and another bag Gisela was carrying. They made room for monogrammed linens, silk pajamas and regretted there was nowhere to hide more. And then they fled to their room, knowing full well that they might have to sell these items in the not-so-distant future in order to survive. The booty was locked in a trunk under Elfe's bed.

One week later, at the end of March, Elfe gave birth to Kirsten. It was a painful, draining labour lasting sixteen hours. And when the baby finally presented itself, in her anguish and weakness, Elfe cried out, in a childish, tiny voice, "daddy," her arms, outstretched. But when it was all over and Dr. Ebner presented the tiny, wrinkled infant to her, she was overjoyed. No tiredness could diminish what she felt. Her own flesh and blood, her own child! Nothing else mattered anymore.

From the first moment Kirsten was put to her breast, mother and child became inseparable. Elfe loved everything about Kirsten. She looked forward to the baths and then wrapping the baby, all soft and sweet-smelling, in a towel. Elfe's heart overflowed with love and enthusiasm. She told Kirsten stories she couldn't possibly understand and Kirsten would coo and gurgle and Elfe would coo and gurgle back to her. Elfe searched those grey eyes as if her entire life was in them while Kirsten sucked on her finger until she fell asleep. Humming endless lullabies, bewitched by the soft, peachy being, she'd remember the Grimms' story of the Six Swans and the steady voice of Katherina telling it, as Elfe nestled against her soft shoulder.

She smiled with satisfaction. Kirsten was the most beautiful baby she'd ever seen, with gold

Chapter Eleven

Bavaria,
March, 1945

flaxen hair, an oval face, tiny features and a cherry bud nose. Elfe was charged with pride and could not believe that Kirsten had not been in her life all along. She was convinced Kirsten had been until birth in her thoughts, guiding her somehow, especially during her pregnancy.

Outings in the pram were particularly special. Now two carriages left the villa each day. Elfe was gay and relaxed as she introduced Kirsten to the world outside. She felt like Sappho, the Tenth Muse, introducing her to the lyrics of songbirds, the fan of a refreshing breeze, and the more pedestrian barking of a dog. The moment Kirsten cried, she was back in her mother's arms, snuggled against her.

Kirsten was, on her very first outing, presented to Josh. Elfe had gone to him with eager footsteps as though to a father. Josh brightened at the sight of the infant, held her and caressed her face.

Whatever the girls could bring to Josh, they did. Always there was bread, a few cold, cooked potatoes, cheese sometimes chocolate, and the hope that each day was bringing them closer to liberation. The thought of leaving Steinhoring worried them. What would life be like when they left?

During one of their outings, Gisela, with a hint of savagery in her voice, shrieked, "Not only will we be hated, so will our children. We'll be ostracized." Thomas is a Lebensborn baby — the child of the SS — an outcast, a black sheep."

Elfe didn't hear her. Bred on luxuries and instant animal gratifications, she was terrified of having them taken away. Never having missed a meal or the pleasures of down-filled bedding and servants to wait on her, she felt it unfair to change that, especially now. For the beggars and peddlers, most of society, life would go on more or less as before. They had no way to tell the difference. But to rob her of what her birthright had decreed she was entitled to, to do that again, that would be a crime. She would not be able to cope with personal indignities. She said to herself, I'll be damned if this princess is going to be turned into a lady toad! Aloud she said, "When the time comes, we'll manage."

"I'm so sorry, Elfe," Gisela sighed and sat down to rest on the dewy grass. "It's just that I get these black moments. Sometimes I wake up in the morning and I feel there isn't going to be any future for me. I'm scared. I've always been such a sturdy wall, rock-solid, no cracks. I don't know what has got into me lately... Yes, I do know!" She was contemptuous. "The villa has turned into a stable and the reassuring lies they tell us, of how the Third Reich will hold out forever, is a pile of manure. Shit is what we'll get when we leave — and it'll be in bucketfulls from everybody! You'll see! The only ones with a pedigree will be the Arabian horses that the women rode here. And, you can bet all your classy manners on it — we'll be left to clean up."

She was smoldering like a log in the fireplace, as she changed her bed as well as something in her attitude, tucking crisp, fresh sheets into the corners, and pounding the feather pillows with her fists fiercely. Somehow, during the remainder of the day, faith for Elfe surfaced like an old, reliable friend she had nearly forgotten.

The early evening was warm, unearthly. This night, as on all the nights this past week, big bonfires burned furiously in the courtyard and round the huts in the park, sending tall trails of sunset smoke, grey, vanishing forever proofs of births and other documents concerning the children's parentage.

Creak, creak, creak. Elfe rocked steadily in her rocking chair by the French doors in her room, looking on, transfixed by the spectacle, the gentle, grey clouds like giant specters in the sky. Suffocation assailed her as she thought of the identities to be no more. Then, her hands folded in her lap, her eyes became distant lanterns, ankles crossed, knees together, dress primly tucked in at the sides, save a hint of ivory, lacy slip showing, as the rocking chair groaned comfortingly beneath her.

She smelled the incense of the chestnut and linden trees and listened to the moonlit echoes of the park and the woodlands beyond, and cried for her own lost memories. They were sweet innocence, belonging only to the seraphs of the sun and the moon. The trees swished and bowed to each other beyond the open doors, and if she listened very carefully, she could hear their dolorous whispering in the rhythm of the lonely rain on this special, vernal twilight. Tides of honey spilled from her graceful head, golden wisps falling onto her neck.

Six-fifteen. Time to go downstairs. She stood, wrapped her shawl about her, straightened her dress and looked in the mirror. A smile flickered across her face, erased quickly. She had a rendezvous with Hans, the caretaker, and could not be even a moment late.

She felt slightly giddy as she glided down the stairs and passed through the jungle of people milling about the dining room, the halls, everywhere. It seemed as if every Nazi who was alive, was here, at Steinhoring, the last Nazi refuge.

Determined, she was out the door and in the garden. Time was so infinitely precious. There, by an ancient chestnut tree, stood Hans. She gave him a wistful smile and walked over. Without any preliminaries, she whispered, "I found Aloyzi. He's in the creche. They call him Albert."

Hans appeared deeply abstracted. The fifty year old common German labourer cared about a baby; a baby belonging to a total stranger. A coarse, simple man. Why wasn't he indifferent?

Hans read the question in her face. He shifted his legs and pulled out a dirty handkerchief from his shirt pocket and loudly blew his nose. Scowling, he looked about the grounds to be sure no one could overhear them, and said, "I am an ordinary man. There is little good I have ever done in this world." Elfe nodded.

"Look, one evening a few weeks ago, as I left the villa to go home, a beggar woman in tatters stopped me in the street. She grabbed my arm and so I pulled away, thinking her mad, but then I saw her eyes. Sorrow was drowning in them! She told me she had not come to beg for food or money, but help." He sighed heavily and blew his nose again. Elfe remained silent.

He proceeded. "She, till a year ago, was a simple woman living with her husband, a farmer, in a village in Poland. They had a two month old boy. One day they were picked up in a raid and became prisoners of the Gestapo in Poland.

"They were deported to Bavaria — she to work on a farm — he to a labour camp. The infant Aloyzi was taken from them. As it turns out, the farmers she works for are sorry for her. Word had it that Aloyzi could well be in a Lebensborn. They found he wasn't in any of the other homes near Munich, and her last hope was to search here.

"She sneaked to the villa here and described him to me. What could I do? Why not help the poor woman?"

Elfe interjected, "He has the birthmarks just as she described. Poor little baby! Hans, what is your plan? He's only a year old!"

"In this mayhem it shouldn't be difficult. Tomorrow evening, when I take the garbage out of the grounds, I'll put the baby in a bag with the garbage. I'll give him a little drink and pray he doesn't cry. I'll take him to the farm."

Elfe had only known Hans for three months. Now they were collaborators, although all she had done was to go into the creche and pretend to play with the children.

"You know, you and Gisela are of the few nice girls here. I felt I could trust you."

The two started to walk about the grounds as darkness closed in. He continued. "Let me tell you something. In 1941 I worked in a slave labour camp at Lodz. I saw the inhumanity. It was a new prison, still in a state of organization.

"Children not considered valuable for the future German Reich, boys of ten, many Poles, are put to work levelling the ground, building huts, putting up barbed wire, digging machine-gun emplacements." Hans mopped his forehead.

"Children arrive every day and undergo regular examinations by the race committee. The few considered 'valuable' are segregated and treated relatively well. The others are starved and the half litre of soup a day is poisoned. They cry bitterly of stomach pains, intestinal cramps, and kidney trouble. Their bodies are swollen from malnourishment. Then there is the beatings, hangings, shootings. And the cold, nevermind the exhausting labour. The children are no longer human. Many have gone insane."

They continued walking together. Each one battling with silent fears and a burdened conscience. Perspiration, like melted pearls covered Elfe's face.

Clumsily he continued. He floundered and flushed deeply as he spoke, fatigue beginning to conquer him. "Bed wetters are sent to Block eight, with no doors or windows. The temperature dropped to minus 20 degrees last winter. They froze to death during the night. The next morning other children were forced to use picks to cut the stiff bodies from the plank beds, load them on to carts, and take them to the Jewish cemetery near the camp. The bodies were thrown into a mass grave, lime thrown over them and it all covered with soil. Those not quite dead suffocated. I, daily, could see the earth over the graves move. I wanted to cry out in outrage, to run to them, to claw the earth with my own hands, to save anyone still alive." He was clawing at his hair, shaking his head in futility.

Elfe was holding in a dam of rage and anguish. Tears streamed down her face. She mouthed the words, "How many?"

"Maybe a hundred a day, maybe more. Once they suffocated, the ground became still. I should never, never forget." He looked incredulous at her. And then the bewilderment in his eyes left him and he appeared drained. Weary, they parted, the worker and the Reich's preferred one.

The next day began with an ordinary morning for Elfe and Gisela. Mechanically they went about their chores. They cleaned their room, they carefully avoided mention of Hans and his mission but their thoughts were consumed with it. When nightfall came and they knew Hans had trudged out of the grounds with the child safely, their hearts sang.

Elfe stood in her nightclothes watching the skies, oblivious to the commotion in the courtyard. All she could hear was a choir of songbirds giddy beneath the brilliant stars, the candles of the angels.

The Third Reich was dying quickly. By February, the Ruhr was in ruins and Upper Silesia was lost. There was a severe coal shortage due to a reduction in production and the inability to move it because of Allied bombing of rail and water transports. Many ships, power plants and munitions factories had to lie idle due to lack of fuel. Fighter planes were grounded and many destroyed on the fields by Allied air attacks. Panzer divisions couldn't move for lack of fuel.

The promised "miracle weapons," were a disappointment. The new jet fighters, the latest generation of rockets and the new electro-U-boats could not be produced in sufficient quantities to make effect. The German atom bomb project, a worry for the U.S. and Britain, failed.

As the news from the front grew worse, Hitler gave way to hysterical rage. At the end of January the Russians had reached the Oder River and were only a hundred miles from Berlin. In March, Hitler, ordered Germany to be turned into a wasteland so nothing would fall into the hands of the enemy. These orders, which would have meant mass starvation, were never carried out. The end was close.

On Sunday, April 29, Hitler dictated his personal will.

On Monday, April 30, 1945, Adolf Hitler and Eva Braun took their own lives. He, by a shot in the mouth. She, by swallowing poison. And then, according to orders, their bodies were burned. Hours later the six Goebbels children were given lethal injections and then Dr. and Frau Goebbels were shot at the back of the head.

In a little red schoolhouse at Reims, Germany surrendered unconditionally at 2:41 on the morning of May 7, 1945. Millions of men, women and children had been slaughtered on a hundred battlefields and in a thousand camps. A greater part of most of Europe's ancient cities lay in ruins, and from their rubble, reeked the stench of the countless, unburied dead.

At the end of April, 1945, the Lebensborn heads and the SS fled, taking with them everything they could, including all the food. Elfe and Gisela had succeeded in amassing a neat cache of their own. A storekeeper in Munich, who had a soft spot for them, let them hide some things in her shop.

One morning one of the young mothers came running, screaming that the Lebensborn was empty. The three of them checked the entire villa from top to bottom, until they found only the devoted Dr. Ebner in his office. All the other responsible people were gone. The women were on their own.

Soon American tanks appeared at the villa and began hunting for the SS. They found only Dr. Ebner and it was an American army doctor who prevented him from being shot.

And so the Americans took over the "last stronghold." They converted the villa into a children's hospital. Dr. Kleinle, a medical officer in the Wehrmacht whom the Americans put in charge, arrived on May 15 and began caring for three hundred children ranging up to four years of age.

Elfe and Gisela decided to wait it out. The handful of mothers who stayed only took care of their own children. The place and the grounds were devastated. Most of the documents and birth certificates had been burned by the SS in a bonfire in the courtyard. And in the last days of April, after the SS left, the villagers, in their loathing of the Lebensborn, smashed and shattered anything they could find, leaving wreckage in the home, in the huts and in the fields.

During the war, at first, the villagers didn't realize what the Lebensborn was, but gradually workers who came to the home talked and with natural curiosity, the peasants paid cautious attention to the home. Soon they saw that the girls were all blonde, very Nordic, not like the Bavarian women who were short and dark.

In time, they discovered that Steinhoring was an SS maternity home for Nordic women who wanted to give a child to the Führer and who were mated with the SS in various SS officers' clubs in the Munich area. The SS with big police dogs, guarded the home day and night. Too many precautions were taken by the SS to keep the goings-on secret. The local people learned to avoid the home, the SS and the women, for they were terrified. Obvious attention could result in being sent to nearby Dachau.

The filth the Americans found in the home was unbelievable. Crying, screaming babies crawling on the floor in diapers that hadn't been changed for days. Illness was also prevalent and the evening of the arrival of the Americans, Elfe became very sick. A sympathetic American doctor took her and Kirsten to a terribly overcrowded and understaffed hospital in the heart of Munich.

Frantic, Elfe begged Gisela to take little Kirsten to her aunt and uncle's farm and with that, Elfe succumbed to a long and serious case of pneumonia. Reliable Gisela had bundled up tiny Kirsten and whisked her off to Aunt Gerda's farm in the car of a total stranger.

"What would I do without you?" whispered Elfe when Gisela came to visit her the next day with little Thomas. Elfe looked ghastly. She had been delirious during the night with a raging fever.

"You're going to be fine. Just try to get better and don't worry about Kirsten — the storekeeper is holding our stuff for us, so you don't have to worry about that either."

She took one of Elfe's hot, dry hands and bent closer to her ear. "You should have seen the celebration when I brought the baby. You know they lost Heinrich in Russia. Kirsten is a gift."

The words smote Elfe as if they were furiously flung rocks. "Can't be, Heinrich was their only son. They adored him." Circular, vermilion blotches painted her hot cheeks unnaturally, making her look weirdly dazzled, rather than sad.

Gisela became alarmed. She grasped Elfe's limp hand pattycake fashion. "I'm sorry. I shouldn't have told you. I didn't know — the responsibility of taking care of Kirsten is a godsend... you've just given them a reason for living. Don't you worry about anything, you hear?"

There were, Elfe realized, many, many more parents whose sons would never come back. She fell back on the pillows in despair, her perspiration-stained cheap, white, hospital nightie clinging unattractively to her body. Staring into nothing, she ventured, "Gunther died too... in an air raid. When I read about it in the newspaper, I felt dissociated, coldly indifferent. I'm ashamed to say relieved. Isn't it funny?" She sighed heavily. A haranguing fit of prolonged coughing assailed her, giving her a brief respite from the deeper wrestling within her.

Leaving the room, Gisela made a point to speak to one of the doctors, telling him that Elfe was a very special friend, that her daughter needed her. The doctor looked at her as if her request for special care was ridiculous but then offered that in about ten days she could recuperate at home — ones so young and strong often recovered, even in these difficult times.

A warm, argent sun smiled benignly as she stepped into the street. It invited optimism among several small children playing ball across the way and in the passerbys, energetic in their gait. Suddenly she stopped. Home, the doctor had mentioned, where was that she wondered.

"Gisela, what will you do? Where are you living?" Gisela was sitting by Elfe's bed in the drab, hospital room. It had three other patients who were seriously ill and the atmosphere was depressing. On the bedside table were a few wildflowers Gisela had brought and put in a jar. They seemed so out of place amidst death and dying, yet they thrived, while Elfe wilted like an ungrateful tenant. She wished for escape. Being deposited into the hospital, catapulted her into incomprehensible lost time. In less than two years, she had lost her parents, her home, became an unwed mother and was still at the tender age of barely seventeen.

She felt so disoriented and alone, in the miserable and alien world of the sick, a world so far removed from her sheltered, patrician senses, so unidentifiable with herself, that the possibility of her own infirmary had never entered the periphery of her consciousness. Thoughts of her homeless state made her so confused and anxious as to her tomorrow, that she unresisting, gave in to the overpowering, all-encompassing fits of coughing, that violated her mercilessly by digging into her raw vitals and heaving forth vile, copious, gangrenous-green phlegm, leaving her disgusted, bereft of hope and panting like an overwrought, benzene-spewing engine.

"Don't worry about me, I've rented a small room. Just big enough for me and Thomas. Meanwhile he can sleep in his pram. We don't have our own toilet but I've got an alcohol stove to cook on, a large double bed and all the loot we both collected. I can't return to my family now. No, meanwhile I stay in Munich and we're not starving. But I can't lie to you, Munich is in shambles. All you can see are gloomy people in tatters wandering through rubble. No street was left untouched. Fallen buildings, others dangerous because they're about to fall over, streets unrecognizable as streets. Miserable people, refugees, cripples of all ages, returning prisoners-of-war with missing limbs, and so many of them!"

Barely taking a breath she continued, "I look into the soldiers' faces and I find skin like old, cracked leather, the kind you see on a reptile, crudely patched with dirty bandages, sometimes just covering missing eyes or flesh. Decaying men and their deformed and missing limbs, hobbling about on their crutches, tapping their canes on the sidewalk. On they go, with their rapping and tapping, like splinters in my ears, they are. Our boys — dwarfed and castrated." staccato clips entered her voice, her watery blue eyes tainted with red from lack of restful sleep. "What keeps them going? What keeps anyone going?"

Playing with the fringe of Elfe's coverlet, she said, "When I see these men, do you know what horrible memory comes back to me? When I was a little girl, the children would catch flies and pull out limbs and wings. The poor, helpless creatures would continue on awkwardly with what they had left. This sight now sizzles and burns in me." Gisela wiped away a tear. "Those crutches, they're like spades for their own graves. I'm sad; I'm repelled. Maybe I shouldn't have told you this." Her freckles were angry, embarrassed, flickering dots, like fireworks.

Elfe thought of the misshapen sentinels who traded in their bayonets and guns for canes and crutches. She was exhausted. The room felt airless. She blended into her pillow.

Gisela saw Elfe's fatigue. "I've done it again. I've been ranting like a silly fool."

"No, I'm a German and I should know what's happening in my country." She made a weak smile.

"Next time, I'll bring you some good news. How's that?" And Gisela was off again, till tomorrow. The next day, she bustled into the room with an armload of daisies and sweet, cooked apples.

"Thank you." Elfe smiled. "This room is beginning to resemble Josh's grotto."

"Elfe, I'm incorrigible. When I left here the last time, I stole a whole yeast cake that was cooling outside a house — a well-to-do-house, mind you." She gave Elfe a sidelong glance.

"And I'm not the only one. People are prowling around the neighbourhoods swiping anything not nailed down. You can't leave shoes on doorsteps anymore. Just yesterday, an entire pot of stew was taken from someone's house. I saw the whole thing with my own eyes. They ran up the steps, walked in and grabbed it. Just like that! You should have seen the spectacle, a big woman running after them with a wooden spoon, no less. A minor peccadillo, compared to starving or going without shoes. Look what's become of us!" Her gleeful tone deceived her, as did the wide, tantalizing smile running from one side of her wide face to the other; she was enjoying every detail.

Elfe burst out chuckling, then coughing, and it seemed she wouldn't stop. Gisela became worried. "We haven't come this far for you to die laughing. I'd never forgive myself."

Composure regained, Elfe asked, "The cake — was it tasty?"

"Very. And so was the stew."

"You're bad!"

"Say, I even brought you a piece." Gisela dunked a slice in the water, and Elfe popped tiny morsels into her mouth. "Delicious. That Frau knows how to bake."

"Yeah, yeah. Listen, conditions here are beyond the imagination. It's a factory here and not a hospital. Did you know they're whisking out frightening numbers of deceased patients — before they're dead, to expire on stretchers, so they can make use of desperately needed beds?"

"I feel faint."

"More water?"

164

Elfe fancied that as her entire world revolved around her illness and her child, at the same time, elsewhere, girls her age were going to school, to parties wearing pretty clothes, the thought made her head smart in pain.

Gisela was holding her handkerchief to her nose. "Every time I pass through these corridors, I nearly vomit from the stench." She plumped herself down on the bed and in a currish tone continued. "Bedpans full to overflowing are piled up for viewing outside patients' doors and beds are lining the halls with the living, the dying and the dead. I nearly slapped a guy for groping, until I realized that the arm dangling off the stretcher was stiff, and so was the rest of him. I could swear his eyes were staring directly at me. Maybe he knew he was going and he wanted his last act to be a happy one. He's lucky he's dead. I would have slapped him silly, if he had still been alive. I have enough troubles without that sort of thing." Elfe was disgusted by Gisela's words.

"Gisela, do you remember Margot, the seventy year old nurse?"

"She's gone home, hasn't she?"

"Yesterday. I miss her already." Elfe shifted her weight in the bed. "She came out of retirement to help the soldiers, toiling day and night in the hospital, until she too, fell ill from fatigue. They said it was angina. When she heard about me not having family, Margot came in when my fever burned, and this frail-looking angel, framed in white hair, cried for me. Those wrinkled, blanched hands sponged me with cool water and she dressed me in a fresh nightgown. That toffee-sweet voice reassured me as she held my head and put cool water to my lips. I listened to her tell me about the homeless cats she adopts and the monkey who shares her apartment.

"A what?"

"A monkey. The zoo in Berlin closed in April. It couldn't be operated any more. After the bombings, the aquarium was destroyed. The reptile, hippopotamus, kangaroo, tiger, and elephant houses, including scores of other buildings were severely damaged. Margot told me the beautiful Tiergarten, the 630 acre park, is now a shambles with room-sized craters and rubble-filled lakes. The luxuriant forest is gone. All that's left are burned and ugly stumps.

"Her sister worked there as a veterinarian and begged her to give a young monkey a home. Margot cried as she told me of how thin the poor animal was when she first took him home. Now he eats well; her grandchildren adore him."

She looked wistfully out of the window. Beyond the walls, she inhaled the sound of children's fresh voices. Spring had erupted in electric, scintillating colours. She squinted shyly at the golden glare of the commanding sun at its zenith. She tilted her nose upward as the ambrosial scent of the grass and roses, wended through the window and were absorbed into her hungry nostrils. The hospital remained a disorganized hive of activity. The stench, of human excreta, came and went, fanned by the air to spread like vast gutter steam from the hospital, diffusing itself all over the city. But Elfe took no unpleasant notice.

The conversation had tired Elfe. She yawned and her eyelids grew heavy. Even the slightest exertion had a soporific effect on her and she drifted off to sleep. Gisela tucked the blanket about her and silently left, with Thomas in her arms.

Elfe was not recovering quickly enough and the doctors decided to keep her hospitalized.

Margot volunteered to come back two or three times a week to help care for the patients. One day, she brought a little German black beer for Elfe who was refusing food. Margot propped Elfe up in bed and held a small mirror to her face. Elfe gasped when the frail, painfully thin reflection whose red eyes rimmed with indigo rings, glared back at her. It wasn't her health that had horrified her. It was the loss of looks. Gone was the face that had made heads turn, that made her feel a cut above most other women. She could survive losing almost anything — but damage to her vanity was a major blow. Thick, black foam met her anemic lips.

"This will stimulate your appetite and help you gain weight. You lost at least fifteen pounds," Margot spoke soothingly.

She succumbed to hot, briney tears for the cruel judgement of the the mirror confronted her as she drained the glass. Mealtime had become a chore — not a surprise, considering the effect of the high fevers. A tray of food arrived, while a pleasant feeling beginning in her stomach, travelled to her head and she giggled. Margot kept coming to see her. She chatted with her while she learned to eat again. It wasn't haute cuisine, but the watery potato soup and chunky black bread with butter looked appetizing. In time, she finished her meals, so captivated was she by the silly antics of the animals, told to her in loving detail by Margot.

From the time Gisela was on her own, the simple farm girl felt bewilderingly transplanted in a dying city, growing increasingly insecure. For a while, she cheered herself up with nature's offerings. She tried to make little cares, happy ones, murmuring to Thomas as he drowsily fed at her breast, drooling droplets of milk, enjoying folk songs on the small radio. Grateful Thomas was unaware of the shabbiness. As she listened to the rapping of the spring rain washing against her tiny, prison-like window, the forbidding rented hovel made the luxury of Steinhoring seem very remote indeed.

She had not planned to reveal to Elfe just how miserable she was becoming, but they had become such good friends, that one day, while visiting her in the hospital, she opened up. Elfe was propped up on her pillows. Her skin was less sallow. "My friend, sit here beside me and tell me how you've been." She patted a spot on her bed.

Gisela sighed heavily. Each night I walk home up the dark, worn, creaky stairs, sticky with years of spittle, to my empty, poor and decaying room. What of this do I tell her?

She thought of the previous night. Thankfully, Thomas fell asleep, the little angel, in his pram. The room seemed so crushingly dismal and loathesome. It always was that way, but it was adding up for her. Just like the water dripping into a fuel can would run out of space, she would lose the capacity to tolerate the ugliness of her living environment. When she went outside it was no better, the bombed out city was a macro scale of her apartment. She scanned the walls of her room, an old, cheaply-painted yellow desert of desolation. There was no hope of salvation in its decrepitude, in the sour stench of stale, amber urine splashed against its faded walls. She prepared a potato soup on her little alcohol stove. The tiny place loomed like an enormous monster, threatening to swallow her into its own miserable fate, sealing it with hers forever.

"I am terribly alone. Can you understand it?"

"Yes, of course I can. Poor Gisela."

"I hate the place I'm living in. I think Thomas does as well."
Everyone hated it, even the golden-brown cockroaches creeping
through the yellowed, stained cracks in the walls looked unhappy.
She watched them, she was no better than they were, her life
worth no more. She started being careful around them, being
sure not to step on one. How could she explain that the
cockroaches had become housepets? How could she tell her
friend that she identified with them?

Gisela was clutching at her elbows, her face a pale moon
spangled with strawberry stars coursing down her taut neck. Her
hair was braided straw, wound about her head like a wreath some
strands sticking out comically. Elfe noticed new lines scribbled
across her brow. Not only had she lost her childhood but she had
skipped over her adulthood. The teenager sitting beside her was
aging. Her shoulders were slouched as if weighted down with
worry and beyond her bare legs, toes were peeping through the
cracks of her well-worn shoes. She was wearing an expensive,
pink linen dress, collared and cuffed in Battenburg lace. Mother-
of-pearl buttons ran down the front proudly boasting its jewel-
like worth. It's simple but expert cut announced that its original
wearer could have been no less than a lady, a Jewish lady no
doubt.

Was Gisela aware of her gaffe? A lady wouldn't have tried so
hard to make a good impression here. Elfe knew she was
oblivious.

Gisela was lost, thinking about her life in a container no
better in her mind than Josh's cave. At least he didn't have to
worry about the neighbours. The noise, the smell... One tiny,
prison-like window, opened onto a ramshackle grey street of old,
tottering buildings. The sagging, metal bed was her only piece of
furniture. She recalled the lovely room they had shared and the
park beyond the window and the lake and felt wretched.

While Gisela sat there she made a silent promise to try to
find Josh. He was her connection to the recent past. She felt
better already thinking about him but did not want to tell Elfe in
case she was unable to find him.

The next morning, Gisela stopped an American soldier in the
street. He must have had many such requests, and suggested
pessimistically for her to try the hospitals. That day she dragged

Thomas to two hospitals. She had almost given up hope when she found Josh in the second one. She ran to his bedside right away. He asked about Elfe before anything else and was upset to hear that she was sick. He had been very ill with typhus but was recovering. Once his immediate danger had passed, he had had time to think about his family. He had lost any hope of finding any of them. His black, punished eyes could melt an iceberg. She felt a rush of pity as she had never known before.

Just then Thomas, who had been asleep in her arms, woke with a loud, toothless howl. When they looked at each other, something happened. Josh uttered the word, "son," and Tommie stopped crying right away. Josh put his fingers to his own lips as if they remembered something he didn't. Gisela got up and took Thomas home.

"That is odd." Elfe yawned tiredly. "Have you seen him again?" Elfe was delighted to get news of Josh.

"Yes, a few times."

A plate of hot food arrived and Elfe's mouth watered greedily at the modest fare of cooked cabbage and potatoes. To her it was no less than a royal feast, a carnival of culinary delight. Ravenous, she gave Gisela an impish look and then attacked the food heartily, alternately chewing then cutting the air as one fighting a duel, with her knife jabbing the air to emphasize her points with each rapid and enthusiastic remark in her clipped, Teutonic, cultivated accent.

"Nice to see your appetite is back," Gisela smiled mischievously. "Josh is as well as can be expected. It's no joke recovering from typhus. He would have died. He was that close," she indicated digitally, showing barely an inch between her thumb and index finger. "And he always, always asks about you. He nods his head as in prayer and says that you are his salvation, that you're an angel that returned to him hope. He gets all dewy-eyed."

Elfe paused, her mouth full. "Oh, I didn't do all that much." She was examining the morsel of food on her fork. "Remember Himmler's beloved porridge we all grumbled about? I bet it's looking very delicious to those women right now. I just happened to be in the wrong place at the right time. Anyone with a heart would have done the same, without thinking twice about it."

Gisela gave her an odd glance. "You really think so? Gisela looked different somehow, purged of anything depressing or unpleasant.

"You're not a mediator between him and G-d, Gisela, and neither am I. You can't take that responsibility." Elfe was wondering with more than a little surprise, at Gisela's expression of messianic feelings and nervous gestures; she was even blushing, eyelids hooded to hide her eyes.

Gisela smoothing her dress looked away. Then, without warning, her voice took on a high timbre and with a sidelong glance, she ventured, "What would you say if we got married?" There, it was out. Gisela seemed to physically shrink, bashful and vulnerable, the muscles of her face tensed. The world too had shrunk. All Elfe could see were Gisela's hands nervously twisting a white handkerchief.

Elfe's sun had turned to black coal. She feared Gisela could see her grief, her own shrivelled spirit and misunderstand that it was a reaction of jealousy. She felt herself spinning through a labyrinth of remembered times. Now she knew for sure that there had been no one more important to her since her parents died, than Josh. He had chosen Gisela. A sickly-sweet taste disgorged itself from her gullet.

Gisela, oblivious, left in a happy, disoriented haze and Elfe's legs became possessed and flung her out of bed and woodenly pulled her outside. Gisela's words had punctured a dream.

She had felt valour in the face of his suffering. The bond they had created, she had truly believed, was a cord of personal affection between them. And she had drunk it in draught after draught, and her love had been concealed until Gisela opened the spillway. She had discovered virtue and selfless intimacy — a mysterious land without a name, an intangible place. A formless divine.

What demon had possessed him to be lured by the vulgarity of the flesh? What failing had pushed her to abandon her parents the day they were killed?

How different was Josh from the soulless Nazis. She was madly enthralled with a wish for Gisela to die! She hated her with her entire being. Gisela had found love and she had discovered a hideous ability which may have lain latent, waiting to surface when the right trigger came along. It was wrong to hate. She thought of their friendship. There was very little else she had besides it and she had valued it. Was it Gisela she despised, or the claim she had on Josh? Uncontrollable tears ran in rivulets down her cheeks. Gisela with the depth of a daisy! When Gisela had taken her hand when leaving, it had burned like fire. She thought of them making love and her stomach writhed in pain.

Gisela bonded to Josh, inspired by a believed innocence — like that of a child. Not that she thought him one, but she accepted life at face value, skimming only the surface. She saw an adult replacement for Agathe, someone helpless and benign and too hurt to hate even the Nazis and what they had done to him. It was his weakness that drew her to him, his naivete. And it was her weakness, her sense of inferiority, he needed to see as compassion. It was their weaknesses that connected them and deluded them into believing they could give each other a place to hide from the punishing world. But Josh was so wrapped up in his need to escape from his past and his loneliness, that with all his education, he forgot that the institution of marriage was not built on sand and even the most desperate attempts to erect castles on it, would collapse, for a foundation had to be solid and real.

Josh and Gisela didn't wait long. Shortly after his release from the hospital, he went to recuperate in her bare and humble room.

A red-eyed sun dribbling fire hung mute in a baby-blue, transparent sky, a splendid fireball. It was Josh's wedding day. He stepped outside, head raised, squinting, and shivered in the passionate warmth. He was moved by exquisite anguish and shrinking, raw doubts, he accepted

Chapter Thirteen

Bavaria,
September, 1945

and drove away, as the prerogative of a groom. The sun could not snuff out the harsh reality, that there were no loved ones with whom to share this day. They had been banished from this earth to a blackened, sooty forest in another sky. Surely the collective mortal wounds bound together and never to heal, would mantle the world, casting great, gloomy, fulminating shadows, such as the universe had never seen, of thick and stinking smoke curled into the shapes of the men, women and children they were just before entering the infernal mouth of the crematoria. There should have been a blighting of the crops in the fields, the buds on the trees, and drying up of every beautiful, living thing in a drought. Yet, none of this had happened. The cheerfulness that had long deserted him was creeping back like vines of roses that stabbed into his sensibilities inflicting an exquisite pain.

Gisela was by his side, taking his hand in hers and they were ready to leave for the simple, civil ceremony at city hall. His thin frame was clad in an old, worn, grey suit, while Gisela was blushing prettily in a tailored pale blue, cotton dress and matching belt, her elation evident in her adoring, forget-me-not eyes of youthful exuberance. There were the things he fought not to think about; His suit, which he fingered nervously, had belonged to a German who had stolen it from a man who had most likely died in a death camp. There was even a name in the lining, in hand stitchery, Michael Klein, to indicate the true owner. Perhaps he had even worn it to his own wedding. By Josh wearing the suit, the occasion also became the funeral of Mr. Klein.

In wearing the suit to begin a new life, an old one was resurrected, its turmoil damply sheathing his body. The original owner, having been cheated of his corporeal body, was transmitting his lack of peace through Josh's veins. The suit had been bequeathed to him only four days before, when he had been strolling in the street. Suddenly voices were shouting to him, and when he turned to look, a group of three gaunt, Jewish men were busy relieving a German apartment of its possessions. Two were on the pavement, arms outstretched to catch the clothing the third was heaving out an upper window. They had recognized him as another camp survivor and, for this reason, he became the beneficiary of a grey suit, almost his size. It was French, the nationality of the dead Jew who had worn it, unknown.

"Wait," one of the rail-thin, living-dead men shouted, "Don't you want something more?" his sad eyes queried with genuine concern. When survivors met on the street, total strangers became instantly bonded. They saw themselves in each other, and every time they met another one, they received a piece of their soul, as if they were all one man, as in the beginning of time, as sparks of soul in Adam. And now, after this apocalypse, all the sparks were searching for each other to reunite, so they would be whole again.

A white, eiderdown comforter had sailed out the window. And on wings of floating, velutinous feathers were the usual, spoken and unspoken dithyrambs — "Do I know you from the life I once had? Can you give me back my identity? Can you prove to me that I once was the person that I now remember? Are you my lost brother, father, neighbour?" And then, in disappointment, but still with a remnant of hope, "maybe you know what happened to this person or that person?"

Some Jews, in the first months after liberation, roamed the streets in their rags with hollow eyes, to claim a few material possessions in a stricken effort to reclaim their stolen lives.

And here was Josh, this morning, wandering into a new beginning, beneath the penetrating eye of the blazing sun and feeling like just so many atoms swarming, bewilderingly, erratic, reaching out for the light. The fugitive from loneliness and the gypsy, each cherishing their own dreams, officially became man and wife, two hemispheres, two worlds. Elfe, at the edge of their thoughts, was still in the hospital. Soon she would be released to stay with friends in Munich.

Meanwhile, Gisela and Josh, began a new chapter in their lives in a modest cottage. She jumped into marriage merrily, anxious to play the role of a doctor's wife and shine in her husband's glory. Dressed like a hausfrau, colourful peasant skirt and white blouse, she busied herself in the kitchen garden and flower beds and chirped to the birds in their love nests in the ripe trees and in the eaves of the wooden verandah. She made herself as busy as a bee gathering pollen. While flies loitered and field mice squeaked, she was building a home.

Josh had gained weight, although he was still thin. He was planning to work in a hospital in Munich. Every day, Gisela gingerly lit the stove and set out simple crockery of blue floral dishes that had been left by the previous owners, and poured out a hearty meal. Thomas slept in his cradle from Steinhoring swaddled in golden fingers of light.

However, it didn't take long for her to wish she were smarter. There were things about Josh she would never understand. At night it seemed he was possessed by the devil himself, and it frightened her. He would shout and scream in a garbled voice. She didn't know what it meant, except that he was reliving the war. She was too afraid and too guilty to ask him in the morning. Her eyes rimmed with dark circles from interrupted sleep, she pretended that nothing had happened.

Black squalls, funnelling in like a tornado, penetrated Josh's sleep. Rabid visions, like sour, projectile vomit, motored wildly, like a hurlybird into the loaded cannon of his mind. Perched precariously at the entrance to Eden, he desperately wanted to believe that hospital work would stunt the flood of apparitions and merge the tormented man and doctor into a peaceful person who had earned his right to coexist with other human beings, on this earth.

Vast herds of sheep and cattle came trampling over the fields of his mind, on their way to the slaughterhouse, night after night, after night, unending, unceasing. Out of his dreams and into his bed, they stampeded, hoofs crushing him until he rolled out of his dreams to the floor and lay there howling, arms outstretched to halt their way to their appointment with Death.

He travelled between two worlds that sometimes collided with each other. Sometimes he saw his parents and they spoke to him. Broken words and very clear images. Once he actually felt his mother's cool breath, gentle and soft as a feather's flutter, on his cheek and he awakened crying out to her. The image of her looking radiant and young draped in a flowing, white robe, stayed with him, as did her showering of love. He would wonder about his sanity and about G-d for having sent her.

Josh would go for walks along unfamiliar streets and scrutinize the glances of the gardeners, housewives, feeling silently condemned. What is a dirty Jew doing still alive? We are Judenrein! Memories of the camps, the hangman's noose, the murdered children, groped back. He clutched his head. He looked at nature's bounty, the plum and apricot trees in the backyards. Leaves fell, children played through Lehar's waltzes on the air waves. He didn't want to think of death and injustice, yet it was his duty not to forget, or forgive.

Josh had no land of his own, no country that he could imagine feeling safe in. He vowed daily to behave with honour for he was an ambassador for the dead. What didn't kill him, he had to show, made him stronger. Only a superhuman could have survived when so many mortals died. Now he had to act like one.

Not only was he reasonably sane, he had a sanctity for human life, a reverence for its value. He would show he was worthy of his suffering. He would show he had not learned the evil of Dachau, that he was not vermin to be exterminated. He measured what he now had left. The Nazis had not taken away the one sure way to his identity. He was a Medical Doctor, dedicated to life. He exchanged his prisoner's striped pajamas for a white coat. One costume exchanged in the parade of life for another.

Now, observing Thomas' baths, as he gurgled and splashed water, Gisela's laughter, the sounds of traffic outside, the memories of his hell hovering over him in the background; this was his reality. This was the life he had been given.

Even sex was not an exertion of manhood but rather a drug of forgetfulness — a grinding, rhythmic ecstasy followed by hot, wet release and an exquisite numbness, but not accompanied by true liberation, for hours later, the black spectres reappeared at the outer edges of his frantic consciousness.

Elfe and Gisela sat at the heavy, ancient, rectangular, oak table in the kitchen by the flickering light of the smoking, tallow candle, eating Gisela's thin, watery potato soup, now the staple of most Germans. There was a pleasantly eerie mood between them. There had been a lull in the conversation and Gisela broke it like glass, "There's no fat in the soup. I know it has little food value. The small supplementary ration Josh gets just isn't enough, but we make do with the vegetables I grow in the garden. We have potatoes, turnips, tomatoes, so we're lucky. I can put decent food on the table."

"You must be delighted with this cottage. Lucky for you, the American doctor can't use it." Elfe looked around. Gisela had obviously transformed the small, drafty, dilapidated cottage into a warm, cozy home. It had been whitewashed and made clean and neat. There was even a fine, albeit old, gold sofa in the living room. Gisela caught her glance.

"I got the sofa from the money I got for the silverware."

"Good for you. You look so tired though."

"We had a lot of work to do." Gisela rested her face in her hands and massaged her temples. There were dark circles under her eyes. "Evenings and Saturdays we work." Pointing upwards, she said, "The blackened ceiling beams were cleaned. The walls were painted and we put bookshelves along the walls. Josh dreams of filling them with new books. His family once had a library. We've felled trees for firewood. There's no end to the repairs we need to do." The troubles with Josh, she kept to herself.

Elfe had only congratulations for her friend. She was attempting to banish her jealousy, her rejection by a man. She was delighted and relieved that she would be invited to their home.

Later, the girls went outside to watch the party-coloured garden. The sun had mellowed to the hue of fading embers. The mountains framed the rural beauty. "You are lucky," Elfe sighed. "You have heaven."

While still with friends for several weeks, in Munich, after her release from the hospital, Elfe's first impulse was to get in touch with her Aunt Gerda and Uncle Frederick and get little Kirsten, so she headed to their farm, waving down a car for the ride. Hot and dusty, it didn't appear likely she'd find anyone home. She stared and stared at the grim scene. The midday sun betrayed the decay of the lovely place she used to know. Death, had paid a visit here, and dried the life out of the grass into yellow hay and withered all the flowers. The friendly home had turned into an old recluse, devoid of vitality, uninviting, detached from life, forsaken. A withering house that had died, unloved, abandoned. Was the farmhouse thinking the same about her?

She found the key under the porch and threw back the familiar bolt allowing her to push the door into the house. Everything was crusted with grey dust. Cobwebs draped the corners of the ceiling. The odor was musty and sweetly foul, like in a room of the dying, yet the family had not left in haste. No, it had been well thought out and soon after Kirsten was with them.

Otherwise, the house was in order; no dirty dishes lying about, and what remained of their clothes was neatly folded in the cupboards. Helplessly, she moved about like an old woman. "Is anyone here?" she asked, knowing the answer. They have left and taken my baby, a lump grew like a giant, hard-boiled egg in her chest. She searched the house and then ran outside, calling, Kirsten, Kirsten, then ran back inside, wild-eyed.

They were kind, knew their place, and kept it. Surely, they understood there was no way to offset their own loss. They were poor devils who couldn't think straight any more. She hated them with all her heart and soul. Had they forgotten hers was a highborn child, one of the select elite! If Hitler had still been in power, they would have been severely punished for such an immoral crime! Hadn't she suffered enough? She was knocking her head in the kitchen wall now, and pulling at her hair. They had no right to her child. She would get her child back. Her surety would guide her.

Her dry throat croaked for help from the lonely house who had witnessed all, but was helpless to answer. Gasping for air, as if drowning in a sightless void, pain clamping her chest, she pulled herself to the cupboard where she remembered there had been whiskey. Shakily, she cradled the bottle and poured herself a glass, and drank. And she broke down and wept.

In shock and frustration, she returned to Munich, wandered the war-torn streets for several days before going to Gisela and Josh's cottage. Alarmed by her appearance, Gisela made her strong tea and Elfe's hands visibly shook as she cupped the warm mug to her chapped lips.

In the whitewashed, scrubbed-down kitchen, blisters of cracked light stroked across Gisela's arms as she worriedly studied Elfe with raised eyebrows, her forehead a series of light and dark hills and valleys. Elfe was slumped in a chair and knew that she looked like an unwashed, grubby, dishevelled, shaggy dog. She was a mess. Her matted, tangled hair had lost its sheen, her shoes were torn, and the hem of her dress had unravelled. The sun's evening light caused her to squint and her breath caught, as a divine, Alpine scent from outside, trickled into her nose, but she was past caring. She was lightheaded, as the smell of food enshrouded her. Gisela was busily heaping food on the clothed table. Her brawny hunger took over, as her senses sampled the delicacies appearing in rapid succession; a sliced loaf of black bread, butter, pungent slabs of goat's cheese and a freshly baked yeast cake. Her friends watched as she sank lascivious, drooling taste buds into the forgotten, gastronomic flowers growing out of Gisela's table garden, and renewed the acquaintance of a satisfied, pacified stomach. For once, its angry, rumbling growl was quiet.

Later, seated on the sofa with her friends, she told them about her efforts to find Kirsten. "I had regained some strength and so I went for Kirsten. But my relatives had moved, leaving no trace. I inquired as to their whereabouts, but found nothing." Her lips were quivering under eyes riddled with profanely fuschia-red, pinpoint dots that bled into thread-like rivers. Her experiences, illness and fears had plucked away her prettiness, her verve, her confidence and were firing away at her spirit. "I believe my relatives decided to keep Kirsten for themselves now that they have no children left of their own." Shrill-sounding, bordering on hysteria, she said, "I've been looking for her day and night!"

"I feel so guilty for not having kept in touch enough," Gisela murmured.

Josh broke his silence. "You must stay with us. You can't be roaming the streets by yourself."

"No, I can't impose on you." Even though it was obvious, that on her own, she was on a self-destruct course, she could not stay in the house with them. She had accepted their marriage by now, but staying in their house would be too much for her.

Like a loyal soldier, she marched on, valiant, stumbling, persistent. Her calloused feet took her everywhere searching for whoever might know something, anything.

The thought of food nauseated her and she ignored the dull, knocking pain in her head and the sandy grit on her arid tongue. She ignored the blue that discoloured her lips and the sharper features of her face, as she grew thinner and thinner. And she ignored the thick coughing and the vomiting. She acknowledged only the jungle drumming in her laden heart.

Once she caught sight of the queer stranger in a window. Reflected there was a waxen, unrecognizable apparition of herself. People around her must have thought she was on the edge of madness. But she understood only her one mission — finding

Kirsten. She thought of the baby who had grown not only under her heart, but in it and her hatred for her aunt and uncle dripped through her veins like poisoned vitriol.

Two months into her search, her gaunt figure collapsed on the pavement. Her meagre strength evaporated as she drifted into unconsciousness, oblivious to the concerned voices of strangers above her. Luckily someone recognized her and informed Josh at the hospital.

"I feel so ashamed, Josh." Gisela was standing in the kitchen by the stove, whipping the mashed potatoes into a white mound. His nostrils were hugging the rim of the bowl. Mesmerized, they followed the aromatic, hypnotic flavour in a steamy trail to sniff, decipher, and report back to him every delicious detail. For dinner, there would be a viscous stew of homegrown vegetables, consisting of green beans, onions, tomatoes, and cabbage. "We've shown her thin charity. What kind of people are we?"

"The sort of people who have to let someone else make their own decisions. Remember, we begged her all along to stay with us. Freedom means the right to make the wrong choices." His ravenous, empty stomach answered in a beastly growl. He was beside Gisela now, soaking a piece of bread in the stew. Minutes later, her open-hearth face looked and listened as he gross-poetically ingested her food. Stretching both cheeks to the maximum with bread and stew, he began chewing in slow motion, slurping up liquid to help it all go down.

Gisela was taking out dishes from the aubergine painted, Bavarian sideboard that depicted colourful birds, their beaks open in song to a spray of flowers. "Well, we're not asking anymore. She's become irrational. Elfe stays with us. I'm going to force-feed her and we're going to search for Kirsten until we find her."

Josh wanted to help, but he said nothing, preferring his efforts to be his message. He owed her. He hated that.

He had moments of sudden contempt, watching Gisela sleeping like a drained and satisfied she-animal with a look of rapture on her flushed face; after having thrashed and convulsed in response to his wild acrobatics. While inside an aroused woman, his addiction, his appetite for hot, willing and pliant flesh, obliterated all else. With detached observation, he noted that almost any female body would do. It just reminded him that he was alive; a fact he had mixed feelings towards. Gisela was entirely interchangeable, the only individuality lay in the fact that he detested her and her people.

Eyes roving ruthlessly over her robust flesh, he was at odds with visible proofs of the pleasure he gave her, the loathsome, gaping mouth, raw and red; he followed the route his teeth took from the lovebites on her neck, and orbits of her breasts, already bluing, down to her abdomen, and on to the furry blond triangle, a paradise island men dreamed of, pouting and wet from his intense cavaliering.

It was an obscene exhibition and he had a murderous urge to raise his hand to smite her and tear her apart with his fingers, the same fingers that only shortly before had sent into ecstasy that healthy animal skin. He longed to kill her. He had compromised himself with the scum of the earth and not with a partner he had chosen. Feeling polluted by her every breath, he raised his hand. Vengeance scorched through his system — he was a fountain of hate.

Yet he was also greedy for the joys of firm young flesh too long denied him. He would not be denied these pleasures ever again. And then he brought his arm like a mutant snake down to coil around her neck. She jumped, her eyes opening to stare at her husband-assailant in marked and deadly fear, and then in terrible confusion. Without easing the noose that was choking her, he viciously kicked her legs apart and drove into her with the fury of a weapon of destruction, unrestrained until the debouk left him and he was weary and spent.

She never spoke of his diabolical side, believing it had something to do with the war and he would get over it. He never apologized, never offered an explanation. That he might eventually kill her roamed somewhere in her subconscious, but she suppressed it and the abuse. The future she didn't think about. The present was, to her, her future. There was nothing in her imagination that could see beyond that.

They brought Elfriede to stay in their home. They posted ads on bulletin boards, in shops, on trees, asking for any knowledge of Kirsten. Elfe, meanwhile, began to recover. She couldn't stand to be left alone with nothing to do but worry. She helped with taking care of Thomas, bathing him and cutting his hair. She helped in the garden. But Kirsten never left her mind for a moment. She ate, slept, walked, talked, and dreamt of her. As she gained strength, she once again began a search for her daughter, stopping people in the streets, knocking on doors, walking up countless stairs of countless apartments. She asked in shops and offices and condemned herself a thousand times a day for abandoning her. She swore that she would make it up to her for the rest of her life.

Josh would reassure her saying, "Give it more time, you'll find her, you'll see. I've asked in the hospital, notices are posted up in too many places for something not to turn up. Some information, something." She loved Josh more than ever. He understood what she was going through more than anyone.

"What if they've left Munich, left Germany? They could be anywhere by now. They shall never return her. She's all they have now." She seemed stretched to the limit and might snap like a worn elastic rubber band. He was worried but didn't let her see his doubts. Secretly he knew that he would be jealous if she were to find her family. He liked her more now that she knew loss, like he did.

Somewhere, in all of autumn's rejoicing fireworks, peacocking nature's intimations of immortality, arrogantly unconcerned of winter's imminent transformation, under the aureate, dimpled sun of a late October afternoon, a diminutive figure was kneeling over the vegetable garden, groping the warm earth as a blind person, filling a wicker basket with greens. A plaster-grey blur, she was, an insignificant speck, a puff of cloud. Her body arched in slow, heavy movements, as if entangled in invisible chains, weighted down, unresisting.

All the russet comeliness of autumn made no difference to her, for she was as blinded as her mother had been. Autumn celebrated life by preparing for the renewal that would come after winter. It purred, it sang, it chattered in trees. But she was defeated and immune to life.

Later Gisela and Elfe were quietly preparing supper, with milk and cheese provided by a neighbour who had a goat, and eggs they had from their own chickens. Gisela was making omelettes, French-style, minus the "champignons." Both women heard footsteps outside the door. "It can't be Josh," they thought aloud, "he just left for a delivery in the village." They listened but there was no knock.

Elfe went to the window but saw nothing. When she threw open the door, through a wash of tears, she could just barely discern an old, battered suitcase and seated on it a kittenish figure in a red wool coat and bonnet. Behind her she could see the stooped shoulders of the elderly, her aunt and uncle, heading down the road. Just once, they turned around to face her, and as her heart thundered, she smiled and nodded forgiveness. Then they, too, walked out of her life forever.

Kirsten was swept up into her arms. She welded her to her own body in a gushing of thankful tears. All the torments, all the hell, the agony and terror so long stored up released themselves. And then Gisela was there and they went into the house together.

A storm was gathering in Elfe, a maelstrom of conflicting feelings. The slow journey to recovery, the search for Kirsten, had not permitted her an excursion into her carefully guarded secret. Now the sharp flairs of lightning and dim emotional rumbles that she had distanced, were ever approaching closer to alert wakefulness. Her jealousy was a fearful, brooding tide that pressed unremittingly.

They were unaware of her situation, her growing despondency and her aristocratic pride never divulged what she felt — that it was coarse and stupid Gisela that was his bride. Not that Josh was around much. Days were spent in the hospital and often he arrived home late, ate and went to sleep.

Josh and Gisela were polite to each other — too much so to be found natural. They went through the motions of spousal courtesy and no more. There were only perfunctory demonstrations of affection — a peck on Gisela's cheek when he left for work and when he came back.

She wondered what went on in their conjugal bedroom, the peculiar sounds it emitted, cries of muffled fear from Gisela and angry curses from him that shocked Elfe, his occasional hurried exists at night only to return the next evening. Lovers' quarrels? Gisela looked glum and moody more frequently these days and would not talk about it.

For whatever reason they cohabited, it was not with passion or tenderness. Two natural enemies joined for their own needs, using the bed as their battleground. Josh had locked her out when he married Gisela and now Elfe was reluctant to disentangle herself from them. What she so badly craved now and had to have at any cost was her freedom. Otherwise she would grow into an organ of hate and jealousy and lose all identity, becoming a despicable creature of ruination and hopelessness. But leaving meant loss.

Elfe stayed only eight more weeks with them. An uncle was willing to sponsor her to go to Toronto, Canada. Her uncle's family were well established and had no children of their own and they promised to help her find work. She had never known them but anything was better than her current life, even the prospect of a new country filled only with strangers.

She was seated with Gisela on the sofa when Elfe read her uncle's letter. Gisela was busy mending. "...such a tragedy... your parents.... You cannot stay in Germany — a woman and child alone. It is settled. You are to leave Germany at once! You both will stay in our Forest Hill home and, once you've settled, can work for us in our antique store... you will learn English... we welcome you with kisses and open arms..." Elfe was comforted by the tone of the letter that seemed to take the decisions out of her hands.

Gisela after reading the letter spoke slowly, "Yes, I think it's for the best. You aren't happy here. I don't believe we will ever see each other again." Both girls began to sob uncontrollably.

While waiting for their departure, the days sped by and winter appeared. In her warm wool coat and button-up shoes, her pink knitted hat a halo about her peachy, cherubic face, her sea-green eyes sparkling like emeralds, Kirsten was Elfe's entire world and the subject of all her dreams.

Part Three

Joshua

The days had been the same falling endlessly one on another. Josh had no idea how long he had been in the cave. He had started by scrapping a small space clear just to the right of the mouth of the cave. In this space he placed a pebble for each day that he was there. The pile grew and he would spend his time counting them sometimes more than once in a day. He added a pebble at the first light each day, at the same time in order to not forget and add more than one in a day. That would have been easy as some of the days seemed to last as long as a week.

During one of Elfe's visits she, without realizing it, swept them away to sit down. He never put the pile together again, although he could have if he had wanted to; that day he knew exactly how many there were. He had counted them at least five times and four of the times his total agreed.

He looked forward to her visits, he lived for them. Otherwise his days were the same. He would take the chance that someone would see him and walk for a few minutes near the cave after he put a pebble on the pile each morning. Then, when he returned, he would read the Bible Elfe had brought by the light from the opening of the cave until he became tired, or the light dimmed. At night he would sleep curled in the blanket the girls brought for him.

Bavaria,
May, 1945

His routine was broken some days, there were times that he could hear people near the cave. Those days he stayed there, not moving, not even reading for fear that his hiding place would be found either by soldiers or a passerby delighted to engratiate himself by finding a hiding Jew. When there were people near the cave he could only remain frozen, unable to concentrate on anything other than his fear. He had acquired a new desire to live and the greater the value he placed on his own life, the more he feared losing it. He was constantly terrified that the girls would confide his secret in the wrong person and he would be found out. He decided to run if he knew that he was to be captured. Better to die with a fast bullet than by hanging.

The spring brought a mixed blessing. One morning he awoke after dreaming that he was a small child again, had wet the bed and that his father would find him and beat him. He woke up soaking and cold and for a moment believed that the dream had been real. The temperature had warmed the day before and in the night, the cave flooded. He built small dams across the front of the cave with rocks and soil making it look natural so nobody walking by would see. For three days he had no sleep while he waited for the blanket and the cave floor to dry out. Finally, on the third day he gave in to slumber after nearly hallucinating. He woke up hours later muddy and cold. Elfe, oblivious, arrived doling out food and chattering endlessly, not noticing that his clothes were wet. After a couple days, she finally noticed and brought dry clothes and a new blanket. He never would have asked.

Eating the food the girls brought him, he grew stronger and more impatient waiting for the war to end. Elfe gave him whatever war news she could obtain. It seemed to him that the Nazis could hold out forever, but Elfe kept telling him that the war would end soon.

Then one day there was nobody there. And the following day again no visit; the same the next day. Had they been captured stealing food for him? Were they dead? After a couple days he became angry. Perhaps they had given up on him. Tired of their pet Jew they had adopted some other being, a rabbit or a wounded bird maybe.

Less than a week passed when, hungry, having run out of the provisions the girls had been bringing, he woke up to a terrific commotion near the cave. There were Germans everywhere diving into the bushes putting on civilian clothes and leaving behind uniforms. He retreated to the back of the cave and hid behind a boulder. The cave was small and he could barely squeeze himself and the remaining provisions into the narrow space. If this were the end of the war, wouldn't it be ironic if he were to be caught and die today at the hands of Nazis furious with defeat?

The front part of the cave lay empty, welcoming to a Nazi fugitive. He didn't have to wait long. An SS officer entered the cave. Josh froze watching as the young man stripped and changed into civilian clothes only a couple feet from him, discarding his uniform by throwing it to the back of the cave, right at Josh's feet. Since the light was coming from the front of the cave, Josh could see him clearly but the Nazi couldn't make out the other fugitive hiding in the gloom. With all the noise from outside he couldn't hear Josh's breathing even though they were at times only a couple feet away from each other.

The Nazi left the cave after an agonizing eternity that probably was only a few minutes. Perhaps he thought the hiding place now too obvious given the number of people around it. Josh stayed wedged into the back of the cave for another day before he dared come out.

He tied his only possessions in the old tablecloth Elfe had brought (a pair of woolen socks, his Bible and the old blanket) and he stepped out into a beautiful spring day.

His wobbly legs, that had seen no exercise in days, carried him into a large field filled with so many colourful flowers. He bent down to smell a blossom and suddenly, out of nowhere, a young, emaciated woman grabbed his hand and pulling it, she told him to run. "The Germans will shoot you, if they see you! Come on!" She spoke endearingly, as if to a small child she'd just taken upon herself to take charge of. She led him to a copse of bushes where three other girls were hiding from the retreating Germans and the artillery fire of the advancing allies. Under cover of darkness they went to a farm known to one of the young women. After feeding them, the farmer told them to go to a nearby airport, Regensburg, which had been recently evacuated. They found an abandoned barracks and it was there they spent the night.

That was the first night Josh had spent in a man-made building since the escape through the wall with Elfe during the bombing of Steinhoring. It was the first time in years that he had slept so close to a woman. He lay there listening to the breathing of the young girls, overcoming the urge to go and lie next to one of them. He settled for the wonderful sound of their breath and allowed sleep to overtake his tired and sore body.

Early the next morning American tanks arrived. Such a wonderful sight it was! For the first time in as long as he could remember, he cried along with the women. The American soldiers, wept with them. One of the soldiers spoke Yiddish. He was a Jew from New York, Arik Rosen. One of the liberators was a Jew! Josh's heart sang, he was with one of his own people.

The Americans took them to a military hospital where Josh was kept because of his weakened condition. A few days later it was discovered that he had typhus.

He did not know how long he was there or how long the fevers raged but at the end Gisela was there. When he was strong enough to leave the hospital, Gisela took him home. She proposed to him and they were married. A new life started, leaving many questions about the old one and a future of uncertainty. All hopes that perhaps his parents or sister had survived were dashed. Often, he still wished that he had died with them.

It was good being a doctor again. He had something the world needed, he was valued, he even had authority, which he used with perverse pleasure. The same authority he took home with him until his marriage to Gisela bent under the strain of his abuse. When Elfe left for Canada, the abuse left the bedroom. He beat her shamelessly, leaving her with visible bruises so that she would not leave the cottage because of the questions it would raise.

Then, for a time, things improved. Gisela would accompany him to the hospital where he worked, to help in any way she could, bathing patients, emptying bedpans, or comforting the destitute, the dying. There was a terrible shortage of beds, medications, staff, food. The patients appreciated there being a person who had time to talk with them. Gisela brought Thomas who would delight them with his laughter.

One Friday it was raining and Gisela rushed across the street to catch the bus home. (Josh had to stay in town to work late). It was pouring. She never saw the car that hit her. Visibility was poor and the car skidded trying desperately to avoid her. It was a terrible death. She was thrown several feet, and impaled on an iron post that had once been part of a fence. She had such a look of staunch incredulity and anguish on her face, her mouth formed in a soundless shout, a battlecry. Gisela died fighting, her hands clasped around the pole.

They were afraid to remove her. She appeared to be staring. Passersby fell to their knees in prayer, in horror. Nobody could decide what to do. A clergyman was found. He came running and cried out when he saw her. Josh was brought and he took her down himself. They tried to stop him. It was so unnatural to see her so still, when she had always been the indestructible one.

After burying Gisela, Josh couldn't stand the cottage. The idea of staying in Germany was repugnant. He wanted to go to the United States but it was impossible unless one had relatives there.

He waited for months trying to get passage to the United States before he discovered that he had cousins in Canada. As a medical doctor and with their sponsorship he was able to go to Toronto. There he completed his residency in psychiatry at a psychiatric hospital.

Only after Josh arrived in Canada did he hear of the conditions in the Displaced Persons camps. If he had not been a doctor working before he left Germany, and had he not had relatives in Canada, he likely would have had to endure the indignities of these places as the only conduit out of Europe for thousands of Jews.

That he was spared the Displacement Camps did not soften the anger he felt when he heard that Jews were often treated no better in these camps than they had under the Nazis — except that they were not exterminated. To make matters worse, the defeated Germans were better treated. In southern Germany, where Josh had been interned during the war, General Patton insisted that the new camps be surrounded by barbed wire and kept under armed guard. Other survivors were left in the same camps the Nazis had built for them. Many were forced to wear salvaged SS uniforms or remain in their stripped concentration camp garb. There they remained for years after the war. At one camp, Rentzschmule, an ex-Nazi was in charge of the Jewish inmates.

The problem for the allied victors was what to do with the Jews that, even after the Holocaust, nobody wanted. The Western Allies had not entered the war to save the Jews, indeed many of their political and military leaders were ardent anti-semites. Their countries feared a wave of emigration by impoverished Jews.

Josh, typically, wouldn't consider going back to Poland. Even while he was in Germany he had heard about the Pograms. (Jews were rounded up and killed by Polish citizens long after the war ended). Besides what was there to go back to? Everything and everyone was gone. Poland was a graveyard for Jews, not a place to live.

Most Jews wanted to go to Palestine but the British government, concerned about its Arab neighbours, restricted legal emigration to there. Josh wanted out of Europe which held nothing but bad memories and hatred. Because of his Canadian relatives he could go to Canada without the indignities of the Displaced Persons camps.

Many of the inmates who remained in the DP camps, as they were called, were broken psychologically and receiving no treatment to deal with the effects of having for years been treated worse than animals while watching their entire families be wiped out. Their dignity and self-worth long gone, and guilty for surviving when their loved ones hadn't, many refused anything that would remind them that they were alive. The camps became filthy while the soldiers in command were ill-equipped to understand why the inmates would refuse to use toilets and practice basic hygiene.

Somehow, out of that misery came a new generation of world leaders, businessmen, doctors, scientists, musicians, for that was the true miracle of the camps. Later nobody would want to remember what happened there, least of all the former inmates.

When Josh first arrived in Canada, he noticed that survivors were often treated rather shabbily by condescending relatives and sponsors, who chose to view a Jew from the camps as a crippled physiognomy, and bestowed on them unnecessary falseness. They were contemptuous of their suffering, for it would have made demands on their consciences. They were afraid of the immigrants.

* * * * * *

"Why didn't you contact me earlier?"

"Pride, I suppose. I wanted to be in a somewhat settled position first. Being pitied would have been more than I could bear."

"Where are you living?"

"I've rented a small walk-up downtown."

Elfe poured them a stiff drink. The visit was both magnificent and tragic. His mind was blurring. He could see himself wandering through a wilderness, unable to see past his groping arms to whatever lay beyond. He had no strength to confront it now, but intuitively knew that one day he must.

After more time he began to relax, even to enjoy the familiar company. Later there was a heartwarming clatter of dishes and trilling chatter of voices as Josh and Thomas finished the delicate chicken consomme at the white, damask-covered table in Elfe's modest, yet charming, kitchen. It was Christmas, December 24, 1952. The mood was festive as wine glasses clanked together, the people were as sparkling as the brightly polished china and silverware and as bubbly as the champagne. The sweetly aromatic scent of the colourfully decorated Yuletide tree drifted throughout the house.

Josh paid homage to the stuffed turkey and deliciously roasted potatoes. He embraced the restorative power of Elfe's heartiness. Flying forks and the unchained hum of conversation brought time to a standstill.

Elfe, finally glided over to the table to join the others, laden with a multitude of questions. She was a blue angel adorned in a royal indigo, form-fitting, wool dress. Her hair was a tamed honey mane in a figure eight twist with velutinous threads sprinting out here and there. Her face was becomingly flushed with curiosity, happiness and a little alcohol. Her Wedgewood blue eyes ran with the words he spoke. She was, in his opinion, the image of lovely form. After nearly seven years, it seemed like only yesterday they had last met. There was an absurdness to time.

He could conjure up the image of a teenager of seven years ago, a sapling with a grazing of worry lines creasing her forehead, and a dimple denting her cheek, giving away that she was still immured in childhood, the war notwithstanding.

Since it was the first time that he had seen her since Gisela's death he knew that they would have to talk about it. Wouldn't it be easier if people in this situation could simply agree not to? Who would bring it up?

Elfe, direct as always interrupted his thoughts, "Please tell me about Gisela, I need to hear this." He saw Elfe brace herself, hoping she wouldn't shrink from him. His face fell. Already?

Josh attempted to form words, but they fell as dry pellets, sand from between his lips. Azurite, lapis lazuli blue stars until he felt it incumbent to blurt out his pain. The red wine, the mood, the music, a candle had been lit inside him. It was indeed intoxicating to be, once again, with his saviour.

He began the story with every detail from that day, as if he could somehow run out of time and not have to finish the story. All the while Elfe waited, without a word, for him to get to the details she needed to know. He paused as he reached the crucial point to get a sip from his drink. If he smoked, this would have been the time to light a cigarette. Perhaps he could start now?

"Go on," she said quietly, not to push him but to fill the space he had left without changing the subject. A shy smile was on her lips, glinting, moist eyes fixed intently on his. For a split second, it seemed almost sensual.

He spared her nothing. He told her everything. Every last detail until it hurt them both. Afterwards he said, "People said she had been chosen as G-d's own child, that it was not by chance. I think that she was punished for others; the sacrifice had to be by someone pure. I laid her to rest." Elfe could only turn away as the dam burst. After a long few minutes she turned back to change the subject.

He mumbled thickly, when asked about Thomas, "He goes to public school and is picking up English well. For the past two years he studied English privately in Munich. I already had thought of leaving Europe."

Elfe encouraged him to keep talking, she leaned back solemnly, listening to him intently. "What are your days like?"

Josh shrugged his shoulders, feeling suddenly tired with all the remembrances. "Early in the morning, Thomas goes to school and I go to the hospital. Evenings are always the same. I make supper and then I study or write."

"Oh Josh, what a drab life you've been leading. Poor Thomas, how awfully lonely he must be!" She nodded her head in stark disapproval. "And I can imagine the meals he's been eating! The poor child!"

"Lonely nights prompted me to write a book about my experiences in the death camps. Only last week, a publisher has shown interest and has agreed to publish it. I received five hundred dollars in advance. I've called the book, 'Life after Death.'"

How could he ever explain his flounderings to make a living and his agony of mind which he could not explain to himself? So vivid, his nightmares hung as oil paintings, evil and grotesque, on every wall he passed. When he slept they came floating in the night, close enough that there was room for nothing else, just far enough that he could see the whole. He could not fling them upon a bonfire, as did the Nazis with literary works and evidences of their shame. A good day was a remission waiting for a relapse. All that was burned in the holocaust, kept that fire alive.

"A thousand thanks to my lucky stars that you had the good sense to think of me!" Elfe spoke wholeheartedly, although her voice had become hoarse, "Oh Josh, you don't know how happy I am that you're both here."

Sounds of children's laughter echoed from Kirsten's room where they were playing; dessert for the spirit. Elfe was worth her weight in gold. "How obtuse I've become. I've been going on about myself, barely conscious of your life." He wanted to listen, not to talk.

She laughed. Guilt, turned inside her. Her friend had helped her find her child just when she was so consumed by jealousy that she had even wished her dead. Oh my G-d! I've done to Gisela what she did to her sister. I've wished her dead. A burning sensation gripped her middle just below the rib cage. There was a glass of milk on the coffee table; she took a few sips.

She remembered that first day of their meeting. They had become the best of unlikely friends. This friendship had become smeared because Elfe had wanted to believe a man could belong to her. Josh had been no one's property; not even his own.

Sitting in the living room, she was sixteen again, able to recall Steinhoring and even more vividly, her parents. This compounded her longing across the gulf between the life she had then, before the bombing of her house, and now. "Mother, how could you leave me to this excruciating solitude," she said aloud softly to no one alive.

"Huh?" Josh wasn't sure that he had heard her correctly.

Josh was alone. Elfe was with him only physically.

Elfe looked around the apartment seeing everything but Josh. She appreciated the fact that Kirsten was too young to recognize the poverty and the absence of a father. Gunther was dead. He would have adored her, if he had lived to see how beautiful she was, and becoming more so every day. Any father would have; she would have melted his cold heart. Honey tendrils of hair curled about her oval face and round, sea-green eyes. Those eyes reminded Elfe of her own mother before the terrible accident. As a little girl, oh, it must have been in another life, she would gaze into those eyes, sitting on her mother's lap and blink at the different facets of green-yellow, sparkling colour. The pilot lights behind those eyes fed her internal flame. A trickle of tears now misted her own and her hand wiped them away. Curtain down, change scene. By the time her hand completed the motion she was back in the present. She looked at Josh and could see that he too was coming back from a trip.

The third floor walk-up was Spartan and cramped. The last tenant had left an old, brown sofa and a coffee table in the living room which doubled as the dining room. There was one bedroom. Kirsten slept in a second-hand bed.

The galley kitchen had a cracked, linoleum floor on which stood a grey-green pressboard table with chrome-metal legs. It was hard to believe that a designer would choose those colours. Did garish colours really cost less than tasteful ones? Four painfully bright, carmine, plastic chairs, also with metal legs completed the decor. To her they looked like raw, hairless animals. Elfe cringed at the memory of her parents' eclectic and elegant traditional furniture. Her parents would have been shocked and would have thought the crate she was living in, barbaric.

Her parents. She had been deeply troubled as to a name and a place for their final rest. Nothing remained to prove they had ever been. This hung like dumb grief, incoherent, trivial, considering the pain of their deaths, but somehow critically important. Their love had replicated itself in her bond with

Kirsten. An unbreakable link in an unbreakable chain, transcending all barriers, even death.

* * * * * *

Just before leaving Europe, Elfe found an old friend of her mother's, living in a dreary boarding house in Munich. Her husband, Carl, had returned from Russia with a chronic chest ailment and her son and daughter were in school. They had owned a small toy factory, now bombed into oblivion. Now, they were trying to manufacture new lives.

Greta was very kind. Their home was a dank and dirty, shabby domain in sharp contrast to the warm, well-lit, lovely apartment she had known as a child. Over a cup of ersatz coffee, she listened to Elfe's story, supporting her every decision. There was nothing left here to salvage — not for a long time. She wished her well and assured Elfe that she had made a wise decision.

That night Elfe stayed with the family, sleeping on a cot on the floor, little Kirsten snuggling in the hollow made by her fetal-positioned form. They shared a meager meal and Elfe poured out her feelings as they talked into the night.

In the morning, after a breakfast of bread and jam, Greta's son made a cross and she burned their names into it. The next day, she took it to the place where her home had once stood. Placing it in the firm earth, she laid them to rest. As she sifted her homeland's soil through her fingers, she wondered if her life would run out the same way.

Then, she boarded the Dutch steamer for America with little Kirsten and all her worldly possessions in two trunks. She surveyed Europe's coastline receding into the distance, knowing she would never return. Defiantly she raised a fist to the sky. As she turned her back to the past for the last time, her face was a white, soggy moon.

Elfe was saving money. Kirsten, two years old, stayed in a nursery with a woman who took care of six other children so it cost very little and she was able to work. Immediately after work, Elfe would pick Kirsten up and they would spend their evenings and weekends together, going to the park and sometimes dropping over at her aunt's house for Sunday dinner. It seemed like every time they went on those Sundays, Auntie summoned Elfe and Kirsten to her bedroom. There they would find heaps of clothes, shoes, bags and linens on the double bed; hand-me-downs from Auntie's rich sister whose own daughters had used and outgrown them. As Kirsten played on the floor with her choice of used yet pristine toys, Elfe rummaged. As a result, the child was a toddler fashion plate, starting with wool coats with Persian lamb collar and cuffs, and on to what would have been pricey dresses, blouses, sweaters, and shoes. Elfe even found a few things for herself, even though the entire idea of wearing someone else's clothes repulsed her. But the fur-lined wool coat and hood, she needed badly and wore with reluctance.

Slowly, surely, Elfe built a modest, comfortable life for the two of them. She learned to economize. She learned to sew when auntie gave her a Singer sewing machine. She knitted and crocheted so well that neighbours and acquaintances commissioned her to make tablecloths, layette sets, all of her own original designs. Her masterpiece was an ivory, crocheted wedding dress with an underlay of white satin. Puffed sleeves intersewn with bugle beads arranged as hearts and flowers matched the same delicate work in the bodice. She had worked nights to complete it.

When she examined her hands one day, they were those of a workman, worn, ugly, honest callused fingers. She was too tired to cry. She had had lovely hands, long and tapered; her mother's pride and joy. These had once been dainty, had worn white gloves to the theatre. These fingers had been kissed by gentlemen, had been flattered by them. These were vain hands, idle hands, evidence of an inborn aristocrat.

Frantically she creamed them with unguent lotions, and when that failed, they hid in her pockets. When she cooked, she glanced over them, around them, never at them. When she had to look at them she saw how her life's heavy artillery had run them over and debased them. She preferred not to see them, like a new generation preferred not to see the veterans of the Second Great War.

She was dying for some fun, to go out on dates like other young women. She was only in her early twenties. The last, and only, memories of sex was with Gunther, and they were sketchy and embarrassing to her now. Even awkward, humiliating sex was better than no sex at all! She realized she had been anaesthetized, apprehensive around men. She thought of her successes, her independence, her growing impatience. There had to be more.

What she did, she did well. Her cooking was good, yet simple and integrated the American traditions too, like apple pie. Hearty vegetable soups remained frequently in the diet, a holdover from postwar years. Like many who had known hunger, her pantry maintained its supply of canned foods and packages of biscuits "just in case."

She had changed from innocent child to exalted symbol of fertility to self-sufficient cavewoman and was still changing. She was a mother without ever having been a wife.

Her country had failed her and going on as a German in America would not do. The respect she had held for her heritage had disintegrated into nothingness, leaving her as an embarrassing symbol of evil she knew she was not. The documentaries on television wore away any sentiment she had somehow harboured, leaving her empty inside. She embraced her new land with open arms. She took night school and learned English. She studied hard and learned quickly, finishing at the top of her class. She would practice trying to sound like a Canadian, less like a German, the unfamiliar sounds warping her mouth until she wondered if it would look any different. She made new friends. And she never, never spoke in German again.

Her thoughts, most of the time, remained on the Western side of the Atlantic. She never would forget that day when they were wrenched across the ocean. Gisela was dead. The messenger of death in the innocent guise of an aged, kind-faced postman, had just delivered the envelope to her letter box as Elfe was about to go grocery shopping. With an air of detachment she had tripped up the narrow, dirty stairs and past the filthy, peeling walls marked with graffiti. She reheated the percolated coffee with chicory, and sat down to read the latest of those rare letters received from her homeland. And then the boiling, black cataract splashed over her rigid hands, scathing her.

Josh's written words were black shards in her stunned eyes. Killed instantly in a motor accident. She felt the blood drain from her body. A shriek of glee pierced her sadness. Little Kirsten had toddled over to the window and pressed her face and hands there to watch the descending snow.

The guilt. This terrible thing had happened because she had wished it. She wanted to phone her aunt, but she couldn't share such knowledge. They knew little of her past and certainly nothing of the Lebensborns.

In spite of herself, she stood and attempted to put her fractured thoughts together. For the sake of Kirsten, happily oblivious to the shabbiness, the poverty, Elfe nursed her stomach with a warm mug of milk. They lunched on mashed potatoes and cooked vegetables and Kirsten soothed her nerves.

In 1953, the two moved to a small, modest, cottage-style house in a lower-middle class neighbourhood. Elfe had greater financial security. Her aunt and uncle let her know that she was their sole heir to their successful business. She combined shrewdness in business and an artistic eye for quality with natural enthusiasm, making her an indispensible asset among business associates and customers.

Sitting over a cup of steaming coffee, Elfe leaned back in the soft, upholstered fauteuil and rested. Outside, the children played, chasing each other around the garden. Across from her sat Linda, thirty years old, pert and pretty with light blond hair tossed into a ponytail and large, brown, serious eyes. Her two little girls, seven and nine, were romping outside with seven year old Kirsten. Elfe sighed. "You have no idea how I enjoy these visits, even though we have known each other only a few, months. If not for that auction, we might never have met."

The up-and-coming interior decorator laughed. She studied her friend, who had all the markings of a complex personality. Superficially, she had the bearing of high breeding. Her tall, straight build and wide shoulders, the darkly intelligent, arched brows, as though perpetually lost in thought, the Greek, aquiline nose, tapering chin and long, swanlike neck. Elfe was like no one else she had encountered. Strains of Doris Day crooning the musical hit, "Lullaby of Broadway" lilted from the radio like springtime vespers. Her own lips moved to the decadent, simple words. Elfe was humming the tune with closed eyes. There was something elusive in the patrician, heart-shaped face that struck her as painfully guarded and it puzzled her. She collected stories, talking was her business. Elfe had resisted every inquiry. Perhaps she had been a Nazi — young women fought in the last days of the war. Anyway, whatever secrets this women held, they were not coming out easily. The gates to her past perhaps were slammed shut forever. Locked, boarded up, and decorated with a do-not-enter sign.

Where had the last seven years gone? She had studied and worked and struggled and endeavored to give Kirsten the best life she could. Today she had a cozy, little house and a thriving, happy child with a green sea for eyes and honeyed hair — who loved her.

Elfe had begun removing dinner dishes to the kitchen sink and Josh insisted on helping. The sound of water running mingled with their talk; Elfe handed him a dish cloth. Wisps of butter-coloured hair sprinkled her forehead and he suddenly had the impulse to brush them away with his hand, as he had often done for his long-lost sister, Sarah.

Elfe seemed to hesitate, choosing her words carefully, as if she didn't have much experience talking about herself. She flushed, looking slightly abashed at being centre stage. "I work hard at my aunt and uncle's antique store. They're good to me, Josh. I don't know what I'd do without them. I scrimp and save. I enjoy my work and I'm with people who care about us. They love Kirsten." She paused. "I count my blessings."

They became firm friends. On weekends when Josh was in the hospital or had to study, Thomas would spend his time at Kirsten's house where the two children rollicked, building odd-looking snowmen and sledding. Sometimes Elfe took them to the movies and being together became a habit.

On this January night of 1956, Josh was a bedraggled remnant of a vanishing race nobody wanted. He felt like a degraded victim and he bore it as a badge of dishonour.

Homeward bound, he trudged in the milky-opaque storm, ploughing the cumbersome snow, coaxing it in places for better footing, his legs stiffened oars, a long, grey scarf roped around his neck, blowing outward wildly like arms flailing, the strong, hawk-like Hebraic features of his ancestors set. Today was bitter-sweet.

In the maelstrom, he was a figure with a tangled existence, twisting through deadness, glared down on by the swollen, yellowy eyes of the streetlamps. In his arms he clutched a package like a prayer book. He couldn't wait to get home and open it.

Huddled, snowy figures fumbled past him, as he neared his walk-up apartment he wanted to cry out with joy and wave back to the trees nodding their approval as he rushed past.

Clashing thoughts tasted like foul ichor in his mouth. He was poor, alone — an outsider. There were occasional condescending generosities in the form of polite acknowledgements of his book in the papers and profit from it was just enough to cover expenses. Invitations to colleagues' homes for dinner were cordial, but nothing more. Everyone likes to

Chapter Fifteen

Toronto
January, 1956

know an author but who wants to talk to one? He lived in a world only he could see.

Each step he took was a page of his life, tattooed between the lines on his body. It was spelled out in outbursts. Startling were those eyes through which people he had known cried for release, revenge; he cried for release, forgiveness. In the senseless chaos of his life, he was a dedicated doctor who still cared deeply for suffering mankind. He understood the fragility of life and sanity.

His caring for his patients was not at odds with the desert that had become of his soul. As his hope dribbled away, he needed a place to put the remnants of everything that had been good about himself. He was seen as a gentle man, generous with everyone. Few people were able to get close enough to see that he spent his love foolishly on strangers rather than risk the returns that would come if he allowed friends to benefit from it. Indeed, he would treat a beggar on the street, or a stranger in the bank with more love than he would allow anyone who knew his name.

Somehow Tommie was exempted. The poor child was burdened with a worse fate than inattention. Josh saw himself in the tender eyes of the child. Yes, he was a German, but he too had known loss, his parents as well had been taken from him by the Nazis — somehow Josh held them responsible for Gisela's death, they had removed everyone and everything else from his life. Josh, in his paranoia, imagined that the driver of the car intentionally murdered Gisela for marrying a Jew. Josh had control over the boy; he could not become the enemy. Thomas, he treated with the love he had for the family he lost, for the hopes and dreams he had given up. For the boy, it wasn't too late. He also treated him to the hatred he had for himself and what had happened to him. The boy represented what had become of himself. The boy sometimes would stand there not knowing whether to run to him or to run away from him.

Josh deposited himself with great flair in his lair, dumping his damp wool coat on a chair in the shabby hall. The flipping on of the light switch jumped-started him into fiendish action at the frontier of his kitchen. Even in the cold apartment, he felt he was boiling, mopping his brow, brandishing the knife to cut the salami, then the fresh bagel. Mustard, he slathered like butter. He made coffee and the ecstatic chewing melted over his face and neck.

When he would feel himself sliding into depression he would eat until his stomach hurt and then, bloated, he would eat nothing the next day. After one of these binges he would lie in bed feeling like he would explode, leaving the wrappings and peels of vegetables and fruits mangled on dirty dishes left as though there had been a boa constrictor convention and not just a hungry Jew trying to escape the concentration camps.

He took his titanic feast: a loaf of bread, thick salami slices, sour pickles, coffee cake and a steamy mug of coffee to the living room and turned on the television — one of few extravagances he had allowed himself. News. It didn't matter what was on; it was there to remind him that it was the nineteen-fifties. There were satisfied gurgling noises as the food slid down his gullet.

Having digested, he snapped his senses to attention as if noticing the rangy abode for the first time. Unfamiliarity surrounded him. His face curled with twitches, pupils were dilated licorice drops giving him a sobering vision of a truth long gone. Frantically he looked about, the pleasurable sensation gone and the awareness of an upcoming flashback in its place.

A photograph of the home in Cracow and scenes of his childhood pleasant memories. It always started this way, as if the producer of his horror had a penchant for contrast. Then the fear and shame would come in, rolling over him like a tidal wave. Not quite in sync., his flashback would give him the sights and sounds of a happy childhood along with the fear, guilt and pain of the camps. Sometimes the flashbacks were sensations or displaced emotions with no fixed memory, sometimes events one sense at a time; a smell, a sound, a picture. Sometimes some or all were scrambled; a sound from here, a picture from there, an emotion from a different time. He would believe himself to be crazy. Othertimes, he would experience every emotion and sense at once, all from the same time. These times, he would not believe he was crazy, worse, he believed he was actually back there, that he was about to witness death, that he would die himself — or want to. He would lose memory of everything that happened after. He would relive the horror complete with the suspense.

After, he would come back to the nineteen-fifties. The sagging, brown upholstered sofa — his time machine — the ratty, threadbare broadloom, the cheap metal table and plastic chairs in the kitchen, for a moment they would all appear unfamiliar. It would make no difference. No success, no luxury could release him. He could have a mansion worth a million dollars. It would never make him feel rich inside.

The ghosts would invade his small apartment. There, standing on his cracked and worn linoleum stood a little girl holding a doll with amber hair. Her face white, her lips blue and her eyes bulging grotesquely, her mouth would open releasing bile and blood onto the floor. "Oh, my poor Sarah. I failed you. Forgive me." His head slipped into his hands. He would cry out but the apparition would continue the play, reaching out a bloody hand to a second young girl, this one naked and bleeding from the side of the head, appeared from nowhere. "Rachel, forgive me." Both girls would stand there holding hands shaking their heads in condemnation until they disappeared. He would stare at where they stood; at the stains they left behind.

Later he would get down on his knees and try to clean the floor but the stains could not be removed. Josh complained asking for the flooring to be replaced but the landlord refused saying that he had accepted the apartment like that, "What do you expect for forty-five dollars a month?" Would he like to move to a more expensive flat?

The next day he would go into work afraid that his co-workers would discover why he had gone into psychiatry — the panic the discovery of his secret would cause. His truth would make them face their own reasons. Yeah, the hypocritical oath — that it was about the good of mankind, to help others. No wonder psychiatrists are such selfish people to work with.

This night an Angel of deliverance, a neighbour, knocked. He was out of coffee. Could he borrow some? Of course. Control was back. He rummaged through his overstocked pantry. There it was. Maybe a tin of sardines, or can of soup? He had more than enough. No? Well, here's the coffee. Food was stacked so high, that the citadel came rumbling down. It had to be rearranged, anyway. Ah, the Campbell's soups, the yummy cereals, chocolate chip cookies to be gobbled two at a time. And the freezer — fish sticks, chicken breasts, and oolala! Thomas' tutti fruiti, butter pecan, slobbery delectable morsels, double chocolate, icecream sandwiches. He would never, never go hungry again. If only he could show the neighbour something that would interest him, keep him there another thirty seconds. The poor confused man retreated clutching his hard-won prize.

Josh glanced around. His other extravagance was the proliferation of books that lined the walls, decorating wall shelves in the bedrooms. Only the finest, they were carefully chosen — Chekhov, Tolstoy, Dostoyevsky, Sholohov — replacements for the novels he had owned. They had been his companions long ago. Now they were the only life-long friends he could claim. For Thomas, he had begun a fine library of Charles Dickens, Mark Twain and Robert Louis Stevenson — lovely, hard-covered collectors' editions. Tonight maybe he could run away into someone else's fantasy. His demons were chasing him around the apartment, while he searched for a loyal friend to save him.

Splatterings of memory took form. They squared and arched to become the rooms of his familial home in Cracow. As each disassociated detail focused, the past confirmed the hold it had over him.

They reorganized to form the packed-to-bursting, human cargo of the dead, nearly dead, and scared to the point of insanity, living. The stench of morbidity dizzied him and occluded his breathing. Again, he was on the cattlecar to Dachau.

Hysterically he writhed and groped for a way out of hell, but he couldn't break the bolts of Nazi steel that locked him. Round and round he went, on derailed tracks, spinning his psychological wheels, embalmed in the anger that poisoned the blood and fueled more nightmares. No universal description of Hell is authentic. Not flames and pitchforks, Hell is custom-made.

The child, Rachel was there again. The child who was his sister's playmate and best friend. He had known her all her life. On discovering that she and he were in Dachau, she watched over him and sneaked him scraps of food — potato peels, carrot bits, a red beet slice — from the kitchen where she worked. How she took care of him, never complaining, offering him the hope he did not have, her soft presence, a truly holy thing.

And then the SS, discovered the relationship, ordered him to defile her with a public rape in full view of the prisoners. Josh, as though smitten with an iron fist, tremored his negation, aghast. The SS thundered; there would be hell to pay!

The dainty girl, who believed in the basic goodness of men, was brought to the centre of the square, uncomprehending. The square fell silent. The SS grew impatient. The place felt hot and close like a massive runny ulcer. The wind delivered a multi-sensory awareness of the decomposing cadavers and their sweet stench poured over the square, over the vacant-eyed prisoners. His body had become a weapon with which to kill his soul along with hers. Overcome by the smell, the heat and the stench he collapsed face first into the dust. An SS officer put a booted foot into the small of his back and wrenched his head up by the hair so that he could see.

The detestable, mutual rape was walked through in a red haze, by another prisoner, Samuel. For Josh, it was as though a pistol were forced down his throat and his mind was concentrating on winding his tongue around the trigger in order to spare himself the continuance of the unendurable, caged pain that raced in him.

Rachel was thus degraded, in her miserable rags and shaved head. The poor inmate Samuel was tied to a post and shot. The next day, when Josh again refused to degrade her, they shot her. The ripping horror of the enactment exploded all of him too, with only a bare shell remaining. His guilt willing him to die was juxtapositioned maniacally with an equal, hateful desire to survive, to see the monsters before him, defeated.

Failing in his summons as a stretching of the enemy's blasphemous arm, he had inadvertently aided wickedness, lacking the objectivity that nothing could have saved Rachel. Forever he would feel a disdain for his impotence — shame and guilt stained him permanently.

Now he was to remain. To remember. Were these enactments sourced in his confused mind his only reason for being? When he died would they die a second time?

In contrast with his weakness, how she had carried herself. She had gone to the post with head held high. The specks of glowing tears that freckled her face unashamedly, turned beams of lights on the cowardice and arrogance of the SS, who cringed as their moment was spoiled by a child who grew tall in the face of death, whose courage was greater than her fear, who composed a horrendous beauty that spread over the camp.

Where all present were assembled to learn an SS lesson in discipline, she emerged the hero. Her eyes near the end, were distracted yet dewy, as though her oppressors were already forgotten, as though she could see what no one else could.

In a dimension where space and time posed no barriers, he found himself inside the core of a wasp's nest — all evilly black and buzzing. His ears smacked and he saw they were actually charred bodies, the size of flies, who swarmed on torn wings. This is maddening, an inner voice told him, as delirium paralyzed his eyes, glazing them over like weird honey pots. He couldn't move as they squashed themselves in droves to him. He thrashed about till he heard their high pitched drone and realized that it was a whistling, shrieking wind winding up his voice box and he awakened bathed in his own cold sweat.

All the suffering, gobbled up children — roasted in ovens — haunted him. They lived only in him, they were dead everywhere else. He felt guilty for wishing they would leave him in peace.

He went to Thomas' darkened room. The lamplit hallway flung wavering, floating ochre wings of light that appeared like swallows alighting on the seamless, navy-black of his bed, wall, ceiling. Thomas, oblivious to his father's presence, turned and sighed, a happy child adrift in the pond of his dreams.

Thomas must not know that his progenitors had taught that murder was a sport. That any life was worthless.

There was no denying that there were evenings he couldn't face without liquor, when he felt he was dying from a slow poison. This was one of them. When clarity of mind came too quickly, a shot of whiskey, or two or three, drowsed him, anaesthetized his nerves — a quick fix and he became less precariously desolate.

He sat staring at the television long after he had turned it off, a drink in his trembling hand. His skin was hot and his thoughts clung like pungent steam and ringed his closed eyes.

Silence inundated the room like a faint and exhausting sound. In the building, doors slammed, feet tread, people laughed. It came from a distance in muffled, discordant notes. He wandered unsteadily into his room and lay down. Even his own footfalls were echoes. A record played undistinguishable music, a child whined, a fishy odour wafted through the walls, all receding in lambswool rolling away. He yawned and his thinking slurred as the door to consciousness slammed shut.

* * * * * *

On a day blighted by sleet-slashed roads, it was a blue-cheeked sky that was puffing on sick lungs. Josh's innermost desires had been relegated to hibernating in their own wasteland. A pleasant, Sunday lunch at Dr. Steinberg's home promised exactly the kind of diversion Josh needed. A picture of the squat, portly doctor curved his lips into a smile. He was a kind gentleman who never failed to exchange pleasantries while passing in hospital corridors and for months, the two snatched meals together.

The picture had been painted with pride-filled oratory. The house, his gem, beautified a steep ravine. It was a must to see, one of the wonders of Dr. Steinberg's world. It had made him a tiller of the soil, brought him closer to G-d. He planted trees and called them his little ones. Their height was measured with the same tape he had used when his children were growing thirty years earlier. Even his synagogue had been chosen according to the proximity to his home, just so he could enjoy and care for it appropriately. When Josh disclosed in brief, the tragedies of his life, the good doctor shed a few tears. It was true, his family had largely been spared, but a beloved aunt and her children had gone the way of the crematoria.

There was a positive sprint in Josh's step that morning. He took extra care in getting shaved and dressed. How he longed for a Jewish taste of family life. He felt happier than he had in years. Artistic dabs into the Old Spice, tie tied to the point of strangulation. Thomas was at the movies with school friends and a sleepover. Josh was off in his car.

The wife greeted him warmly with a hug at the door of the attractive, sidesplit house. An engaging lady that, to him, was achingly reminiscent of aunties and other relations from Poland. The garden indeed dropped to a ravine and the bedroom windows did have an amazing view.

Dr. Steinberg offered a glass of red Manischewitz wine and spoke benignly about the history of the house, from behind his hornrimmed specs perched low on his ample and imperious-looking nose. Josh luxuriated in the Jewish familiarity, not that they were particularly religious — merely traditional. How he had missed any semblance of haimish flavour in his life.

The sunken living room, moon-shaped, with white, custom-made sofas, was voluptuously sumptuous. He was served red wine so sweet, it could have been frozen, cut, and distributed as candy condiment. His uvula twitched and heaved as more of the syrup was pressed on him so politely, that he had no choice but to let glass after glass refill his hyperglycemic gullet.

Somehow, in the slurring of speech and dulling of vision, their daughter, Luba, came into focus. A langorous collection of fat stuffing... She was homely. The adipose tissue had to make do with the short, squat body, lumping itself shapelessly in fallen breasts and bulging thighs and edemous ankles. Trapped, in her company, he made every effort to be kind, but not overly so. Pity. She was a pity to behold. Her black satin dress was an entreaty to the bereavement, and obviously so, to the state of old maidenhood she would soon endure, if a man, any man, did not rescue her. The doom bell was ringing, ever so loudly between his ears: save me, words like a metal mallet beat, save me, the jelly lady with mouse-coloured eyes begged. Oh, how the jiggling and beating hurt his head. For all of her at least thirty-five years.

Unsteadily they headed to the mahogany dining room for lunch, he, crutched on her padded arm. Between the last course, sweet-baked noodles in cinnamon, and dessert, the atmosphere was one of synthetic cheerfulness. He sat there sauced, nursing his constantly refilled glass and evaluated the most unnubile Luba through nascent hostility. Did he know she had a steady, well-paying job in a travel bureau? She had travelled extensively, spent summers in the finest resorts. In fact, this year they could all go together to the Catskills. Wasn't that nice? He nearly choked when she said she went there because it was family oriented and so she could enjoy the children. She just loved children!

A vortex of nausea whirled in him. The earlier pleasantness had been a sham. They were matchmaking. He fumed at their Colgate commercial smiles, at the ruse.

It became too close and he couldn't wait to leave. Rubber burned on the way home. What kind of fool did they take him for? Trying to peddle second rate wares off on him — a doctor! He kicked his ancient car in anger when he reached home. That those thick legs, as heavy as stone pillars could actually entice him! That he'd crawl into her hole! They took him for a tank of hormones with no brains. His anger percolated and he was about to boil over. What, did they think he was so inexperienced, so provincial, he didn't know good merchandise? That he was a little ghetto Yiddel?

Josh had hardly been in his apartment fifteen minutes, when a car drove up and Luba was at his door. With a grin as wide as a train tunnel, she was bestowing on him, the jacket he forgot — and herself. He didn't know what to do. After all, her family had been gracious hosts. "Would you like to come inside?"

"Uh, well, all right, mm, maybe for a few minutes." She was blushing and it was most unbecoming. As she stepped into the living room, she spotted a baseball mitt. "Your son's?" They chatted about baseball, school. Why didn't she just go?

Later, he wouldn't be certain what exactly triggered his wrath, made him lose control. Was it her direct question as to his romantic life and her pressing the matter. "If you're not serious about anyone, then maybe we could take in a movie or..." Luba moved a little closer to him on the sofa. She gently touched his arm. He could feel her fingers running up and down. What the hell! He made a swift move, grabbing her ample waist and cupping a gelatinous, warm and satiny breast in one hand. And dumbfounded found himself splattered on top of her as she pulled his head to her face. At first, he couldn't extricate himself, her hold was so strong and unbelievable — Miss Goody-Goody? And then ensued a primeval, meaningless, dirty dance of groin on groin, as they fumbled at underwear, ignominious in its execution. The kiss she had puckered for, was rejected as he flung her back, separating her legs. Panties were torn and with lecherous abandon he drove into her over and over, onward at a galloping pace. A half hour passed. She shuddered, cried out, "Please stop." He was a contortionist gone insane in a fit of complete abandon. As he came in loud exhortations, he refused to retract his organ until it was delectably as hard as bone again.

She remained jammed against the sofa helplessly straddled as flesh tore flesh and he writhed and pulsed and dug deeply inside her as though she were a subterranean mine. Her nipples were chewed raw and started to bleed. And then, deflated, emptied, he crumpled in a heap on the floor. "You filthy sonofabitch," came garbled to his ears through a fog of bleary lids which flipped like loose tent flaps over his bloodshot eyes. He was awfully sick but nothing would come, until a feral scream regurgitated the fine lunch turned sour slop onto the floor which he was scratching like a dog at his food bowl.

When she left, he wasn't sure. But the sun had set for it had brandished its redness on him briefly, even on him, a ragweed. He lay expended and imagined himself back in the cave. Just around the corner it always waited, a memory field, a sink hole. Now he was inside it, too tired to crawl out. Too tired to care. Ashamed and riddled with self-loathing, he lay in his own filth until he was sober.

In lucid, terrible reassessment of the Sunday fiasco, undistorted, Luba became a tactile symbol of his current self. She was a floundering whale, upstream, in a pathetic half life without the support of the proverbial "better half." In some acceptable way in his mind, he saw they were both searching for someone to love.

Their spirits were wilting from waiting — they were orphans till love would condescend to direct its wondrous, soul-feeding gaze upon them.

* * * * * *

New Year's, 1958, rolled in on a sudsy medley of champagne bubble bursts, fuzzy recollections, and roaring hangovers. The morning after found Josh stranded in a Toronto hotel, glassy-eyed and nursing a gritty tongue while listening to his hungry stomach growl, even though the thought of food made him sick. His brain clambered to get itself into gear. He then lurched to the unfamiliar bathroom, vomited, then turned on a cold, cold shower. Ah, it was all coming back. Double trouble. Doctors and their damn parties! The hospital staff had organized the dinner dance in the banquet room. Women wore strapless black numbers, men black tie. The crowded, overheated room seethed with alcohol-shed inhibitions and bodies gyrating to cha-chas, tangos and racing hormones.

The food was good, the company pleasant, although in the towering Babel of voices, conversation was drowned out. When people got up to dance, a redhead appeared swathed in a haze of tobacco smoke. He hated cigarette smokers, their yellow teeth and foul breath. Yet here was this va-va-voom creature slinking over to him and into his chair. "Light my fire," came provocatively through, loud and clear. He coughed appreciatively, "And it isn't even my birthday."

Cloudy circles enveloped them as they drank and talked. She was a receptionist in one of the doctor's offices, she shared an apartment with a friend, wasn't this party fun...? Boy was she dumb. He did note that her boobs danced in the long V-cut of the velvet dress. She followed his eyes. "Doc, (you don't mind if I call you that, do you?)" She giggled foolishly. She's a goddamn moron, he thought. "A friend and I just got back from Florida. I have a sister there..." The rest was lost on him until, with a start, he felt her hand press against his thigh and move upward and realized it held her hotel key.

He thought, in a liquefaction of emotions, dizzying from the narcotic-like stupor of alcohol, that he could do a lot better, that he would prostitute himself if he bedded a bimbo who picked men up. In the dim light, she glowed like cheap, dyed tinsel. That they would be in the same room as each other, struck him as ridiculous. Cantilevered over each other, they jollied their way to the nameless girl's room. His libido was so suddenly urgent, so hot, it felt like coagulating sap coursing through his veins. Sirens of alarm screamed between his ears in chaotic, unreadable messages. Josh was horny to high heaven. He could read that message from his panicking synapses singing their inebriated song.

What delectation ensued, a sumptuous feasting of flesh on flesh, his teeth ivory keys playing her sexual chords, shorn of all shame, galloping in whooping, groaning frenzy. He let out a roar when he entered and partook of her breasts like two dumplings in a Sabbath soup, chewing in a fracas, every miniscule inch of her, like freshly baked bread. Her buttocks may as well have been two coffee cakes right out of the oven. When they came, in howls and shrieks, he turned her over and kneaded her rump into a roast, until their mutual orgiastic convulsions turned to unsubsiding horror, for Ms. X, as she wished to be called, had not reckoned on his dangerous take-off from sanity.

Ah, what Jewish cuisine she was, he salivated in utter delirium as he munched on her neck, licked behind her ears voicing the gutturals of a wolfman. Her anguish replaced joy. Limbs stiffened. The fornication turned bloody, as he tramped over her and she bit on her own lip and tasted blood.

During the fantastical dawn, when he went to piss in the sink — She could see him through the open bathroom door — she fled in tatters and fear.

The slide into athletic, carnal madness left him weirdly bereft, perplexed, troubled, and compellingly self-accursed. Self-revulsion faced him in the mirror as an enemy he didn't know, glared back. He shook in a feverish rapture of disgust, hurling foaming obscenities. He lurched to the shower, turned it to cold but couldn't disentangle himself from the chalky reflection staring at him in the mirror. He smirked stupidly back. He hated that monster and so he spat and then recoiled like a snake from the detestable image, crying hoarsely, "Go away, go away."

Breaths came faster, harder, the allegorical mountain he was climbing was higher. He grappled with the sink for balance. The slippery surface was sleek Alpine stone whose summit he could not reach. If he fell, it would be to the bottom of the earth, alone, where no one could save him. On bended knee, he rasped, his heart roaring violently against ribs, "Help me out of this ruinous life." Raucous disjointed thoughts swayed and rushed with electric fury. Josh was seething inside. Boiling his flesh in oil was the least he deserved. Sorrow swept through him in waves with the swift, sobering currents of contempt and wild bewilderment at what he had done. He lifted halting hands to his face and then rushed into the tub as if to a waiting friend with kind answers. But what greeted him was a steely pummeling ice bath that drained him totally, leaving only blinding bright emotional emptiness.

Afterwards, he collapsed into an armchair, where he briefly dozed and was frighteningly seized in a twisting, churning dream of mud and rocks sliding in a dust bath and he helplessly falling yet reaching for a multitude of children's hands growing out of that disintegrating mountain, ever just out of his grasp, the sounds of children's cries high yet muted, as though trapped in shattering glass embedded in his heart. Pulled ever faster away from the smoggy image, berserk and baffled, he awoke with a crash, his shirt soaked with new sweat, on the floor, the overturned chair on top of him, in stupefying disorientation. His profession was a holy thing, his hands were for healing, giving comfort. But the lion in him had become unleashed; it roared, charged — grew stronger than him. He could only do his best to keep the beast at bay.

The phone rang and rang. Nobody bothered to answer its harsh notes as it broke the calm in the dimly-lit, somber atmosphere of the apartment. Finally, they both made a dash for it, Josh got the receiver first and Thomas went back to his homework.

"Hello... yes..." and then a sudden "WHAT!" Thomas dropped his pen and ruler startled, running into the room to see what happened. Josh cupped the receiver with his hand and excitedly, said, "Tommie, someone knows your Aunt Sarah — my sister — my little sister Sarah. She's alive! I was so sure I had lost her in the war. Is it possible?"

"Dad, get all the details." Thomas was handing his father a pen and paper, while Josh screamed into the phone.

"I'm shocked! You spoke to my sister?"

When Josh finally put the receiver down, he had changed. He grabbed Thomas tightly in his arms and hugged him. "My sister — your aunt — the dearest person to me in the whole world — is alive!"

Josh and Thomas sat down. Thomas' mouth was gaping. "How?"

"Our Canadian cousins, the ones who've ignored us all these years, were recently in Israel. They inquired at the organization of camp survivors of Cracow to see the lists of those who had survived and immigrated to Israel after the war. There they discovered that Sarah, their first cousin, is alive, married, and living in Rishon le Zion."

Josh sat right down and composed a letter to Sarah. He seemed to have been brought back to life and the modest apartment vibrated with a new-found vigor. Ten days later, came the reply. A photo fell out of the envelope. Josh's hands shook as he read the letter.

My dearest brother!

G-d gave you back to me! If only I had known you were alive. A part of me died during the last years of the war. I felt so guilty and unworthy. Why me to live and you and mama and papa to die? But this is a moment of rejoicing and I cannot tell you what I feel in my heart. That little girl of eleven you last saw is no more. I'm a twenty-eight-year-old married woman and the mother of the love of our life, a girl of nine we called Ayelet.

So much has passed since we last met, that I don't know where to begin. But I must begin with the saddest time of my life, a permanent shadow on my soul. When mama and papa entered the ghetto, they tried to save me. It was unspoken, but we wondered if you even were alive.

I faced our parents' death while hidden away. I was at the brave Jasinskis. G-d let no harm befall such good people.

When I knew our parents had died a vile and horrible death, at least they had joined the same earth beneath the same sun that embraced the fallen, mighty tree and strangers who, after all is said and done, are one in the eyes of the Lord. This gave a small measure of comfort.

I never saw anything in the same way ever again. I would see everything with the intensity of a hundred riveting eyes. I knew if I'd hate, I'd slowly turn to a cold and barren stone. It was a furious acknowledgement, that I too, could become a brute bent on vengeance. That I too could learn the fanatic language of the enemy. Rather, I gave myself that singular important lesson, to never love without pain, nor hate without pity.

I greet each day knowing I have my husband's kiss and there is wind waving my child's hair. I worship all this. And I wonder, if tragedy had not been so great, would I be flooded with so great a love?

At times I had felt that the weight of my sadness was so heavy it would collapse the ground and bury me far under the earth. But the tides of life that delivered tragedy, also brought Ayelet to me — a raven-haired angel in abundant joy on wings of renewal and promise. She is the beating of my heart, my consolation, my humility, my purpose in being.

My husband, Henry, I met while in hiding. He is my best friend and my family. And a dedicated physician. I have leaned on his strength, on his sweetness and gentleness. Henry and I are one soul, one love. One great gift to each other.

Enough of singing praises. I want you all to meet.

From your letter (I read between the lines) you sound so lonely. I'm so sorry about Gisela. To die so young and for Thomas to be denied a mother. Next year Thomas, the nephew I didn't know I had, will be bar mitzvahed. We want Thomas to have his bar mitzvah in Israel. It would mean so much to us. Ayelet was so excited when she heard about Thomas. Please come. I want to meet my nephew. It's been too long.

Write me soon with your answer. Kisses and love,
Your loving sister,
Sarah.

"Oh dad, can we really?" Thomas asked. "I've been going to Sunday school for three years and I'm good."

Josh was glad that he had sent his son to Sunday school, to have the cantor himself teach him. It had been costly, but worth it. The idea of a bar mitzvah in Israel would mean so much to all of them. In the months that followed, Thomas studied his lessons with a renewed fervor. They made plans and when Josh told Elfe she was happy for them. When the time came, she went to the airport to see them off. They boarded an Air Canada flight to New York and then flew El Al to Tel Aviv.

On the eve of their departure, Thomas received a Bible which he was to keep for the rest of his life from the Adath Israel Synagogue where he studied the Hebrew level necessary for him to read from the Torah. He had learned well. He knew the reading and the rhythm.

After a long night's flight, they arrived at Lod Airport to a typically hot June morning. As Josh and Thomas walked out of the terminal to a throng of people waiting for friends, Josh saw his little sister, Sarah, coming towards him. He winced in irresistibly pleasurable anguish. He embraced her, burying his face in her mahogany hair, suffusing himself in time-suspended rapture. The pages of his life flipped back, way back.

Josh had barely noticed the man with the compassionate eyes, looking on nearby. Henry led them, insisting on carrying the luggage, to his waiting Dodge. "Sarah just couldn't come. I think emotionally, it would have been too much." Henry, glancing in the rear view mirror as he drove, spoke with such understanding that Josh felt completely comfortable with him. "She wanted to stay home and get used to the idea that you two would finally be here, on our soil."

Thomas added, "You should have seen Dad as we were landing. Wow, then it really hit home, you know, that it wasn't just a dream."

Henry looked Israeli as did Ayelet. Both were tanned, very healthy and robust. Henry wore jeans and short sleeves and Ayelet sported a long ponytail. She was bouncy, aggressive and eager to practice her English on Thomas. Josh said little during the short twenty-minute drive to Rishon le Zion.

Soon they arrived at the bungalow, cast in the crowning glory of a mid-morning sun. That poets had deemed heaven to be a blue island proved true, for from out of a heart-stopping splash of powdered blue sky, came the quickening, so familiar foot taps. Josh was afraid to look, afraid if he did, if he reached out, the illusion would disappear. Then he caught a glimpse of a figure running down the garden path and into his arms as if she had sped from the ends of the earth for them to be hurled together.

They hung on as though standing on the edge of a precipice, sure of death if they dared let go, hearts pounding. Older but still Sarah; older but still Josh.

Josh and Thomas were in the house being introduced to a typical Israeli breakfast turned gala affair, and then some. "Aunt Sarah," Thomas gasped. "I don't think Dad and I can eat all this."

Ayelet broke into a charming fitful of giggles and Thomas stared at her quizzically, as Henry clattered about in the kitchen. Sarah couldn't restrain herself and chuckled, "I guess we overdid it." Their eyes and noses waltzed over the aromatic and colourful array. Fresh pumpernickel, yoghurt, heavy bouquets of vegetable salads of every variety, chopped into small pieces and mixed in oil; plates of sour herring, sardines, and Sarah delivering hot egg omelettes in mushrooms. As they all sat down, Thomas' stomach gave a happy rumble. Glasses clinked endless toasts, plates were passed around and easy chatter ensued amidst not-so-sober bursts of laughter from Ayelet and Thomas. When Josh and Thomas were certain they would explode, coffee and cake were brought in.

Later Sarah and Henry showed them their garden. The modest house took on a fairytale aura nestled within the dense fruit trees of pear, orange and avocado. They showed off the vegetable patch of potatoes, tomatoes, carrots, cucumbers, zucchinis and green peppers. But the flowers — these were Sarah's pride and joy. Rose bushes of red, white and pink blossomed profusely. It was a small Garden of Eden. "Food supplies cannot meet the needs of the growing population," Sarah said to Josh as they walked about her mini-orchard. "We're so fortunate to have a house and garden. We use a barter system with the neighbours. We give them avocado and pears, whatever they don't grow and they give us eggs and chicken. There's rationing here because Israel is still a new struggling country."

"Would you like to see the town?" Ayelet looked directly at Thomas, eager to show off her new, Canadian cousin to her friends. And off they went.

The next door neighbours, Haim and Tova, dropped by to say hello and stayed for coffee. There was small talk, politics inevitably, since it was a brief two years after the Sinai campaign. Sarah and Tova talked of their volunteer work for Wizo, which operated daycare centres for the poor who had no one to leave their small children with during the day.

Tova said, "Sarah and several other women who own houses bring fruits, vegetables, anything we can to these poor homes.

Some of these people live in terrible apartments. All these children have ever known, is misery and deprivation. It means so much that we can do something."

Finally, sister and brother, sitting on the gently swaying porch swing had each other to themselves. The time apart had been so long; at first they didn't know what to say. They were so close and yet so far apart. They wanted to reveal everything and yet both held back.

Sarah had filled out into full womanhood and she looked, to Josh, like a sabra — tanned, self-confident, healthy — not like the delicate, fragile, quiet little Polish girl he had known, light years ago. Good health radiated from her like a golden halo. Snowy-white teeth gleamed in sharp contrast to tanned skin and black eyes shone like highly polished diamonds. Her thick, ebony hair, tied back in a ponytail, gave an interesting symmetry to the strong curves of her long neck and the proud, bold profile of her prominent nose. She was a twenty-eight-year-old woman who could never be unnoticed in a crowd.

"We've been through some tough years, haven't we, Sarah." Josh looked at the peace and serenity in Sarah's little Eden. "How inviting the garden looks!" he said with a sigh.

Sarah smiled to him. "A real home has been created here. I wouldn't ever want to leave it." Such a look of contentment crossed her face, a contrast with the stark reality of his own life was unavoidable. He envied her, but he didn't begrudge her anything. Sarah's eyes followed Josh's.

"Josh, we planted everything here with our bare hands. I would say to Henry 'Over there we'll plant orange trees, there pear trees and there, in the sun, the rose bushes.' I wanted every colour of roses, pink, white, red and I planted them in such a way Ayelet could see them from her bedroom window and smell their fragrance and at night, hear the whispery rustle of the trees. I wanted desperately to become attached to things, material things, I could call my own. Something I could see and touch and know is really mine.

"Since we first moved here I remind myself that I have freedom of choice with my life. If I build, I have; if I plant, I reap. I'm a free human being with all human rights. I could never, ever, live any other way, again." Sarah sounded confident and secure as she sat surrounded by all she and Henry had built together. Her eyes were shining. Again, he noted the extraordinary resemblance between mother and daughter.

He let himself luxuriate in the painted canvasses of Sarah's existence. A smile crossed his face. He thought of Elfe, for she would have seen a house in a sea celebrant of life and peace. She would have loved this place. Plump roses sailed through the wavy grasses, floating up the walls, blowing perfume that smoldered with seduction. Pluck me, inhale me and dare not be inspired by romantic notions. His sister had used a most beautiful palette — a positive imagination, guided by love and courage.

This was not the chaotic picture gallery he kept framed in his mind. Confronting him again and again, from the depths of an immense pit was a boneyard of fleshless people in all manner of posturing, human branches groping upward in extremis — a dark mountain range extending for miles. "I died in the holocaust, in the fires of the ovens, and I was buried in those pits," he wanted to say to Sarah. The words roared in his ears dancing as if they were cardboard in a wind, and fell, impotent and dry, on his silent lips.

She detected the utter despair, the starvation and degradation he had known. She gleaned it from pieces of him; a fresh horror in his eyes. He was an icehouse of dread things that she feared would pour from him as a fountain of life's blood, if he ever let them go. It would take a special woman to be a willing receptacle, to receive so great a personal responsibility. No one other than an angel, could answer such a calling.

They regarded each other with a leaning of eyes, hardly breathing, held together by the links of their ancestry, by the names of their parents, of blessed memory.

She was anxious to help him. "I have something irreverent to confess — I supposed I ought to be ashamed." She glanced away. "I challenged G-d when I thought I'd never find you. I told Him He was too selfish in snatching the best away for Himself. And I said, He had our parents and that was enough. I was left behind. I said that until my death, I could not forgive Him." She turned to him as sharp as lightning, "My heart knew I wouldn't lose you. I didn't always listen."

Josh's head spun. Who was this woman of such courage and maturity? "I wish I had been here for you."

"Oh Josh," she said hugging him, "what counts is that my prayer was answered." She had the expression of a girl again, soft and surrendering.

Words ached in his throat, unarticulated. The sensation of long, lonely, bitter years coming to an end, was overwhelming.

Two days later, bright and early on the Saturday morning of the bar mitzvah, the one hundred and twenty guests consisting of acquaintances of Henry and Sarah and old friends Josh knew from Cracow, assembled at nine in the morning in the synagogue on Rothschild Street.

Ayelet had slept over at a friend's house and Thomas and Josh used her room. "Girls! Yuk." Thomas had said as they had gotten into her pink painted bed, gazed at her pink painted walls and turned out the light of her pink frilly lampshade. Several dolls smiled at them from a chair in the dark. Their pillowcases had pink crocheted trim and hand embroidery. It was an oppressively frilly, silly, feminine, doll-infested, ribbons-and-lace boudoir whose bold feminine statement did not diminish even in the dark while they slept. The frilly-edged sheets tickled and the heavily sweet scented rose sachets dispersed abundantly throughout the room, had both Josh and Thomas sneezing.

"I couldn't take two weeks of this," Thomas said, lying on his back in the middle of the night.

There was a hushed motionlessness as the services began. And then it was Thomas' moment. Proudly, he read from the Torah and then the Rabbi spoke to the congregation, he said full of emotion, "This is no ordinary bar mitzvah." He paused meaningfully and gazed at these people whom he had known for many years. There was a hushed silence as all eyes rested on him. "I feel that all assembled should know the history of this family, of their enormous losses, of finding each other only recently, of how they were at all able to survive the Holocaust.

"It is a time," the rabbi went on to say in his deeply resonant voice, "to honour the Horowitz and Reichman parents who perished, whose lives were so tragically cut short.

"It is also a time to honour those two brave Christian families, the Jasinskis and the Bolewskis, who at great risk to themselves, and their families, found it in their heart, to change the course of these lives who would otherwise not be all here today. These people, all of them, must never be forgotten. The memories of them must never diminish." His voice broke, guests shed tears. So many of them sat there, lost in memories they normally suppressed since it hurt too much to remember.

A day of sorrow and a day of rejoicing. The rabbi bestowed on Thomas another Bible and just after noon, in the blistering heat, the lightly clad guests went to Sarah's house for the reception.

The garden had become transformed. On the lawn stood several picnic tables that Henry and several of his friends, one a carpenter, had built with wooden planks from a lumber yard. There were three long tables with attached benches.

"For three days a horse and wagon delivered planks to the house and it took five men to put it all together," Henry told Josh.

The lunch was buffet style, consisting mainly of cold cuts, a salads, sandwiches, Swedish meatballs, and a rainbow variety of cakes and cookies, all prepared by Sarah, Ayelet and their friends. Red and white wine flowed freely, courtesy of the Carmel Winery, plus brandy and liquors. Homemade falafel in pita was also served. Wine glasses clinked together in hearty toasts.

The sun went down and many guests departed for home. Sarah had made a point of inviting people whom she met yearly at the gathering of survivors of Cracow. It was a particularly emotional experience for Josh; the last time he had seen them was before the war.

The next day Henry took the family to see the sights. They drove first to Tel Aviv. Josh was charmed by the main street, Dizengoff, known as "The little Paris," with its sidewalk cafés and quaint boutiques. They later drove to Asaf Harofeh, the barracks-style army hospital where Henry delivered babies. Here Josh met Henry's colleagues.

As they strolled side-by-side along the hospital grounds, Josh said, "I couldn't help comparing the open friendliness and warm camaraderie of an Israeli hospital to the more formal attitude and colder atmosphere I've experienced in Toronto."

Henry pondered a moment. "We're all Jews on the staff, we have a feeling of belonging. We value each other. You won't find too many religious Israelis, most don't even bother to adhere to tradition. It's a casual life here — the way we dress, for instance, the way we think."

Solemnly Josh added, "At least here one is liked or disliked for himself and not because of his race."

"Maybe so, but there's a price to pay. It's a hard, hard life, Josh." The men walked on in silence, each in his own private thoughts.

Standing at the top of the mountain, looking down to the sea, Haifa, known as "Little San Francisco" was breathtaking. But it was Jerusalem that Josh fell in love with. There she stood, atop a region of broken hills of Judea, 2,500 feet above sea level. The sun fell like golden rain as they approached the city of the seven hills.

First they visited the Old City and then the New City. The two and a half mile long and thirty-eight foot high walls made the Old City look like a fortress. Single file they made their way through the network of cobblestone alleys and the souks, bargaining for souvenirs. Since 1948, the Old City and the suburbs east and northeast of the city walls belonged to the Hashemite Kingdom of Jordan. Donkeys and camels plodded through the alleys too narrow for cars. There were Arabs in loose, flowing robes alongside Westerners wearing the latest fashions. The population of New Jerusalem had doubled since the State of Israel was established in 1948. New suburbs were spreading like a pink-layered cake over the hills.

Josh was conscious of the very heart of Judaism. It appeared to reside in depthless meditation and prayer, enrobed in majestic light, strawberry against the coral and grey stones of the buildings built from pink "Jerusalem" stone blasted from the Judean hills.

Apartments were beseechingly braced in high form, each individual dwelling trimmed with a small balcony from which wafted the happy, puppy-like sounds of children's voices.

Casually-clad civilians trotted beside crisp, uniformed men and women soldiers, flourishing tanned bodies with confidence in their stride. It was the finest sight — a young generation of Israelis, in the service of their own country. Thomas grew more and more inquisitive of the country's history. His thirst for knowledge seemed unquenchable.

"Dad," Thomas said, as they stood on Mount Herzl at Yad Vashem, where the murder of six million Jews by the Nazis is documented, "I feel like I've become a different person. I really admire what these people have done."

His face held so much feeling so much youthful idealism. At that intimate moment, Josh was overjoyed that they had come here at such an important milestone in Thomas' life; Jerusalem — the heart of Judaism, the city where the Jewish tragedy is recorded, the ancient ways and the contemporary ways, the Mount of Olives, the Wailing Wall, now a part of Jordan and inaccessible to the Israelis, the Mandelbaum Gate dividing Jerusalem West and East, Mea Shearim and the pious Jews, sects born out of anguish as the result of massacres in the Middle Ages. Israel, the bright, enduring light, the eternal flame a light that will never go out again.

The sun shied its face to beneath the earth for the last night. One final peek, one final orange, citrus, poignant burst and it left the family to themselves. The stifling furnace-like heat gave way to a waving breeze that spread the earth with perfume from Sarah's garden. As Josh and Thomas were walking up the path to the house, they were dusted by the large, emerald splayed fingers of the palms. They followed the glow in the eye of the lantern above the screen door. A choir of crickets cheered them on.

Inside, the small house was in a bustle of activity. The glossy, apple-green salon with its cherry-red, upholstered sofa pranced in spangled colour from the candlelights burning everywhere. It coloured those at the table in rich greens and surrounded them like a decorative fortress. Drapes with a design of juicy, chartreuse apples dangling from brown branches on a white, cotton background, were poised at the window. Family pictures in black and white, paved the walls. The room was bedazzled by a two-tiered, Czechoslovakian crystal chandelier (an extravagance Sarah wouldn't, she said, deny herself) which cast a silvery sheen.

The grey, stone floors gleamed beneath the profusely laden table clothed in white, starched cotton. The cooked food steamed in steel pots — chicken stew and brown potatoes in onions, baked eggplant in tomato sauce, chopped salad greens and warm applecake fresh from the oven, teasing the taste buds with its heady cinnamon scent. Henry served and refilled plates and tea cups, so brother and sister could indulge in their last hours together.

Tova dropped by with a chocolate cheesecake and was urged to stay for dessert. Conversation was lively, Thomas helped with the dishes, and then Josh mentioned something about the good fortune Tova and those like her, had been spared the Holocaust horrors. Sarah, Henry, and Tova, all exchanged cryptic looks. Tova's face greyed with pain, as though Josh's comment had been meant as a thoughtless rebuke. In her expression he felt his guilt. No person could maintain such a permanent engraving of hurt, as he had spotted from the first meeting, without having been abused in her early years.

Her eyes now held bemusement and compassion and she began to speak, "Let me tell you a true story. I was a child in Bergen-Belsen, when the Rabbi of Bluzhov, arranged for matzot. Seventy inmates signed a petition, asking to be given flour instead of the daily ration of bread, so they could bake for Passover."

Tova trembled along the length of her slender, boyish body, in her recollection of Jewish sacred Time. They watched her smarting eyes from which tears fell like quicksilver. He understood well how the barbarous world of the Holocaust made the wonder of salvation and its implausible dream, a valiant reality, yet still leave a waking dream. No matter what else would happen in their lives the dream would be endless.

"Who had a watch then?" Tova poured herself a glass of wine. "When our adherence to tradition relies on time. So the moon and the sun guided us. The Sabbath and holidays begin and end at a precise time. The phases of the moon, new moon coinciding with the new month and the full moon with the fifteenth of the month. Even for us in the camp, the moon remained faithful.

"The matzo was a black and tasteless pancake. One of the barracks was used for the Seder. There was almost no other food (someone had procured a few boiled eggs which we shared), but we children believed in the special holiness of the holiday. The rabbi said that this was our darkest hour and that G-d himself would lead us into the light. That next year we'd be in Eretz Israel. That G-d was the fountain of life.

"In keeping with tradition, the youngest child asks the Four Questions, Why is this night different from all other nights? For on all other nights we eat either bread or matzot, but tonight only matzot, especially on a night such as this of unspeakable suffering. The rabbi added 'Yet it is also the beginning of our redemption.'"

Tova looked at everyone seated. "We are in that wondrous promise, in the hallowed light in Eretz Israel."

Henry asked the children, "Why is this night different from all the others?"

Thomas said, "Ayelet, you're the baby, tell us." She kicked him under the table, fumbled for a moment, then grinning widely, answered, "It's a celebration of our Exodus out of Egypt and the Holocaust and into the promised land."

Thomas added, "That we're all here together, in freedom at this table — our cup runneth over. It's awesome!"

Sarah passed her hands over her face. The house had become a magnificent and strange pulsating organ, amplifying the rhythm of each beating heart. Each face reflected the light from the lamps.

A vase filled with water overturned accidentally and it cued Sarah to emit: "It is because of our bitter tears that when filled to overflowing, signals the end of our suffering."

Henry started muttering, "The paths of redemption... ah yes, it's been years since I thought of it... from Sanhedrin 98a. The paths of redemption are flooded with the blood of our brothers and the sufferings of the generation of Masiach are as great as the sufferings of the generation of persecution. Rabbi Yochanan said: 'If you see a generation upon which numerous disasters pour like a river, expect Him.'"

Sarah finally spoke again, formerly in keeping with the occasion, almost trancelike, "Everything I do, everything that happens, I view as through a looking glass — fruit is sweeter, bread is fragrant in my mouth, the desert in its aridity, holds the promise of the ages and the inner lands of our souls, find its mirror-image largesse in the Mediterranean sea and sky. I can never be despondent, for the great blue sky then gazes in its clear steadfastness as G-d's visionary. The children I teach, grown from this land's bounty, from bellies that cried with the emptiness of children whose tears of hunger and hopelessness are a permanent shame of what we call humanity. They eat food tilled from the soil by hands that once plead for a crust of stale bread while others of similar age elsewhere in the world, beheld nutritious meals and life's comforts. We are no ordinary settlers. We are seasoned veterans of hell — the chosen children of Hashem. We have come from the slaughterhouses of Hitler to create a new voice from our hearts and with the sorrowful echoes of our dead loved ones, sainted be their names, who collectively should so laden the heavens, that they should have collapsed from the sheer weight." There were faint, pencil lines around her mothering eyes, soft and convoluted as dark crush velvet.

She continued. "I feel elation and exhilaration with each new classroom of innocent children's bright young lives entrusted in my care, for me to help mold — untamed, undisciplined yet soft and yielding. They become columns of little soldiers, of long-gone ancestors, out of the Diaspora, at long last, in a country to call their own. The school is a great cathedral and I have an awesome responsibility to our forefathers, to our singular history. The children are our hope and reason for survival." The room held its solemn, collective breath. Sarah appeared translucent and shining, like a solitary star ascending, ever watchful. She was beautiful in that light, vital. He saw the modern day heroine in her and he found himself looking up to her.

Then the radiant orange sun, unfurled as it rose, a great, boiling lake igniting the day, the poetic words blazed long and tall as glittering rays of the cedars of Lebanon. Like naked truths written upon the tabernacles of eternity and falling before his mind's eye in a showering of scarlets and golds. It was time to leave.

At the airport, Sarah gave Thomas the talit, the prayer shawl, that their father had worn, the very one their mother had sent with Sarah when she went into hiding. Everyone was choking back tears. The engines of the plane were revved up, the stairs attached, hurried hugs.

Josh said, "I thought I had lost you."

"You never lost me. I never forgot you."

The plane circled as if hesitating, then rose and soared into the great vastness, leaving smoke-filled memories behind.

J osh drove into the driveway of his red brick, two-storey house, a modest building in comparison to the brand new, shiny sidesplit and backsplit homes on his affluent street. He had bought it a year before along with the cumbersome furniture and was still attempting to rid it of the mustiness and drabness with coats of white paint, working a room at a time. He was exhausted from the heat and his workaholic hours. It now seemed an ugly ruin, suffering from his intrusions, whose door finally gave in and creaked, complaining, open. He entered and went straight to bed and collapsed there.

Rivulets of perspiration trickled from his forehead and neck; his head ached like a damaged clock still ticking, though arrhythmic and fatigued. His arms felt like worn upholstery, functional, if tired. A shot of gin would oil the mechanism. Ah, but wasn't he a dead man? He was grateful that Thomas was with Elfie. Now, he could come unglued in complete privacy.

Soon he was surrounded by dead things: dead men, dead women, death mongering eyes made from swastikas wielding deadly weapons. And the stench and the sight and taste of atrophy and its tight-fisted embrace, crowded around him. Obscene, fetid, it burned his nostrils, his eyes, his throat. He had to cry out in order to breathe. The enemies would be

Chapter Seventeen

Toronto
Autumn, 1956

temporarily drowned — those adversaries and his reactions. Gin, not oxygen, was taking effect.

At last he was almost comatose, gurgling infantile greetings to his visitor. If he could only rest his longing and spent soul on the wide banks of his mysterious devil-woman's shoulder, and commune without the need for words. He felt inadequate and helpless immersed in another of his dreams. She was so familiar, so intimate, that she had assumed soulfulness, and could simultaneously arouse fear, passion, guilt. Face averted, her image would zoom in as a rushing wind bearing fire. Hair aflame, ends singed and smoking, crushed, red pomegranate juice squirted from her head, arms, legs and from between her legs. She didn't speak, but made him understand that the soul of her sexuality would be entered through an opening made by sexual wounding, and would be healed only by sexual wounding.

She was so transparent, light passed through her. He gasped, for she had exposed herself utterly. She was fire; he was the flint. He passed into her, joining her dream, her breath, her heart with his soul.

Josh awakened with the disturbing feeling that he knew her, always had. Man for Woman. Beast for Beauty for he had learned to see himself as a beast. Had not well-intentioned people in the early days of the war, inquired about the alleged abnormal, priapic appetites of Jewish men?

Gisela. It had become easy to believe, after she died, that she had signed her own death warrant when she had bequeathed to him her lily-white body to lie with him in bed and let him pollute her with his putrefaction, with the heat of his blood, with the outcries of his lust even as he was killing her, filling her up with his poison.

She had died in the bonfire of his careful camouflage. I am a doctor, he declared, a healer; I will protect you. I am not a wolf in man's clothing. He had just as surely snuffed out her life, as if he had driven that car through her. Their marriage bed had become her grave. Yes, he had done all that. He hadn't just failed one of them. He had lost one of his own because of his weakness. Rachel. That last rifle shot would still be echoing between his ears when his blood would finally grow cold and his lungs expel the last of their unconsumed oxygen.

And what had he done since he returned from that memorable trip? He had transmigrated into the lowly serpent of Biblical days. He had desecrated Tova's splendiferous fountain of life, a psalm that sang with the verity of G-d. Only through Him, could there be salvation. Could even the serpent be saved? Did He forgive filthy, perverse acts, when Josh had trouble forgiving himself?

Would Josh still be welcomed into His house, His sanctuary and domain of His mercy and grace, mercy to overflowing, in the paradisaic river, or one common source, with its spring in G-d, yea, "G-d is the fountain of life, the one and only fountain of life with all life flowing forth from Him." Did He cringe at a covering of prisoner's stripes, a blight on the collective consciousness of mankind, and cry out, "On his judgement day, he will appear before Me and I will join all his suffering?"

The very salt of the words thundered inside the bestiality of his heart. He could only visualize being led to the light, all-illuminating, with divine knowledge and spiritual joy. Josh wondered, if the Lord knew of his loneliness and pain, of his suffering, of the reason for his descent into frightful darkness.

With what ease he had seduced a twenty-year-old girl, half his age, he had met at a bar and taken to a motel. They were both so inebriated, they were in and out of consciousness, boundaries between dream and reality, blurred. Denise, somebody or other, willing and eager; she was Rachel — oh, he had to save the child — with his body, with his being.

At first, in their mounting excitement, her fingers pulled at his hair, hard brown nipples pressed against his teeth, she begged him to go harder, faster, deeper. Then, the convulsions of consensual sex turned into assault and, when he wouldn't let up, lunatic metamorphosis.

Josh had pushed her legs back against her chest, rummaging frantically with his hands everywhere, probing with a lupine intensity and then came violent thrusts until he was done. Denise whoever, had become the unwitting prisoner of his madness and lay beneath him in meek submission, mesmerized by a Halloween expression of inchoate rage. She listened to his gargled gutturals, his teeth grind, felt pummeled by his cannonball propulsion, speeding tempo, and was rained on by his sweat. She saw nothing as her eyes that closed in excitement, remained closed out of fear.

She tried to rescue herself through her vocal chords and when she found voice, it was a high, strungout, endless wail.

What promises her cooing anatomy had held, what appetites had been roused, what a meal his mouth had made of her flesh.

Then the old, dull, misery was back. His red and swollen face paled as before him materialized a young and frightened girl sentenced to death. He embraced her on that bed the way a man embraces a loved one who had died — with desolate, gentle kisses and whispers, cuddling her superimposed image on the body of Denise, pressing his cheek against a body, rigid with fear. The sound of her strangled vocal chords sobered him and he shuddered, allowing her to extricate herself from his brambly arms and retreat to the bathroom.

"I've been dreadful," he said half aloud, to the creature who came out with the wariness of one being caught in a cave with a rabid animal. His shaking hands proffered $500 at which she stared bewildered, then grabbed, and ran.

Later, his body heaved with a vengeance. His madness had set him on a perilous course of self-destruction. Josh had to empty his stomach contents in the toilet. It was frightful, what he had become. Bent like an octogenarian unused to walking, he ambled about demoralized. He wrestled with self-loathing, he could neither stand nor sit, think nor let his brain idle. Was there anything in him worth salvaging? The question hung over him in mute, echoless space.

He grieved his obscene assaults with an immeasurable sense of loss of his identity. Shame lay in him like foul excrement, loathsome beyond all telling. Lower, he plummeted, in his turbid sinkhole. He had believed himself to be a paragon of virtue, anthropomorphic, who, to his shock and dismay, had surreptitiously become umbilically corded to his former encampment and he was infected by it.

Nagging constantly with commanding metronome exactness, was the staggering responsibility he had towards centuries-old martyred forebears and the generations after him. It was to their reputation he owed to correct his moral behaviour.

Work in the next several days consumed him, the psychotherapy for his patients lending a break from his own worries. At night his body thrashed about restlessly.

Josh sought moral authority and explanation for his hate in his faith and found none. After the war, the Jews liberated from the camps, did not cry for German blood. Nor in Palestine; in kibbutzim and Palmach camps, vengeance was denounced. The basic principle was that Nazi crimes must be opposed by humane justice: hate must not be fought with hate. Jews had to show the executioners a moral superiority, prove to other people that Jews are incapable of deeds of hate. Hatred of the enemy — especially in his defeat — has never been a Jewish habit. "Rejoice not on seeing thine enemy struck down," Solomon teaches.

Josh knew that in the few places where hatred does figure in the Bible, it is always of family, of tribe, or of neighbour — not of foreigners. Jews are suspicious of foreigners, they do not hate them. In modern times, the ghetto Jews expended upon the "Judenrat" a more concentrate hatred than upon the Germans, and during the British occupation of Palestine, the secret political organizations hated each other more than they hated the English.

Where was the greater wonder? With the submission to their slaughter, to the extent they could be called collaborators? Or the ease with which the murderers nearly annihilated the race? Josh was a learned, introspective man branded with terrible events, and crippled by them and he knew that well.

Guilt, guilt, more guilt — so dreadful, that the beleaguered heart went on punishing itself, carrying on what the SS no longer were present to do. With passing time, still thinking himself an individual, he was merely following a behavioural pattern that could have been calculated by the Nazis. Left like a timebomb to destroy; like a psychological virus that would slowly consume and destroy its hosts, penetrating the consciousness that the SS could never reach directly. The experience of the camps would never end. Even in death, its effects would be endless. Had Josh not passed on to Thomas the paranoia, distrust, hatred and fear he learned in the camps? Would he teach the boy self-loathing?

Other vessels for hatred would inherit the virus. They would be the carriers, not necessarily the ones to suffer from the disease, but capable of infecting a new generation of haters, bigots, anti-semites. There would be new generations of SS officers. G-d's testing of the Jews was endless. Walking between the parted blood-red sea was reinacted, so was pharoah's oppression.

Deliverance was always only temporary. Strength was about stamina, resilience, recovery, faith, wisdom and remembering not about might. Goliath wasn't Jewish. But, David, Daniel, Solomon, even Samson's physical strength was in his hair, his heart even stronger. What was G-d trying to tell him? There was no virtue in being a brute; no justification either.

He was alive. His comrades were dead. Thus death would be a deliverance from the evil he propagated by staying alive. It was staggeringly obvious in the camp, that he was part of a forsaken and doomed collectivity. He was a dehumanized, nameless number. Every day someone will die and someone will continue to suffer. It's nothing personal, makes no difference who it is. He's only a number. Each selection, when he was spared, there was relief. And after all the selections, eternities of them, there was a cumulative effect, together with fear and anxiety, of guilt. "I am happy to have escaped death" is synonymous with "I am glad someone else went in my place." So, if wishing death on another is evil, so was the act of survival and gratitude for surviving. Partial atonement could only come by wishing himself dead in place of someone more deserving of life.

Josh's preoccupation with man's evil and recent bloodthirsty history was evident in the frightful selection of Holocaust literature. Books on Auschwitz, Treblinka, and other camps inflicted a morbid atmosphere. He stared at them now. No reading or immersion could trade his life for any one of the six million worthy lost lives.

A corner of his room was a loving shrine of framed photos of Sarah, Henry and Ayelet, taken at their home and different beaches. Their smiling faces seemed spiritually linked to the events that the books contained. Now, they were strong, worthy, Jewish. He was vengeful, angry, animal. If G-d had saved him to prove that the Nazis were wrong, he had failed G-d as well as the person whose place he had taken by surviving.

At the depth he reached, Josh once more looked to Elfriede for salvation. He was drawn to her, the only woman who attracted him as a man as well as a beast. Only she could save him. Only she could reach the man and give salvation to the beast.

Josh tried to think of her as would a gentleman. In spite of himself, when he was lately near her, he'd stare at the nape of her smooth neck and want to kiss it — more than anything in the world. The thought of her soft, firm breasts was disturbingly vivid and left him struck and disbelieving. What was love, romance, lust? Would he pollute and kill her before she could save him? The telephone brought him back from such a distance that he almost did not recognize the technology. He stared at it quizzically before picking it up as if using one for the first time.

It was Elfe's priggish very German aunt, Juliana. While Josh could avoid seeing Elfriede as the Nazi enemy, he would never be comfortable with her aunt. The woman was German from the tip of the feather in her Bavarian hat to the disciplined German step that brought her clipped, critical, voice closer than he could tolerate, so that she would stand judging him, one of the Jews that the camps had failed to exterminate. He never doubted that she would have been capable of ordering the deaths of Jews.

With marked alarm in her voice, she sounded gentle, human, almost caring, "I thought you should know that something bad has happened, and maybe you can help..."

For a fleeting instant, he imagined Elfe's lifeless body in a road, covered with tire marks. He barely managed, "Is she...?"

"Oh, mein Gott, no, let me tell you what happened. Kirsten was at my house. I made lunch, wiener schnitzel, cooked carrots and mashed potatoes, but the child wouldn't eat, complaining of stomach pains. She didn't look so good, pale and had feverish red smudges on her face. I asked 'Honey, did you eat something bad before?' and she said 'No, no, auntie. Don't mention food. I can't eat since yesterday.' So I thought, maybe some sort of flu. So I said 'Honey, go lie down.' Maybe half an hour later, I have a bad feeling. I go to the bedroom and she is all doubled up and groaning and she had thrown up. I touch her head and she's so hot and she says the pain is tearing her apart and shows me the right side of her stomach. Oh, I tell you, I got so scared. I say, 'Honey, I'd better call your mommy.' And she cries 'No, no, mom will be so upset.' And I say 'You need a doctor right away.'" At this point, Josh had difficulty catching her words, for she was crying. He wanted to ask her to get to the point but was afraid of insulting her and delaying even further the transfer of critical information.

"Then I remember, Elfriede went to the boutique with Linda. After I call there, Elfe come double quick, only Kirsten was much worse. She was shaking with such pain, the ambulance people had to carry her out of my house, all twisted in half! Elfreide wanted to change her damp, soiled shirt and she couldn't unbend her arms. She is at the hospital now."

"Juliana, I'm going there right away. Tell Elfe I'm coming!"

"G-d bless you, I'll tell her."

Josh could feel the auricles of his heart squeeze together like two fists, so rigidly stricken was he with worry and guilt. Blood throbbed his hot temples. He rubbed them self-accusingly. He was a narcissistic shit, bad, selfish, unforgiving, self-absorbed, the centre of no universe. Worse, by holding Juliana's Germanness against her he was no better than the Nazis.

Driving winds almost prevented him from getting into his car. The door handle was frozen and the windows may as well have been painted white — there was virtually no visibility. Cursing, he got out, scraped away the snow, then took off in a slippery swerve that rearended a parked vehicle.

The oscillating swish-swish of the windshield wipers drove home his transgressions. Damn! How long had it been since he had paid any attention to Kirsten? He couldn't remember. He was as devoid of compassion as a statue. That's how Elfe had to see him.

At the hospital, he was quickly confronted with the mighty figure of Elfe's Aunt Juliana elaborately hailing him in a frenzy. If she were in a dark alley with two thugs, they'd be knocked unconscious, if not with her sizable fists, then with her breasts. It amazed him how this hefty, powerfully muscled woman, who in her heyday could have wrestled (and won) with the best of men, could be intimidated and bullied, crumbling like a piece of porcelain, the kind she collected. He mustered one of his warmest, compassionate smiles for her.

With quiet dread, she directed him to a room, only uttering, "The doctor's right there, but he won't talk to me."

The young MD, recognizing Josh said, "The young lady is very sick. What can I tell you? She has one red hot appendix, dancing around in her belly with pus, maybe a perforation. That little, wiggly sucker has got to come out. I've started an IV with antibiotics. I can bet the problem is localized, but won't be for long. Peritonitis we don't need." The doctor saw the distress in

Josh's face. He smacked him on the back. "Don't be so glum. Old Doc Bergman, that old fart, he'll take it out for her. That Neanderthal is nuts, always was. He went into the wrong patient's room the other day and yelled at him for complaining of abdominal pain, when he could see no reason. He caused quite a ruckus, let me tell you, trying to evict the guy. But as a surgeon, he's A-1, no question! She's scheduled for OR in a couple of hours. No use wasting time. Oh, I'd keep the senile old bat out. She's bad for the nerves." The doctor had an athletic manner, sharp and capable.

"She is a strong woman. Her grandaughter needs her."

Josh entered the room to an atmosphere of emotional turmoil, standing on the brink of battle. Elfe was braced in her unnaturally still and stoic manner. She was turned to the window, lost in thought, her blonde mane an incongruous thing of beauty in the place's stifling drabness. He had never paid much attention to the ugliness of hospitals. Now, it announced its essence — beware, this is neither a safe nor happy place. It is a stage set for the enactment of misery.

When she turned, she had an expression that barely contained the crisis she was undergoing. For a moment, he was embarrassed, seeing her so helpless and sad. She had been the strong one. Now she withered before him, the proud shoulders slouching. "It's so good of you..."

"Say no more. I'm here for you." He took her outstretched hand in his. There was a rustling in the bed as Kirsten moaned softly. The glazed, sea-green eyes, so feverish, illuminated Kirsten. She seemed to disappear in the large, white bed, so tiny and fragile. Her lilac-white skin was translucent to the touch.

"How is the little dove?"

A small voice, like breeze over grasses offered, "I feel sick." Her cut and parched lips moved slightly, like an autumnal leaf. The artificial light glowered at her. Her fingers were little twigs as he rubbed his thumb over the knuckles. There was a bad odour of stale vomit mixed with the earthly fragrant scent of a child in the springtime of life.

Another attack grabbed her with invisible clawing hands and refused to let go. "Oh mom, I have to throw up again." A kidney basin was placed to the side of her mouth as Elfe smoothed the sprays of yellow hair. From another room came lilting strains of Rodgers and Hammerstein's 1956 movie, "The King and I," Deborah Kerr was singing, "Whenever I feel afraid, I whistle a happy tune, And the happiness of that tune, Convinces me that I'm not afraid."

The notes lingered as Josh watched Elfe's composure falter. He rushed out and brought a hypodermic needle and injected it into the girl's right buttock. Ten minutes later the pain dissipated, Kirsten was wheeled to the OR. Josh then scrubbed and gowned, capped and gloved, joined the surgical team as an observer. (Elfe had begged.) He then rejoined Elfe.

"I sent Auntie home. She protested, of course." Reflecting, she mused, "Whenever something bad happened in the family, my mother prayed. But I refuse to. A sick child is sacred ground and G-d is there anyhow. Her life hasn't even begun..." her voice trailed off.

The evening stretched itself into the long diminuendo of night. Elfriede knew the appendix had perforated and a small amount of pus had begun to ooze into the surrounding tissues. It was a dangerous complication, for if unhalted, general peritonitis could occur — an infection in the abdomen — people died this way — but, the doctors reassured her that the vigorous dozes of antibiotics would fight the disease.

She stroked Kirsten's damp, aureate hair with such care, that her fingers spoke a language of their own. For a moment, Josh fancied those tangible words softly fluttering just within his reach and he blinked at their implicit tenderness.

Elfe seemed so out of place in the unrefined surroundings. She was a lady with delicate sensibilities. She could never be comfortable around the various ugly vessels of degradation that reduced man to beast and left blatant evidences in the vicinity of sight and smell. Embarrassing odours and private bodily functions were public domain here.

Kirsten, too, had always been sheltered and was so very young. Children had no place here and yet so many were. It came as a cruel initiation, to have seen her being borne on a gurney into the room, right past Elfe, yet barely conscious, her eyes tightly closed, as though to ward off the hostile world of her pain. Kirsten had been Elfe's strength; her childish mirth had buoyed her many times. Full of mischief and life, they somehow expected her to sit up and laugh at their grim faces.

There had been a flurry of activity around her bed, adjusting the IV and urinary catheter. Kirsten had gasped in pain and Elfe had cringed as if it had also been transferred to her. A nurse returned promptly and gave her an intramuscular shot of Demerol. Elfe leaned over the bed and whispered in her ear, "I'm here baby. The pain will go away and I'll be right beside you."

A procession of nurses came every ten minutes to monitor blood pressure and check vital signs. Josh had an easier time reassuring Elfe that the prognosis was favourable, than reassuring himself. As far as they knew, the infection was localized.

This would be the worst of it and then day by day she would begin to feel a little better. He was saying this to the petrified, frozen expression on Elfe's face. She had thought, until now, that her love had been a moat around Kirsten, protecting her from all danger. That belief was dashed when her temperature rose dramatically in the middle of the night. As the child writhed deliriously, the doctors upped her antibiotics. Josh had been sent home by Elfe against his will. When peritonitis was mentioned, she sat sullenly by the bed and applied cold compresses to Kirsten's forehead and rubbed ice chips on her chapped lips and held her head against the kidney basin when she retched.

In the phosphorescent light, the carefully constructed moat lay in ruins. The stench of sour vomitus pervaded the air as Elfe's confidence crumbled. The two were closer than most mothers and daughters, for she was an orphan and Kirsten had no father. They were keenly attuned to each other's feelings. And so she sat and massaged the child's cold feet and kissed her hot cheeks. She had wanted to summon Josh, even have him stay, but he was not her husband; she could not treat him as one.

By morning, the awful night had left Elfe exhausted and her stomach crying from hunger pains. She was dreaming when a nurse touched her shoulders and told her Kirsten was on her "way out of the woods." She looked at Kirsten, a lily among the tumescence of tubular weeds that seemed to grow from the bed.

Kirsten's temperature was down, miraculously, but now a fire roared in Elfe's insides. When she glanced up, Josh was there with a conspiratory smile. "You're coming with me." She was too weak to resist and let him lead her out of the hospital ward and to the cafeteria. He deposited her at a table and soon returned with scrambled eggs, hot porridge with milk, toast and jam. He had coffee and a bran muffin. As they ate, he assured, that the tide had indeed turned, although Kirsten was still very sick.

When they went back to the ward, Kirsten had been sponge-bathed and had had her bed changed and even been given sips of flat gingerale. A small victory had been won in this dismal location. Elfe hugged her daughter. The sun entered, falling on the embrace outlining it making even the unpleasant contraptions seem a minor distraction. And Josh felt human.

*I*n the days that followed, Elfe kept vigil, in dark shade, hinging on exhaustion, a weeping willow, great and protective, wilted. Kirsten remained weak, her voice, a kitten's whimper; her delicate constitution, a deposed water sprite.

There were small forward steps and then mild relapses. Elfe hung on with fortitude and steeliness. Kirsten basked in the love from mother to child and the child began to respond slowly. She was now able to sit up in a chair for a half hour in the morning with a lap blanket about her legs, breathless, dizzy and frail.

Mother and daughter took a daily walk in the hall and Kirsten pinked in her mother's presence as though she were a wellspring from which flowed healing waters. Her skin was no longer like iced milk, her limbs less like slender birch. One morning she questioned the weariness printed on Elfe's face.

Josh came upon them when Elfe had just washed and dressed Kirsten in a new, carnation pink bedjacket of satin with pink buttons. For all her fourteen years, the wide eyed, green candor, void of complexity, was soft and still that of a child. For a moment he felt a tremendous sadness, all too aware of the inevitable heartbreaks that would one day mar this sweet life. As was usual for him, sad thoughts coexisted with every joyous one.

Chapter Eighteen

Toronto
Winter, 1957

Elfe and Kirsten were victorious over a formidable power, they were unvanquished, if weakened. They had at last dominated a faceless oppressor and Kirsten had reclaimed authority over her own body. When she had needed to, she had done what animal instinct told her to — and fought.

Linda brought Kirsten and Elfe home. That night Josh dropped by. It had been two weeks since she had last been home. The house had faded discreetly with the night, as he turned into the curving driveway lined with tall pines. Lights of honeyed pink gleamed kindly from the dormers and shone on the snow as polished stone. Out back the snow-covered lawn tumbled downhill and the blackened trees congregated in shivering silence, pacified by the night. The rawness of winter was exposed by streetlights illuminating a brutish display of bare trees with snapped and broken branches.

Crooked in Josh's arm was a gift for the child — from Thomas — a selection of science fiction stories by H.G. Wells. Elfe showed Josh into the living room, her finger to her lips in deference to the napping girl curled up on the sofa. She offered to make coffee and he went to make it, motioning her to stay with the child, noting the tiredness in her face.

He could see the drawing room from the kitchen, and he found himself drawn to the rush of citrus colours widening in the space like a brightening moon. Elfe was at the centre of this lunar vision, in a rocking chair, crocheting. The champagne-coloured wool rug beneath her feet seemed to reflect moving light, like a river. Elfe flowed in its midst, rivettingly beautiful, her face composed of light rather than soft flesh and bone, yet oddly guarded, the firm set of the chin, a drawn moat for the world. Josh yearned for her to lower that guard to him.

The room was a celebration of elegance and fine taste, exquisite in execution. A lemon-yellow, smooth brocade sofa stood against yellow-glazed walls, two large windows were draped in canary yellow, Shantung-silk drapes and graceful valance. Two yellow armchairs faced each other in front of the crackling fire set in a grey fieldstone fireplace topped by a slab of natural oak. Antique blue and white Kangxi porcelain decorated the mantel but the crowning glory was a magnificent, classical, gilt convex mirror with eagle ornament. It was very old, early nineteenth century, from Boston or Salem, Massachusetts — one of Elfriede's astute buys. She had explained, bursting with enthusiasm, a year before, that this was a superb work of art, combining remarkable delicacy, balance and sculptural perfection. Indeed, as he studied it now, the eagle seemed poised in preparation for flight and held in his beak, a drapery of chains with tassels. He thought of Cracow and the coat of arms of Poland. How much he had learned about material things, discovering their soul and history. Elfe had lovingly acquired an eclectic mix, piece by piece.

The eagle. He pondered over the emblem of power, courage, and freedom soaring high above the earth. Yet it was also a predator. The Romans used a golden figure of an eagle to represent bravery, strength and skill, as did Russia, the German emperors and the Austrians. A black eagle was the emblem of Prussia. An important decoration was named after it, but he couldn't recall what it was. The newly formed United States took as its emblem a bald eagle with outstretched wings, a shield on its breast, an olive branch in one foot, and a sheaf of arrows in its other foot. In its beak, it held a banner with the Latin words, E pluribus unum, meaning one out of many. There he was, one left when many had died. What was he to live up to? How could he possibly live for so many? Sarah was another one. She had succeeded; their dead parents could be proud of her, married, established. But what of him? He had lost one wife and could only be ashamed of the other encounters with the opposite sex, for that is all they were, brief, shameful and humiliating for both. He shook his head as if to erase, or at least relocate what it contained.

In the corner was another prize possession, a Queen Anne walnut corner chair with four cabriole legs and cabriole arm supports, made in Philadelphia, in the mid seventeen hundreds.

They drank their coffee and he picked Kirsten up, placed her arms around his neck, and took her upstairs to bed. On his return downstairs, Elfe was ensconced on the sofa. She gave him a wan smile. "You've been wonderful to us." Her hand reached out to touch his as he sat down beside her.

I'd like to be more, he thought. His cheeks felt hot and her hand was as a cold as Carrera marble. If only he could warm it in his flesh. Had he looked into her face, he would have seen the raspberry flush crawling up her neck and the extreme discomfort at her unfolding emotions. He would have seen the shyness, the vulnerability.

Josh didn't know what to do; feeling like an awkward adolescent, he muttered something about it being late. They stood and went to the door. He turned to leave and at once he became aware of her sapphire-blue-sea eyes tunneling through him.

He violently pulled her to him, crushing her round breasts. His mind shut off from thinking. All vitality poured to his groin. He could hardly contain it. His brain worked feverishly, pumping hormones into his system. Desire plucked at his loins. She was a great, bosomy sea and he was lapping at her shore. He could always rely on it, whether the Baltic at Zakopane, or the Mediterranean, it stayed the same, always young, always rejuvenating itself.

Her long legs that he pressed against unresisting were quivering waves and he had to swim into that womb as though into a secret cove. Ah, to grow again there! His hands were tentacles and he was the sea monster that would ravage her, drink her dry. They were pulling her dishevelled hair, backward, his gaping mouth released his tongue which snaked its way from beneath her earlobe, down her neck, to the cleavage between her breasts.

Frightfully, she tried to break loose, shock crossing her facial muscles, then brief submission as he dragged her back to her sofa, fell on top and forced her legs apart, hiking up her dress. One of her arms swung free and he thought if she dared resist, he'd assault her, rather than let her prevent their mating. He was a part of this sea and the sea was part of him.

The slap came, swift and stinging. He raised his hand to strike her and then paused; she was speaking softly. "Joshua, not this way, not this way." She wasn't saying no. She grabbed his arm now waving aimlessly in the air and kissed his hand, his arm. She arched her torso to him and drew his face to her and kissed his mouth, his chin. For the first time since he could remember he was running his fingers gently through a woman's hair, gently stroking the quivering muscles of her neck. The fever abated. They remained together holding each other gently but firmly. It felt so good. Time did not stand still, aches eventually reminded them that their position was unnatural and uncomfortable, his back was twisted, her arm and shoulder crushed. Their bodies had to move even if their hearts wanted no distraction. The movement woke up something in both of them. Hungry and animal, they came together again — mutually aggressive and aware of each other.

Her silk panties were off and that locked safe, velvety and wet swelled and opened and he went inside in deep thrusts with increasing ferocity until he groaned to climax and she screamed as orgasmic spasms convulsed in her. They struggled in each other well into the night until they were drained and aching.

Elfe was in love for the very first time in her life and all her inhibitions had become unlaced. Did he love her? If he didn't, she would prefer that he keep it a secret. For the first time, it was three of them and not just Kirsten and herself. And if Josh was with her in order to hide from the world, it was all right with her.

All her thoughts were candied, glazed with rampant sexual urgings. If she were a carnal toy, it had never tasted better. It was an all-out, seven coursed, luscious, libido delight.

A week later with Kirsten better and in good hands, Thomas also with friends, they took the night train on impulse to New York City and sequestered themselves at the glittering landmark hotel, the Plaza, on the corner of Fifth Avenue and Central Park South. The weather was brisk as they strolled through the park, then headed for the bright lights of Times Square snapping pictures before catching a Broadway show.

To the strains of a violin duet, they supped in the European sumptuousness of the Palm Court in the heart of the Plaza. Great palm leaves glowed beneath immense chandeliers and mirrored walls, spotlighting the couple with their eyes and hands molded together. Elfe wore a form-fitting, red silk dress and red and gold brocaded bolero jacket — to him, a living conflagration of flamboyant flame, her skin in the birdlike swerve of her neck, seemingly oiled and coppery.

With an air of mystery, she disappeared from the table just before coffee was served. They had dined on grilled sole, baked potatoes, string beans and white wine. When she returned, draped in her arms was a square object about two and a half feet square, covered with paper. She jauntily placed it on a chair. "From me to you." She saw his bemused expression and laughed, "Go on, open it." her blue eyes shimmering like painted glass.

As he undraped the bundle and feasted his eyes upon the painting, his facial muscles quivered involuntarily, he could not move, nor breathe, nor utter a syllable. Eyelids grew hooded, and as though a button had been pressed, his head began to move slowly from side to side, like the windshield washers of a car. Knife-edged pain lengthened his profile. His knees faltered and he sat down. After a time, he returned to the sanctum of her presence.

Sweeping him away was the opaline, phantom river, rising on emeraldine tiers, to the castle's tower. In it, ran his life, love profound, welling, flowing with his blood. When he reached out, it was though his heart leaked. Her hands, the dam. She rose before him, a seraphic conduit between what he had and lost and what still could be. Leaning forward, he hobbled on a few inadequate words. "You're my life's searching."

She fixed her gaze unblinking on him. "You're my prayer answered." There was a pause. "I went to the New York City Library for a photo of the Vistula. When I found one, with the Wawel in spring in the background, I knew what I had to do. I painted it for you. It is the first painting I have done since I was a child. I hope the colours are right."

She didn't know it, but she was reshaping his image of womanhood. Her caring fingers ran through his greying hair — and he smelled the river, sombre and beautiful. His meanderings and blunderings were over and when he looked up again, it was with the air of a man sure of the path his future would take.

They left the table and floated up the stairs. He rested the painting against the window ledge of their room and stared as Elfe busied herself preparing for bed.

She was delicate, ghostly, swathed in an ivory nightgown of swirling satin snowflakes that seemed to have grown from her voluptuous curves. No living creature was so irresistibly beautiful, so translucent and perfect. He was afraid that she might dissipate into mist before the lit matches of his eyes.

In a blinding haze, he demanded union with this new, ripe, Alpine fruit. He imagined the wintry heights they would climb and he was already short of breath. The transparent snow lace slid to the floor. Obsessed and insatiable, they grappled on the bed.

In the middle of the night, Tia Maria and profiteroles were ordered. In the quiet even as heart-beats slowed and flushes retreated, Elfe's guilt about Gisela made the room sombre. She admitted the jealousy that had corroded her when he had married Gisela. "You can never understand." Her throat was a hard stone and her voice low and unrecognizable.

He reached for her hand. "I had no idea how I hurt you. To go back in retrospect, it's so difficult, she wasn't a real person to me — nobody was then." Gisela had been a sex object, something to tell him he was still alive. It was physical pleasure — how could he say this? "I had nothing else to give to anyone." He let his hand rest on her knee. "I loved you from the first day in the cave."

Elfe wiped away tears, blurting her words between sniffles, "I wished her to die. I had never done such an evil thing before. G-d forgive me." Then she gave in to crying. Taking a tissue from the Kleenex box, she mumbled, "I murdered her."

Josh thought of the years with Gisela. He believed that the time had not been right until now, for him and Elfe. What he had once thought too late, had in fact been too early. Quietly he whispered, "It was Gisela's time to go. She didn't expect to live long. She always said she wanted to get what she could out of life now — the only reality was the present. We have to let her go, to leave her in peace."

Josh had been anaesthetized during and immediately after the war. That's how he survived. Don't feel the pain, a voice inside had said. Gisela was an analgesic. With her, he could avoid Rachel. No, he wouldn't think of her now. He had to be alive to be with Elfe. The radio was turned on. Brahms was being played — music from a dead composer. One day we will all be dead.

Elfe's eyes were wet, her skin taut, her neck whiter than her face. He was staring at the gilded hair falling across her face, a face as familiar to him as his own body. He took her hands and kissed their tips, smooth and cold as paraffin. He rested his face on them. There had to be more to life than suffering — more than guilt for unavoidable events.

That night Josh dreamed of Rachel, infinitely tiny, like the most delicate of fairies, nubile and so beautiful. She looked expectantly at him. He was moved and her face reflected his happiness at seeing her. She seemed so close that he reached out to touch her and found himself on the other side of the glass. He was in her kingdom, facing her. It was like hearing exquisite music. "Why didn't our captors take me, Oh, Rachel, I thought you were dead." He woke up weeping from sadness and joy.

Then he dreamed of himself as a little boy at home in his mother's kitchen with no thought as to the purpose of his existence. "Why am I here?" he asked.

A voice answered, "That is for you to find out. We are not plants that live, die and grow again. We have responsibility. Our purpose is greater, more honourable and profound than one existence on earth, than all our material possessions and what we are to ourselves in our small selfish world. Beyond flesh, its gratifications, beyond physicality."

"Forgive me," he wailed as he returned to his body. He was still crying from without and within, as Elfe turned to him and held him.

Slumber for Elfe had for too many years been equated with the lonely darkness of night, unsheltered and closed. She had somehow cushioned the uninviting night with late TV shows and mugs of hot milk, sometimes drifting into unconsciousness on the living room sofa. She felt small and insignificant and her fate inescapable.

That Josh now installed himself in her bedroom, changed her routine. Everything was planned with ceremonial exactness — even the baking of small cakes and preparation of cucumber sandwiches with midnight snacking in mind. She went out and bought black lacy lingerie.

There was nothing tame about the sex. Whatever Josh favoured, she eagerly complied. She so wanted to make him happy. He heated her relaxation dose of milk, brought the mug, a cup of Sanka coffee for himself and the freshly baked desserts to the coffee table, where Kirsten also partook. Later, back in the kitchen, amidst dish soap, rinsing, and drying of dishes and putting plates away, before they knew it, they were dancing to their own private music. They relished in their homemaking.

Every room in the house was baptized with exoticism; risk taking was an added aphrodisiac under a tree in a garden, in the park during the day where they were almost caught, in the back of a movie theatre. Like Adam and Eve in the Garden of Eden, they ate freely of every proverbial tree, bush, and blade of grass. They were revelling in their own Big Bang.

He bought her a diamond ring of one carat at Tiffany's, a solitaire surrounded by sapphires. She was dazzled as she turned it on her fingers. But it was his shimmering, black diamond eyes that were her proud gemstones. She was the centre of his life.

He kissed her hand. "I'm tired, Elfe. It's time to set down roots, to make a home for all of us. I'm too old for a vagabond existence. I don't expect you to love me. You're just barely out of your twenties and I'm almost fifty..." He began to choke. "The war scrubbed away any such fairytales." The glass of water he took a sip from, trembled.

Elfe looked into those black, spherical orbs as though they were twin crystal balls. "Do you know what I see? The two of us growing old together — two codgers in rocking chairs. There! Journey with me. Imagine! Sitting with our grandchildren on a porch stoop."

He nodded his head, moved, disbelieving. Her hands encircled his wrists. "Be an architect. Design your, our, future. Look into my eyes. Use them as mirrors; tell me if you don't see the very same things." She leaned closer. "We're not so different."

It had been a wonderful three weeks since their coming together. When Josh thought of Elfe, he shivered with excitement, the hairs on his arms bristling. He even caught himself singing in the shower for the first time ever.

Josh swerved into Elfe's winding, paved driveway and sprung out into her private dominion. She had composed paradise, a wonderland to take the breath away. Brought to life was her artistic and idealistic vision of domicile perfection, the countrified city place, with all the city perks, the hearth and home she had kept in incubation for so long.

Elfe. She was the embodiment of femininity, provocative in her exuberance and subtle sexuality. He felt like a young sun perched on the edge of a brand new and irresistible world. He idled to the kitchen window and peered inside — like a spy only moving too slowly and comfortably. And this was his own life that he was observing. A wonderfully ravishing aroma of supper — roasted chicken, the smell of coffee and cinnamon, the clatter of dishes, the sounds of laughter, enticed him. Yes, he was happy to live here. The intermingling scents of food and a freshly waxed floor, were the smells of home. His day had come. A time of harvest, a time of love, a time of quiet peace.

The front door burst open and Elfe, her expression wide with girlish surprise, said, "Josh, what are you doing home already?" She came into his arms and the press of her breasts pillowed against him, making him hot with desire.

"I had a couple of cancellations at the office," he said casually — could he get used to this life? They kissed in mutual circumlocutory flicks of tongue searching mouth in mock oral intercourse. Then she tousled his salt and pepper hair, he shed his car coat, and fingers intertwined, they went into the living room. Elfe went into the kitchen and brought them steaming coffee in delicate, Aynsley, floral cups.

A little later they snuggled on the sunny sofa in front of the crackling fireplace. Her wool dress of pale yellow sung over her like a ballad and his eyes and hands danced in a tracery that was definitely less than kosher, and she had to remind him that there were two teens in the house. Even as she uttered those words, her nipples grew rubbery beneath his fingertips as he laughingly assured her of his staid sense of propriety and decorum.

A few hours later, after supper, with the children doing homework upstairs, they talked seriously of the many matters that involved their future together as husband and wife.

Josh poured himself a brandy and fed newspapers to the metal jaws of the fireplace. As it ingested its dry food, it became a simulcrum to bones cracking and vanishing in a floribunda burst of orange fire. Gone were the blooms that once were children.

The portals opened and the homeliness of the hearth became the crematoria. That the demons could trespass here like vile marauders, was momentarily depressing, but he reminded himself that he was only freshly healed and reentering that nightmare world would endanger not only his health and happiness, but the quality of other lives that he had taken upon himself to be responsible for.

Epidermal manipulation on her part, the stroking of the back of his neck, enticed him back to the loveliness of the glamorous surroundings, his present swimming in greens and golds, her proximity tangy and good. He nuzzled her with hungry nostalgia, the bad spell broken.

She was juicily sheathed in a banana coloured dress, hair combed into a snood. He scanned the classical slant of her cheeks, the pure luminosity of her eyes, and the arch of her neck, where he kissed its hollow.

Two weeks later, to the astonishment of everyone, Josh and Elfe got married. There was no fuss. After the many interwoven years of great platonic friendship, like the finest of tapestries, the formality of the simple marriage ceremony at City Hall was a final formal signature. It was a touching study of best friends, an end to alienation and austerity for him and the making of a family for her. The riches of her being she would share with him generously. Their home would be a fortress against an indifferent world.

Elfe looked stunning in a simple, cream silk dress, a wide suede belt, brown suede pumps, and a small, cloche hat and short, tulle veil. The only jewelry she wore was a single strand of cultured pearls and pearl stud earrings, all from Josh.

Later that day, they, and a few guests, lunched at an elegant restaurant downtown. Champagne flowed. Elfe and Josh had never been happier. Linda and Andrew, Josh's partner in the office, a few doctor friends, and last, but not least, Kirsten and Thomas were present.

Thomas looked grownup in his suit and tie. Kirsten looked soft and feminine, "like a young lady out of the Victorian era," Josh had said, appraising her attire, and Kirsten had flushed a deep crimson, matching the raspberry colour of her sophisticated velvet frock and matching velvet shoes.

It was settled. Josh was selling his house, and at a neat profit. "Josh, I want to keep my house. I've put so much love and work into it. It's my first real home since childhood," she had said beseechingly to him.

He thought of each tree, each flower with her name on it, the kitchen garden with tomatoes, potatoes and green beans. "This house is already blessed, Elfe."

On a late spring day, the house rollicked with Josh moving his belongings in and redecorating. Kirsten's room was papered, transforming it into a romantic, English garden of tiny bouquets of pink roses and white snowballs. The new, white, wrought iron, Victorian daybed was smothered in coordinated, striped bedding and carnation-pink, wool broadloom was laid, wall-to-wall. A pine dresser stood in the corner.

Thomas had the attic converted to a messy "guy's digs," with his stacks of rock and roll records the main decor. New French doors were installed to the upper balcony outfitted with black lanterns.

When they finally collapsed on the deck, dirty and exhausted, the promise of forever was sealed. They now had it all.

*E*ven in this idealic setting; married, a house, a good job, Josh could not escape his past. Fits of anger would overcome him turning him into a ruthless abusive brute. At other times he would break down guilt-ridden, grateful that Elfe stood by him. She doused him with love unconditionally.

He would go and sit in her meadow-like garden, comforted by its brilliant hues studding the expanse of glossy grasses that contrasted the greyness of his soul and his memories. Being able to respond to such beauty meant that some scintilla of goodness remained and that too comforted him. The songbirds perched in the trees were to him singing angels. Some days just sitting there he would be filled with happiness such as he had not experienced since his teens.

Travel dominated the first months of their marriage. These trips were pleasure mixed with lucrative buying trips in New York and Los Angeles. Elfe was among the legion of savvy dealers at major estate auctions. When he had to stay home, long distance calls to her hotel were frequent as he reassured her that he was managing adequately.

The children were doing well. Thomas would be spending summer as a camp counselor up north. And Kirsten was ardently practicing the art lessons her mom had began. Armed with

Chapter Nineteen

Toronto
Winter, 1957

pad and pencil, she'd cock her head with a studious expression, measuring the shape and form of her subject.

Kirsten's girlfriends slept over, pizzas were delivered. Giggles reverberated through the walls, as Josh's breath would nearly stop, while plucking with the adroitness of a violinist, the inspirational vegetables arrayed in neat rows, ripe and luscious, for the casseroles and salads.

Elfe and Josh had been together for more than a year. It was the late 1950s and affluence was the defining social value. The war, and the following lean years, were the poor relatives everyone wanted to forget. Modern sidesplit, backsplit houses were cropping up along middle class streets and teens rocked and rolled to the American Bandstand. Sentimental songs alluded to every man's need for a Shangrila and the innocent promise of Mr. Sandman. Movies gave and recognized heroism of the ordinary American and Englishman, but the war years were mostly relegated to TV documentaries.

Josh even tried to cook for the children. The first time he made breakfast, Kirsten stared at the heaping food on her plate. Thomas chortled, "Think of it as conquering a mountain. Or running a marathon with your teeth." On two pieces of toast, were swimming scrambled eggs, cheese, green peas, bordered by avocado and tomato slices.

"I'll be sprouting grey hairs by the time I get through this." Kirsten looked worried. Worse, Josh was humming, because he was preparing more food.

Thomas winked at her and lowered his voice. "It's a war thing. He puts his whole life experience into a plate. It's a big, cosmic occurrence." He set his fork to demonstrate with a large, expansive gesture with his arms. "Dad always says a silent prayer before meals, or a barely audible string of curses to enemies. I think G-d is being very patient."

Josh poured himself a soupbowl-sized mug of coffee and buttered a single slice of bread. "An entire hut of inmates could sustain themselves for a day on just one such portion." Then he let out a sigh. "How many times I ate something that fell out of someone else's mouth!"

Kirsten didn't know which way to look, so she rivetted her eyes on her monstrously sized plate. Thomas uncomfortably cleared his throat. Josh cupped the steaming drink to his nose and inhaled deeply.

After Josh left the room, Thomas turned to her, "He tries not to show it. He can't forgive himself for surviving. He gets this look whenever he sees food. He actually begins to fall to pieces."

Kirsten winked, "Mom will take care of him."

Family life was interrupted by a beautiful honeymoon trip to Switzerland that brought out the colour and youthfulness in Elfe. After the holiday, life continued with Josh coming home later each evening and the children heard petty arguments over everything from their school to what major appliances they would buy. Josh appeared remote and would sit only one room away from the family brooding silently.

Snow was falling silently, heavily outside. Elfe's fingers gently traced the decorative designs frozen on her windows by the frost. She felt soothed by the idealic Christmas scene and at the same time, troubled by affairs at home. Her nose was pressed against the cold windowpane, eyes squinting, just as she had done when she was a child, waiting for her papa to come home. Maybe, Josh would be seen trudging home in the early darkness. She so loved, looked forward to, that familiar sound of the car, turning into the driveway, the sound of his footsteps on the stairs, and the sound of the key in the door. This ritual was so dear to her, it was vital.

Seven months had passed since their honeymoon and Elfe was growing more and more insecure. Tonight, as on many recent nights, the supper was growing cold and Josh would once again be late home. "Hey you guys, supper's ready!" Elfe called to the two sixteen year olds.

A few minutes later, they were all seated at the table in the new eat-in kitchen and Elfe was putting up a brave front. Dishes were passed and Kirsten asked, "Mom, Josh's late again. He's hardly ever here for supper." There was a whining tone to her voice. Both children were looking at her for an explanation.

The sound of a key in the door meant deliverance and Elfe, in a flash was there to greet Josh, love in her heart. "You look so pale and tired," she said, planting a kiss on his cheek.

"Late appointments, I guess I got lost in a paper I'm writing." His face and his voice were detached. Elfe said nothing and the evening went on as usual, each of the adults in separate rooms.

A few days later, Kirsten and Thomas, who had been away on a skiing weekend were being driven home by Linda. They were still some distance from the house and caught up in the glow of the festivities of the last hours. There had been music, dancing, great food, and the company of schoolfriends. The slopes had been perfect and the magic seemed to follow in the car as the dark streets whizzed by, but they remained stationery locked in with their reminiscences that were visually moving in frame after frame outside the car's window. Before they knew it, they were in the driveway and carrying their overnight bags through the door. All at once they were in the vortex of a ferocious emotional storm. From upstairs with minimal filtering, came Josh's hoarse voice, "You and your breed are murderers and thieves!" And then the thud of a fist banging on wood and something being smashed. Thomas ran up the stairs to the master bedroom, but the door was locked. He called out, "Please let me in," while trying to force the lock. There was only the sounds of things being broken coming from the room.

Inside, Josh's face was a sinewy twist of pulsing muscles and bluish-red veins, an abominable visual Frankenstein. "This isn't your Germany, polluted with the blood and ashes of Jews! I could kill you just like that!" He grabbed a pair of scissors lying on the dresser and came at her wielding them menacingly.

She was livid, her lips a thin, tight line. "You lousy son of a bitch. If not for me, you wouldn't be here now, in the luxury of your hatred. If not for me, you'd have been finished — kaput — nothing — ashes!" She was pointing a finger at herself while jabbing at the air. "Have your revenge! You had to lie in your own filth. I should have left you there to rot. My mistake!" She lunged toward the sharp blades.

They struggled in a macabre dance, she pushing the weapon to her breast, he resisting, the scenario peculiarly reversed. Disarmed by her icy fortitude and confused, he stormed out of the room and out of the house, slamming the front door behind him. Kirsten burst into tears and ran up to her room. Thomas asked Elfe if he could help. She said she just wanted to be alone, but could he be with Kirsten?

Lately, the kids were emotionally tip-toeing around as though the floors were covered in glass shards. They were embarrassed at the loss of dignity of their parents. Thomas felt like an unwelcome houseguest and Kirsten found herself disoriented — in unfamiliar territory, as though the house had been moved to a country she didn't know.

With all the sunny, warm colours in the home's decor, the atmosphere was cold and the flowers on the walls, furniture and rugs false. Only the limp carnations, dying and unattended, were authentic. The precocious youngsters were gaining the understanding that the wickedness that had occurred in Europe somehow affected them.

Thomas and Kirsten who usually were preoccupied with adolescent hormonal ups and downs, were witnessing what they had hoped would be a near-perfect Utopian home, become as uprooted as if an evil tornado had been sent to deliberately destroy the sacredness of the home that they had been enjoying for so brief a time.

Thomas kept Gisela's silver locket in his room tucked away in a drawer. Periodically, he'd tenderly take it out and study the two photos. A miniature of Gisela was in one of the twin compartments, Elfe in the other. Elfe's picture covered an even smaller and older one of a baby he knew was his aunt, who had died young. Whenever he had a major decision to make, he'd clutch the locket and silently ask, "Mother, if you're listening, I hope I'm doing the right thing." The father was dead he was told. Josh almost never spoke of his parents, not even of Gisela. And Thomas didn't need the words — It was the looks, the vibrations which gave him the feeling he had.

If Elfe was a surrogate mom to Thomas, Josh was a pseudo-relative too. Josh had never spent recreational time with him — they didn't catch ball nor go fishing like with other dads. Thomas knew he had been adopted, the biological father never mentioned. Josh's outlandish ideas seemed cruel and unfair for they were coming from a world Thomas couldn't imagine, yet was required to participate in. If he ate his dinner too slowly, Josh called him ungrateful; if he couldn't eat — or eat enough — Josh would go on a tirade about how undeserving he was. He was called names — a criminal wasting good food, a pig. Early on Thomas believed that the food he ate resulted in the starvation of others less fortunate and more deserving. Josh saw a dead zone that existed in a place of continual human suffering. A knock at the door meant the Gestapo, chimneys meant Jews burning, black limos — more Gestapo. Josh did not join a Men's Organization nor come to study groups at the synagogue and he was reserved with members of the congregation — a suspicion of collectivity. Phobia after phobia. And half the time that he would go to sleep, he would wake up screaming.

Thomas, unable to confront his father, picked fights with other kids to channel the frustration. He had temper tantrums, and Josh who worked all the time, condoned the bullying, telling him not to be a pushover, a victim.

Thomas had been dismayed at Josh's warped sense of propriety. It was as though Thomas were a medieval knight on the battlefield, fighting for honour and country. He may have been raucous and belligerent in school, but he was a brilliant student who needed to prove that he was better than the others who had rejected him socially during the lean years. He knew he'd go into medicine. In as much as he rebelled, he also increasingly claimed as his own, altruistic emotions and ambitions that grew out of his father's neurosis. Josh always said that he worked hard so Thomas could be a somebody, for you could not trust the world. Given the right conditions, everything you ever worked for could be taken away, you could be robbed of livelihood and life.

Josh always said that as long as there would be people, there would be wars and that was the evil nature of man. That war was about greed — and industry its collaborator, making rich those who worked for it. Armaments, machinery would decay just like dried blood, life and death being good for business. Tyrants were very dangerous, for they had no illusions about man's dark soul. A Hitler could make your kindest neighbour hate you and want to kill you.

Josh's soul took on the colours and shapes of its place of incarceration. It was a mutant creature in striped rags, filtering the present with it in all its distortions. Thomas saw a loaf of bread — Josh saw a lifeline to dying inmates. An excavation for building a house was a burial pit for filling corpses. Supper was no less than Passover every night. A freshly baked cake was excruciating glory, a prayer answered.

Thomas well understood the power of money and the rejection lack of it would bring.

Kirsten appeared small, ashen-faced and too delicate, more of an eleven year old child than a teen. Her eyes were guileless, like the squirrels and chipmunks she chased after and fed in the garden. She thought of the times Josh carried her when she was too sick to walk and was astonished at the contrast. There had been a tender feeling of protection and she had wondered if this was how it felt to have a father.

Kirsten recalled how they had explored the garden and beneath the corkscrew willow tree, amidst tangled vegetation and floppy rhubarb leaves which trembled like velvety fans, he had spoken as though she were grown up. He had impressed on her, that throughout history, Jews were hated and persecuted for reasons that had no connection or rationale. At times they were hated for being too poor, while at other times they were scorned for being too rich. They were hated for being capitalists and for being communists. They were hated for being too successful and for being failures. For segregating themselves and for trying to assimilate. The only common thread was the hatred itself. And now she could see that he too hated, indiscriminately.

It wasn't new. At least three months had been like that — Josh increasingly distant or so horrible that the family longed for the periods of quiet distance — their own private cold war. Elfe, each day, lived with a new hope, a strong desire, that the next day would be different. The poorer she felt emotionally, the more she added to her wardrobe. There were so many dresses, suits, cocktail outfits — and shoes to match everything, that she not only filled up her own closets, she stuffed Kirsten's, Thomas' and had new ones built downstairs. When they would go to the grocery store Josh would see an item on sale and buy so many that a basement room was turned into a second pantry, an extra fridge placed there to hold the perishables. Kirsten and Thomas would hear people at the store whisper about the "cheap" Jew who would turn his house into a warehouse to save a penny. Only other survivors understood the need to have so much food secured in the house.

Snow fell on Elfe and her world. Loneliness materialized and gathered dust, waiting like Elfriede waited. In the dim pewter night, by the frosted window, she was as invisible and all she wanted was for things to be the same as in the beginning. All she wanted was for Josh to come home and lie with her under the feather quilt and keep her warm. The silent driveway was unforgiving, until suppers had gone cold. She would jump at the sight of the headlights coming into view, run down the stairs to greet him and she'd throw her arms around his neck, kiss his cheek and receive only coldness in return.

Then there was a charity banquet, held at the Georgian mansion of a diamond importer. Guests milled about the vast, marbled and mirrored rooms as a string quartet played to the clicking of champagne glasses and subdued conversation. The black and white colour scheme was a perfect setting for the magnificently dressed women, their jewelry sparkling and adding prisms of light from the crystal chandeliers. Elfe was acquainted with the wife through meetings at her home and the hostess breezed in proudly bearing her two month old infant son. People crowded about and Elfe took the sleeping child in her arms.

The ebullient mood, the vast lawns shining beneath the moon and the stars, the food and champagne intoxicated Josh and when the baby was handed back to the mother, Josh put his arm around her waist and murmured, "What about a baby?"

She disengaged herself, "Please, I don't want to think about that now!" Her exclamation made him jump as though he'd been punched in the chest. She was his dream woman, on her he had hung all his hopes and beliefs, one German who was different, who loved him as a man, who was appalled at what Nazi Germany had done. He was amazed at how empty he felt. And how betrayed. With all her blue blood upbringing, she could only be comfortable with a man who was beneath her — Gunther had been low class and Josh — was a Jew.

With sweaty palms he gulped down his bourbon. She was silent, suddenly tired and feeble, as though she had inhaled his fury and had to lean against a wall. Through clenched teeth he hissed, "What did you marry me for, you Nazi?" He gripped her arm and pushed her outside.

He turned to look at her and expected to find anger and remoteness, but instead there was sadness. Her black velvet cocktail dress merged into the sea of night and beneath the

Japanese lantern, her head appeared like a skull. He felt apologetic and annoyed.

"What is it you want," she demanded.

He thought of his patients and how they gave their lives over for him to tend to, just as he had turned his life over to Elfe; how they were locked together in solitude, close yet so far away. If they had a child something to connect them everything would be better. A child was the only triumph over death. And death was all that linked them.

He sensed her serpentine curves provoking him, mocking him and a snake was writhing inside, telling him to strike out at her. He grabbed her by the crotch. "You belong to me!" She tried to push him away. "You sick pervert." He slapped her face viciously. He had learned well from his teachers. Tears were running down her cheeks; she kicked him. "Get away from me, you lunatic." She tried to scratch his eyes.

The moonlight cast a soft glow on their struggle. "I could wring your neck, just like that," his arm made a circular motion. She staggered backward. He let out a cry that was only part human. He wanted her dead with a passion. "So I'm not good enough for you!"

Her heels dug the ground but she was not defending herself from the man she had saved. Gripping his hands she yelled in eager madness demanding that he get it over with.

"For all we know, I may already be pregnant," she said after a few minutes. "Remember, I'm the fountain of life, ripe with golden eggs and golden babies begging to be born. I am magic."

He stopped asking why she married him. His thoughts were incoherent. His entire life felt like a ridiculous mistake. As far as a Jew is concerned, she was a product of Nazi Germany — a pure-blood Aryan of self-designated selective breeding. It was inevitable that the merry-go-round they had stepped onto, would speed up, out of control until they faced the truth of their life together. He couldn't see that two children born in an unspeakable regime, were being bred in a free country — by two victims of that regime. If they won their wars, Thomas and Kirsten would grow up with uncrippled minds, compassionate. Had Hitler won his, their children and grandchildren would have converted the earth into a Dante's Inferno.

Something in Elfe was breaking. Loneliness had always been her greatest fear. "I must run away!" she said. She hurled herself into the bleakness of the night. She wanted to get out — away from the fear she learned from him and her own guilt that he played to. Children. How could these two handicapped people bring a baby into their tiny space able to join the rest of the universe? She broke into a sprint, made it to the main road and hailed a taxi. She had to get home. She would talk to Josh. Men had betrayed her. Her father with conditional love, Josh for preferring Gisela.

Josh had run after her, then went back for a few more drinks. Fuck. He'd never gotten that close to killing anyone before. The idea made him miss the urinal and piss into his patent leather shoes. Elfriede knew how to press his lunatic buttons. That goddamned Nazi!

Why had he ever believed he loved Elfe? Spent years thanking her for hiding him in a cave? What was he — a lion, a bear, a groundhog? His life was hers, the house and daughter hers. He was another trophy, along with her antiques. He had been obsessed with finding the good side of a German. Her ease with friends, her laughter — how he had needed it. Any Aryan woman could have fit the bill.

He drove back to the house. It was shawled in a low, black haze but he noticed that the outside light had been put on for him.

Inside, he found himself with a decanter of whiskey, sitting on the sofa in the salon with an emptied glass, watching the fireplace. He couldn't recall how he got there. His body was exhausted, he felt rooted in the armchair, the crackling fire was an avenging madness bent on consuming his house, the city, the world.

He thought of how he cursed her people and how she had become an outlet for his rage. He knew he must leave her while he still had any nostalgic memory of the idol he had worshipped. The teenage Madonna with child who had swept him into relative safety, rendezvousing in the forest of Bavaria with food inextricably fused with goodnaturedness, had become decadent. The fact that she continued to feed off her charity to him didn't mean he wanted it. He would tell her he was moving out. He'd have to prepare Thomas. Through his fury he remembered the honey blond with twinkling blue eyes bringing him a Bible she had stolen for him to peruse in a cave.

Josh's body grew heavy and weak. He felt dizzy and cold and shortly he fell asleep on the sofa. He dreamed fitfully that he was back in the cave, hungry, lonely and scared — and calling to Elfe.

Josh woke up. Two children he didn't know were there with him. The boy was speaking to him in a foreign language, the girl was staring at him wide-eyed from the doorway of a magnificent room. This isn't heaven he thought. Was this what it was like to die? Had a German shot him while he was still sleeping? He grabbed for the blanket Elfe had brought him the day before and found one he didn't know. He looked into the boy's face and realized the child was as scared as he was.

"Dad" Thomas pleaded, "What is wrong with you? Why are you acting as if Elfe were your enemy? She wasn't a Nazi, why are you treating her like they treated you?"

As the years flooded back to him, Josh was struck by Thomas' bravery. Clearly he was frightened but he was standing up for his family. Josh saw the best of himself in the boy — and the best he had never been. The girl at the door made him think of Sarah. He had never been there for his own family.

Now Thomas was talking about love, a concept that only further confused him. He mumbled something about being tired and asked if they would leave him for a while. He was so very cold and his eyes stung. He didn't know how long he had been alone but now Elfe was bending over him, covering him with a blanket. She appeared so white, ghostly and he smothered a cry. She held a lighted candle in a brass holder.

He spoke quietly. "It's best we go our separate ways. I'm no good for you." As soon as he said it, he was overcome with terror and sadness.

"Isn't that for me to decide?" There was genuine surprise. She stood there awkwardly fiddling with the sash around her waist. "I don't know what I'll do, Josh. I can't imagine life without you. I couldn't bear to be alone. It was always my greatest fear."

He could not declare that he knew that he loved her. He could not speak any words.

Coffee was served on the gay, floral, chintz-covered sofa, the silver tea service sparkling on the oak, octagonal coffee table.

Later that night, in their bed, Josh fell immediately asleep beside her and Elfe snuggled close to him. In the dead of night, he woke screaming "No, no, no, please, no Rachel — no!" The piercing outburst awakened the entire household.

"Please Josh, you can tell me." Elfe implored but Josh, rubbing his eyes in the dim light, only seemed bewildered. "Why did you wake me up?" he grumbled.

"Something's tormenting you!" Elfe was pleading, gently stroking his forehead. "Please don't shut me out! And who's Rachel?"

"What? I don't know any Rachel." And that was that and he rolled over. She was losing him. She knew that now. His ignoring her, his remoteness, and there had been no sex for months. Another woman? That seemed absurd.

In the morning, at breakfast, Elfe greeted Josh with a hug and a kiss on the cheek. He stood with his arms stiff by his side. When the kids left Elfe said, "Josh, I know something's wrong. Please tell me, whatever it is, and who's Rachel?" He hadn't heard a word she said. She repeated herself. Josh stood up looking through her and walked out the door slamming it behind him. Elfe looked out the window as he got into his car and drove to work. Long after the car was gone she stood staring out the window feeling helpless.

In a dreary, foul mood, he headed for his office, fuming at the nagging and badgering he was getting at home. Rachel! Damn! What was Elfe trying to force him to remember. He didn't need her anymore. She had changed since their honeymoon.

The day at his office was long. Wednesdays, he had six afternoon appointments. Mrs. Weinberg — a pain in the ass. He glanced at his watch. It was only four and he needed a drink. No, he needed a Valium to quiet his nerves. Elfe had been making him too nervous lately. He looked at his hands. They were shaking. He hardly felt like going home.

He slipped into his small kitchenette and made himself some black coffee and popped a Valium. Somehow, he made it through the next appointment. Mrs. Weinberg was the last. He opened the door.

"Hi, Mrs. Weinberg. Please come in." They both sat down and he looked at her; a fat middle-aged housewife, whom he'd been seeing for two years. She had migraines that she said were triggered by relatives she was always complaining about. She had an annoying, nervous twitching of her eyes, a habit of waggling her crossed legs which she crossed and uncrossed all the time and a compulsive scratching of her face, legs, and arms, the degree depending on how upset she was. Today she was having a bad day. He could barely contain himself from giving in to the impulse to twitch, waggle and scratch. He was itching like crazy all over. She was going on and on. A pain in the ass! Thank goodness the Valium was working.

Chapter Twenty

Toronto
Winter, 1957

"Dr. Horowitz, my eldest son doesn't want to continue in university and my husband blames everything on me..." She went on and on with her usual grievances. The two Valiums were making him drowsy. He was going to nod off. If only this session were over! Then he could lie down on his sofa and catch a snooze.

"Dr. Horowitz. DR. HOROWITZ! Are you listening?"

Josh's head was spinning. He was barely able to stay upright in his chair. The room had begun to spin. The oriental rug seemed to rise from the floor, right before his eyes, like a magic carpet. He watched the rug rise and sway, the rest of the furniture seemed to be levitating on their own and he sat there mesmerized.

"Doctor, are you all right?" He looked at her. She was obviously concerned.

"No, I'm fine." His mouth felt dry as he licked his lips.

"You sit right there. I'll be right back." Mrs. Weinberg disappeared for a couple of minutes and came back with hot coffee for him. "Here, drink it down. I thought for a minute, you were going to faint." Her voice was motherly.

"I'm not feeling well. I'll go home. Thank you."

She said, "I'll let myself out. You take care of yourself."

When she left, he flopped down on his sofa.

The phone woke him up. He stretched and glanced at the clock. He had slept the entire night in his office and in his clothes. "Hello?"

"Josh! Where have you been all night?"

"I haven't been anywhere. I've been right here."

"You could have at least called! You don't know how worried I've been." Elfe sounded both worried and angry.

"I'm sorry, but I've got a patient who'll be here in a little while." He hung up and shakily went to clean up. He felt no guilt. He had become hard, insensitive. And the behaviour became a pattern. More and more frequently, he stayed away for nights, offering no explanation. He went to bars, then he'd take a cab to his office and sleep or try to write.

"Josh, we've got to talk this out. The situation is impossible." It was Sunday morning and the children were out.

Josh stood up and walked to the door turning only to look through her. His face was hard and grey, impassive as if carved.

"How dare you?" Elfe shrieked accusingly at him. "You owe me. You owe me an explanation! Where the hell have you been all these nights you never give an account for?" Her face looked like it would burst from the pressure.

"I have to get out of here." As he opened the front door, Elfe ran towards him screaming, "No you won't. You owe me. You owe me an answer, damn you!" She never knew if she hit him, pushed him or if he tripped, but there was the terrible sound of the door slamming and an agonizing shriek of pain. Josh reeled backwards in pain, his hands shielding his face where fresh blood was oozing from his nose over his hands and down his face. She hadn't even realized that somehow in those few seconds her right knee had gone swiftly up catching him in the groin. Josh was doubled over in agony.

Elfe was consumed with an overpowering maternal feeling. "Dear G-d! Oh my dear G-d!" She was engulfed with shock and horror at what she had done. She ran to him, arms outstretched. "I didn't mean it!"

"Get away from me! Don't you ever dare come near me again!" His hands were still shielding his face and he was cowering in a corner.

She knew he was more dear to her, than anyone had ever been in her entire life, other than her own child for whom her love she knew to be immeasurable.

"Please, Josh, I implore you, let me help you, let me help us! We can't go on like this!"

"Well, my dear, you don't have to. I'll be happy to give you a divorce." He hadn't even looked at her. Abruptly he left the house and did not return for five days.

All that time, Elfe was despondent. Memories of her short life with him as her husband monopolized her thoughts. The storage of extra food supplies they didn't need, his need to be covered with three extra blankets at night, and most of all those horrible nightmares when he'd cry out, often incoherently, yet increasingly, the name Rachel. Who was she? And the absences. Where was he going? She knew it would be easier to end the marriage than to save it. She had never had control over the other major events in her life. This time she would not give up. She would save him, or die trying.

When Josh returned she didn't question him. Instead, she showered him with affection, all the while bleeding inside. She was so afraid of the conversation going wrong or him leaving that she left him a note: "Darling, I love you and I'm going to help you. Don't answer right away. Think about it. I've taken a few days off from work and I want you to make yourself free for me, for these few days. I won't let you go, ever. I want you to know that I need you. This isn't charity."

It seemed like an eternity but it was really only a couple days before Josh came in to the room she was sitting in, sat down and said he wanted to talk. It seemed as if they didn't get anywhere that day — but they didn't lose ground either. The next day they spoke for a shorter time but they remained talking. About the children, about his work, about coming to Canada, about his missing his parents. Elfe was waiting for the dam to burst. She knew that one day it would and Josh would talk about the camps. She wanted to tell him what it had meant to her to be German knowing what her people had done, she wanted to tell him that not all Germans were involved. She wanted to express her shame on behalf of her country, on behalf of the father of her child whom she loathed. Elfe waited, knowing that one word too early would squander everything she had gained by her patience. Josh was coming home earlier than he had ever before and he was telling her more about his days.

One day he came home in a rage. An administrator at the hospital by the name of Herman Krugel had been difficult for months. Everything Josh tried to obtain for his practice or patients was held up. His patients always seemed to stay in admitting longer than Josh felt reasonable before being transferred to their wards for treatment.

Now, one of his patients, Leo Rosen, was dead. He had committed suicide the previous night by hanging himself in the garage of his home. Rosen had been found by his distraught wife and their six year-old daughter still turning on the end of his rope. Josh, believing that Leo was safely under supervision, had left his office early. Hours later, the patient wanted to be released but Josh had ordered that he be kept overnight for his own protection. Krugel, as he had many times before, referred Josh's decision to the Medical Superintendent who released Leo in the middle of the night. Then he failed to inform Josh, who had been at home and accessible by telephone. That was an administrative error as the hospital's policy insisted that any doctor whose patient was being released against his orders would be called — day or night. Josh would have tried to help Leo outside the hospital as he had become a friend of the family and both Rosen and his wife were survivors. Now, Leo was dead and Josh faced an appointment the following morning with his widow who had called angrily blaming him for not preventing the discharge and demanding an explanation. He also faced a report to the administration of the hospital for the loss of his patient. Krugel rarely had any of the other doctors' medical decisions reviewed. If he had let Josh's decision alone, Leo Rosen would still be alive.

There had been too many administrative errors lately and Josh's decisions had been questioned too many times. Josh was beginning to question Herman's Austrian roots. What was he doing during the war? He would have been thirty-two when Josh's parents were killed. Where was young Herman then? Josh had nothing solid — just a German-sounding accent, and the feeling that this man had trouble with Jews. What was he doing here? Nearly half the doctors were Jewish. Administrator! Isn't that the favorite career of a Nazi? Efficient little bastard.

Two weeks earlier he had confronted Herman in the common room and asked him point-blank just what he had done during the war. The fear in that little rodent's eyes betrayed more than his words. He came from Linz he said. He had been a clerk working for the municipal government. He had opposed Hitler. After the war he came to Canada. Before the end of 1945 he had bought a small triplex in the west end of Toronto and had made enough money to buy several more. Now he was a rich man and worked "to keep himself occupied." His tenants purchased about one new building a year for Herr Herman. Josh asked him about Vienna but Herman had never been there. That was the only thing about Herman's past he believed. An Austrian who didn't know Vienna?

Josh poured out his feelings to Elfe. She sat impassively. When he was finished she wanted to ask him if he believed that everyone with a German name and accent had to have been a Nazi. Instead, she suggested that he report his concerns to the police. Weren't they always looking for leads? Elfe thought silently, perhaps they would reassure him that the man was an Austrian nobody whose greatest crime had been to allow the release of a patient without his doctor's knowledge. But her job was to support Josh, no matter how crazy he became. Josh smiled at her and went into the kitchen to make his call.

Later that evening they were sitting in front of the fireplace. Josh had spent an hour on the telephone and came back looking and feeling victorious in spite of the fact that he had only secured a promise to look into one Herman Krugel.

He suddenly moved to sit directly by the fire, adding more logs, as if the fire could help him remember. "You know, when I first worked in Canada, I rejoiced in a feeling of exhilaration, for I was dealing with other peoples' problems. The volume and variety of them somehow meant that I wasn't alone. Do you know, I had a forty year old man in my office certain that he had been meant to be a woman and his life was a lie. I get one of those every month or so. I had a woman who had been locked in a basement for fourteen years because her father was afraid she would grow up. It's easy to forget one's problems when every file opens with another's tragedy." He spoke to the fire, an eerie glow flushed his face as the outside temperature of his skin rose. "Yet, I didn't know how to enter the world of the living. It became more comfortable to be in my office where my fucked-up life was normal and a healthy mind the aberration." Josh paused. Elfe said nothing, knowing that one wrong word would close the door that was finally opening to her.

"You can't understand what I'm talking about. You weren't there and most who witnessed what I witnessed, aren't alive to tell the tale. Do you realize what I saw? Arriving at the gates of Dachau — a German officer with a stick in his hands separating us, mothers and babies from their fathers, women from their children, and the shout of 'right, left, right, left' — the hell, the inferno — the screaming — oh the screaming that I will never forget or cease to hear — parents crying, begging — mothers torn from their children, a young, six year old crying, 'mama, mama,' as she was ripped out of her mother's arms, and the child rushing to her mother at the other side of the barbed wire fence only to be electrocuted on the spot. I'll never get away from that mother's face. I hear those children, I see it all — over and over." His face was writhing in agony, his hands were tearing at his hair.

Elfe was frightened to the core — frightened for him. She was also relieved that he was talking to her about a period of his life he had never mentioned to her.

He continued, still staring into the fire. "The first day in that inferno we were sick from the smell of human flesh and bones burning in the crematoria. People waiting in line, families clinging together, mothers singing to a frightened small child, together in line to the gas chambers. I can never forget that smell, nor the realization that I actually got used to it. It became a part of my life like the smell of fresh manure to a country boy.

"I got to empty the bodies from the gas chambers, you could recognize the families — nearly always huddled together, as one, mothers, fathers, grandparents — oh G-d, why didn't you take me too?" He was rocking back and forth. Elfe was stroking his hair and the back of his neck. "Dear G-d, why did you save me? Shouldn't you have let me go with the others?" Josh broke down, his face in his hands.

"As painful as it is, maybe you lived to remember them — to live for them. You have to make the most of your life because it was given to you. You have to live for them. If G-d wanted you to die for them, you would have gone then." Elfe had chosen her words well. She measured his face with every word she uttered hoping that they would not shut him down. She had to say something or he might think she wasn't listening, or worse.

Outside, the smooth, thick blanket of blinding white snow was unsettling in its peaceful contrast, its quiet, stark beauty. There was no sound except for the odd car driving by. They were locked up, together, in this hell revisited. The kettle whistled and Elfe made tea and brought fruit cake to the table.

Elfe poured, handed him a cup and said, in a voice of confidence, simply, unwavering, "Please tell me everything." Josh looked at her face. There was an unyielding look of strength in every contour. Her jaw was firmly set. Her gaze was even and direct when it met his vulnerable, quizzical one. There was the pure beauty of the fresh snow, the scent of tea, the scent of pine from the Christmas tree. Could he trust her with his terrible secret? He was ashamed and suddenly afraid he would lose her.

He didn't speak for several minutes. And then he whispered, "Can anyone who didn't go through this hell ever understand?" He looked at her. She sat quietly, hands folded in her lap. "Liberation," he laughed bitterly. "Liberation woke us from the nightmare, and was perhaps even more painful than the captivity. We were no longer preoccupied with survival. You don't think of much when you believe you will die the next day or, if not, the day after. With liberation, we had to face what parts of our lives had not survived — we had to face what we had lost, who we had lost. Before, our interest was reduced to a bowl of watery soup and a crust of bread." His voice was strained. Elfe sat quietly, watching him.

"Then, the happy liberation day, a mass of emaciated scarecrows, huddled together in wooden huts, no food, no blankets, no medicine — all in dirty rags, eaten alive by lice gain their freedom. Thousands of naked and emaciated corpses, all decomposing, lying all over the camp. Many of the surviving inmates were so sick they did not know that the liberation had happened. I saw them, days later and still stunned, some didn't believe the war was over, others thought they had died already. I went back to the camp to see if anyone I knew had survived. Everyone I knew was gone even though it had only been a couple months since you helped me through that wall."

Josh told her his story for the first time His agitated words ran over her until her ears ached. He described the scene when Hitler came to Austria. Flags were hoisted over the city, particularly in the main streets. The Mariahilfer Strasse where the Führer and his staff would pass, was beautifully decorated. Every three or four yards there were white pillars with wreaths of green leaves and gold swastikas; banners stretched from streetlamp to streetlamp. The air was electric with anticipation. There was a parade. During the first days, the Nazis celebrated their victory. But very soon they began to round up the Jews, at first to scrub the streets and barracks. Jewish stores were smeared with 'Judah Perish!' and similar slogans. Nazis made Jews wear humiliating signs and drove them through the streets. Non-Jews enjoyed the spectacle. Nazi maids accused their masters of 'Race Shame.' The accused ones were promptly taken to concentration camps with no opportunity to defend their 'innocence.' Jews, having lost their businesses and jobs, had to pawn possessions to survive and Austrians bought things, like jewels and silver for a fraction of their worth. The Nazis appointed a commissioner for every Jewish shop. He took charge of all the property belonging to that particular Jew and sent him to Dachau.

Those who had relatives abroad desperately registered for affidavits; lineups to consulates were long and there were quotas. Jews were no longer allowed to keep a gentile maid, Jewish children were forbidden to attend regular classes in order not to 'contaminate' Aryan children, so they were transferred to special Jewish schools. They couldn't go to parks; if they did, they were thrown out by the Nazis. Poverty and starvation now affected all Jews including those who had been affluent.

After the Evian Conference, any Nazi in uniform could seize a Jew from any place and do whatever he liked with him. They were hunted like beasts and lived in constant fear. The Gestapo took husbands and fathers away to concentration camps. All Jews had to appear at police stations to receive identification cards with fingerprints. All women had to adopt the name Sarah and all men, Israel.

Josh's face tightened as he told Elfe how he escaped to Switzerland but returned to Austria on his way home only to be captured by the SS.

"I was driven back to Vienna by a friend of our family. Joseph Müller was doing business back and forth between Austria and Switzerland. I stayed with the same people I had known when I was at the University. That was my mistake. The head nurse, Gayle Blum, a Christian, was fond of me. She and her businessman husband were in their fifties with grown children. There was a small room just off a ward where I slept and she'd bring me weiner schnitzel and poppyseed cake from home. She was a great lady, who cared about the suffering around us. The cook liked me too. He left something cooked for me in the kitchen each day where we'd chat briefly over soup and bread.

Heavy booted footfalls from the corridor woke me that day. The door was kicked open as I was getting into my trousers. Two SS men ordered me to go with them. I was taken to the courtyard where SS and SD men in black uniforms were hurrying into waiting trucks the small Jewish staff, consisting of about ten doctors, five or seven technicians and maybe twenty nurses. As I was pushed into the crowd, I noticed some were bleeding from the nose, others from the mouth. The bedridden were wheeled out and flung into trucks with the rest of us. Two trucks were piled with the patients on top of each other. Once we were inside an old man began chanting a prayer, 'Shma Yisrael, Adonai Eloheinu, Adonai Echad!' A young woman whispered to me that she had helped evacuate the Jewish patients in the still of the night. With the doors of the truck, the door to my former life slammed shut behind me."

Elfe was crying. She asked him to stop for a few minutes and excused herself. While Josh sat in their living room, silent, motionless, suspended like a taperecorder on pause, she escaped to the kitchen where she poured a glass of water and sat on the edge of her chrome and vinyl kitchen chair, one hand worrying a hole in the material, pulling at the newly exposed foam stuffing, the other gripping her glass. She must have been there at least ten minutes but Josh continued on her return as if he had never been interrupted, ignoring the glass she had placed on the table which sat there sweating. For a moment she worried that the glass would leave a mark on the cherry surface and almost interrupted him again so she could fetch a coaster, but instead she sat, trying to take in as much as she could. There were no magic words that would make it better or speed the healing. The act of listening meant that her husband was not alone anymore. That was the most she could hope to contribute.

"We were taken to the railroad station, then driven into freight cars, each car with a small barred window. The few belongings people had were seized and thrown to the ground and picked over for valuables. The stench was overpowering — the smell of sickness, the smell of those who let their fear escape into their trousers. Some went insane right there, shrieking and clawing at each other. By the time we got to Dachau, we were raw sewage, covered in slime. To get even one gasp of befouled air, we had to suffocate those beneath us. When the freight doors were opened, we were driven out by the SS amid beatings and curses, the sunlight stinging our eyes. Though we didn't know it, many were only moments away from the crematorium. We were being pushed, some to the left, others to the right. Men were separated from the women. We looked around us to see corpses hanging with the noose around their necks, queer-looking inmates in striped pajamas."

This time Josh paused on his own. He picked up his water glass and took a long gulp letting the water soothe his sore throat. He noticed the mark it had left and rubbed the wood in a futile effort to remove it. Cursing, he covered the stain with a Bible that had been left on the sofa.

"Soon, friends, co-workers and people I would never get to know were reduced to ashes dusting the sky and irritating our mouths and noses. Our hair was shaved off, and we were dressed in striped fatigues. We were kept like farm animals, our days filled with work, starvation, exhaustion, and the terror of the guards. As soon as a person became unable to work he was converted into smoke — pollution. You can't imagine what it was like. When you found me, I was no longer human, hadn't been for months."

Josh's tongue hurt. It undulated as a savage hill, ignited by a volcanic fire. His lax cheeks hung in shabbiness on the bony promontories of his face. His confidante looked tired but together in the gnarled acres of remembrances and entwined pasts they were welded. He could see the connection and it momentarily angered him. She hadn't earned the right to this past that had cost him his youth, his family — everyone he had loved — counting himself. He stood up as if preparing to leave the room. "Wallowing in the mire with me, Elfe?"

Elfe lost the control she had maintained for hours. "Why must you punish us? Why must you deform what we built together? Here," she hissed, tearing off her sweater and bra, baring her chest, "take that belt and lash as many times as you need, until you're satisfied we've been punished enough."

He stared at her naked breasts. Josh knew she had deliberately humiliated herself. They had always made love in the dark. Even when alone in the house, she never paraded nakedness. Josh sat down again and looked away. Elfe covered herself shocked at what she had just done. When he spoke again it was in a whisper. "I'll tell you about Rachel."

She put her fingers to his face, moving them over his creased forehead and eyebrows then to his temples, as though the heat of her hands could stop the times of his life. As if the timepiece of the world could be brought under a lover's control and into sharp focus — and alter the rhythm of the world. Josh was struggling with a blizzard of feelings. He seemed belted by cold and shivered. Elfe noticed, and took his hand in hers lifting it to her cheek. She led him to the kitchen. There, she let his hand fall only long enough for her to reach for the bottle of sherry. She poured two glasses, placing one in his hand. Carrying her glass in one hand, with the other she led him back to their living room, pausing just long enough to pick up two coasters for the table. "Drink," she said firmly, as she arranged pillows so they could sit. Then more gently, her voice not more than a hush, "Tell me about Rachel. It will help us both."

His face hardened. "Do yourself a kindness, let me leave you."

"Have you forgotten? I save lives. Maybe I can save yours and mine. What comfort is there for me in an empty, unloved life?"

"I never loved you, never, I was grateful."

Her mouth made an O, like a startled child but said nothing.

Her response was not what he had expected, he had been expecting something aggressive — for her to scream at him or hit him. Not this. He thought of his sister, he thought of Rachel. He felt sorry for her and remorse for his cruelty. There had been no victory, no relief in causing pain to Elfe. He knew what the SS officer had felt when he had shot Rachel and hated himself. Josh swooped his face across her lips and ears. Her rapid breaths were the kisses of life. "I am the devil," he gasped. "Don't die. I love you, I do love you."

He had not killed Elfe. He had, though, almost destroyed her. Lacy snowflakes fell outside their window. They seemed to crash silently into the bottom of himself and he held onto her.

"You want to know about Rachel." She couldn't see his face for his lips were at her ear and he was whispering his secret into her head. Elfe's eyes were closed. "After a few days, who should I see, but a fifteen-year-old girl from home. Rachel, my sister Sarah's best friend."

"My parents and her parents were long time friends and I knew her from the time she was a baby. I loved her as I loved my sister. The two even looked alike. They were inseparable; the same mocha skin, black eyes, strong nose, full, arched lips. Of course, at first we didn't recognize each other. Skeletons tend to appear alike, and that's all we were. Then one day we met and she recognized me. I had said something to her, I don't remember what — it can't have been important. She wasn't looking at me and had only my voice to recognize. I became (as best I could) her protector, her big brother. We were each other's only link to the past. She was lucky. She worked in the kitchen as a vegetable cleaner. Whenever she could, she brought me a potato or peels, a carrot. I made a small fire and cooked them. To her I gave some of my bread and margarine. She was an innocent, selfless child. People stole food from each other so I cooked in secrecy. With time I got other jobs — toilet cleaner and also commando. Usually these people were physicians, rabbis. Our job was, early each morning, to go to each barrack and carry out the dead bodies and put them in a two-wheel carriage and bring them to the forest where ditches had been dug. The job sounds worse than it was. It was horrible, grisly, but it meant that they needed me, that as long as I could do the work, I wouldn't become one of those bodies myself."

Josh was now unconsciously stroking her hair as if trying to soften the effects of his words.

"I kept up my struggle to survive. Anyhow, one day an SS guard approached me and told me to rape my surrogate-sister Rachel. I refused, revolted to the depths of my being." At these words Elfe recoiled, ashamed of how she had pressured Josh into telling her. She had presumed Rachel to have been a lover and her own fears and jealousies had raped the memory of that little girl who was no older than her own daughter.

"The next day, another medic I knew was given the same order. He complied and then was shot. Later, the SS guard brought Rachel and me to a place in the square and with the other inmates forced to watch, he told me that although he recognized 'a dog's restraint at mounting a bitch, even a Jewish mongrel hunde had to understand his place.' I was in no position to disobey orders. 'There were consequences,' said the fat face, greased with sadistic pleasure. But I was unable. The SS shot her in front of me. Her eyes, I'll never forget those eyes. How do I live with that? If I had obeyed, she would be alive today, just maybe — I was the cause of her death. Nobody can forgive me."

"G-d, no, it wasn't your fault! She may have preferred that. Josh, they would have continued torturing her until they killed her. At least she died knowing that you would never defile her. If you had obeyed, that would have hurt her, she would have watched you get shot and then after being raped many more times they would have killed her anyway. You have done nothing to forgive. You showed her honour. You gave her one final victory." Josh was quiet. Elfe brought him a pillow comforted him on the sofa and left the room to wrestle with her own soul.

Josh dreamt he was in Cracow, amid his beloved lush fields and flowers, but the red horizon was now the blood of the Jews, the clouds — ghosts, flesh and bones — fertilizer. The breeze was a collective breath a final exhale. I am still touched by emotion. I am you and you are me. I am alive and so are you. Their nearness followed him. Someone remembers us.

When Josh opened his eyes again Elfe had returned and was sitting next to him. She spoke softly, "I will not spend the rest of my life alone. I saved your life then and now I want you to do the same for me. Josh, its time to bury the dead. We don't have a perfect life but we have life."

He had saved none of them — not his mother, not his sister, not Rachel, nor Elfe. She was the saviour. She would not let him throw away the life which she had fought to preserve and she alone valued. She deserved whatever it was he had to give. She was offering herself to him and, deserving or not, he was obliged to accept.

The fountain of tears. He wept for all the retreating heroes and heroines who would have told him that his life was not his to give up.

He took her hand in his and kissed it. "I choose life. Together we will be until this world can no longer have us. It won't be easy, but nothing ever is."

He thought of the fountain of life and the children whose mouths already filling with ashes, sang "I Believe" Ani Ma'amin. If those children could believe perhaps he could to.

Epilogue

Josh's eightieth birthday had been a celebration. His small extended family had come for a party and were not disappointed. Food was laid out on a long table in the garden and sunshine bathed the gathering with the warmth and promise of spring. Sarah and Elfe had organized a day to remember.

Josh remembered another day: his grandmother's eightieth. There had been so many people there he couldn't count them nevermind remember their names. That had been a happy time. So was this, although there were fewer to share it with.

Sarah had been living with Josh and Elfe ever since Henry died. The cancer had taken him suddenly and, two days after his burial, Sarah made the decision to come to Canada. Ayelet had moved to the United States years before and just recently had taken a job in Toronto. Torn between her family and her beloved Israel, Kirsten's constant e-mails of pictures of cute North York bungalows had swayed Sarah. A top selling real estate agent, Kirsten had rightly pointed out that Sarah's modest bungalow in Israel would fetch a small fortune — enough for her to buy a house in Canada and leave plenty of money left over. But, in the end, it was decided she would live with her brother and her sister-in-law. Josh couldn't have been happier.

Kirsten and her husband, David, were there to help with the clean-up. Glasses and plates had to be boxed and taken back to the caterers, the tent that had been pitched on the lawn had to be struck and returned. David was humming happily putting the boxes in his minivan — usually used for transporting smaller antiques. He was accustomed to spending time there. Elfe had made him a full partner in her business. He did most of the travelling now, but she still reviewed all the major purchases. They stayed in touch when he was away by fax and e-mail. Elfe would slow down but never retire. She often looked at Josh and loudly affirmed, to anyone who would listen, her passion for "old things."

Inside the house, Josh was playing a game of chess with Gisela while her father looked on with mild interest. Kirsten and David complaining that there were two many cooks, had kicked them out of the work area. The dishes were rented to reduce the work — there was nothing to wash and the mess would be gone in another hour. The game was a foregone conclusion, Josh hadn't won a game of chess with her since she was fifteen — she now wanted to stretch her unbeaten streak to six years. Thomas was unsympathetic — he played her more often and hadn't won a game since she was thirteen. He looked at her with pride. She had turned out well, he thought.

For a time he had been worried; her mother had left them abruptly promising never to speak to Thomas again. Gisela's marks in school plummeted and he found drugs in her room later that year. This month, she had finished her second year in law at the top of her class. Her drive to change the world and to fight injustice had saved her, but he hadn't done such a bad job as a parent either.

By early afternoon, the house was quiet. Elfe was working outside on a small old mahogany chest she was refinishing, Ayelet had picked Sarah up to see a movie and Josh was lying on the couch. He hadn't felt well all day. He now regretted the second helping he had had of David's Tandoori chicken. He always overdid it when David cooked.

Several times, he got up thinking he would be sick only to eventually have diarrhea so violently that he was now sore and exhausted. This was the worst case of food poisoning he had had in years — hadn't they checked the meat first? Perhaps, it had been left out in the sun too long. Now he was sweating profusely, his curly silver hair so wet that it stuck to his head as if he had just taken a shower. He got up to change his shirt which was now soaked and had to sit down again because pain shot up through his spine from the arm he used to steady his rise off the sofa.

Damn. His arthritis, aggravated by the physical abuse he had endured in the camps, was bothering him, worse than it had in years. His doctor had told him that there was nothing he could do. Fifty years after the explosion that opened the hole in the wall that Elfe had dragged him through, he still picked pieces of shrapnel out from under his fingernails, slivers that came from within.

When Elfe came in carrying the newly refinished antique, wooden box in both hands, proud as if she had just made it from scratch, he glanced at it and then, complaining of the Tandoori chicken, made his way upstairs to their bedroom to rest. Josh's aches and pains were nothing new to Elfe. She pecked him on the cheek and told him that she would come back in a couple hours after she had brought the box over to the store and picked up some supplies.

Only minutes after Elfe left the driveway, Josh realized that he was having a heart attack. Disoriented by the pain he slipped the first pill under his tongue. Two minutes later the second. By the third pill, Josh knew that it wasn't going to work. With pain running down both arms and streaming from his wrists, elbows and neck he wandered about the house, confused — unable to concentrate on anything but the fire within him. He tore off his sweat-soaked shirt. He couldn't remember ever being so hot.

He woke up on the floor staring down the stairs from the hall in front of his bedroom. It took a few moments to realize where he was and that he must have passed out and collapsed there.

Somehow in his confusion, he decided that he couldn't let Elfe find him this way. The best place to die would be in his bed. Josh wrestled his screaming body back to the bedroom and lay there staring at the ceiling, waiting. For a few minutes he accepted his death, but then he found the will to fight.

Blinded by pain he got out of his bed and struggled down to the first floor, to the cordless telephone. Sitting on the floor, he pushed the buttons, frustrated that he couldn't figure out how to make it work. Suddenly, the phone lit up. It was like a candle — hope — life. He stabbed at the large numerals 9-1-1. He barely remembered to lift the telephone back to his ear.

"Please, I'm having a heart attack."

The woman on the telephone was calm, professional. "What is your address? — Allergies? — Medications? — Stay with me. They are on their way. Don't put the phone down." Almost immediately, Josh could hear the ambulance through the roaring in his ears. Holding the telephone, he told the angel on the other end that he was going to the door to unlock it. After doing so he struggled upstairs. Somehow, he thought that he could put together his own overnight bag. Where was that medical card?

The door opened and a voice asked where he was. "I'll come down, you can't get a stretcher up here." Josh made it to the stairs and part way down. He saw warm, kind eyes and the softest french accent telling him that he would be okay. Then the eyes got closer and closer, and he was floating. This must be it he thought.

The attendant must have caught him for he was now on the floor a hand-held ECG taking his vitals, the attendant talking with someone over the radio.

The next thing he remembered was the bumps as the ambulance took him to the hospital and then the banging of the emergency doors as he was whisked into the building out of the cool evening air.

When Elfe arrived Josh was conscious although he was receiving morphine intravenously. "I'm so sorry for leaving this afternoon. I thought you were okay." Elfe was crying but trying to keep her emotions in check.

"I saved myself."

"That you did." The nurse pulled at Elfe's sleeve whispering that Josh had to rest. The next few hours were critical.

* * * * * *

A shy May dawn blushed tentatively into existence, sun-washed and rejuvenated. It yawned through the shutters, cast zebra stripes on the walls, then stretched voluptuously into a gorgeous, daffodil-coloured morning. But Elfe saw none of it. She, half reclining, hid her head in the cotton sand of her blanket.

The hellish waiting had made her ravenous, but she couldn't eat. The mental exhaustion had fatigued her, but she hadn't been able to sleep. Monstrous waves heaved in her stomach, invisible boots pounded her aching head. In spite of this fine May sun, her teeth were rattling like castanets, her bones were ice columns. I'm a summer snowman, she thought.

It was eight in the morning. She went dazedly into the bright, country kitchen and prepared cooked oatmeal and milk, a formula that had kept her stomach ulcer under control for years. She brought the food back to her room of forever budding, blooming flowers and leaves, always alive and crisp, never to wither, like her and Josh's love and their memories together. She had endeavored and succeeded, to bring light into darkness and peace where there had been turmoil. She saw her marriage as her shrine.

When the phone rang at eleven, she jumped. The operation had been a success; Josh was awake and talking with the staff. Could she bring today's *Star* and some real pajamas? Elfe arrived, flopped the newspaper onto the bedside table and hugged him.

"After all these years you're not leaving me now," she exclaimed holding on to him. "Thomas, Kirsten and Gisela will be here in a couple hours. You read your paper and I'll be back in a few minutes." Elfe went out to the nursing station to talk to the staff.

When she returned, Josh was clutching his chest gripped by pain. Unable to speak he pointed to the newspaper he had been reading. The headline read "Neighbours Defend Mass Murderer Accused of War Crimes." Herman Krugel's photograph was unmistakable although the caption read "Klaus Schaub, alleged Einsatzgruppen officer and mass-murderer." The article went on to say that Schaub had been personally responsible for the deaths of thousands of Jews, communists and gypsies in Eastern Europe. The newspaper claimed that there was evidence that Schaub had lied about his past to Canadian authorities when he arrived under the name Krugel.

Membership in the Einsatzgruppen was equivalent to being a war criminal. This was the special force of mobile SS and police units that entered behind Hitler's armies with the single purpose of rounding up and killing civilian enemies of the Reich. Schaub had had a good life in Canada. Coming here in 1946 while thousands of Jews waited in squalid Displaced Persons camps, he had received the red carpet treatment. Now he was an old, and very rich, man.

His neighbours were quoted as saying that he was a model neighbour who grew beautiful roses and couldn't have been a murderer. One man was quoted as saying "That was so long ago and war is so crazy anyway. He is an old man. Why can't we just let him live in peace?"

A crown attorney was quoted wondering if the country would have the stomach to prosecute an old man of eighty-seven. "Prosecuting and deporting an old man for things that happened fifty years earlier would be a miscarriage of justice," he had said.

None of his victims got to be old, thought Josh. Am I too old to understand what is right? The fact that Schaub had had the opportunity to lead such a privileged life and become an old man — now that was the perversion of justice!

* * * * * *

Josh had been home for two days making slow and steady progress. The doctors called him a fighter, a survivor. Elfe stood up from the edge of the bed where he was still recuperating. On stiffened legs she stepped out on the balcony overlooking her two acres of woods. Her body felt like a dragged, heavy sack while her suddenly soaring spirit buoyed out of her, floating effortlessly into the puffy, white clouds swimming in the budding spring sky.

Author's Recommended Reading List

1) *Hasidic Tales of the Holocaust*, by Yaffa Eliach, published by Vintage Books, copyright 1982. A unique and sensitive collection of true stories that shed light on the inner spiritual world of the Holocaust victim.

2) *Avenue of the Righteous*, by Peter Hellman, published by Atheneum, copyright 1980. Shows the greatness of spirit of gentiles who risked their own lives and those of their families, in order to save Jews.

3) *Shoah* — A Jewish perspective on tragedy in the context of the Holocaust, by Rabbi Yoel Schwartz and Rabbi Yitzchak Goldstein, published by Mesorah Publications, Ltd. in conjunction with Art Scroll, Jerusalem, Ltd., copyright 1990. An inspiring book that delves into the meaning of events and attempts to discern their purpose.

4) *The Town beyond the Wall*, by Elie Wiesel, published by Avon Books, copyright 1964. The story of a young Jew who survives the holocaust and is compelled to return to his home town.

5) *A Jew Today*, by Elie Wiesel, published by Vintage, copyright 1978. Reveals philosophical, moral and political implications of the holocaust for the Jews in today's world.

6) *Of Pure Blood*, by Marc Hillel and Clarissa Henry, published by McGraw Hill, copyright 1976. The story of Hitler's secret program — The Lebensborn (Fountain of Life) plan to breed a master race.

7) *Master Race*, by Catrine Clay and Michael Leapman, published by Hodder and Stoughton, copyright 1995. The Lebensborn program, it's implications and its aftereffects

8) *Man's Search for Meaning*, by Viktor E. Frankl, a Touchstone Book, published by Simon and Schuster. Dr. Frankl gives a moving account of his life in the Nazi death camps and his theory of logotherapy.

9) *While Six Million Died*, by Arthur Morse, published by Ace Publishing Corporation, copyright 1967. Chronicles the apathy of the world during the plight of the Jews in the 1930s-1940s, in order to gain understanding of how it happened in the past in order to prevent genocide in the future.

10) *The Wiesenthal File*, by Alan Levy, published by Constable and Company Ltd., copyright 1993. It is an examination of one of the greatest Jewish figures of our century at a time when anti-Semitism is on the increase throughout Europe.

11) *Concentration Camp*, by Eugene Heimler, published by Pyramid Books, copyright 1959. A true account, vividly documented of man's inhumanity to man during the Holocaust.

12) *The Rise and Fall of the Third Reich*, by William Shirer, published by Crest, copyright 1959. A History of Nazi Germany.

13) *A Friend Among Enemies*, by Janet Keith, published by Fitzhenry and Whiteside. The story of Arie van Mansum.

There are many good books on this subject. These are just a few.
R.K.

About the Author

Roma Karsh's parents survived Hitler's death camps and it was the painful descriptions told her from early childhood that inevitably found voice in this novel.

Her late mother, Stephanie, survivor of the death camps Ravensbruck and Dachau, and her late father, Israel, survivor of the death camp, Buchenwald, and other notorious camps, were to her, living memories as she compiled this book.

She was born and raised in Toronto, graduated from Humberside Collegiate Institute, later moved to Israel where she studied Nursing and then worked in a large hospital. She now resides in Toronto, Canada with her family.

There was more room in writing this book as fiction, giving soul a greater arena and imagination a wider range.

While the Holocaust formerly ended more than fifty years ago, its effect continues not just in the gaps it has created: uncles, aunts, brothers, sisters, parents, children, friends, colleagues — whole families lost, but in the lives of those who continue to cope with its aftermath. It touches new generations born long after the Third Reich ended and lives vividly in the tortured dreams and memories of victims who can never leave it behind.

Roma hopes that this book will help preserve the memory of not only those who died but those who carry the burden of survival — and their children. She also hopes that for some it can help explain as well as comfort.